Shojo Beat

NANA Vol. 13

Contents

The Story of Nana

Nana "Hachi" Komatsu and Nana Osaki meet by chance on a train headed for Tokyo. Their personalities and the environments they grew up in are very different, but by fate or by chance, they meet again and become roommates...

The Blast members eagerly await Hachi, who emailed them an invitation to the fireworks festival. It's been a long time since they last saw her, but after hearing that Hachi is afraid to see Nobu and knowing she's about to get married, Nobu realizes he can't deal and doesn't partake in the gathering.

Then Ren suddenly proposes to Nana and she accepts. They hold a press conference announcing their engagement on the day Blast's debut single hits the streets! All eyes are on this press conference...

For the sake of Trapnest interests, Hachi agrees to postpone her wedding until after Nana's wedding. Feeling sorry for her, Naoki invites her at the last minute to a party for Shin's and Reira's birthdays. Hachi wonders if she should go...?

♥For the complete story, please check out *Nana*, volumes 1 - 12. Available in bookstores everywhere!!

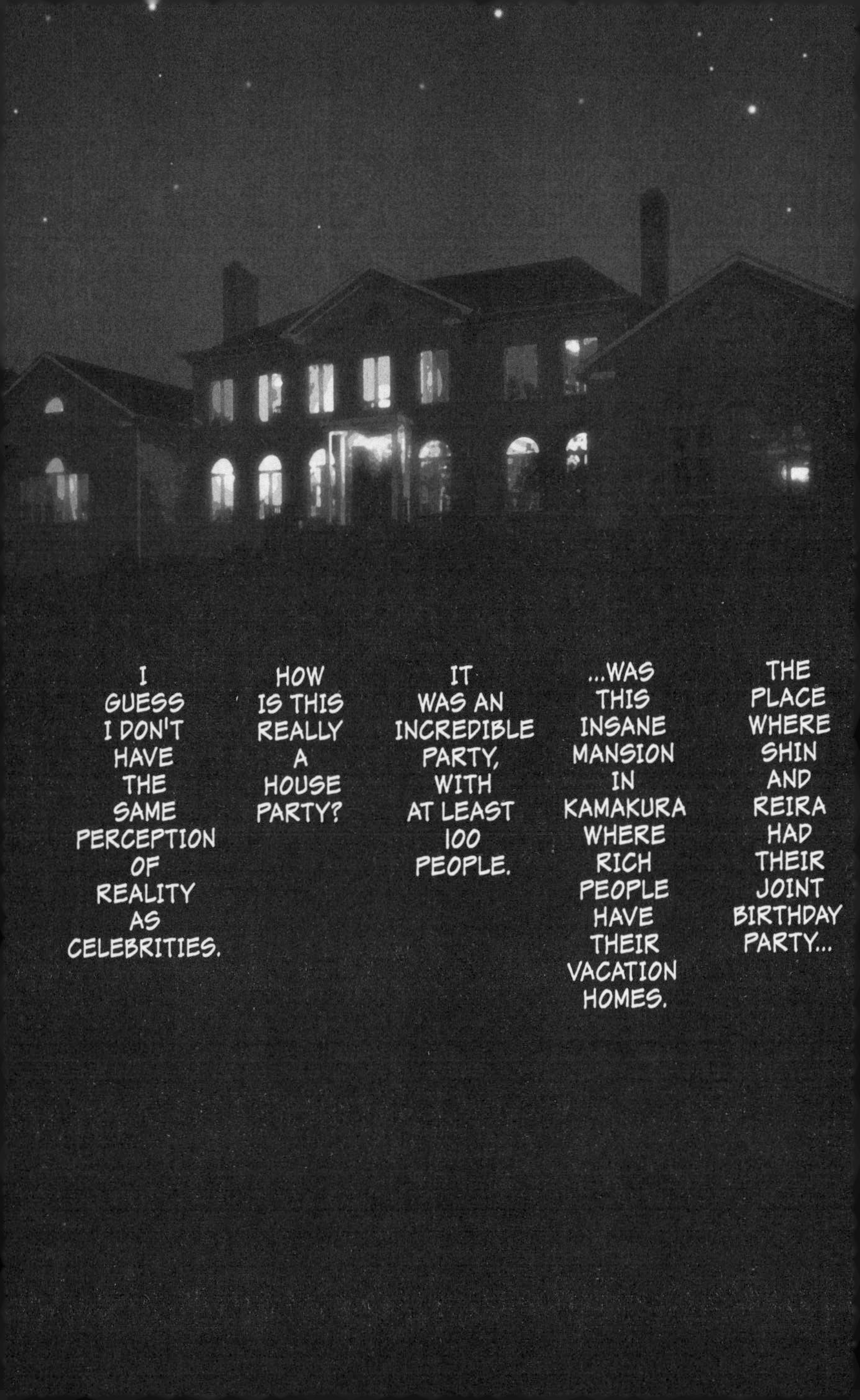
THE PLACE WHERE SHIN AND REIRA HAD THEIR JOINT BIRTHDAY PARTY...
...WAS THIS INSANE MANSION IN KAMAKURA WHERE RICH PEOPLE HAVE THEIR VACATION HOMES.
IT WAS AN INCREDIBLE PARTY, WITH AT LEAST 100 PEOPLE.
HOW IS THIS REALLY A HOUSE PARTY?
I GUESS I DON'T HAVE THE SAME PERCEPTION OF REALITY AS CELEBRITIES.

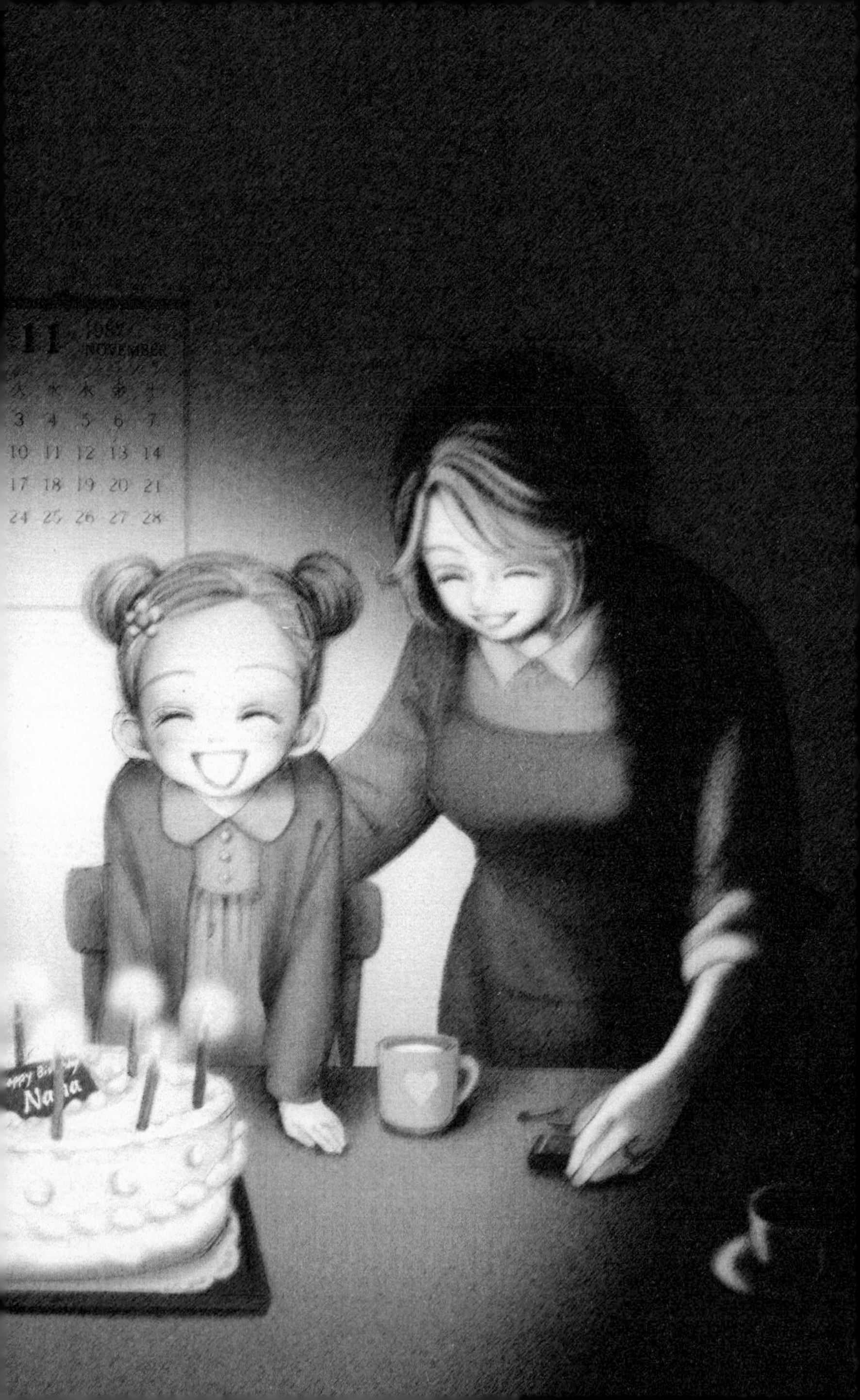
11
NOVEMBER
3 4 5 6 7
10 11 12 13 14
17 18 19 20 21
24 25 26 27 28

[Chapter 46]

NANA
ナナ

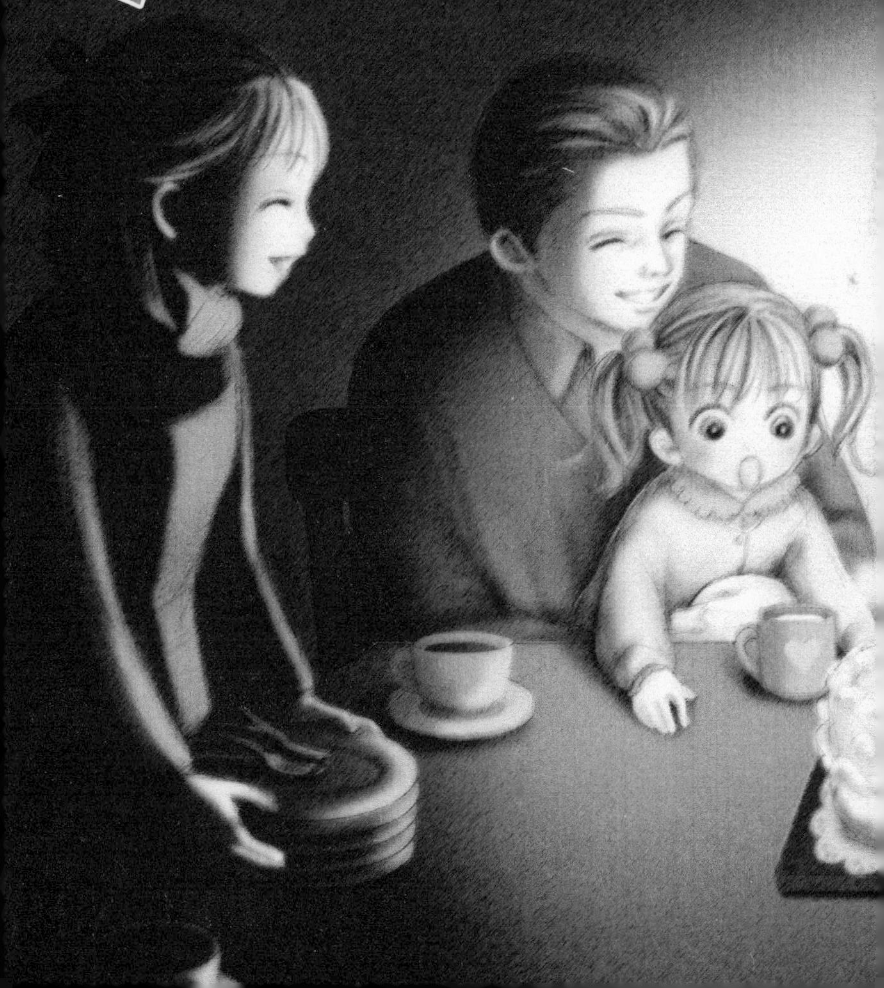

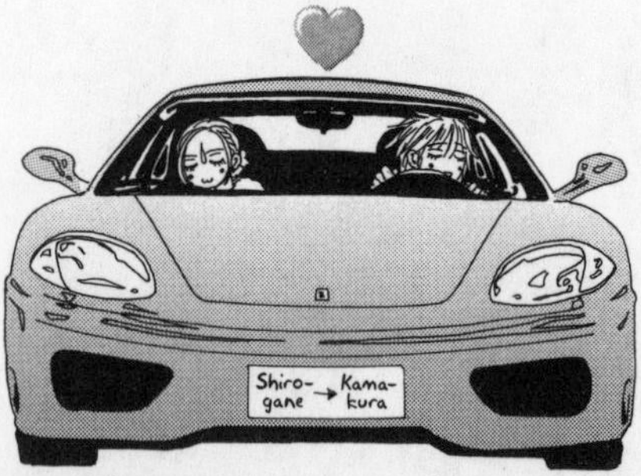
Shiro-gane → Kama-kura

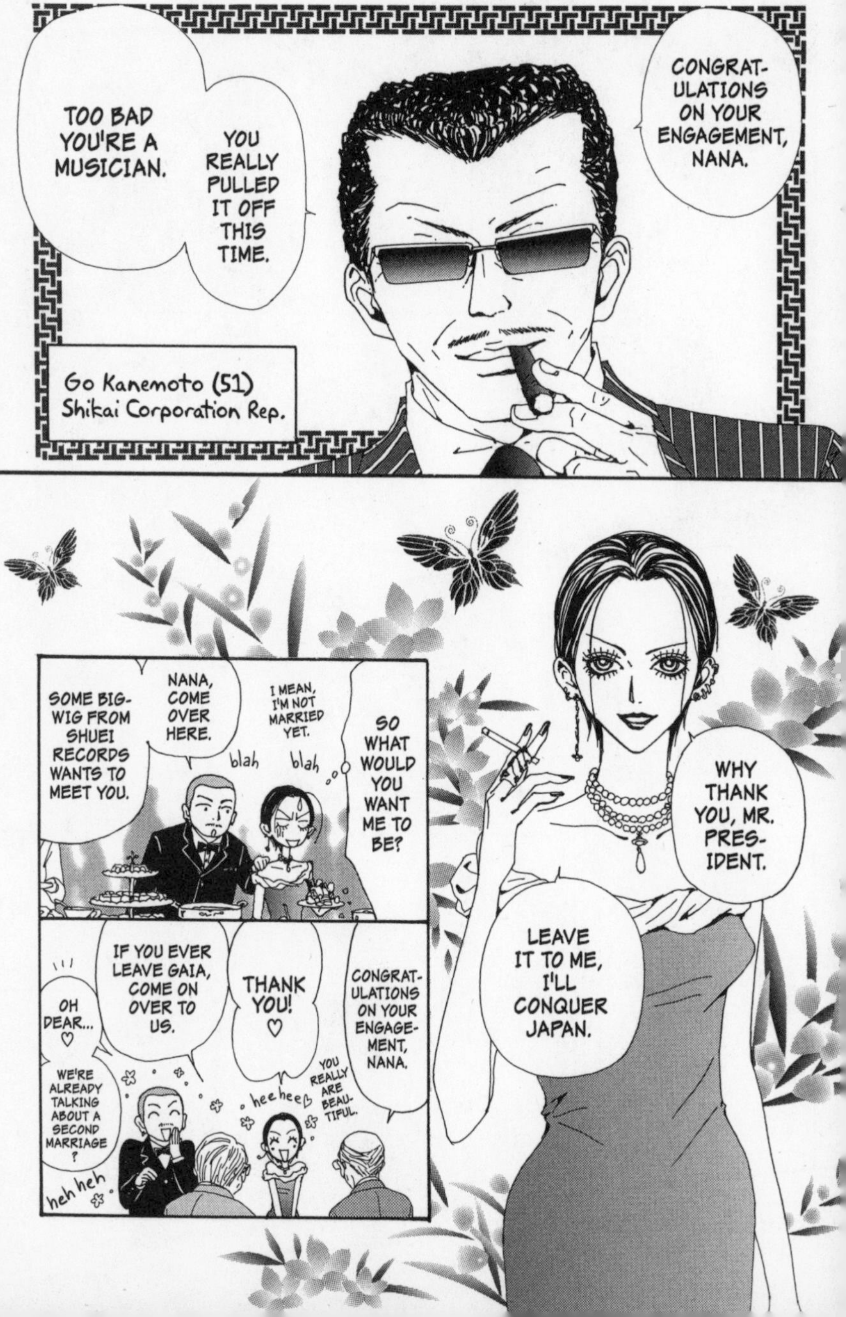
CONGRAT-ULATIONS ON YOUR ENGAGEMENT, NANA.
YOU REALLY PULLED IT OFF THIS TIME.
TOO BAD YOU'RE A MUSICIAN.
Go Kanemoto (51) Shikai Corporation Rep.
WHY THANK YOU, MR. PRES-IDENT.
LEAVE IT TO ME, I'LL CONQUER JAPAN.
SO WHAT WOULD YOU WANT ME TO BE?
I MEAN, I'M NOT MARRIED YET.
blah blah
NANA, COME OVER HERE.
SOME BIG-WIG FROM SHUEI RECORDS WANTS TO MEET YOU.
CONGRAT-ULATIONS ON YOUR ENGAGE-MENT, NANA.
YOU REALLY ARE BEAU-TIFUL.
THANK YOU! ♡
heehee
IF YOU EVER LEAVE GAIA, COME ON OVER TO US.
OH DEAR... ♡
WE'RE ALREADY TALKING ABOUT A SECOND MARRIAGE?
heh heh

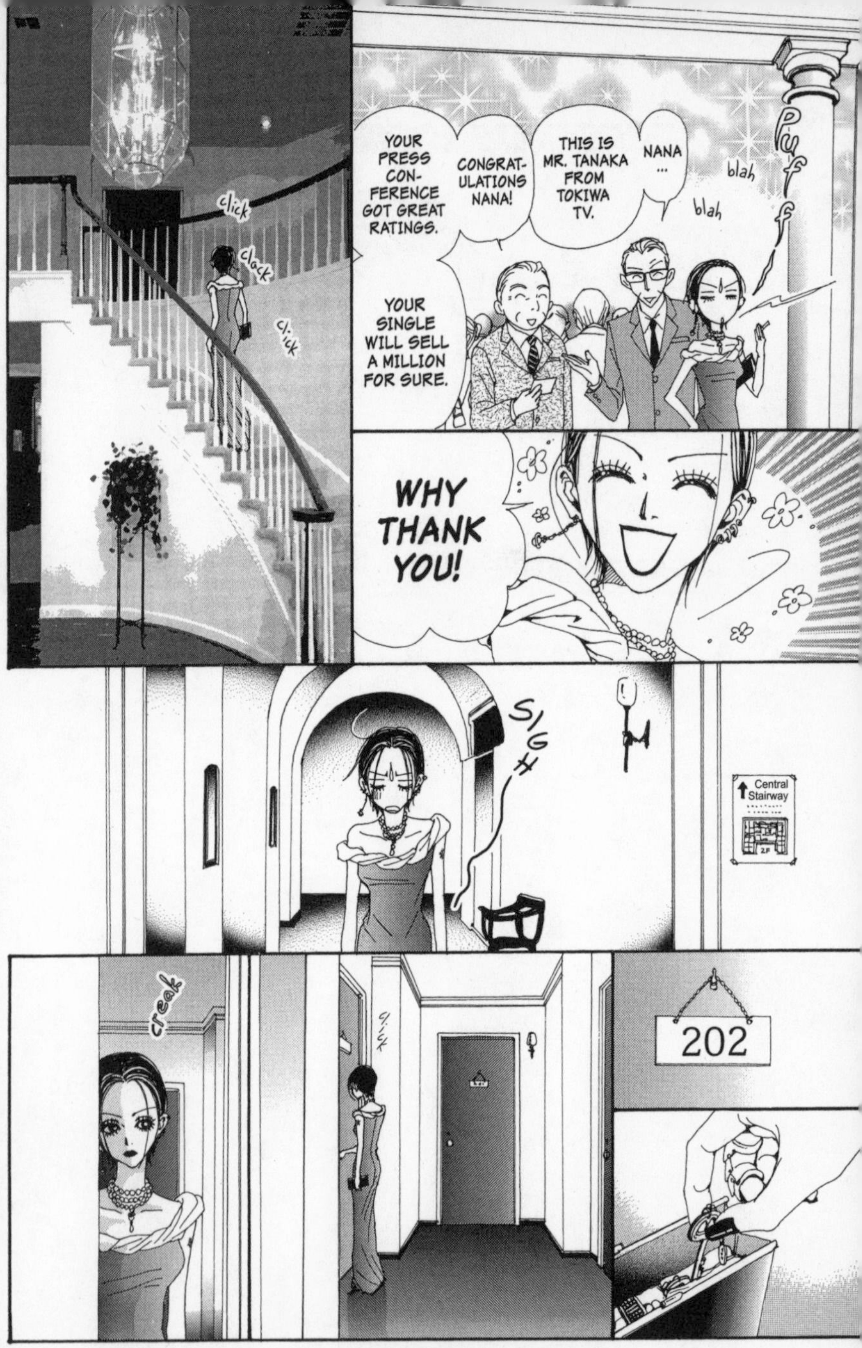
Puff
NANA ...
blah
blah
THIS IS MR. TANAKA FROM TOKIWA TV.
CONGRATULATIONS NANA!
YOUR PRESS CONFERENCE GOT GREAT RATINGS.
YOUR SINGLE WILL SELL A MILLION FOR SURE.
WHY THANK YOU!
click
clack
click
Central Stairway
2F
SIGH
202
click
creak

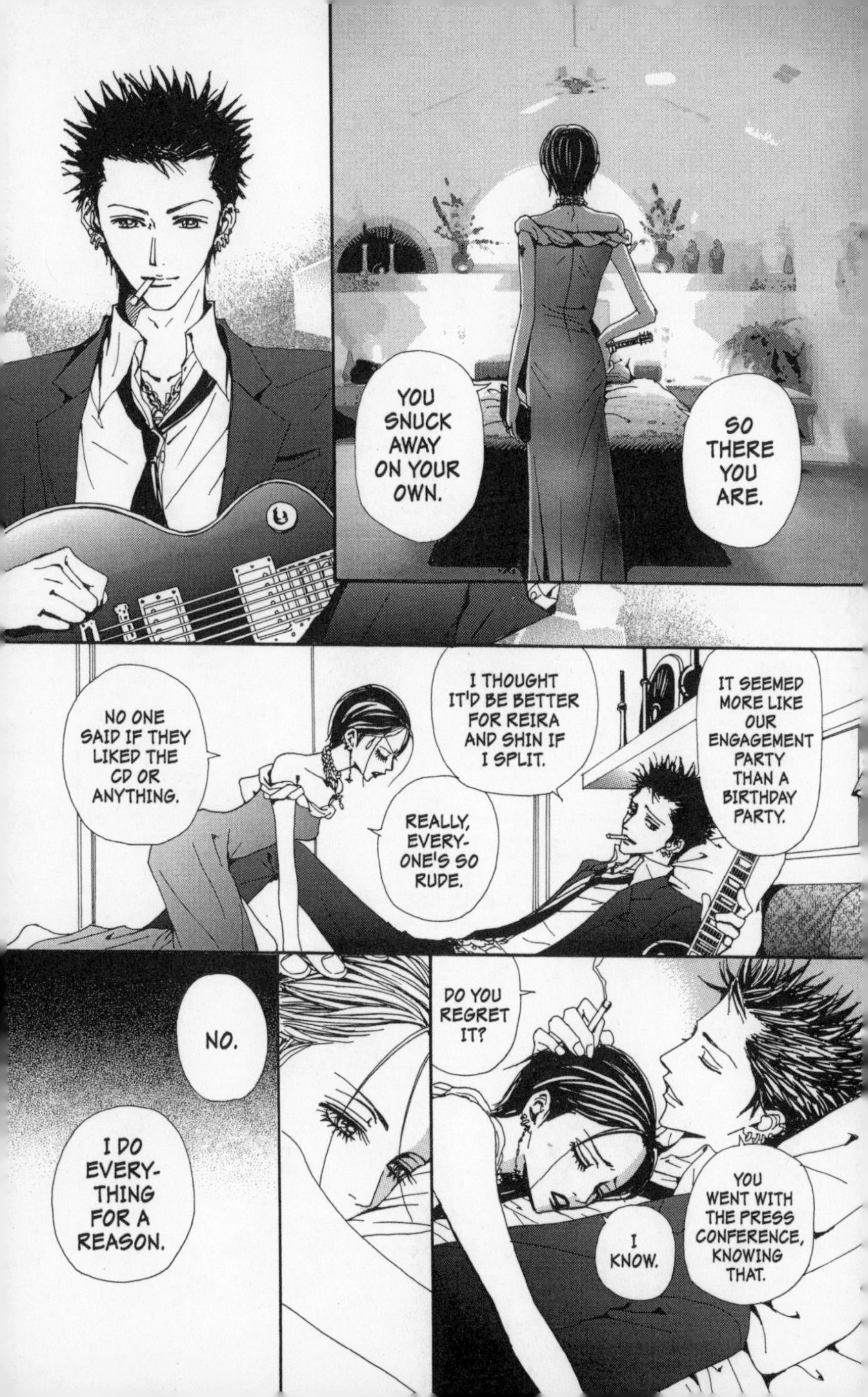
SO THERE YOU ARE.
YOU SNUCK AWAY ON YOUR OWN.
IT SEEMED MORE LIKE OUR ENGAGEMENT PARTY THAN A BIRTHDAY PARTY.
I THOUGHT IT'D BE BETTER FOR REIRA AND SHIN IF I SPLIT.
REALLY, EVERY-ONE'S SO RUDE.
NO ONE SAID IF THEY LIKED THE CD OR ANYTHING.
DO YOU REGRET IT?
YOU WENT WITH THE PRESS CONFERENCE, KNOWING THAT.
I KNOW.
NO.
I DO EVERY-THING FOR A REASON.

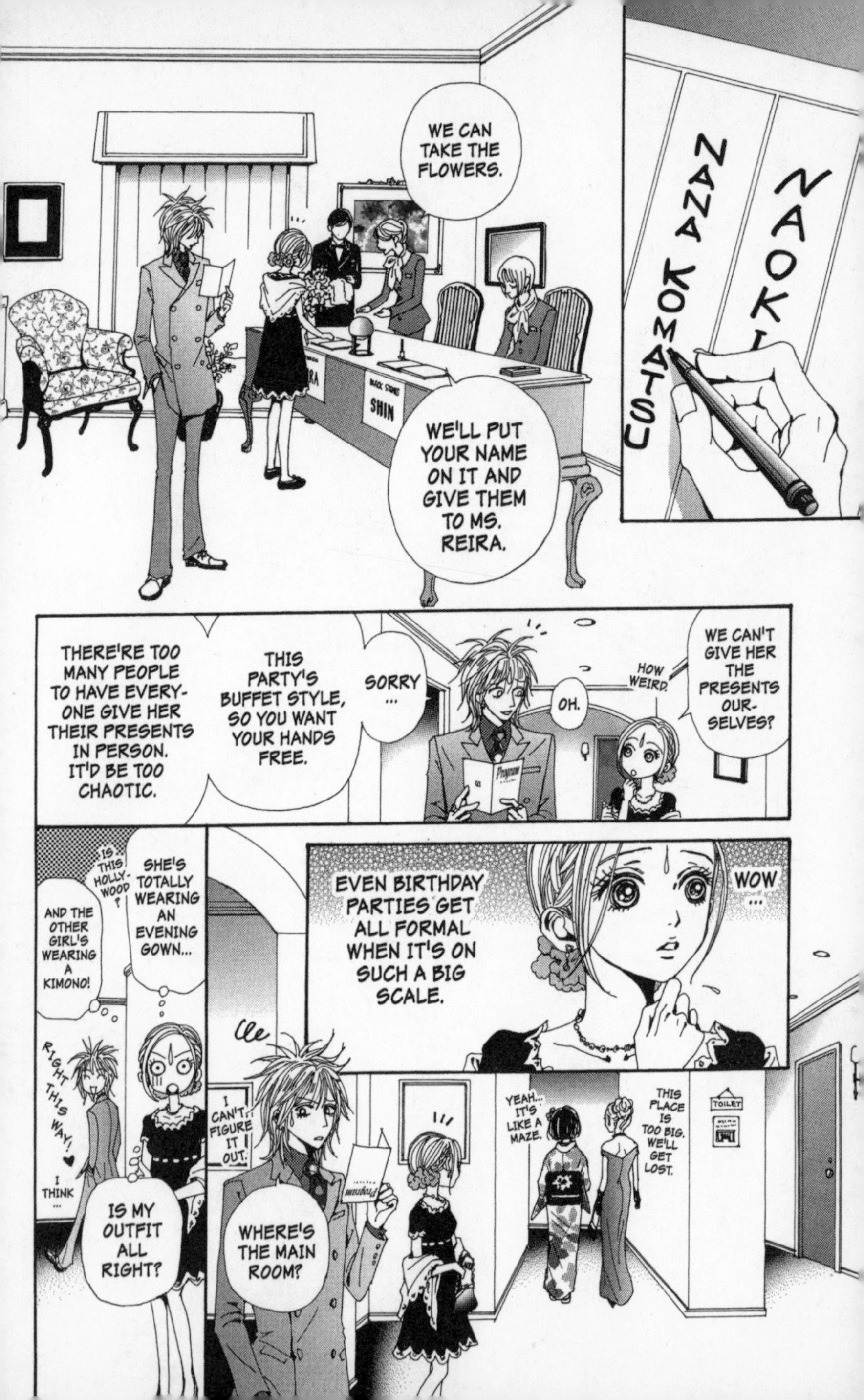
NAOKI
NANA KOMATSU
WE CAN TAKE THE FLOWERS.
REIRA
BLACK STONES SHIN
WE'LL PUT YOUR NAME ON IT AND GIVE THEM TO MS. REIRA.
WE CAN'T GIVE HER THE PRESENTS OURSELVES?
HOW WEIRD.
OH.
SORRY...
THIS PARTY'S BUFFET STYLE, SO YOU WANT YOUR HANDS FREE.
THERE'RE TOO MANY PEOPLE TO HAVE EVERYONE GIVE HER THEIR PRESENTS IN PERSON. IT'D BE TOO CHAOTIC.
WOW...
EVEN BIRTHDAY PARTIES GET ALL FORMAL WHEN IT'S ON SUCH A BIG SCALE.
TOILET
THIS PLACE IS TOO BIG. WE'LL GET LOST.
YEAH... IT'S LIKE A MAZE.
I CAN'T FIGURE IT OUT.
WHERE'S THE MAIN ROOM?
SHE'S TOTALLY WEARING AN EVENING GOWN...
IS THIS HOLLYWOOD?
AND THE OTHER GIRL'S WEARING A KIMONO!
RIGHT THIS WAY! ♥
I THINK...
IS MY OUTFIT ALL RIGHT?

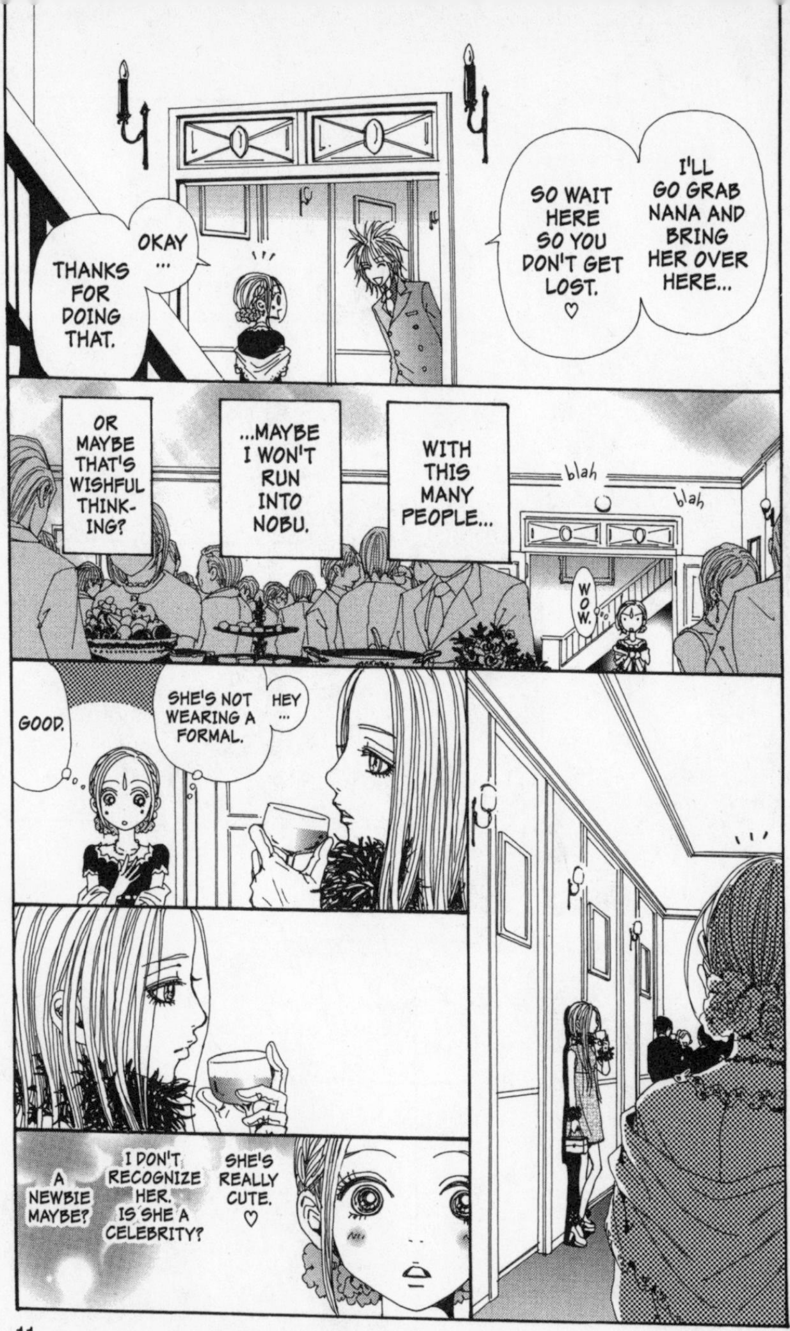
I'LL GO GRAB NANA AND BRING HER OVER HERE...
SO WAIT HERE SO YOU DON'T GET LOST. ♡
OKAY ...
THANKS FOR DOING THAT.
WITH THIS MANY PEOPLE...
blah
blah
WOW.
...MAYBE I WON'T RUN INTO NOBU.
OR MAYBE THAT'S WISHFUL THINKING?
HEY ...
SHE'S NOT WEARING A FORMAL.
GOOD.
SHE'S REALLY CUTE. ♡
I DON'T RECOGNIZE HER. IS SHE A CELEBRITY?
A NEWBIE MAYBE?

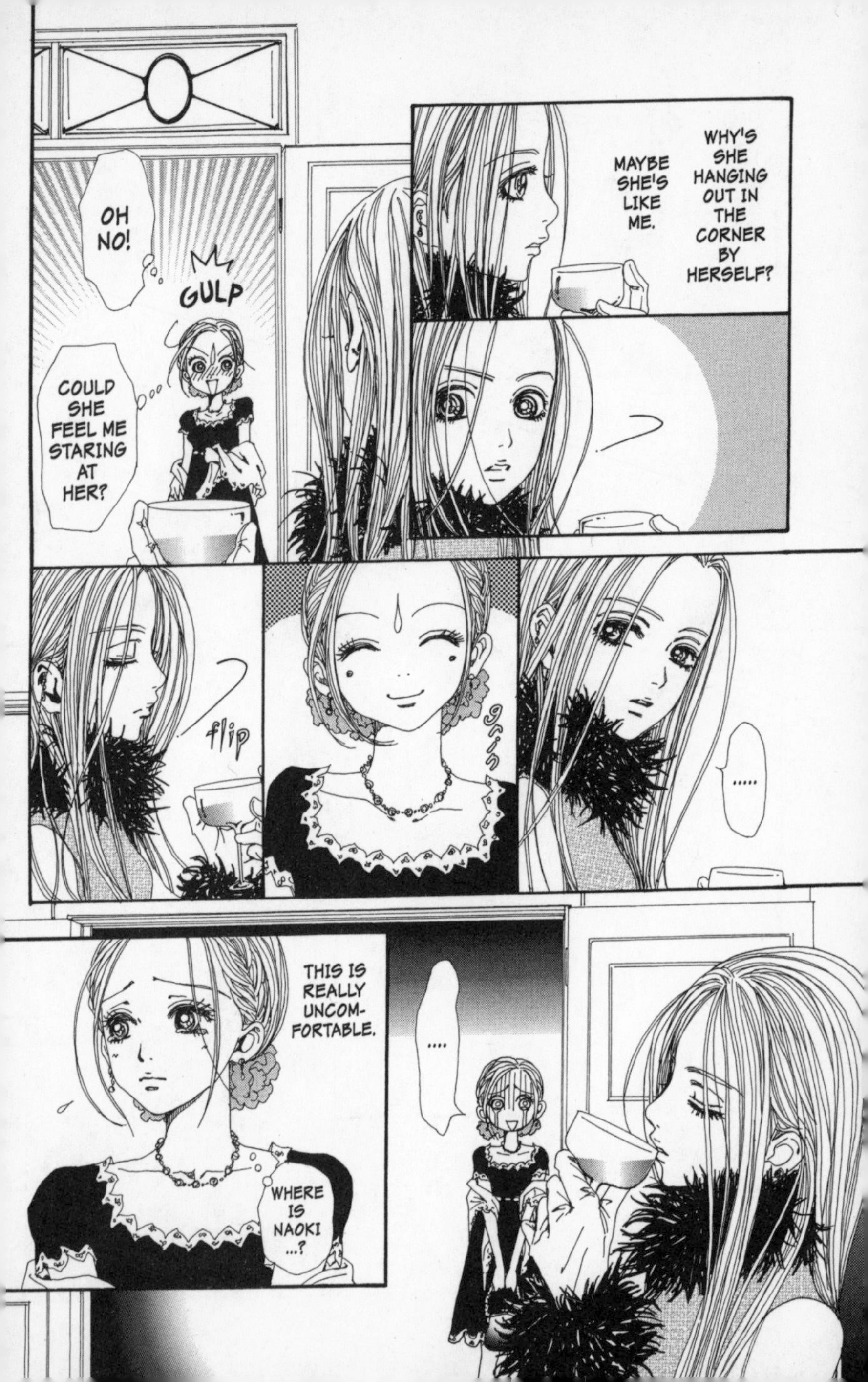
WHY'S SHE HANGING OUT IN THE CORNER BY HERSELF?
MAYBE SHE'S LIKE ME.
OH NO!
GULP
COULD SHE FEEL ME STARING AT HER?
.....
grin
flip
....
THIS IS REALLY UNCOM-FORTABLE.
WHERE IS NAOKI ...?

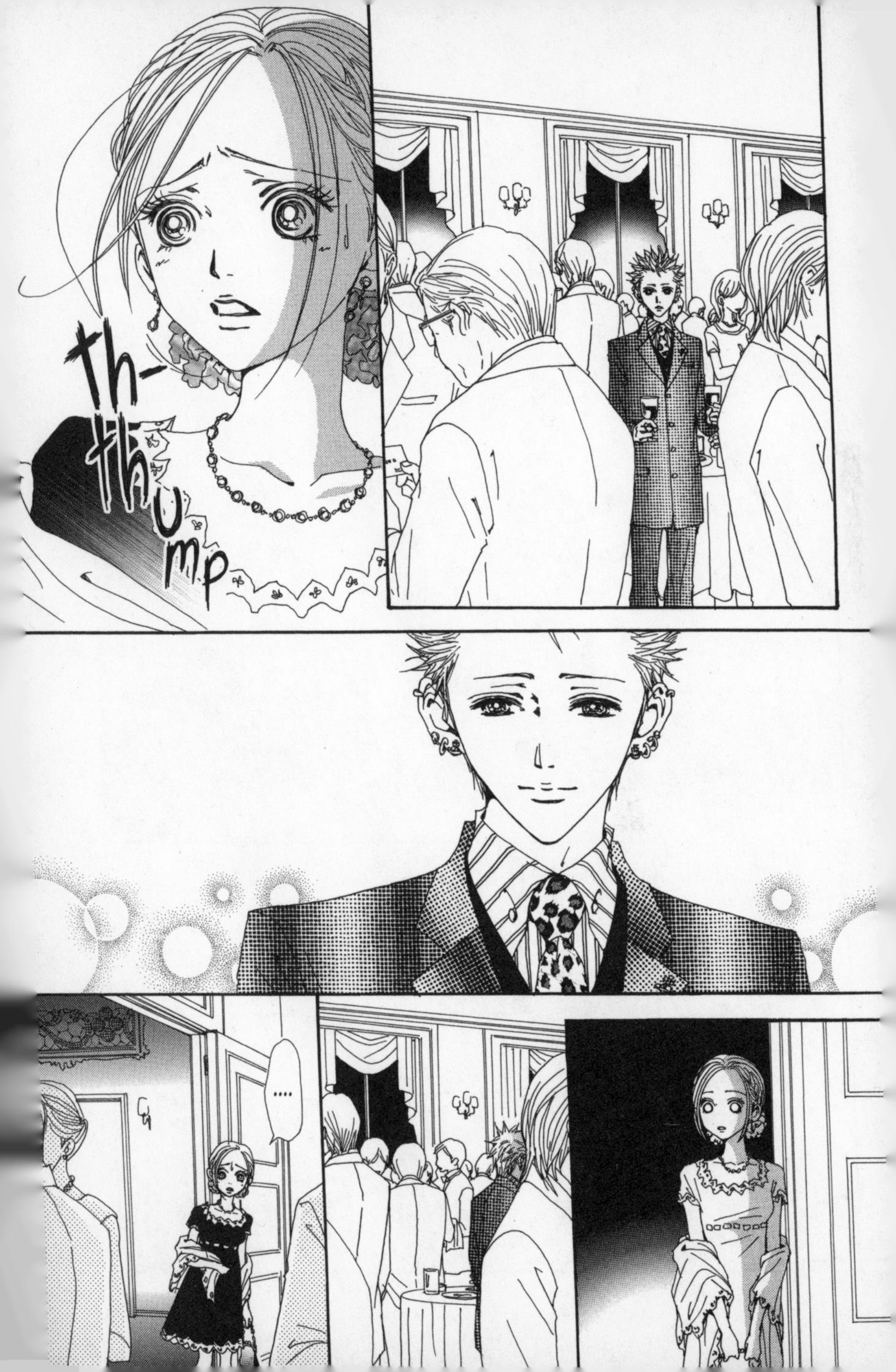
th-thump
....

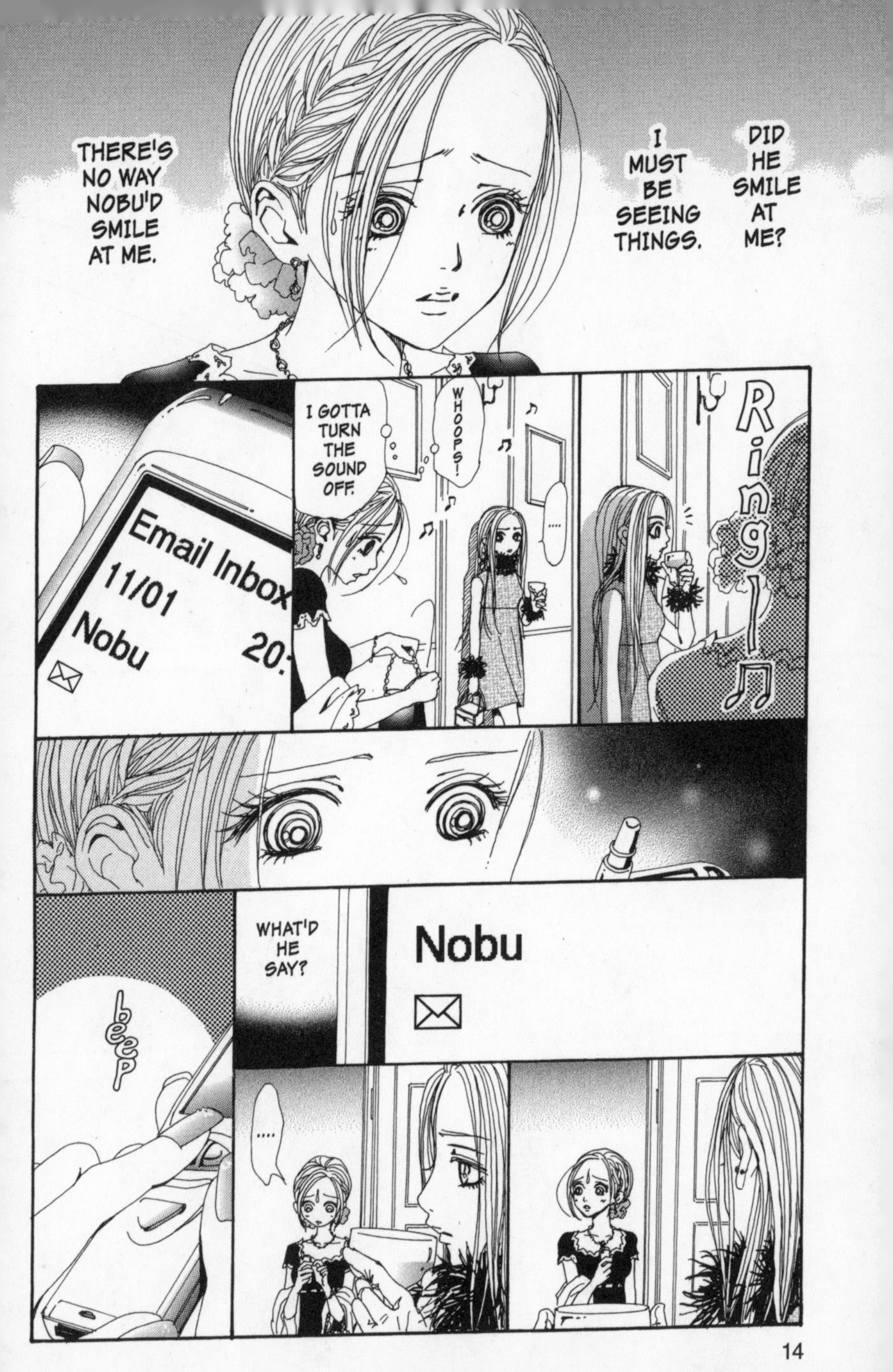
DID HE SMILE AT ME?
I MUST BE SEEING THINGS.
THERE'S NO WAY NOBU'D SMILE AT ME.
Ring♫
....
WHOOPS!
I GOTTA TURN THE SOUND OFF.
Email Inbox
11/01
Nobu
20:
Nobu
WHAT'D HE SAY?
....
beep

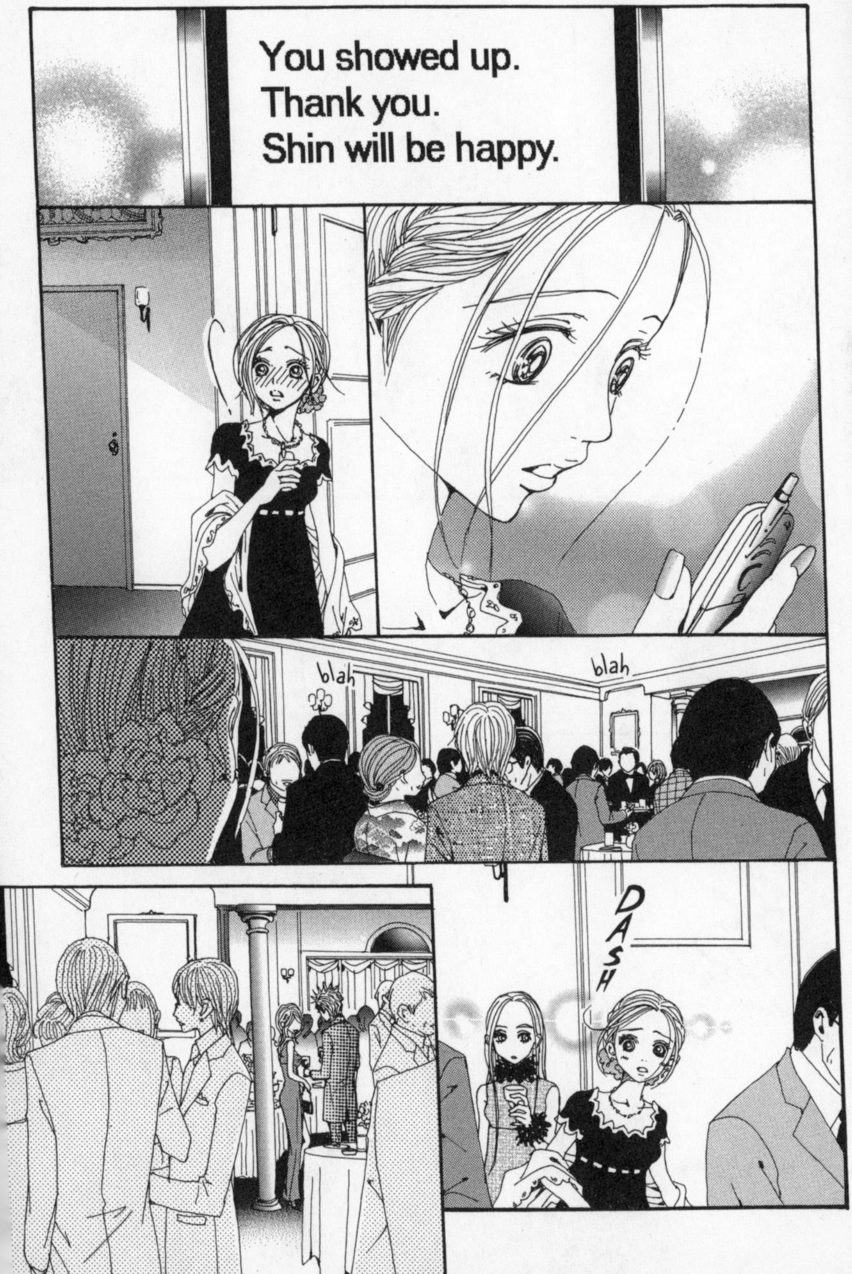
You showed up.
Thank you.
Shin will be happy.
blah
blah
DASH

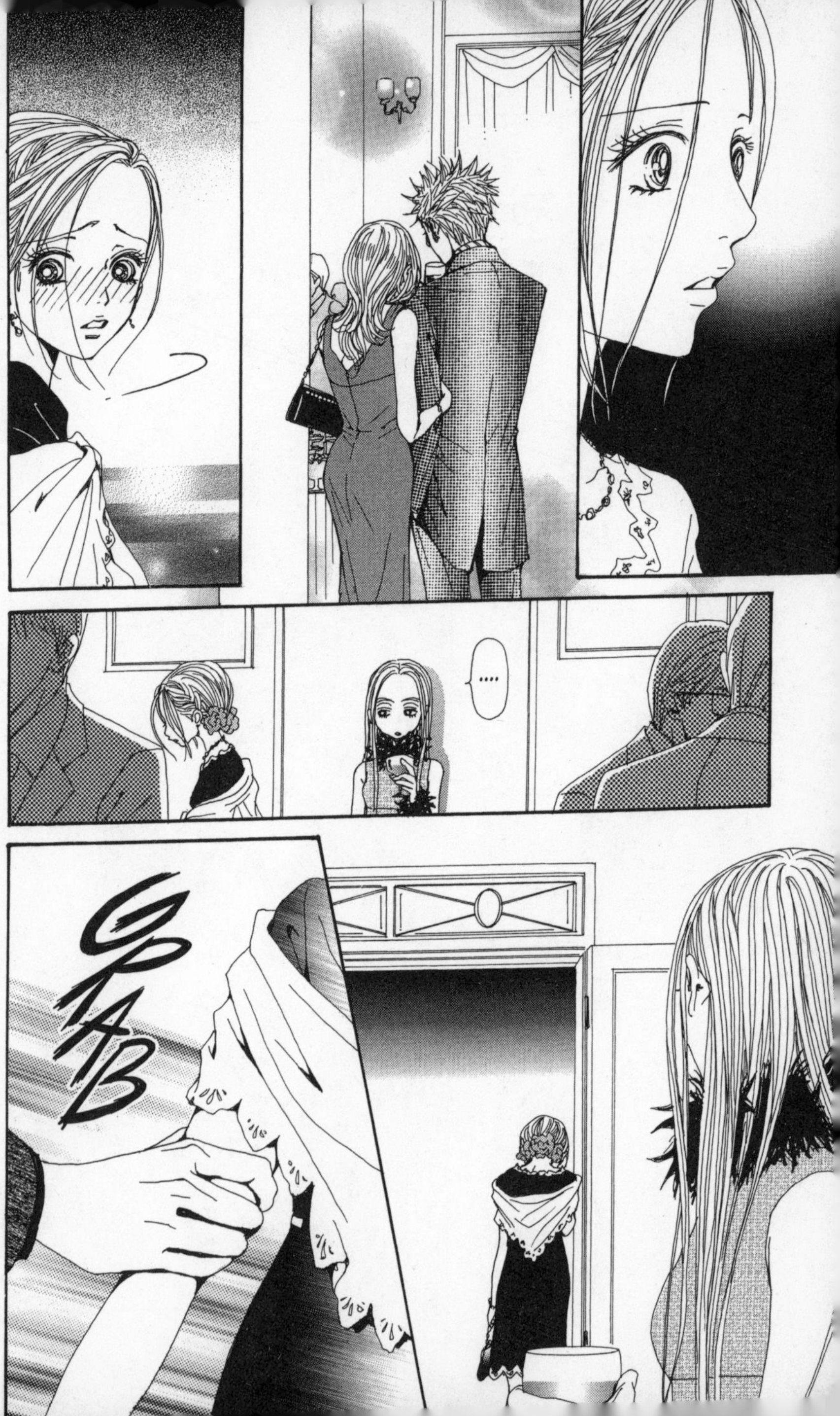
.....
GRAB

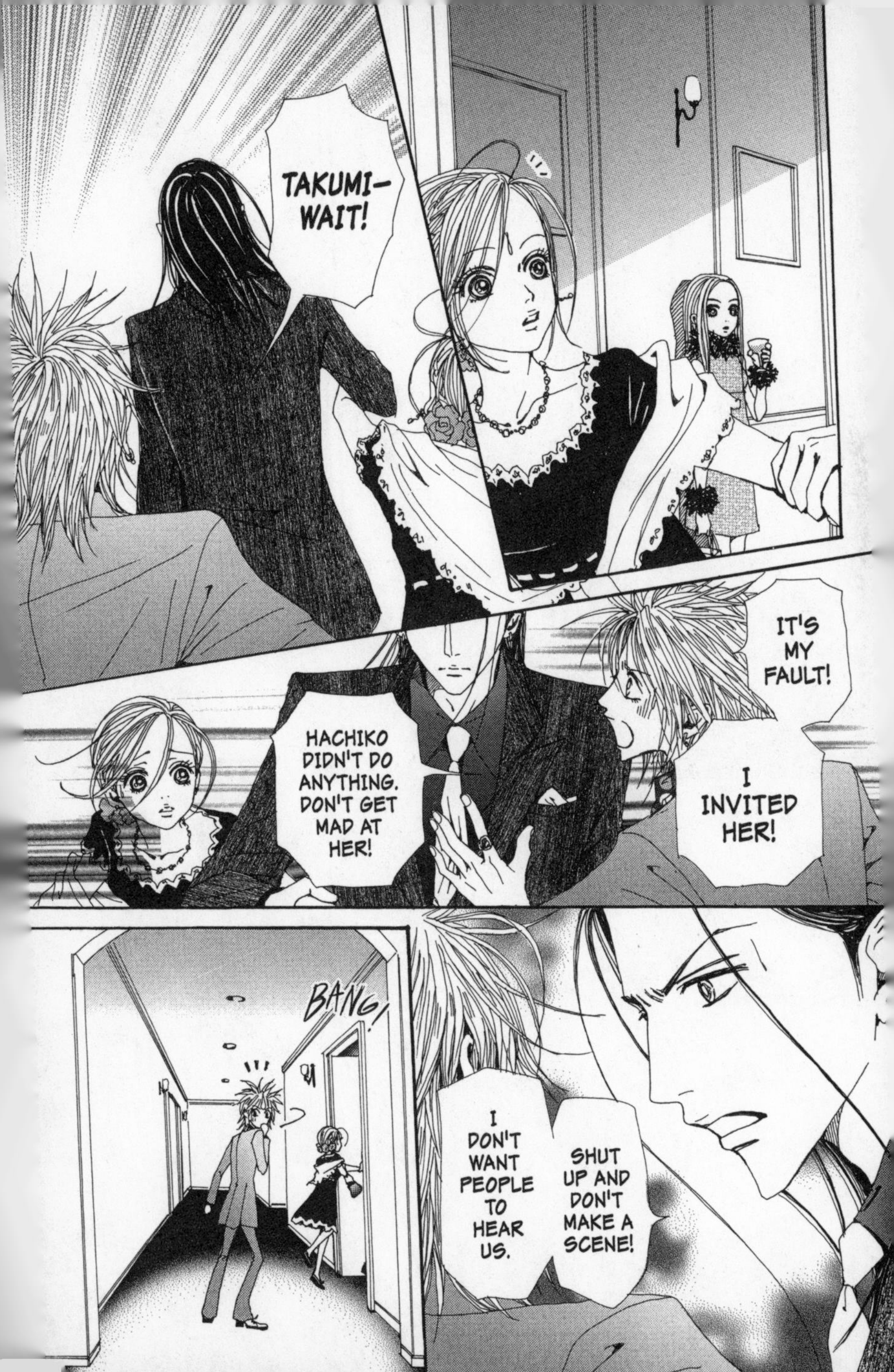
TAKUMI—WAIT!
IT'S MY FAULT!
I INVITED HER!
HACHIKO DIDN'T DO ANYTHING. DON'T GET MAD AT HER!
SHUT UP AND DON'T MAKE A SCENE!
I DON'T WANT PEOPLE TO HEAR US.
BANG!

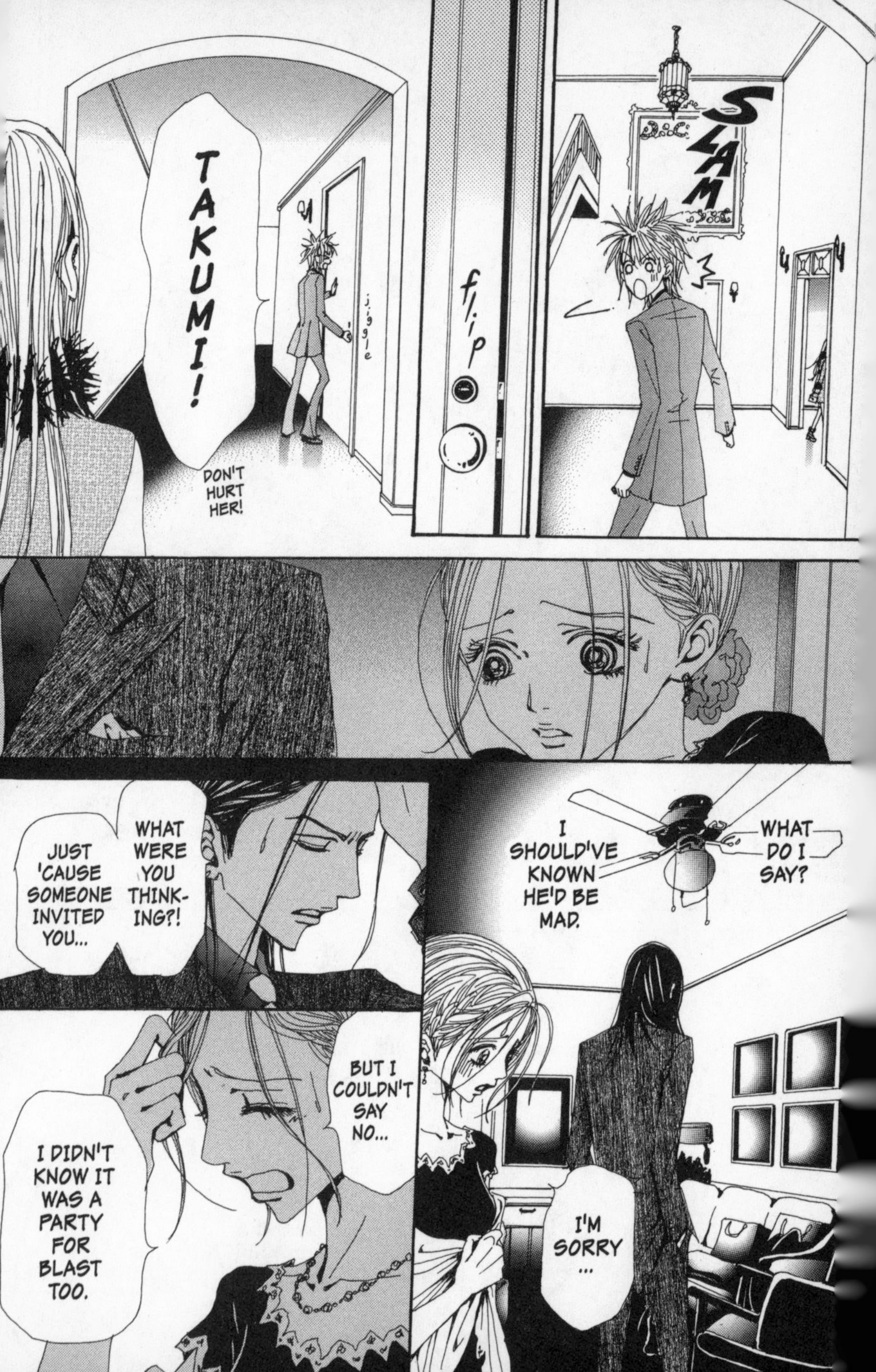
SLAM
flip
TAKUMI!
jiggle
DON'T HURT HER!
WHAT DO I SAY?
I SHOULD'VE KNOWN HE'D BE MAD.
I'M SORRY...
WHAT WERE YOU THINKING?!
JUST 'CAUSE SOMEONE INVITED YOU...
BUT I COULDN'T SAY NO...
I DIDN'T KNOW IT WAS A PARTY FOR BLAST TOO.

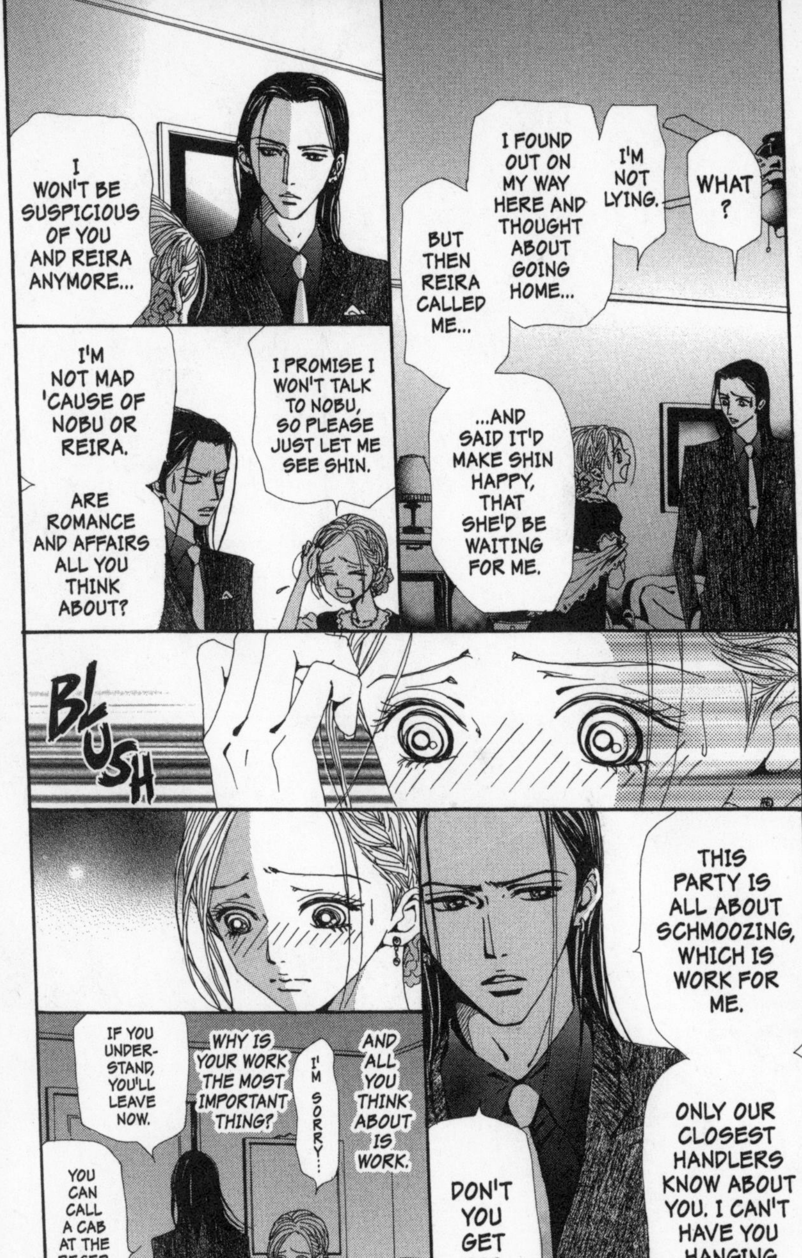
WHAT?
I'M NOT LYING.
I FOUND OUT ON MY WAY HERE AND THOUGHT ABOUT GOING HOME...
BUT THEN REIRA CALLED ME...
...AND SAID IT'D MAKE SHIN HAPPY, THAT SHE'D BE WAITING FOR ME.
I WON'T BE SUSPICIOUS OF YOU AND REIRA ANYMORE...
I PROMISE I WON'T TALK TO NOBU, SO PLEASE JUST LET ME SEE SHIN.
I'M NOT MAD 'CAUSE OF NOBU OR REIRA.
ARE ROMANCE AND AFFAIRS ALL YOU THINK ABOUT?
BLUSH
THIS PARTY IS ALL ABOUT SCHMOOZING, WHICH IS WORK FOR ME.
ONLY OUR CLOSEST HANDLERS KNOW ABOUT YOU. I CAN'T HAVE YOU HANGING AROUND.
DON'T YOU GET IT?
AND ALL YOU THINK ABOUT IS WORK.
I'M SORRY...
WHY IS YOUR WORK THE MOST IMPORTANT THING?
IF YOU UNDER-STAND, YOU'LL LEAVE NOW.
YOU CAN CALL A CAB AT THE RECEP-TION DESK.

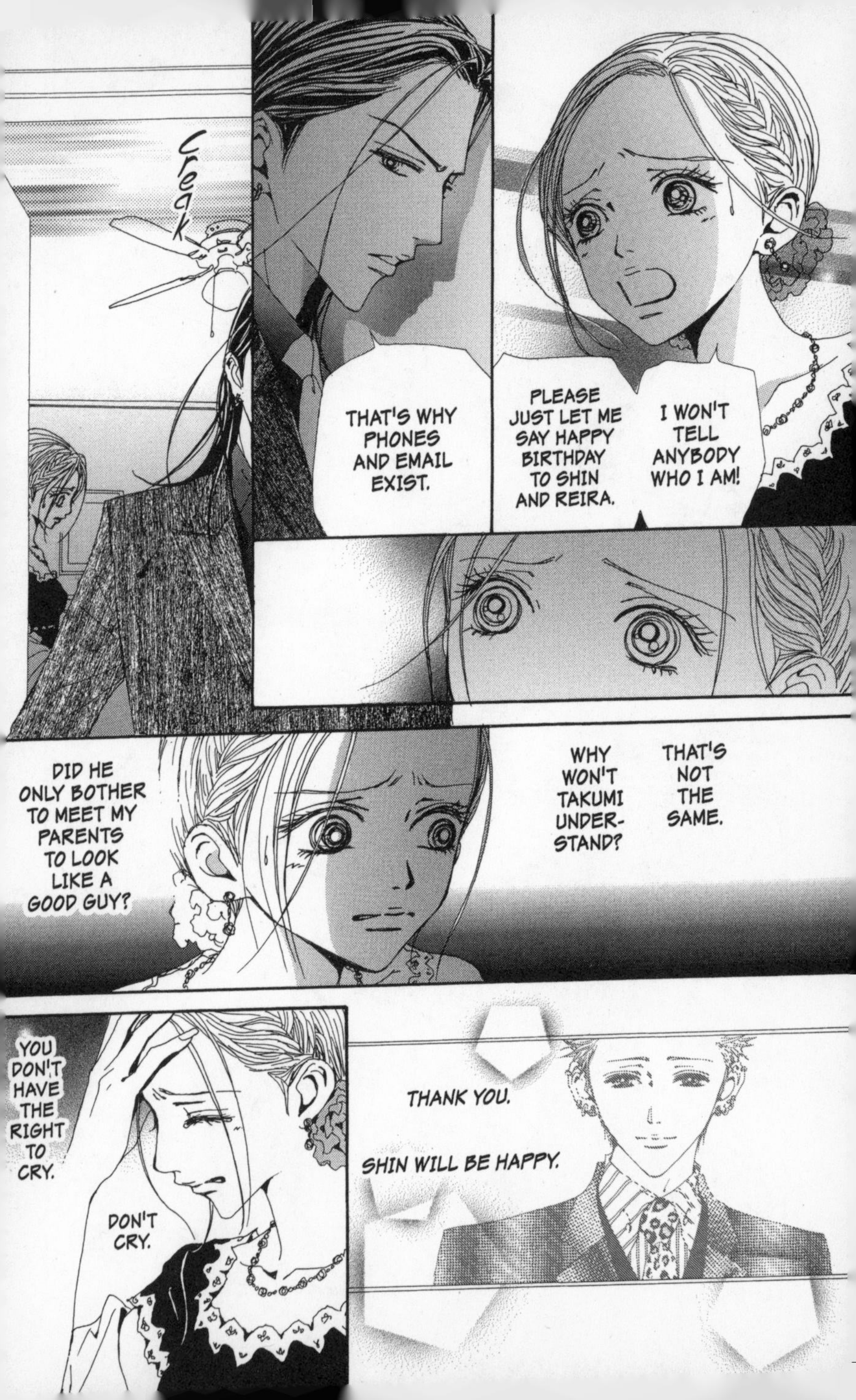
I WON'T TELL ANYBODY WHO I AM!
PLEASE JUST LET ME SAY HAPPY BIRTHDAY TO SHIN AND REIRA.
THAT'S WHY PHONES AND EMAIL EXIST.
Creak
THAT'S NOT THE SAME.
WHY WON'T TAKUMI UNDERSTAND?
DID HE ONLY BOTHER TO MEET MY PARENTS TO LOOK LIKE A GOOD GUY?
THANK YOU.
SHIN WILL BE HAPPY.
YOU DON'T HAVE THE RIGHT TO CRY.
DON'T CRY.

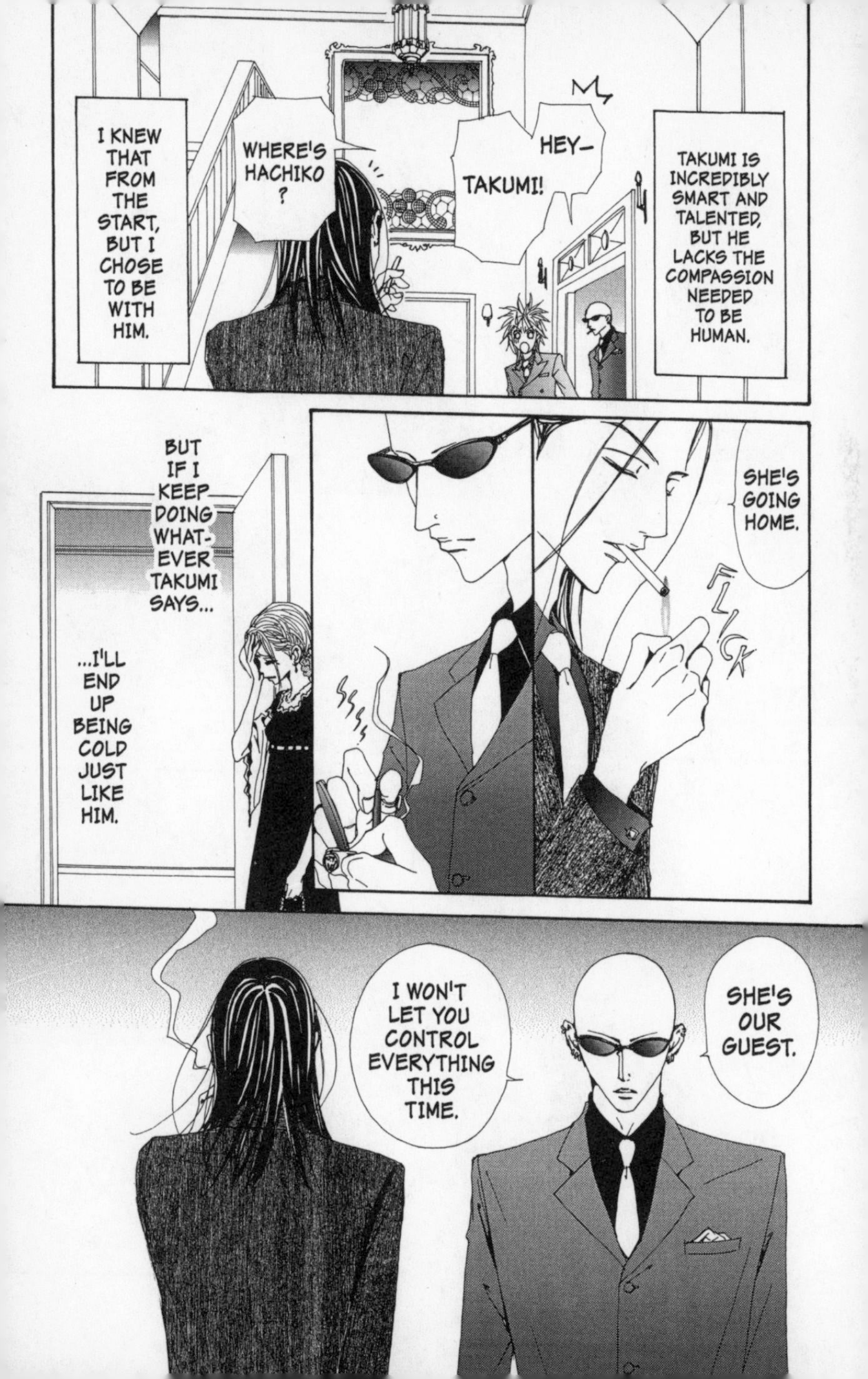
TAKUMI IS INCREDIBLY SMART AND TALENTED, BUT HE LACKS THE COMPASSION NEEDED TO BE HUMAN.
HEY— TAKUMI!
WHERE'S HACHIKO?
I KNEW THAT FROM THE START, BUT I CHOSE TO BE WITH HIM.
SHE'S GOING HOME.
FLICK
BUT IF I KEEP DOING WHAT-EVER TAKUMI SAYS...
...I'LL END UP BEING COLD JUST LIKE HIM.
SHE'S OUR GUEST.
I WON'T LET YOU CONTROL EVERYTHING THIS TIME.

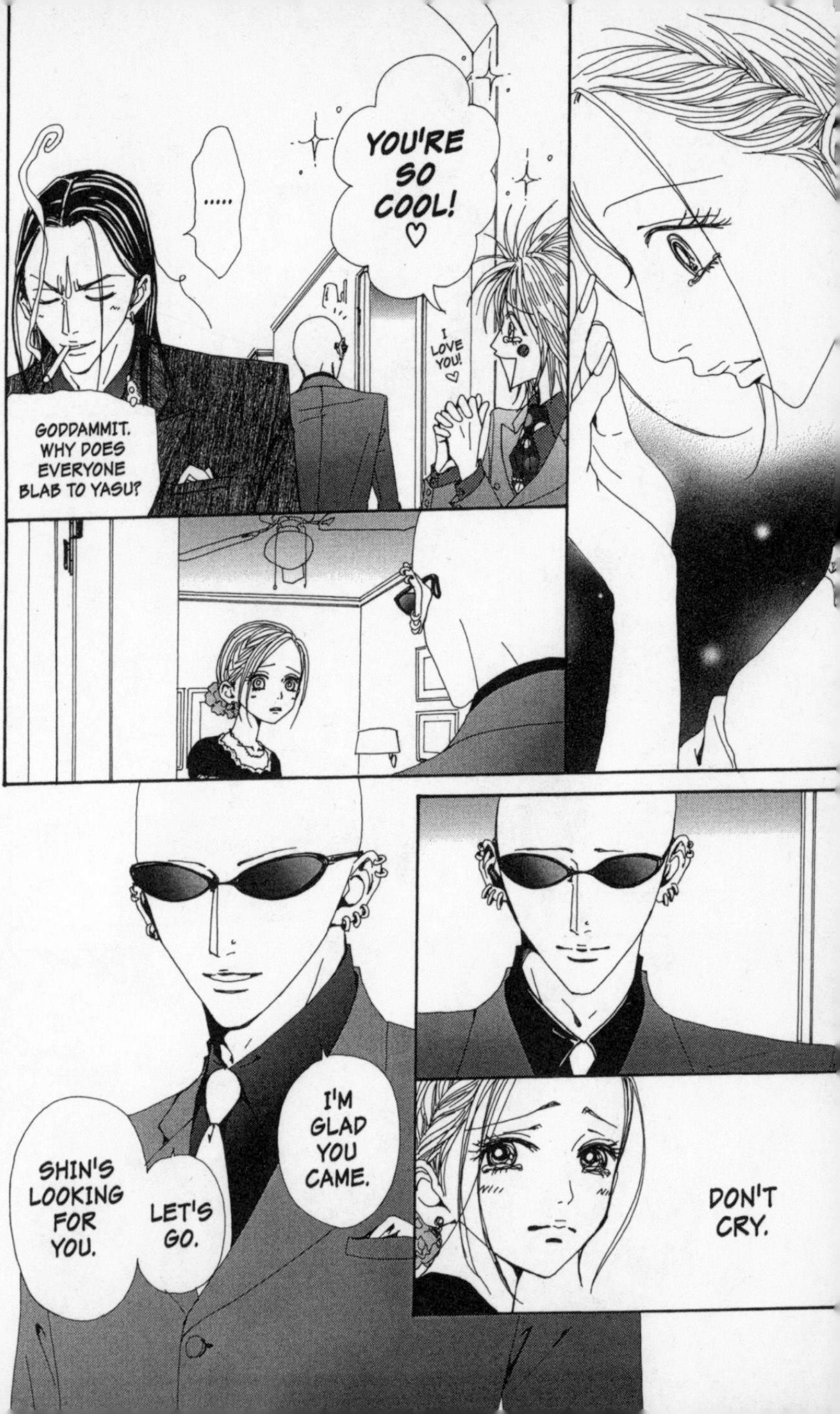
YOU'RE SO COOL! ♡
.....
I LOVE YOU! ♡
GODDAMMIT. WHY DOES EVERYONE BLAB TO YASU?
DON'T CRY.
I'M GLAD YOU CAME.
LET'S GO.
SHIN'S LOOKING FOR YOU.

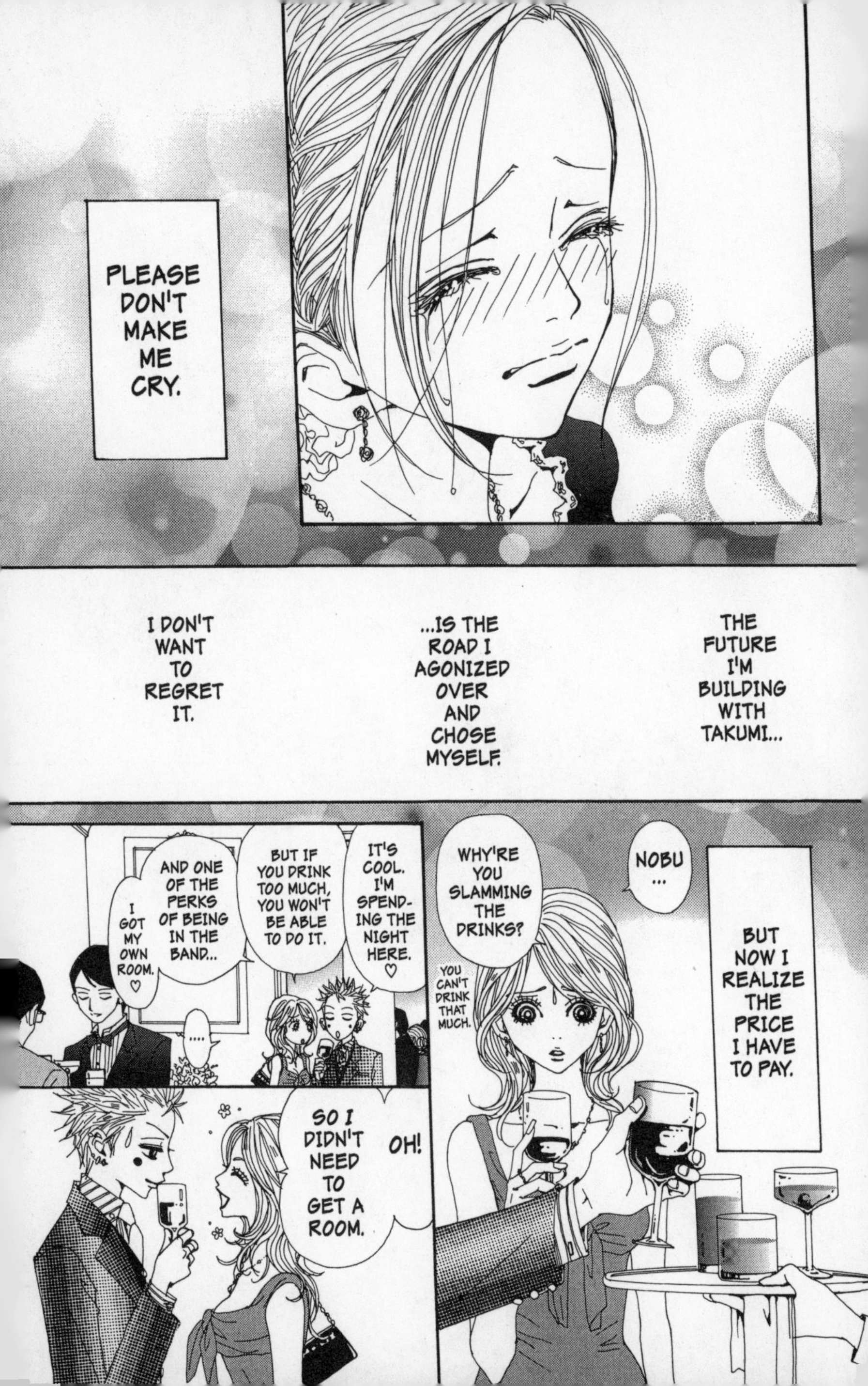
PLEASE DON'T MAKE ME CRY.
THE FUTURE I'M BUILDING WITH TAKUMI...
...IS THE ROAD I AGONIZED OVER AND CHOSE MYSELF.
I DON'T WANT TO REGRET IT.
BUT NOW I REALIZE THE PRICE I HAVE TO PAY.
NOBU...
WHY'RE YOU SLAMMING THE DRINKS?
YOU CAN'T DRINK THAT MUCH.
IT'S COOL. I'M SPEND-ING THE NIGHT HERE. ♡
BUT IF YOU DRINK TOO MUCH, YOU WON'T BE ABLE TO DO IT.
AND ONE OF THE PERKS OF BEING IN THE BAND...
I GOT MY OWN ROOM. ♡
.....
OH!
SO I DIDN'T NEED TO GET A ROOM.

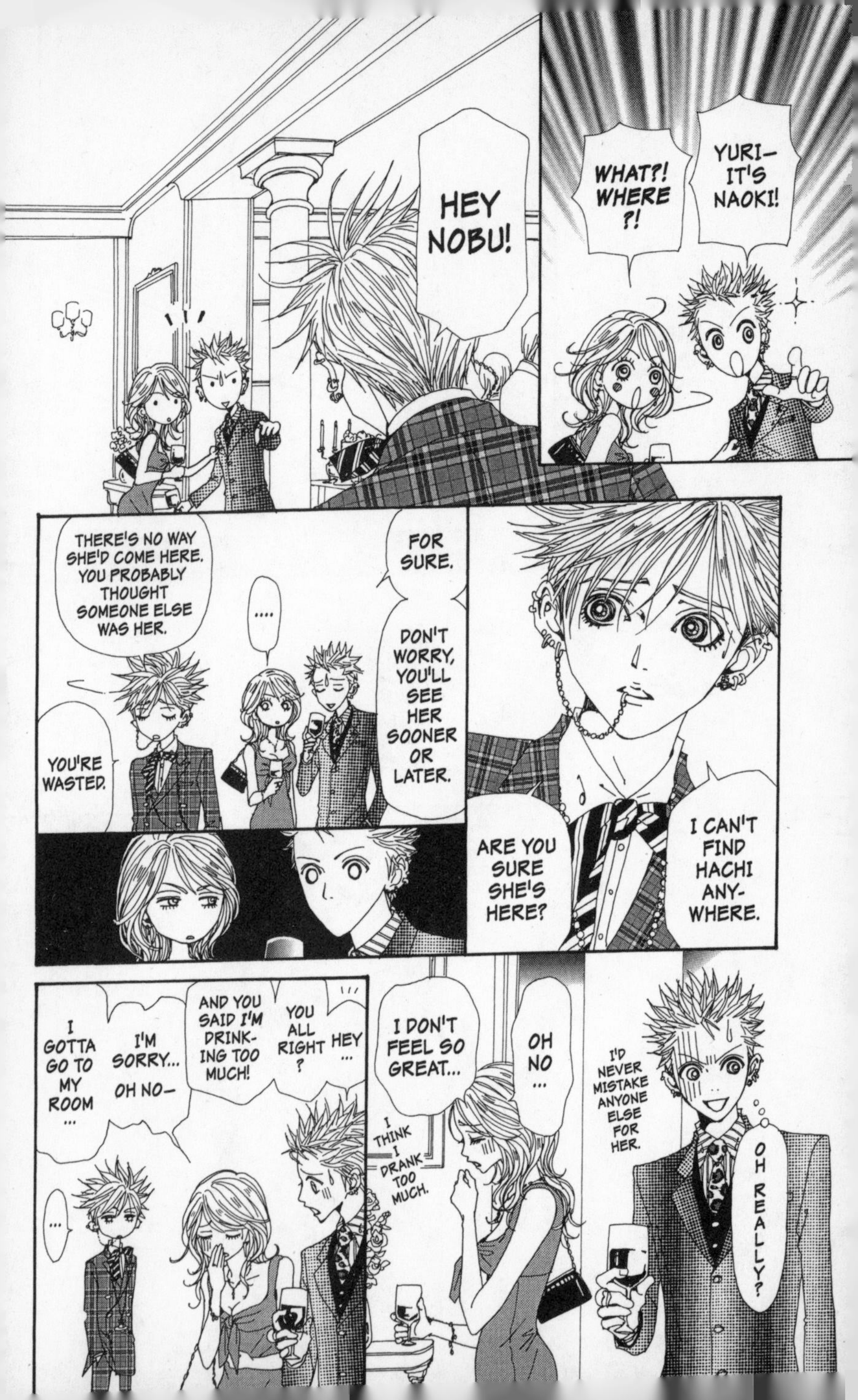
YURI— IT'S NAOKI!
WHAT?! WHERE ?!
HEY NOBU!
I CAN'T FIND HACHI ANY-WHERE.
ARE YOU SURE SHE'S HERE?
FOR SURE.
DON'T WORRY, YOU'LL SEE HER SOONER OR LATER.
....
THERE'S NO WAY SHE'D COME HERE. YOU PROBABLY THOUGHT SOMEONE ELSE WAS HER.
YOU'RE WASTED.
OH REALLY?
I'D NEVER MISTAKE ANYONE ELSE FOR HER.
OH NO ...
I DON'T FEEL SO GREAT...
I THINK I DRANK TOO MUCH.
HEY ...
YOU ALL RIGHT ?
AND YOU SAID I'M DRINK-ING TOO MUCH!
I'M SORRY... OH NO—
I GOTTA GO TO MY ROOM ...
...

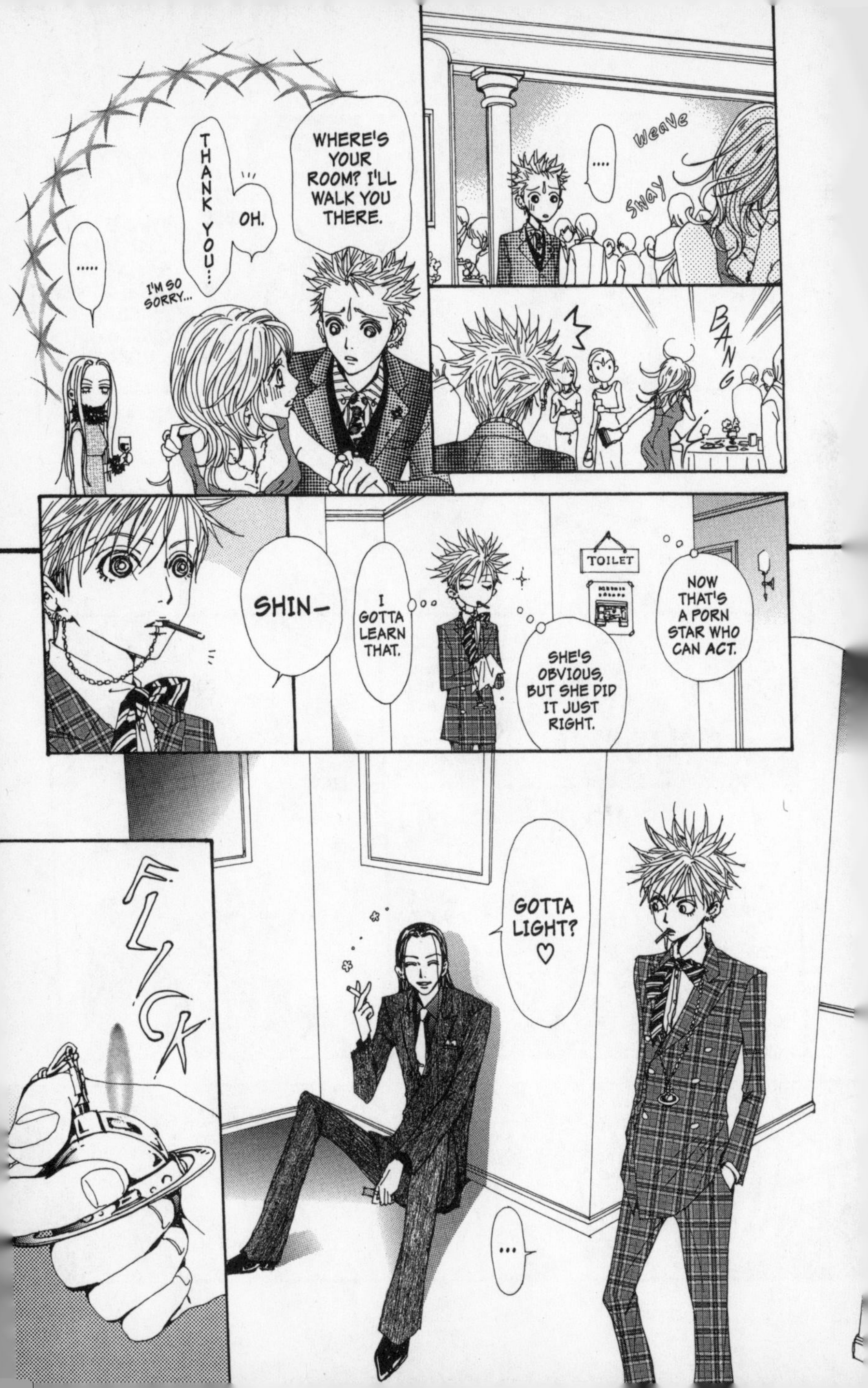
....
WEAVE
SWAY
BANG
WHERE'S YOUR ROOM? I'LL WALK YOU THERE.
OH.
THANK YOU...
I'M SO SORRY...
.....
NOW THAT'S A PORN STAR WHO CAN ACT.
TOILET
SHE'S OBVIOUS, BUT SHE DID IT JUST RIGHT.
I GOTTA LEARN THAT.
SHIN—
GOTTA LIGHT? ♡
...
FLICK

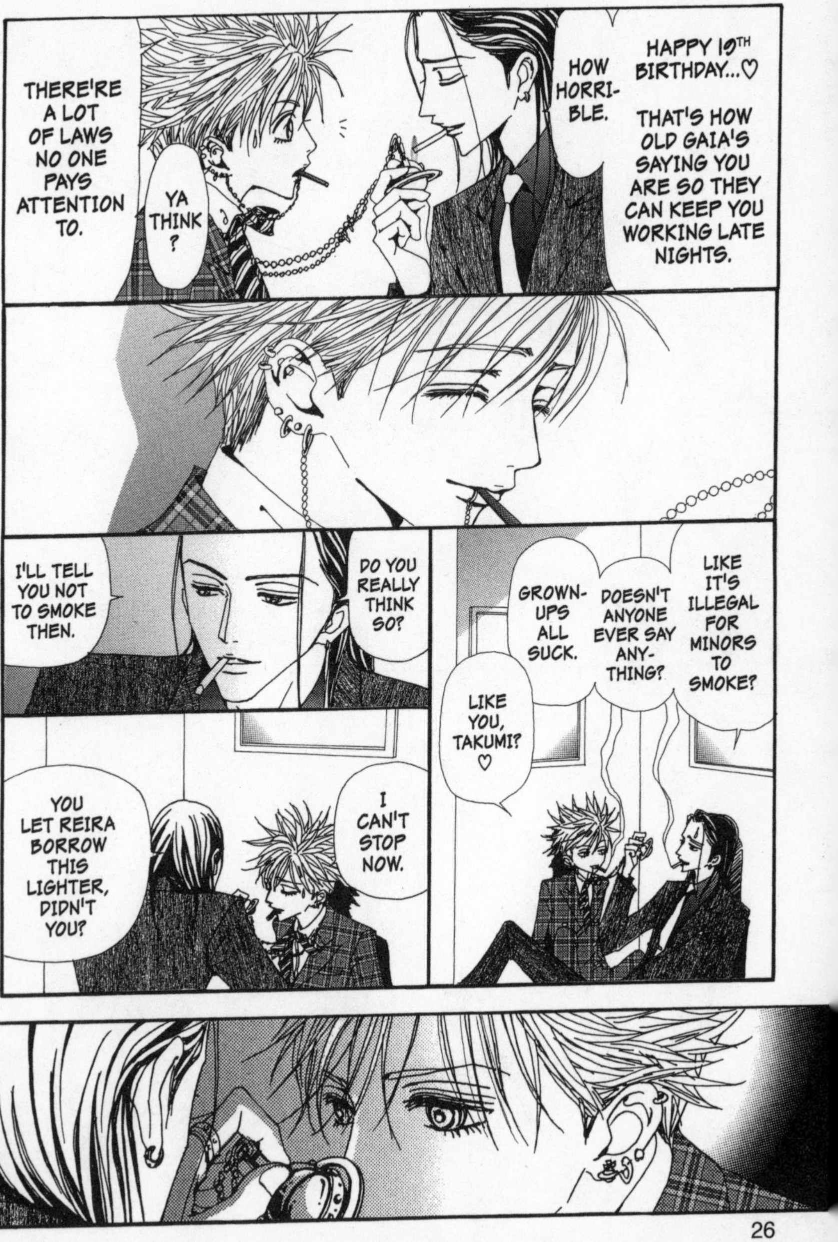
HAPPY 19TH BIRTHDAY...♡
THAT'S HOW OLD GAIA'S SAYING YOU ARE SO THEY CAN KEEP YOU WORKING LATE NIGHTS.
HOW HORRI-BLE.
YA THINK?
THERE'RE A LOT OF LAWS NO ONE PAYS ATTENTION TO.
LIKE IT'S ILLEGAL FOR MINORS TO SMOKE?
DOESN'T ANYONE EVER SAY ANY-THING?
GROWN-UPS ALL SUCK.
LIKE YOU, TAKUMI? ♡
DO YOU REALLY THINK SO?
I'LL TELL YOU NOT TO SMOKE THEN.
I CAN'T STOP NOW.
YOU LET REIRA BORROW THIS LIGHTER, DIDN'T YOU?

HUH?
I DON'T REMEMBER DOING THAT.
REMEMBER IT.
REIRA SURE WAS HOLDING IT TIGHT.
YOU'RE SO COLD.
....
SHE MUST JUST HAVE THE SAME LIGHTER.
I'M SURE THERE'RE OTHERS OUT THERE.
IT'S A LIMITED EDITION, THOUGH...
AND IT HAS THE SAME SERIAL NUMBER.
....

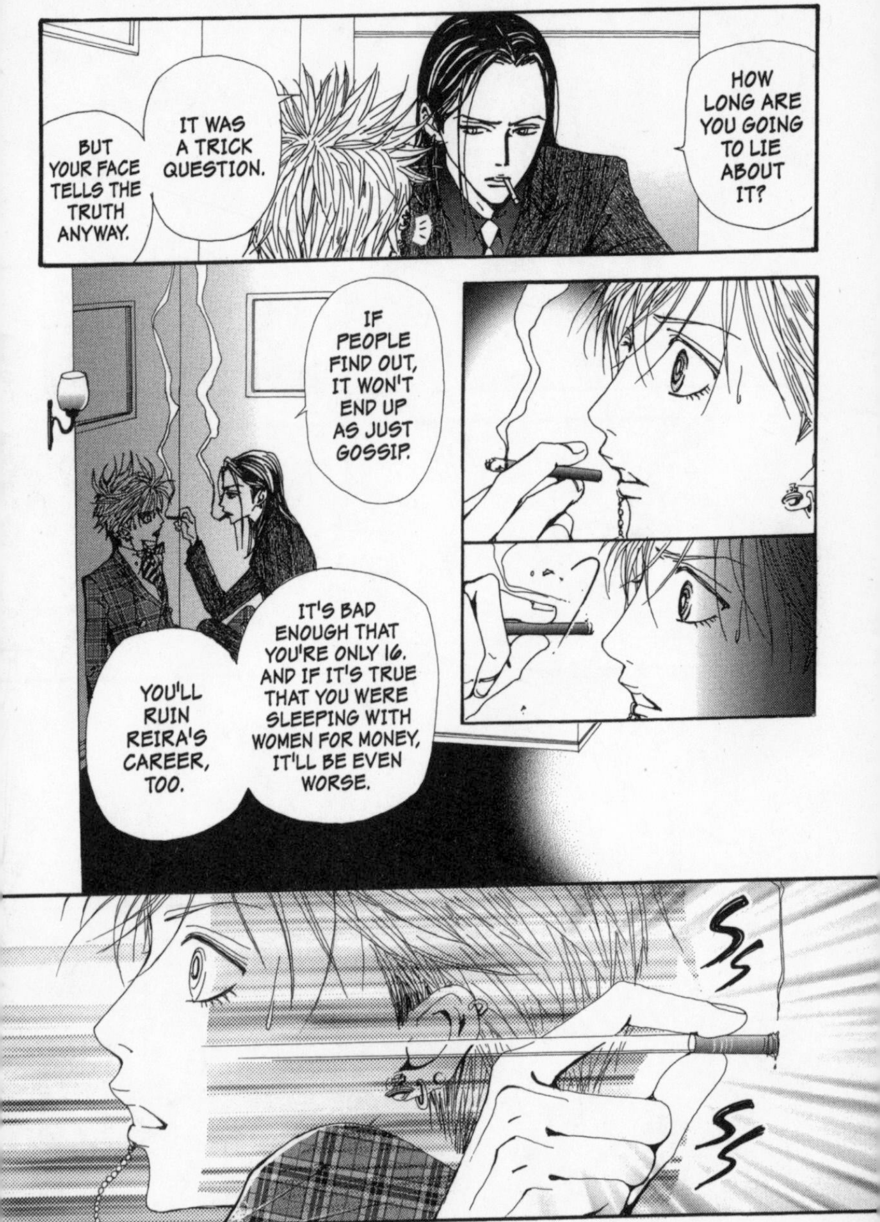
HOW LONG ARE YOU GOING TO LIE ABOUT IT?
IT WAS A TRICK QUESTION.
BUT YOUR FACE TELLS THE TRUTH ANYWAY.
IF PEOPLE FIND OUT, IT WON'T END UP AS JUST GOSSIP.
IT'S BAD ENOUGH THAT YOU'RE ONLY 16. AND IF IT'S TRUE THAT YOU WERE SLEEPING WITH WOMEN FOR MONEY, IT'LL BE EVEN WORSE.
YOU'LL RUIN REIRA'S CAREER, TOO.
SS
SS

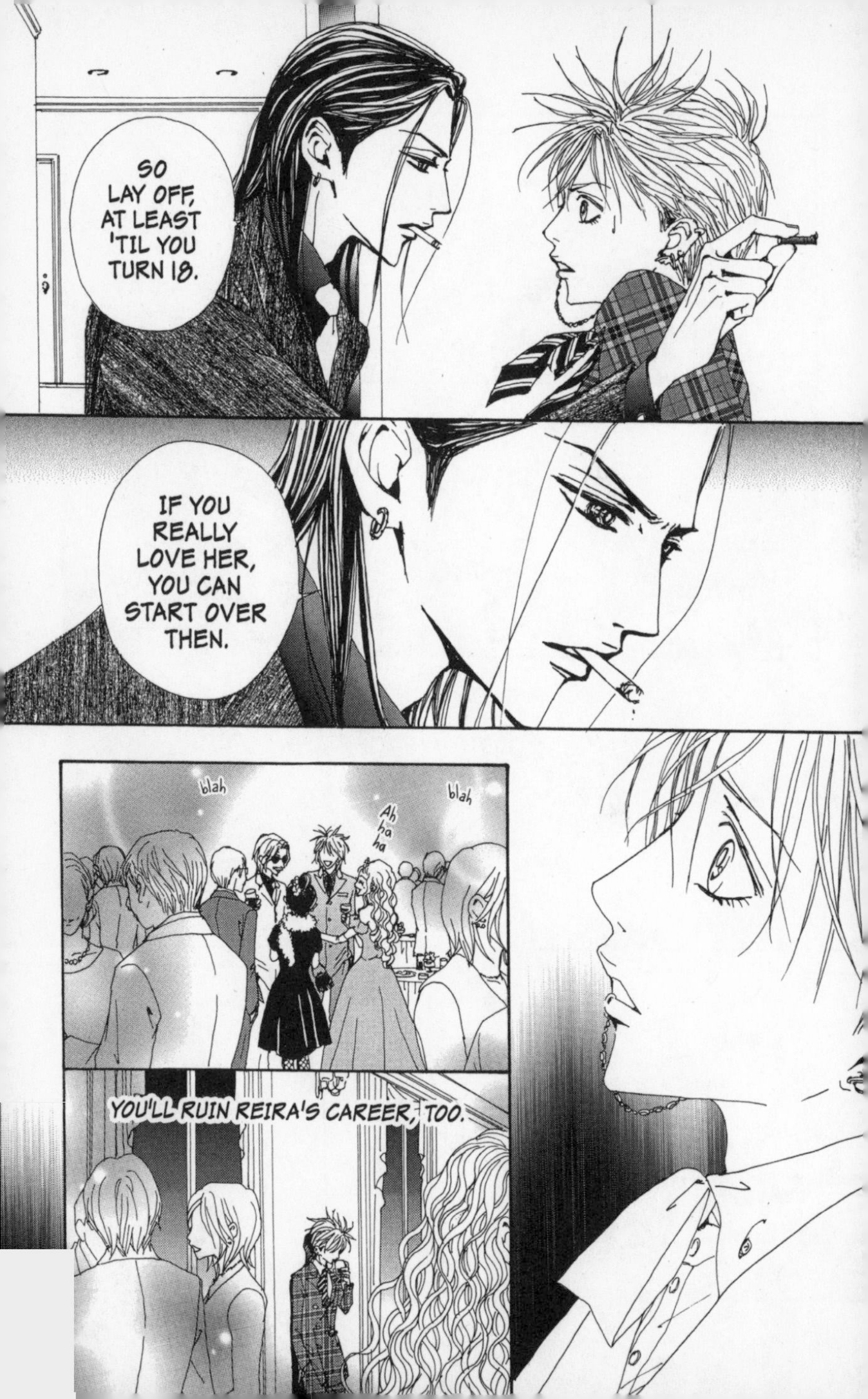
SO LAY OFF, AT LEAST 'TIL YOU TURN 18.
IF YOU REALLY LOVE HER, YOU CAN START OVER THEN.
blah
Ah ha ha
blah
YOU'LL RUIN REIRA'S CAREER, TOO.

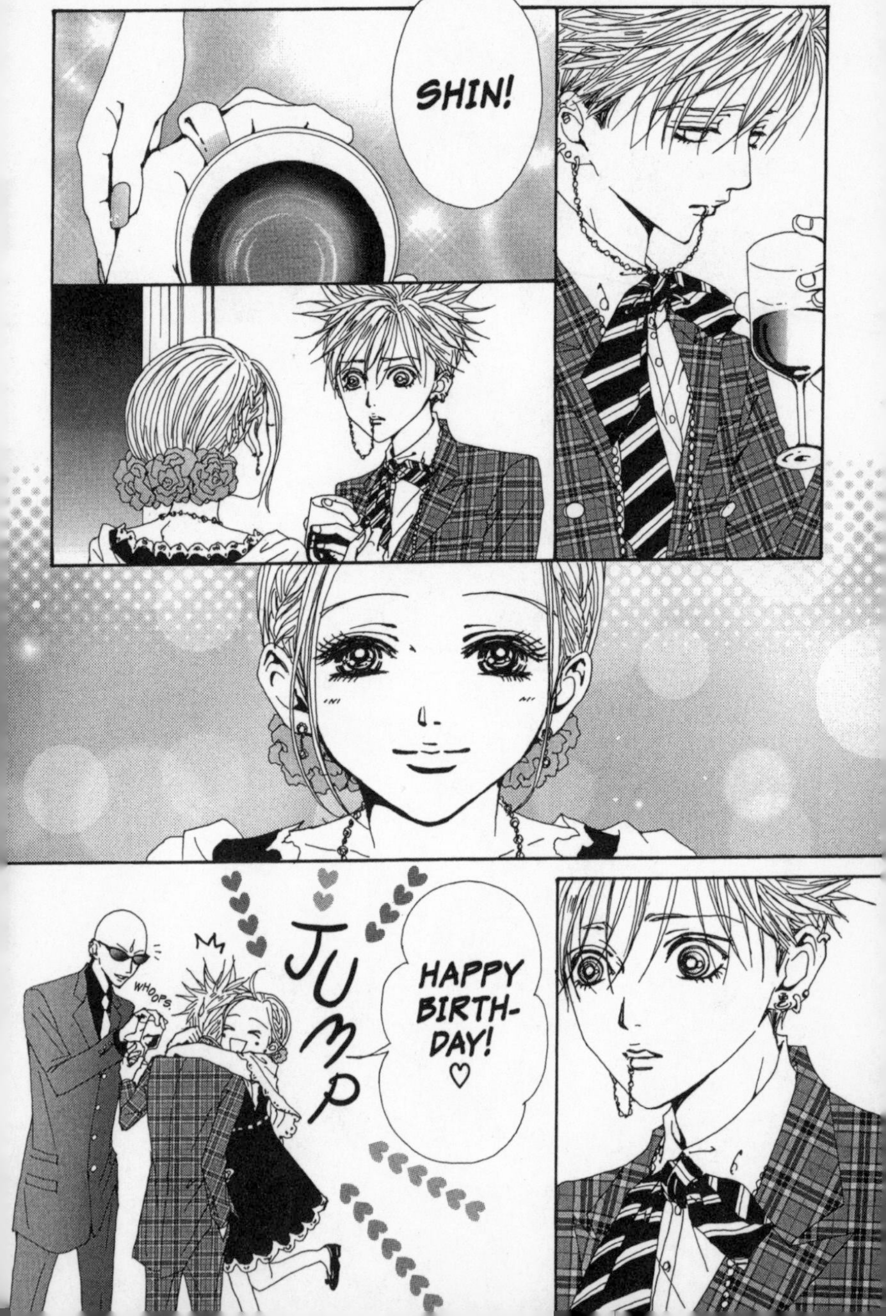
SHIN!
HAPPY BIRTH-DAY! ♡
JUMP
WHOOPS.

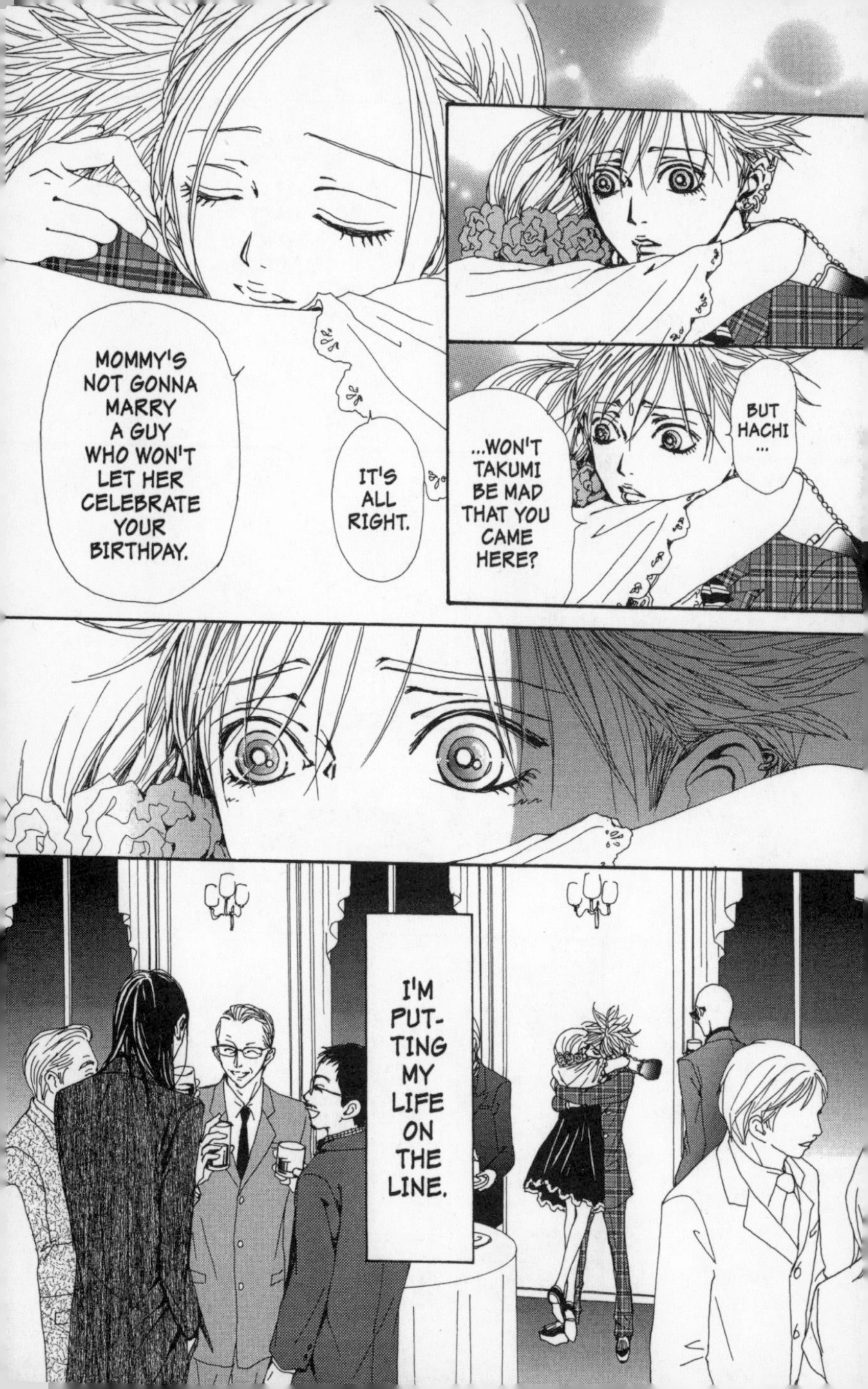
BUT HACHI ...
...WON'T TAKUMI BE MAD THAT YOU CAME HERE?
IT'S ALL RIGHT.
MOMMY'S NOT GONNA MARRY A GUY WHO WON'T LET HER CELEBRATE YOUR BIRTHDAY.
I'M PUT-TING MY LIFE ON THE LINE.

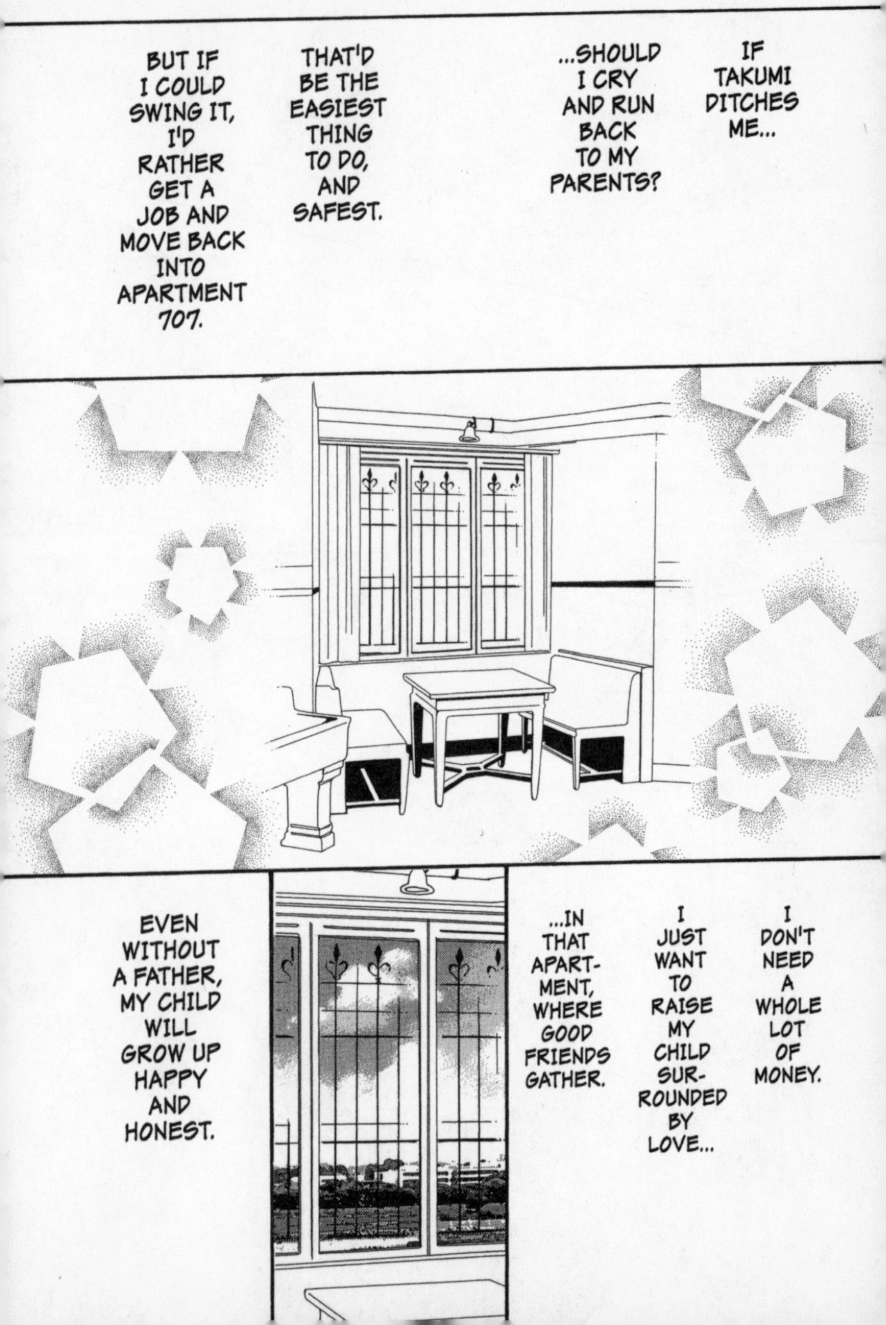
IF TAKUMI DITCHES ME...
...SHOULD I CRY AND RUN BACK TO MY PARENTS?
THAT'D BE THE EASIEST THING TO DO, AND SAFEST.
BUT IF I COULD SWING IT, I'D RATHER GET A JOB AND MOVE BACK INTO APARTMENT 707.
I DON'T NEED A WHOLE LOT OF MONEY.
I JUST WANT TO RAISE MY CHILD SURROUNDED BY LOVE...
...IN THAT APARTMENT, WHERE GOOD FRIENDS GATHER.
EVEN WITHOUT A FATHER, MY CHILD WILL GROW UP HAPPY AND HONEST.

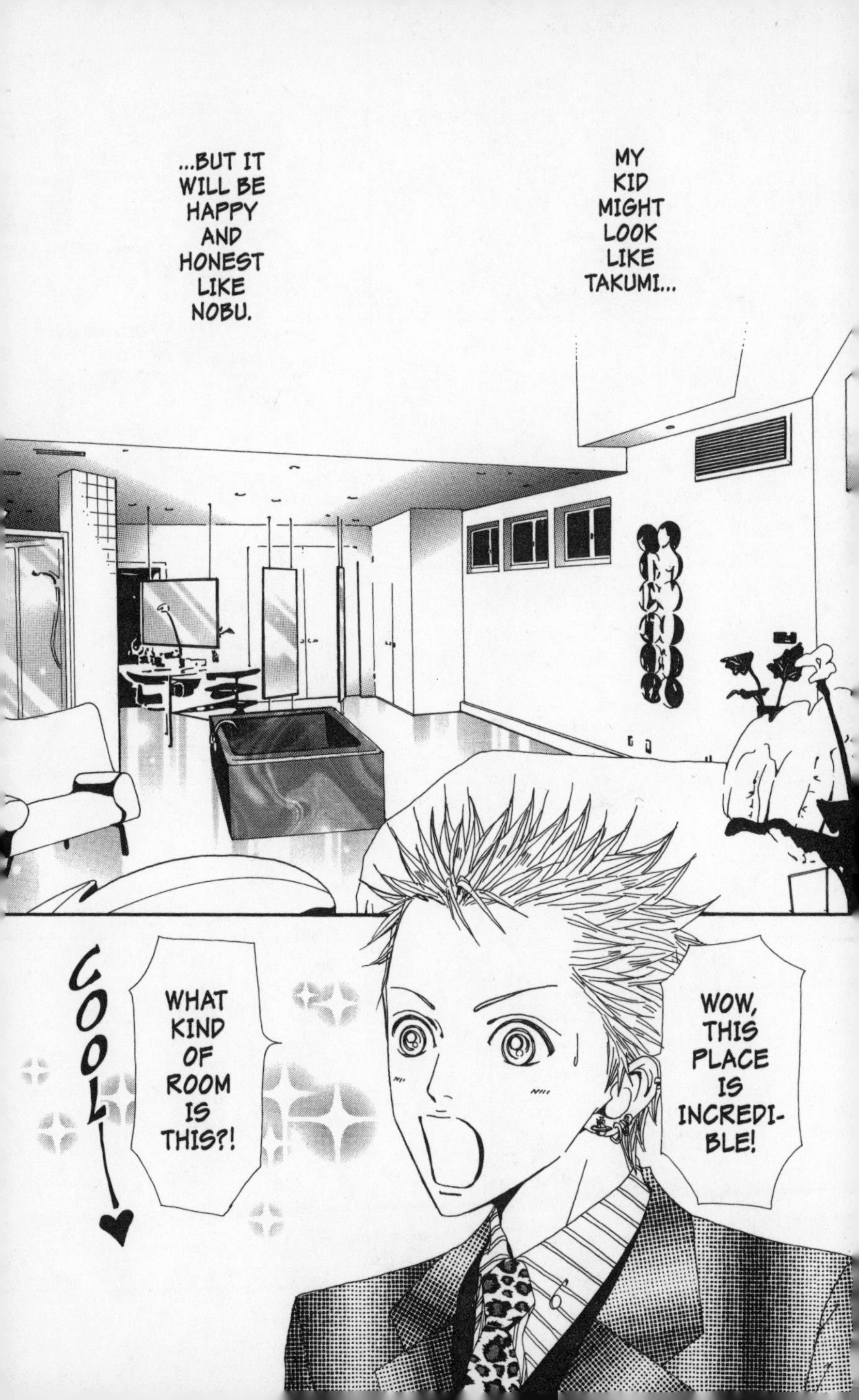
MY KID MIGHT LOOK LIKE TAKUMI...
...BUT IT WILL BE HAPPY AND HONEST LIKE NOBU.
WOW, THIS PLACE IS INCREDIBLE!
WHAT KIND OF ROOM IS THIS?!
COOL!♥

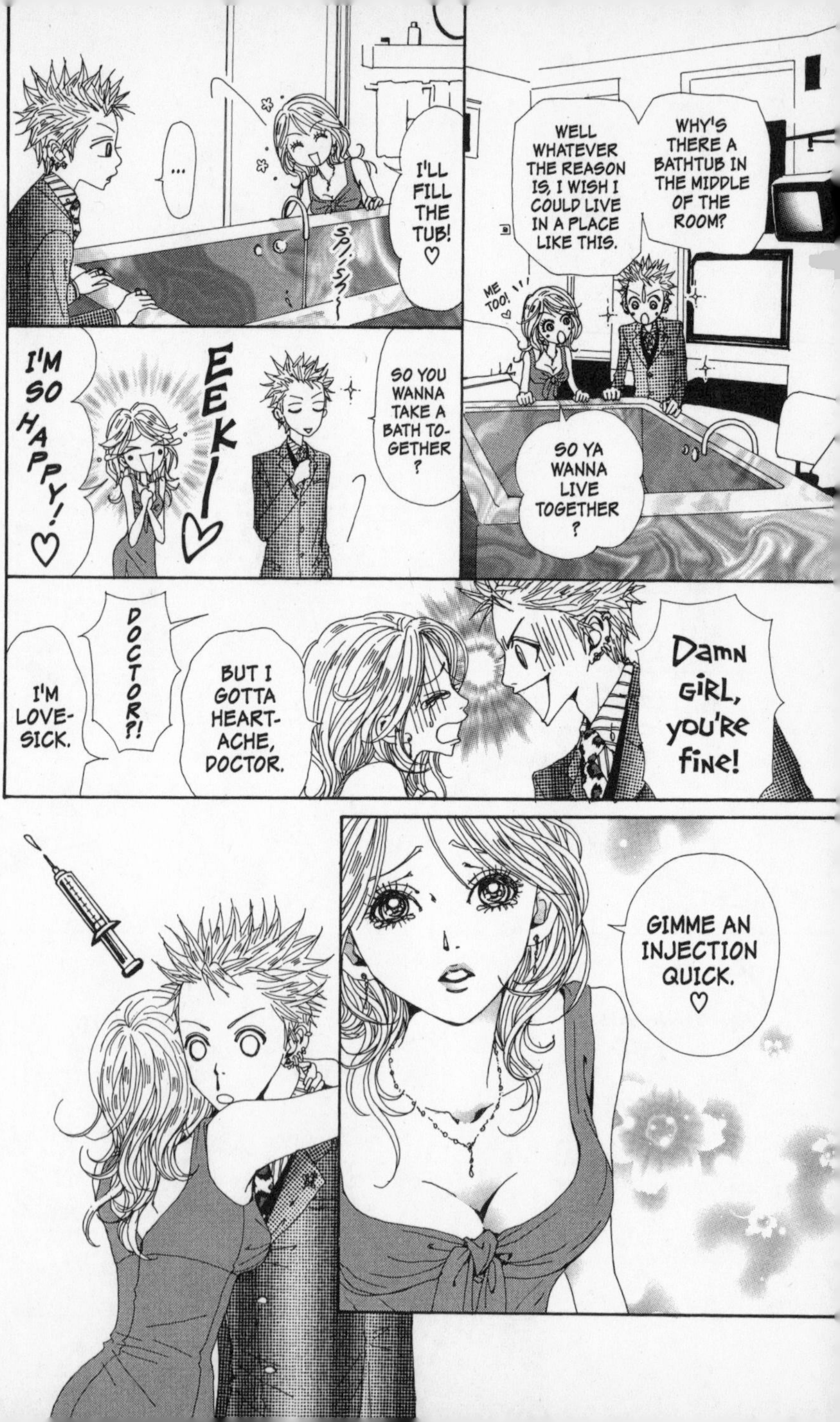
WHY'S THERE A BATHTUB IN THE MIDDLE OF THE ROOM?
WELL WHATEVER THE REASON IS, I WISH I COULD LIVE IN A PLACE LIKE THIS.
ME TOO! ♡
SO YA WANNA LIVE TOGETHER?
I'LL FILL THE TUB! ♡
...
SO YOU WANNA TAKE A BATH TO-GETHER?
EEK! ♡
I'M SO HAPPY! ♡
Damn girl, you're fine!
BUT I GOTTA HEART-ACHE, DOCTOR.
DOCTOR?!
I'M LOVE-SICK.
GIMME AN INJECTION QUICK. ♡

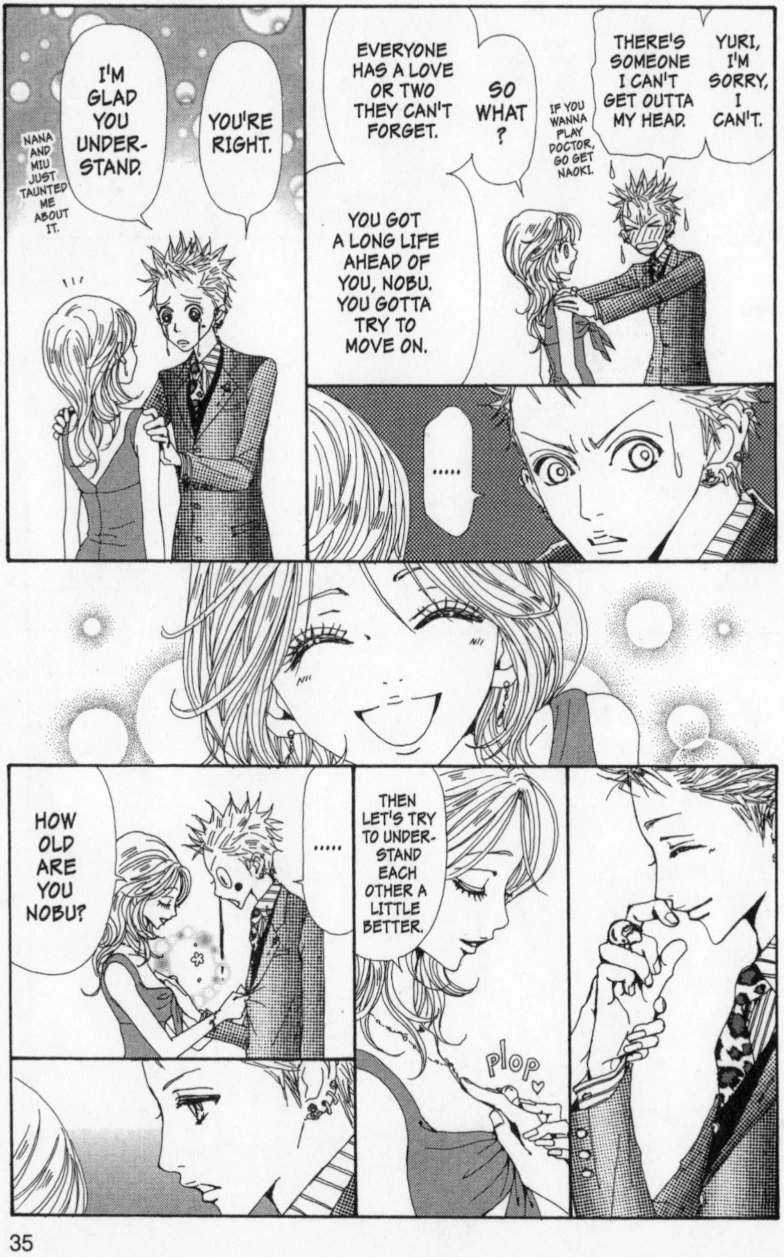
YURI, I'M SORRY, I CAN'T.
THERE'S SOMEONE I CAN'T GET OUTTA MY HEAD.
IF YOU WANNA PLAY DOCTOR, GO GET NAOKI.
SO WHAT?
EVERYONE HAS A LOVE OR TWO THEY CAN'T FORGET.
YOU GOT A LONG LIFE AHEAD OF YOU, NOBU. YOU GOTTA TRY TO MOVE ON.
.....
YOU'RE RIGHT.
I'M GLAD YOU UNDER-STAND.
NANA AND MIU JUST TAUNTED ME ABOUT IT.
THEN LET'S TRY TO UNDER-STAND EACH OTHER A LITTLE BETTER.
plop
.....
HOW OLD ARE YOU NOBU?

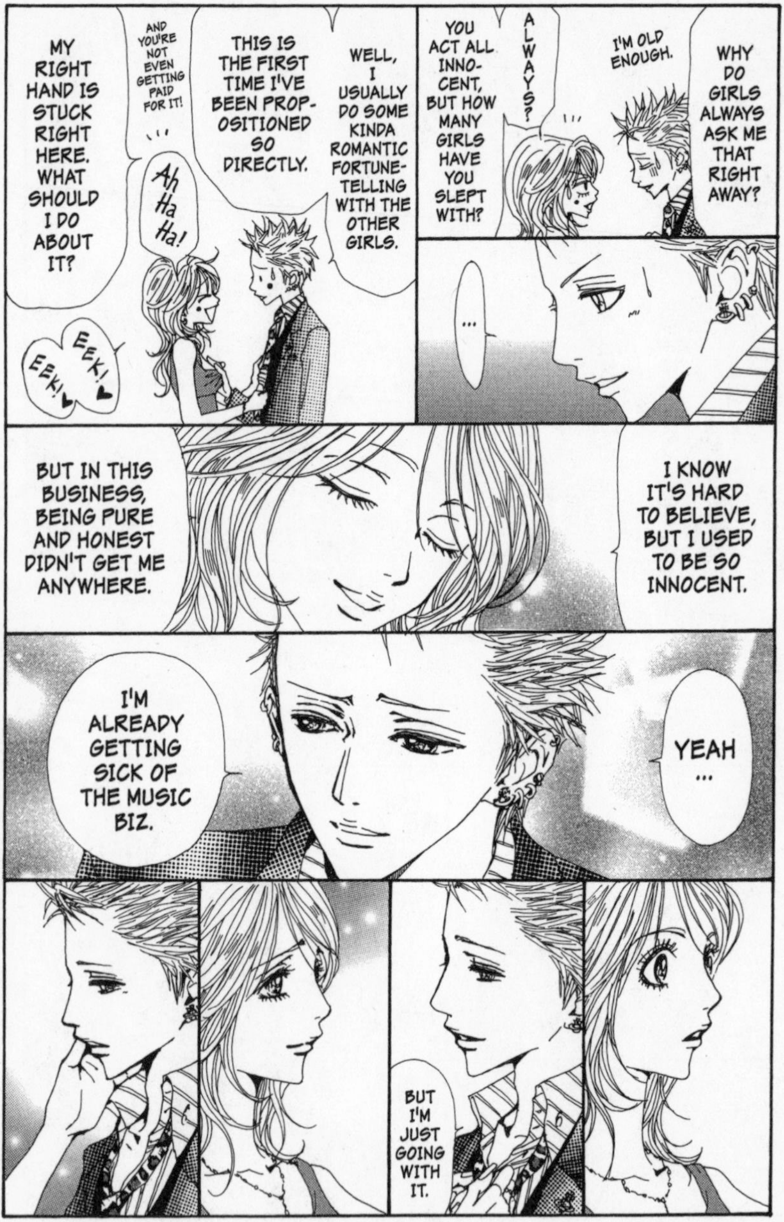
WHY DO GIRLS ALWAYS ASK ME THAT RIGHT AWAY?
I'M OLD ENOUGH.
ALWAYS?
YOU ACT ALL INNOCENT, BUT HOW MANY GIRLS HAVE YOU SLEPT WITH?
...
WELL, I USUALLY DO SOME KINDA ROMANTIC FORTUNE-TELLING WITH THE OTHER GIRLS.
THIS IS THE FIRST TIME I'VE BEEN PROPOSITIONED SO DIRECTLY.
AND YOU'RE NOT EVEN GETTING PAID FOR IT!
Ah Ha Ha!
MY RIGHT HAND IS STUCK RIGHT HERE. WHAT SHOULD I DO ABOUT IT?
EEK! EEK!
I KNOW IT'S HARD TO BELIEVE, BUT I USED TO BE SO INNOCENT.
BUT IN THIS BUSINESS, BEING PURE AND HONEST DIDN'T GET ME ANYWHERE.
YEAH ...
I'M ALREADY GETTING SICK OF THE MUSIC BIZ.
BUT I'M JUST GOING WITH IT.

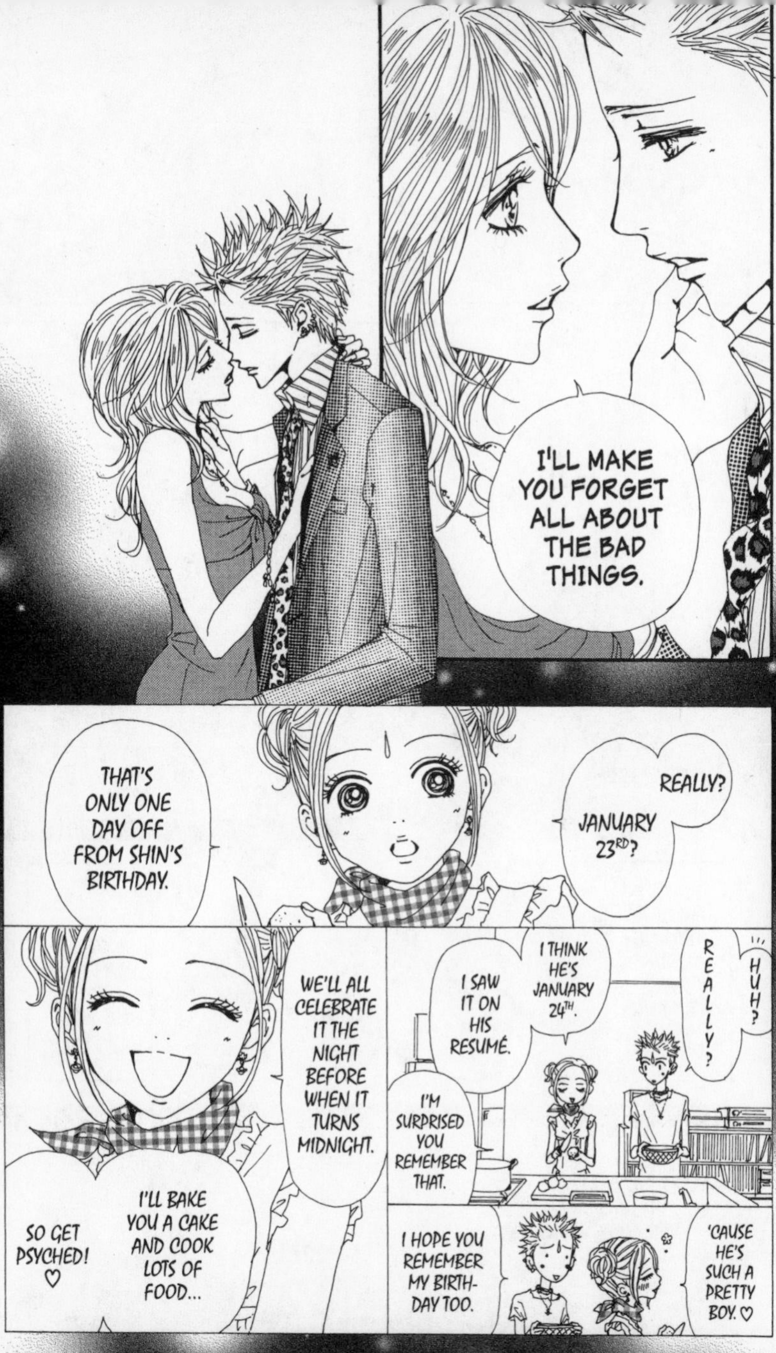
I'LL MAKE YOU FORGET ALL ABOUT THE BAD THINGS.
REALLY?
JANUARY 23RD?
THAT'S ONLY ONE DAY OFF FROM SHIN'S BIRTHDAY.
HUH?
REALLY?
I THINK HE'S JANUARY 24TH.
I SAW IT ON HIS RESUMÉ.
I'M SURPRISED YOU REMEMBER THAT.
'CAUSE HE'S SUCH A PRETTY BOY. ♡
I HOPE YOU REMEMBER MY BIRTH-DAY TOO.
WE'LL ALL CELEBRATE IT THE NIGHT BEFORE WHEN IT TURNS MIDNIGHT.
I'LL BAKE YOU A CAKE AND COOK LOTS OF FOOD...
SO GET PSYCHED! ♡

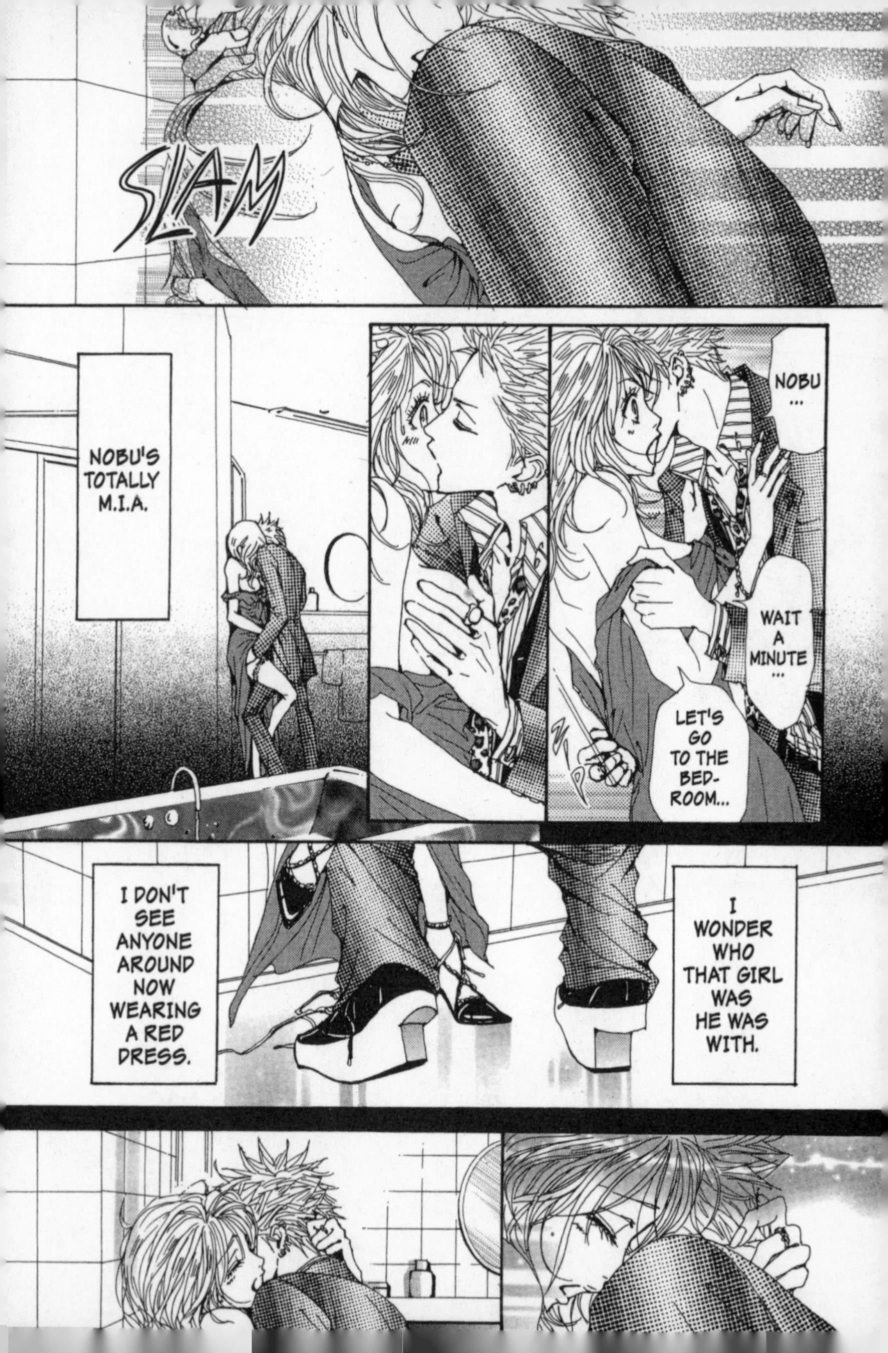

SLAM
NOBU ...
WAIT A MINUTE ...
LET'S GO TO THE BED-ROOM...
NOBU'S TOTALLY M.I.A.
I WONDER WHO THAT GIRL WAS HE WAS WITH.
I DON'T SEE ANYONE AROUND NOW WEARING A RED DRESS.

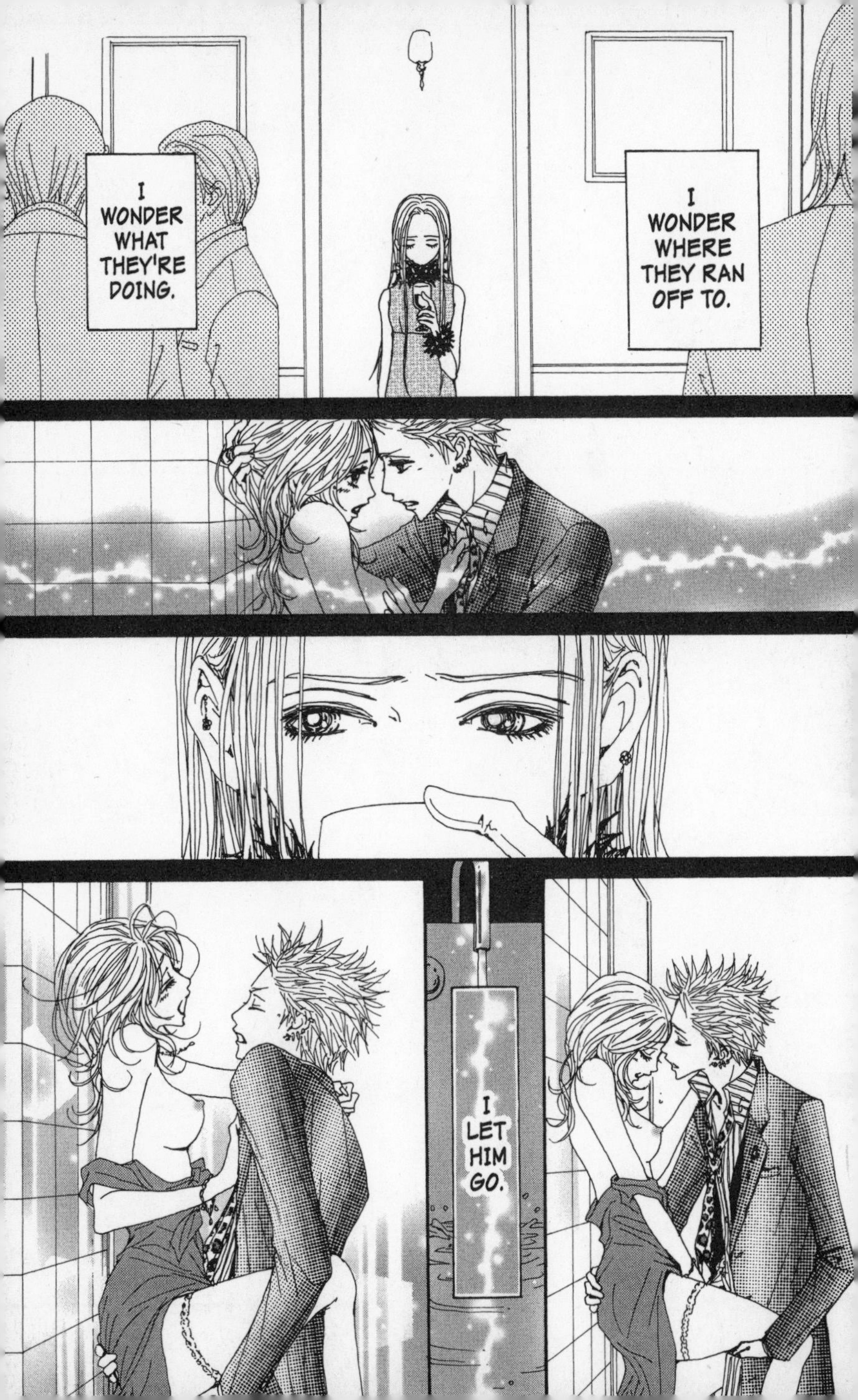
I WONDER WHERE THEY RAN OFF TO.
I WONDER WHAT THEY'RE DOING.
I LET HIM GO.

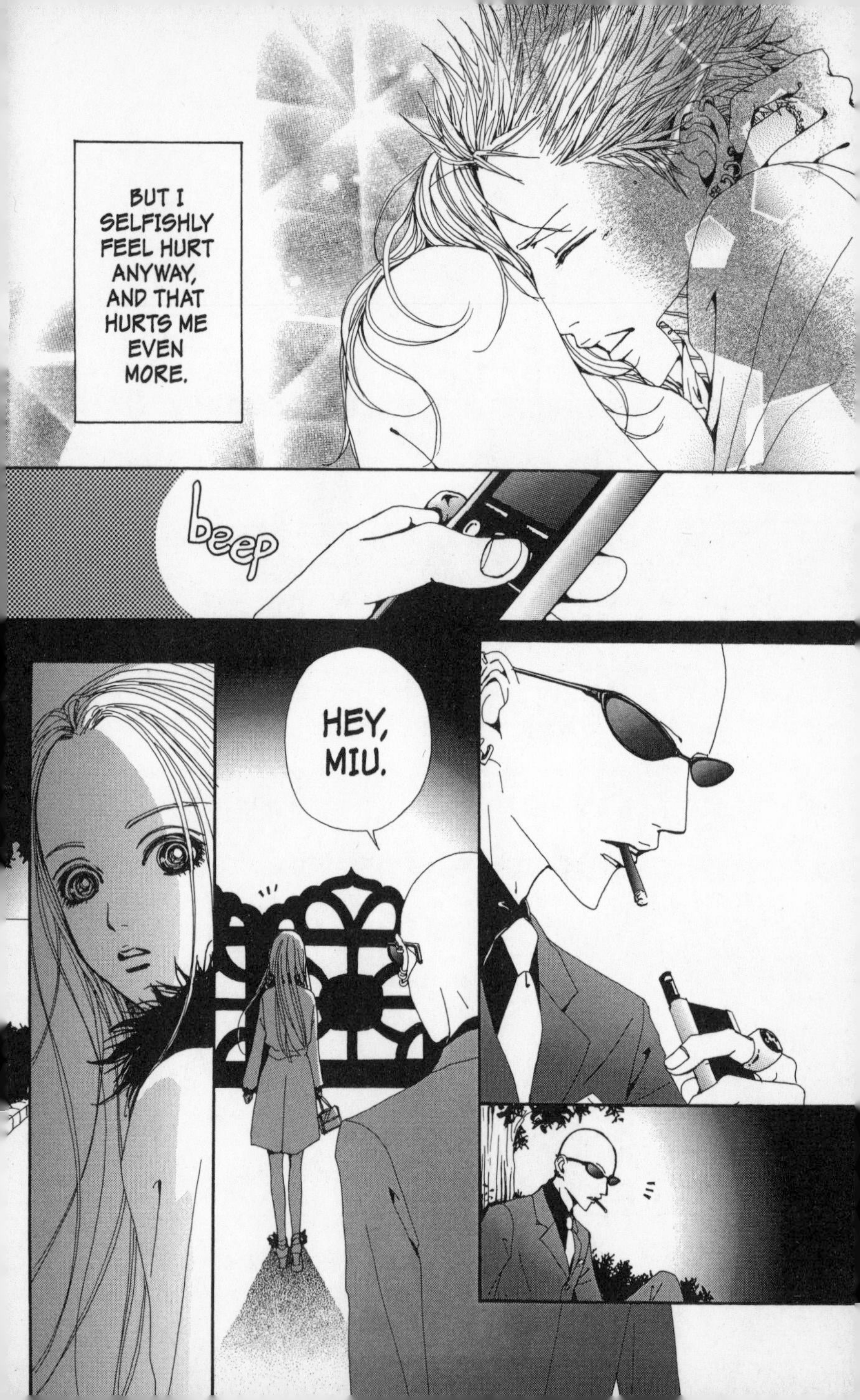
BUT I SELFISHLY FEEL HURT ANYWAY, AND THAT HURTS ME EVEN MORE.
beep
HEY, MIU.

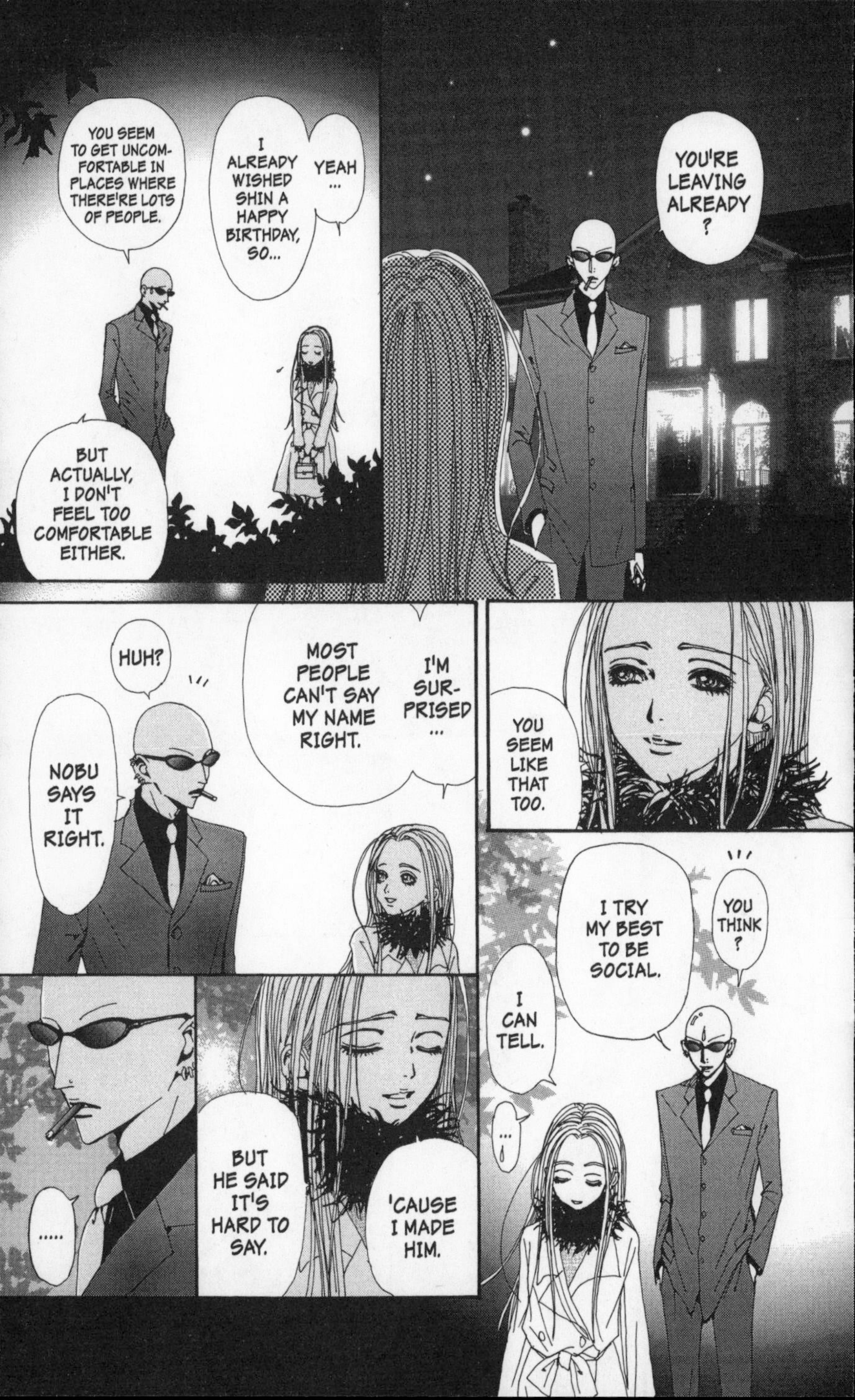
YOU'RE LEAVING ALREADY?
YEAH...
I ALREADY WISHED SHIN A HAPPY BIRTHDAY, SO...
YOU SEEM TO GET UNCOMFORTABLE IN PLACES WHERE THERE'RE LOTS OF PEOPLE.
BUT ACTUALLY, I DON'T FEEL TOO COMFORTABLE EITHER.
YOU SEEM LIKE THAT TOO.
YOU THINK?
I TRY MY BEST TO BE SOCIAL.
I CAN TELL.
...!
I'M SURPRISED...
MOST PEOPLE CAN'T SAY MY NAME RIGHT.
HUH?
NOBU SAYS IT RIGHT.
'CAUSE I MADE HIM.
BUT HE SAID IT'S HARD TO SAY.
.....

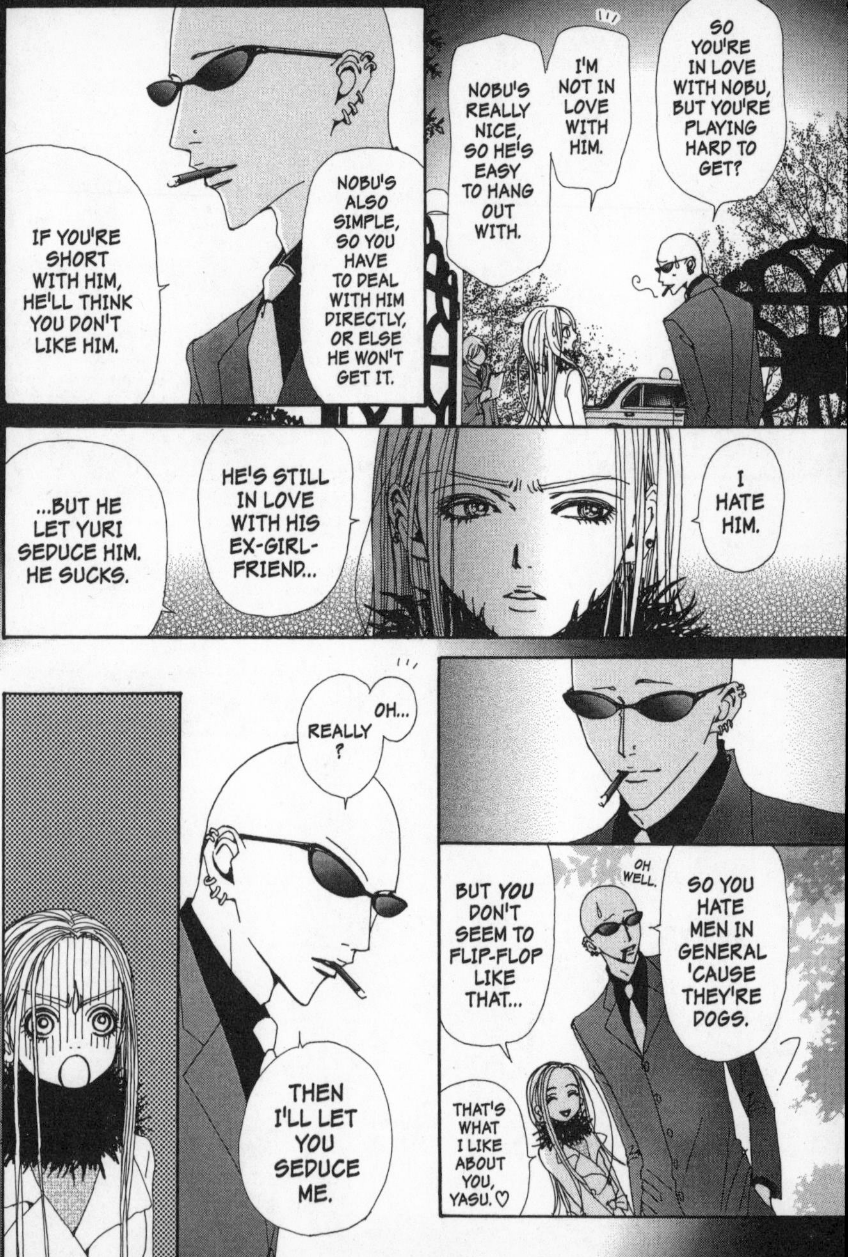
SO YOU'RE IN LOVE WITH NOBU, BUT YOU'RE PLAYING HARD TO GET?
I'M NOT IN LOVE WITH HIM.
NOBU'S REALLY NICE, SO HE'S EASY TO HANG OUT WITH.
NOBU'S ALSO SIMPLE, SO YOU HAVE TO DEAL WITH HIM DIRECTLY, OR ELSE HE WON'T GET IT.
IF YOU'RE SHORT WITH HIM, HE'LL THINK YOU DON'T LIKE HIM.
I HATE HIM.
HE'S STILL IN LOVE WITH HIS EX-GIRL-FRIEND...
...BUT HE LET YURI SEDUCE HIM. HE SUCKS.
SO YOU HATE MEN IN GENERAL 'CAUSE THEY'RE DOGS.
OH WELL.
BUT YOU DON'T SEEM TO FLIP-FLOP LIKE THAT...
THAT'S WHAT I LIKE ABOUT YOU, YASU. ♡
OH... REALLY?
THEN I'LL LET YOU SEDUCE ME.

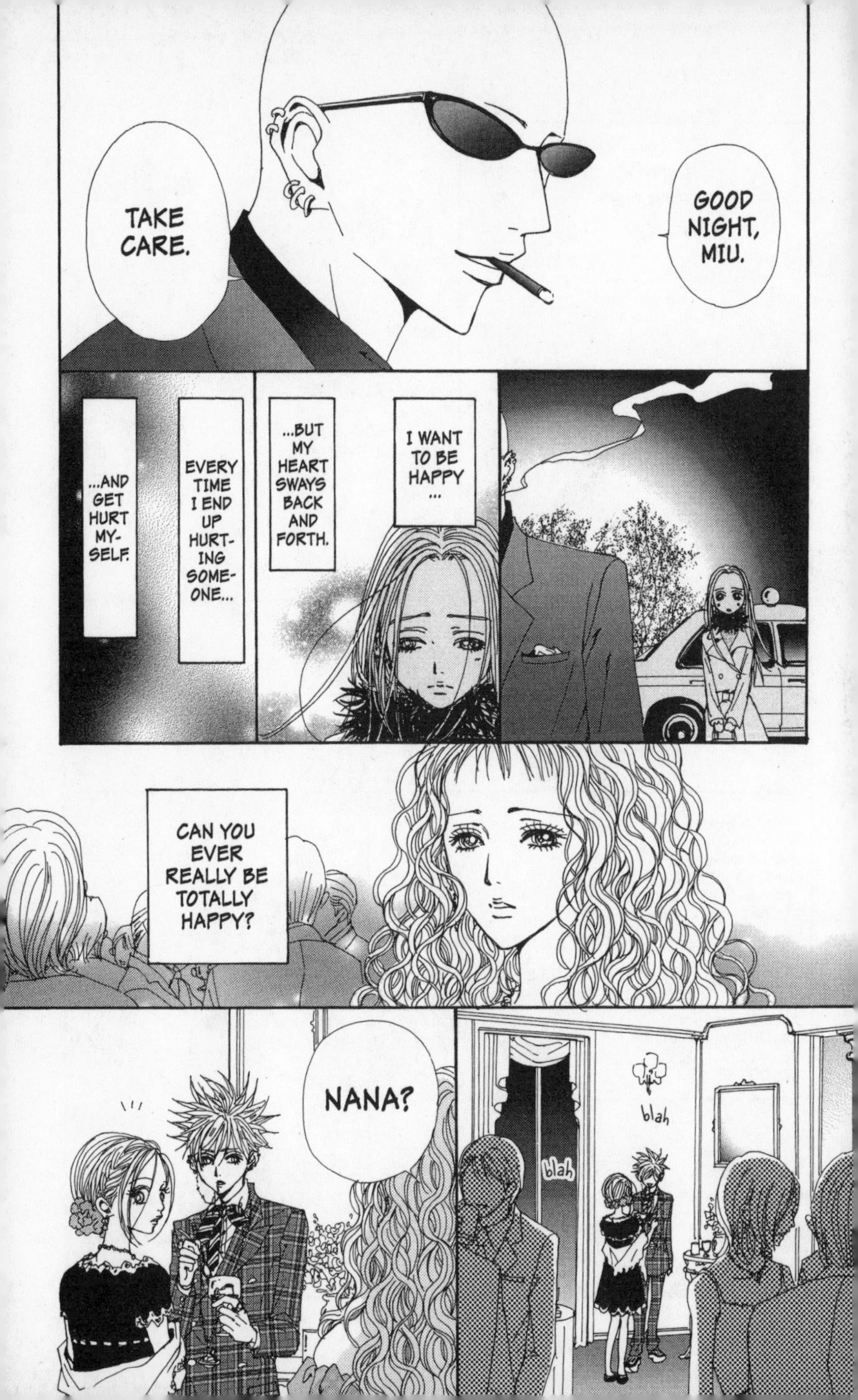
GOOD NIGHT, MIU.
TAKE CARE.
I WANT TO BE HAPPY ...
...BUT MY HEART SWAYS BACK AND FORTH.
EVERY TIME I END UP HURTING SOMEONE...
...AND GET HURT MYSELF.
CAN YOU EVER REALLY BE TOTALLY HAPPY?
blah
blah
NANA?

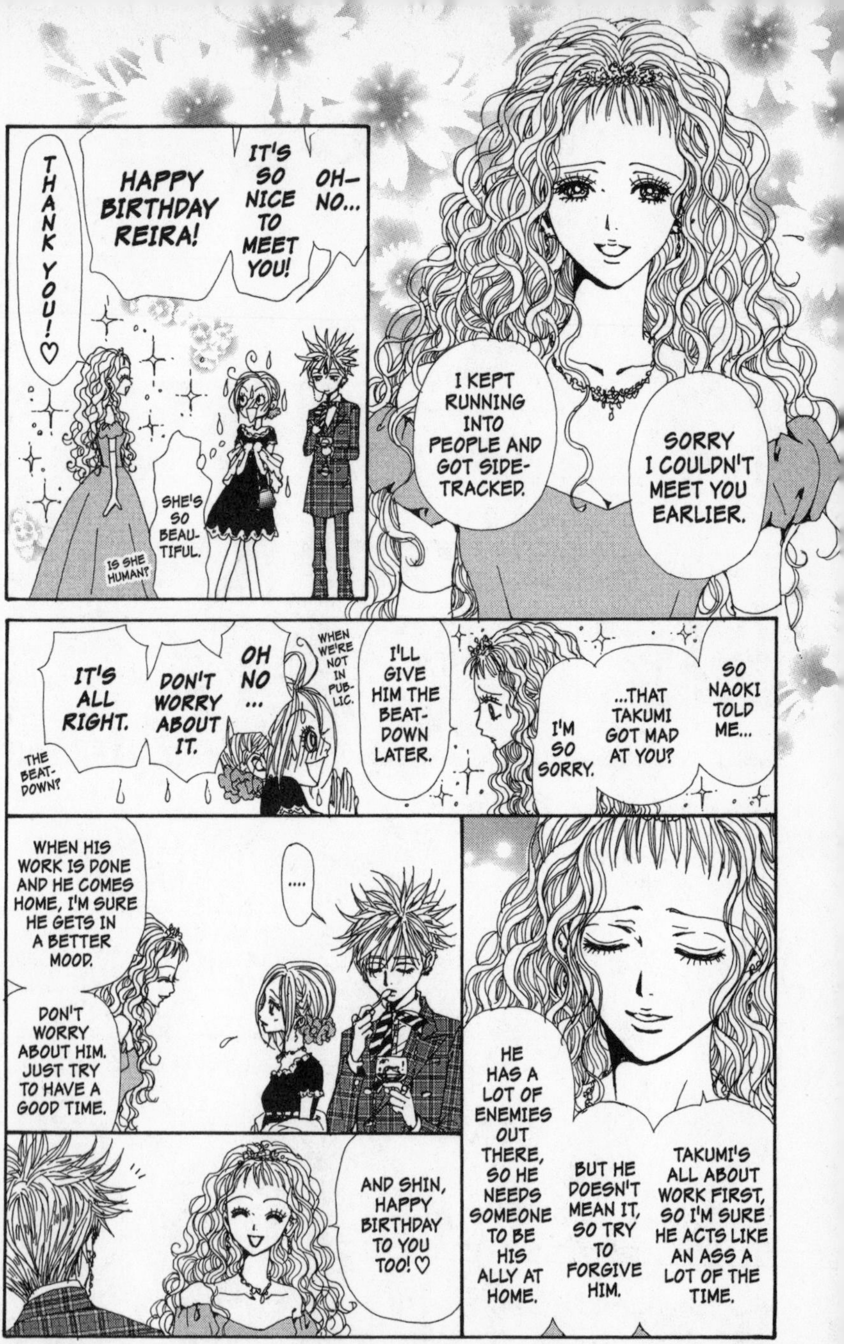
SORRY I COULDN'T MEET YOU EARLIER.
I KEPT RUNNING INTO PEOPLE AND GOT SIDE-TRACKED.
OH— NO...
IT'S SO NICE TO MEET YOU!
HAPPY BIRTHDAY REIRA!
THANK YOU!♡
SHE'S SO BEAU-TIFUL.
IS SHE HUMAN?
SO NAOKI TOLD ME...
...THAT TAKUMI GOT MAD AT YOU?
I'M SO SORRY.
I'LL GIVE HIM THE BEAT-DOWN LATER.
WHEN WE'RE NOT IN PUB-LIC.
OH NO ...
DON'T WORRY ABOUT IT.
IT'S ALL RIGHT.
THE BEAT-DOWN?
TAKUMI'S ALL ABOUT WORK FIRST, SO I'M SURE HE ACTS LIKE AN ASS A LOT OF THE TIME.
BUT HE DOESN'T MEAN IT, SO TRY TO FORGIVE HIM.
HE HAS A LOT OF ENEMIES OUT THERE, SO HE NEEDS SOMEONE TO BE HIS ALLY AT HOME.
WHEN HIS WORK IS DONE AND HE COMES HOME, I'M SURE HE GETS IN A BETTER MOOD.
....
DON'T WORRY ABOUT HIM. JUST TRY TO HAVE A GOOD TIME.
AND SHIN, HAPPY BIRTHDAY TO YOU TOO!♡

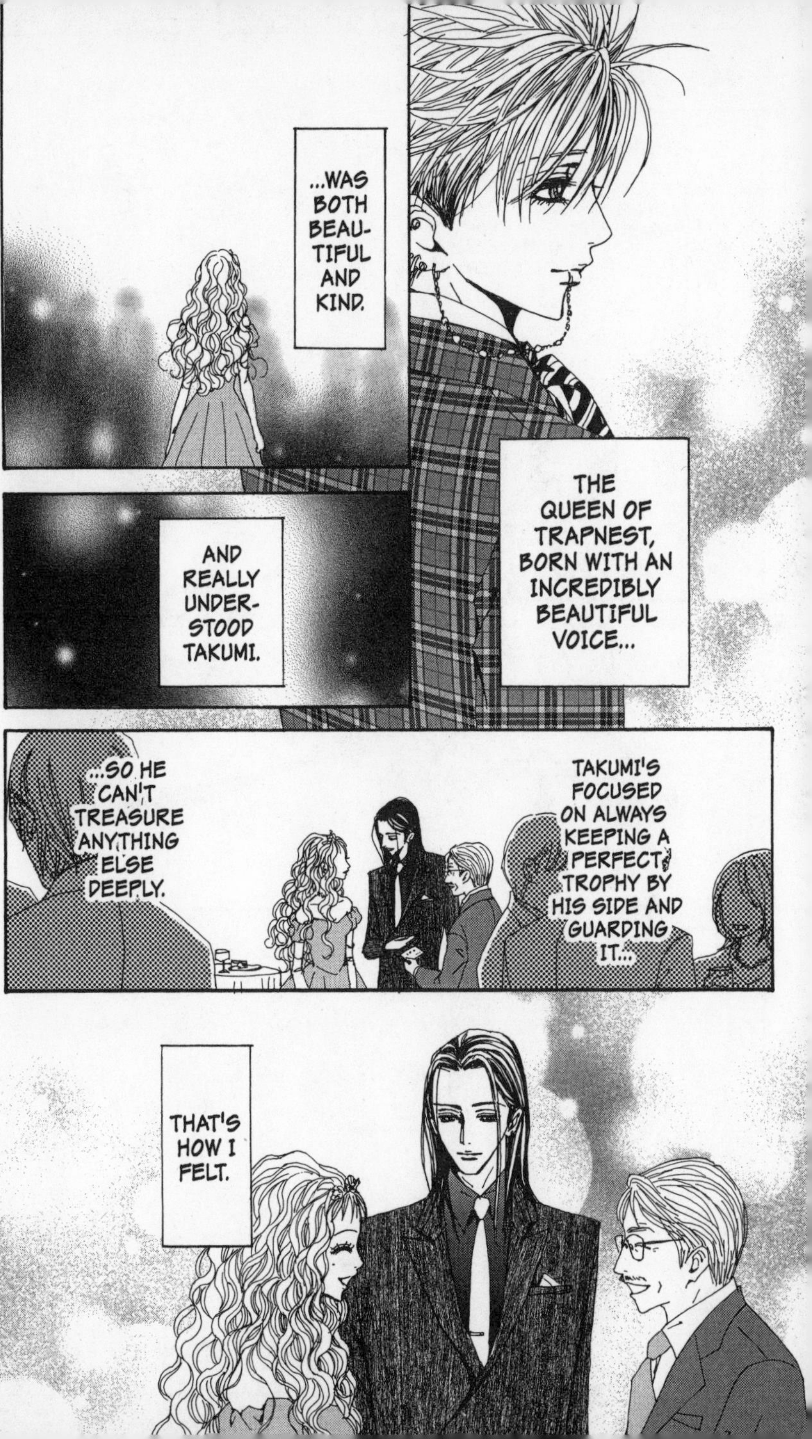
THE QUEEN OF TRAPNEST, BORN WITH AN INCREDIBLY BEAUTIFUL VOICE...
...WAS BOTH BEAU-TIFUL AND KIND.
AND REALLY UNDER-STOOD TAKUMI.
TAKUMI'S FOCUSED ON ALWAYS KEEPING A PERFECT TROPHY BY HIS SIDE AND GUARDING IT...
...SO HE CAN'T TREASURE ANYTHING ELSE DEEPLY.
THAT'S HOW I FELT.

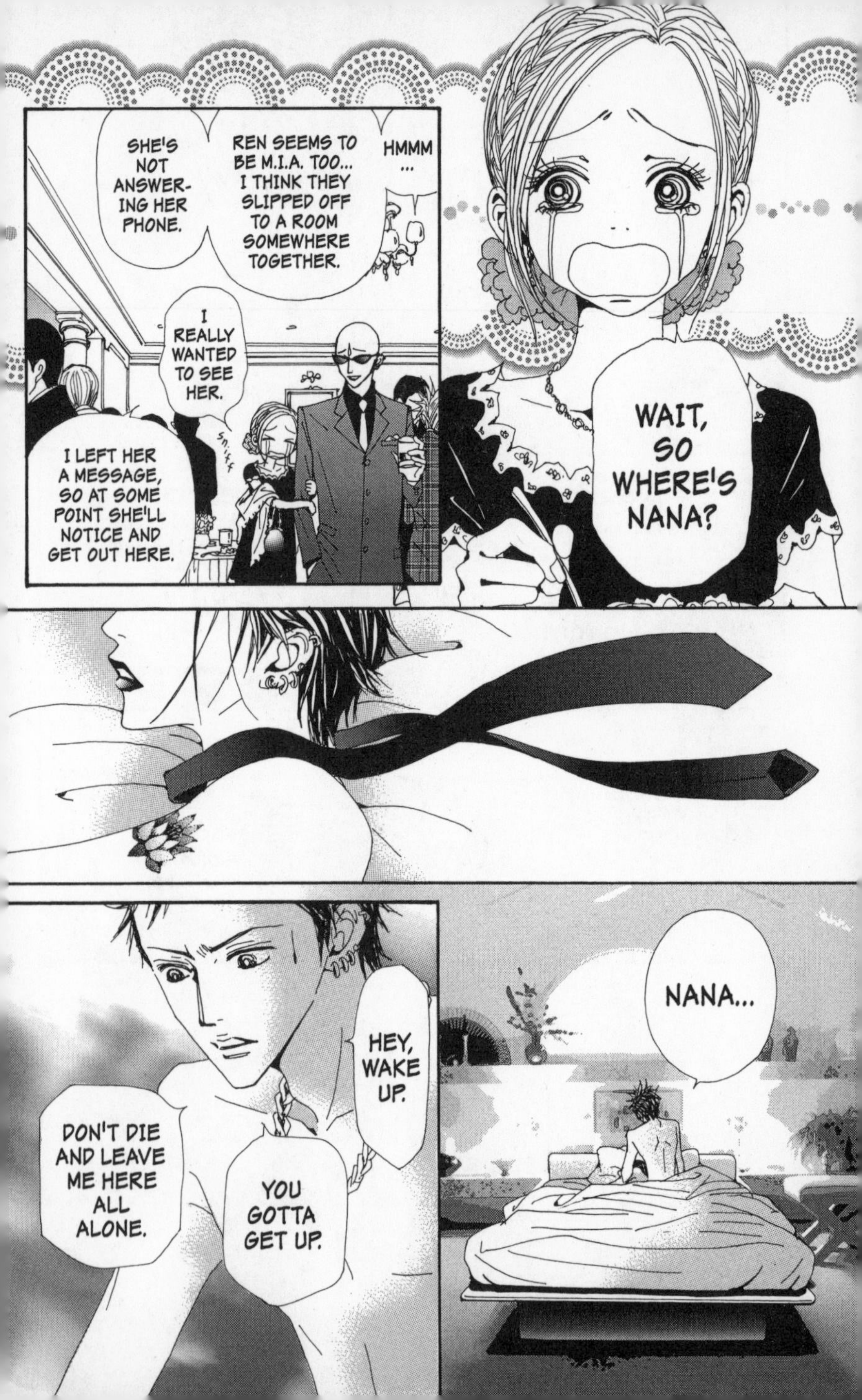
WAIT, SO WHERE'S NANA?
HMMM ...
REN SEEMS TO BE M.I.A. TOO... I THINK THEY SLIPPED OFF TO A ROOM SOMEWHERE TOGETHER.
SHE'S NOT ANSWERING HER PHONE.
I REALLY WANTED TO SEE HER.
sniff
I LEFT HER A MESSAGE, SO AT SOME POINT SHE'LL NOTICE AND GET OUT HERE.
NANA...
HEY, WAKE UP.
YOU GOTTA GET UP.
DON'T DIE AND LEAVE ME HERE ALL ALONE.

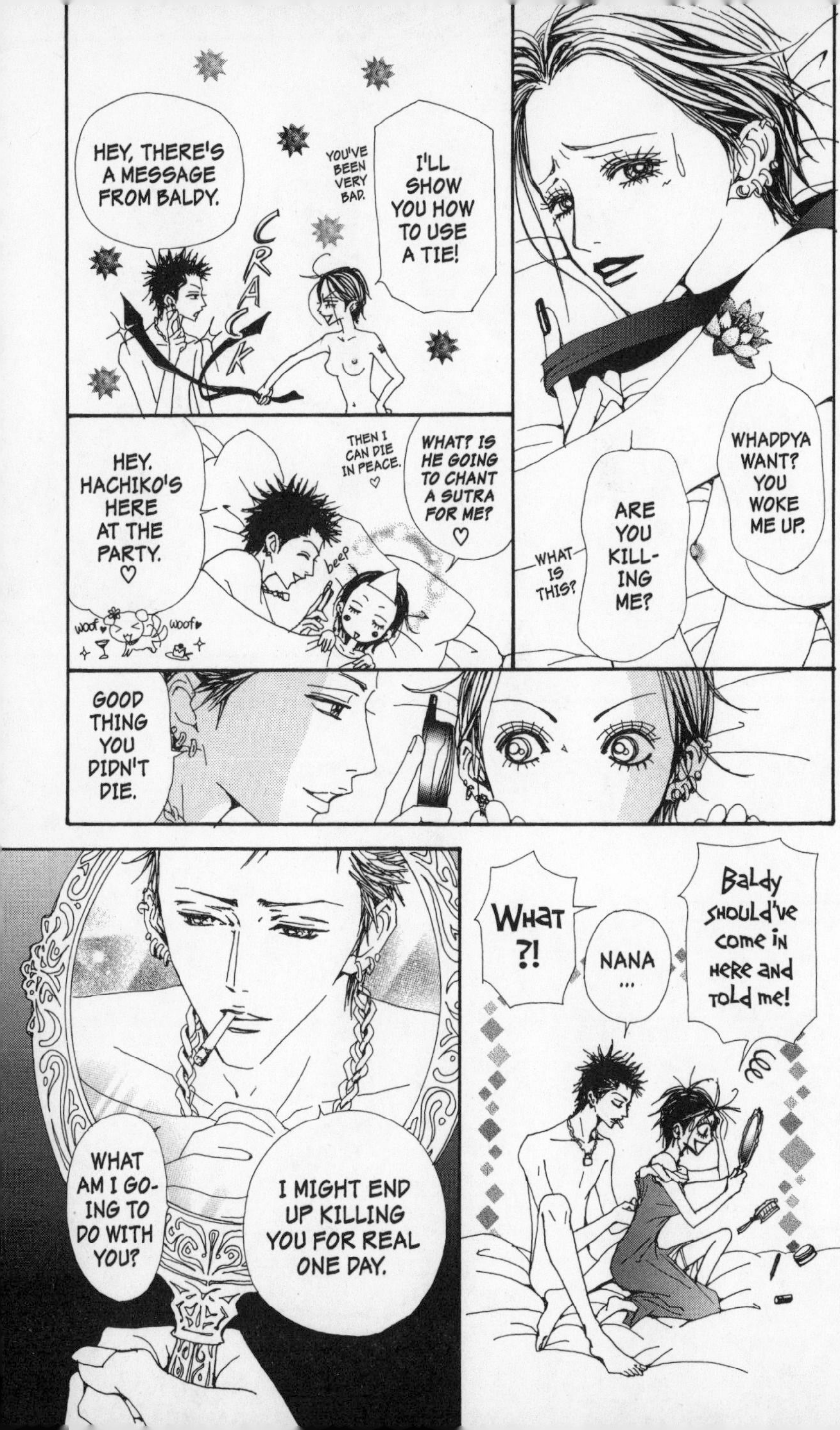

WHADDYA WANT? YOU WOKE ME UP.
ARE YOU KILLING ME?
WHAT IS THIS?
I'LL SHOW YOU HOW TO USE A TIE!
YOU'VE BEEN VERY BAD.
CRACK
HEY, THERE'S A MESSAGE FROM BALDY.
WHAT? IS HE GOING TO CHANT A SUTRA FOR ME? ♡
THEN I CAN DIE IN PEACE. ♡
HEY. HACHIKO'S HERE AT THE PARTY. ♡
beep
woof♥ woof♥
GOOD THING YOU DIDN'T DIE.
Baldy should've come in here and told me!
NANA...
WHAT?!
I MIGHT END UP KILLING YOU FOR REAL ONE DAY.
WHAT AM I GO-ING TO DO WITH YOU?

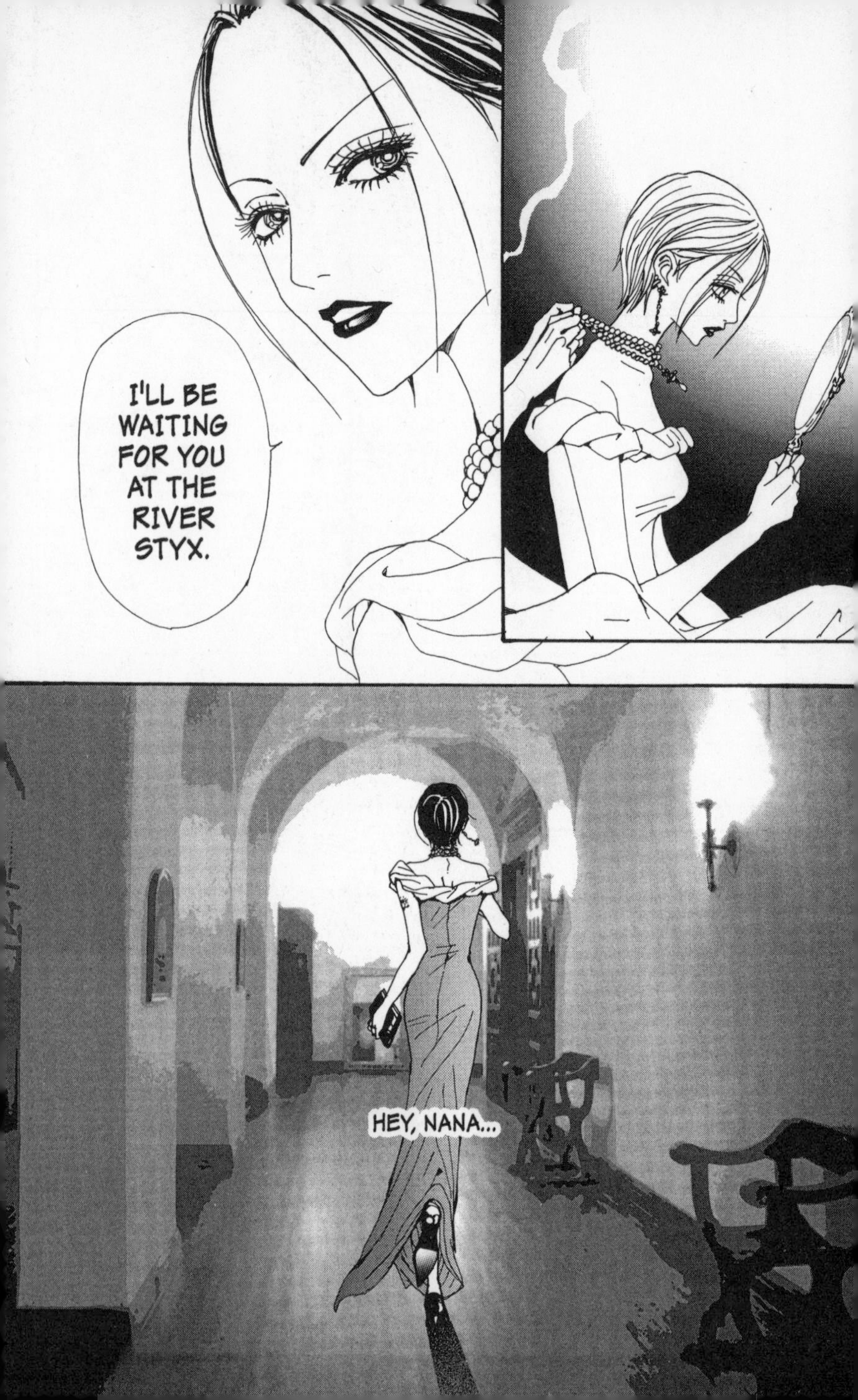
I'LL BE WAITING FOR YOU AT THE RIVER STYX.
HEY, NANA...

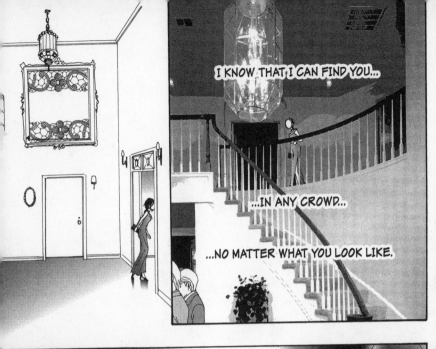

I KNOW THAT I CAN FIND YOU...

...IN ANY CROWD...

...NO MATTER WHAT YOU LOOK LIKE.

blah

blah

NANA!

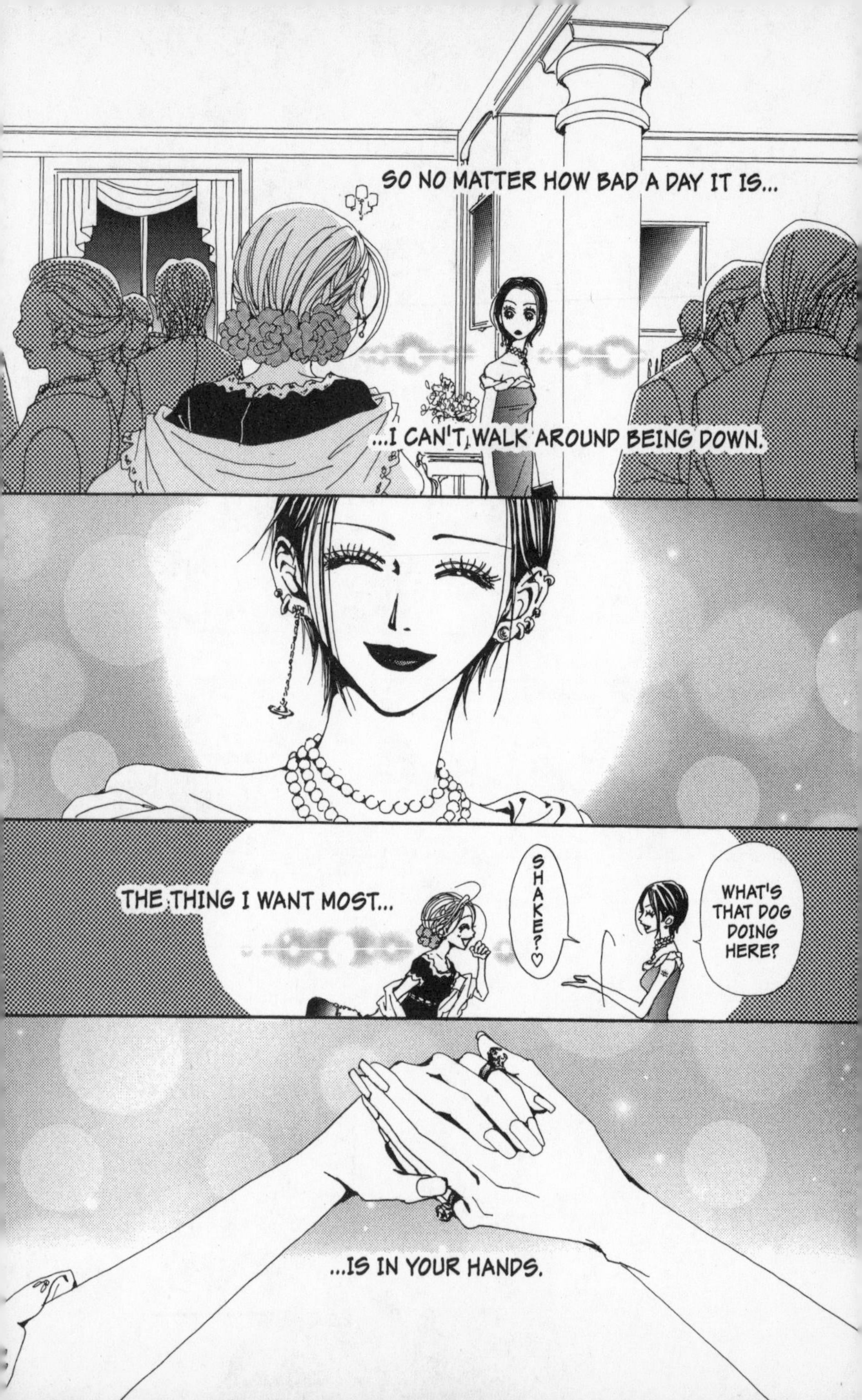
SO NO MATTER HOW BAD A DAY IT IS...
...I CAN'T WALK AROUND BEING DOWN.
WHAT'S THAT DOG DOING HERE?
SHAKE?♡
THE THING I WANT MOST...
...IS IN YOUR HANDS.

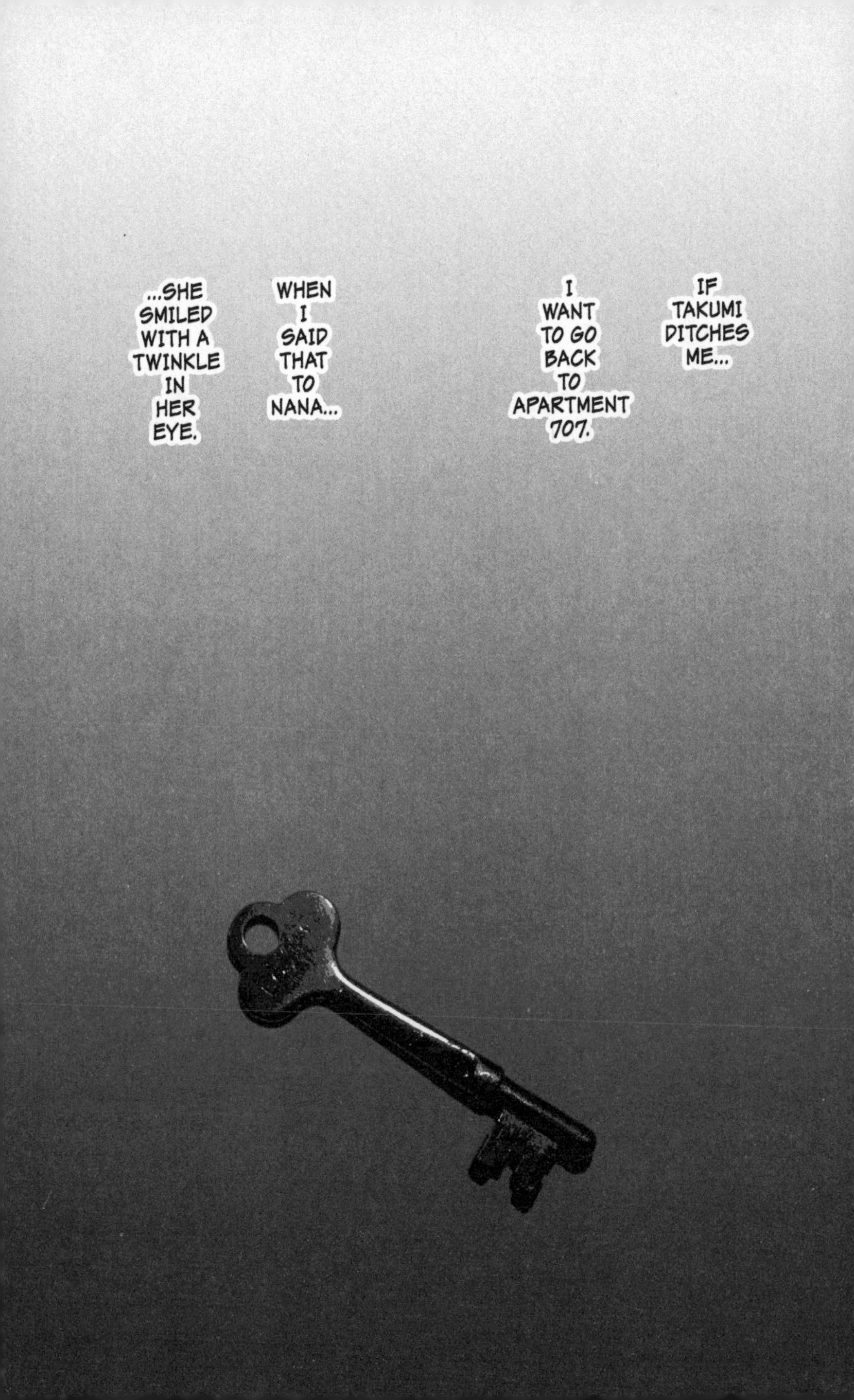
IF TAKUMI DITCHES ME...
I WANT TO GO BACK TO APARTMENT 707.
WHEN I SAID THAT TO NANA...
...SHE SMILED WITH A TWINKLE IN HER EYE.

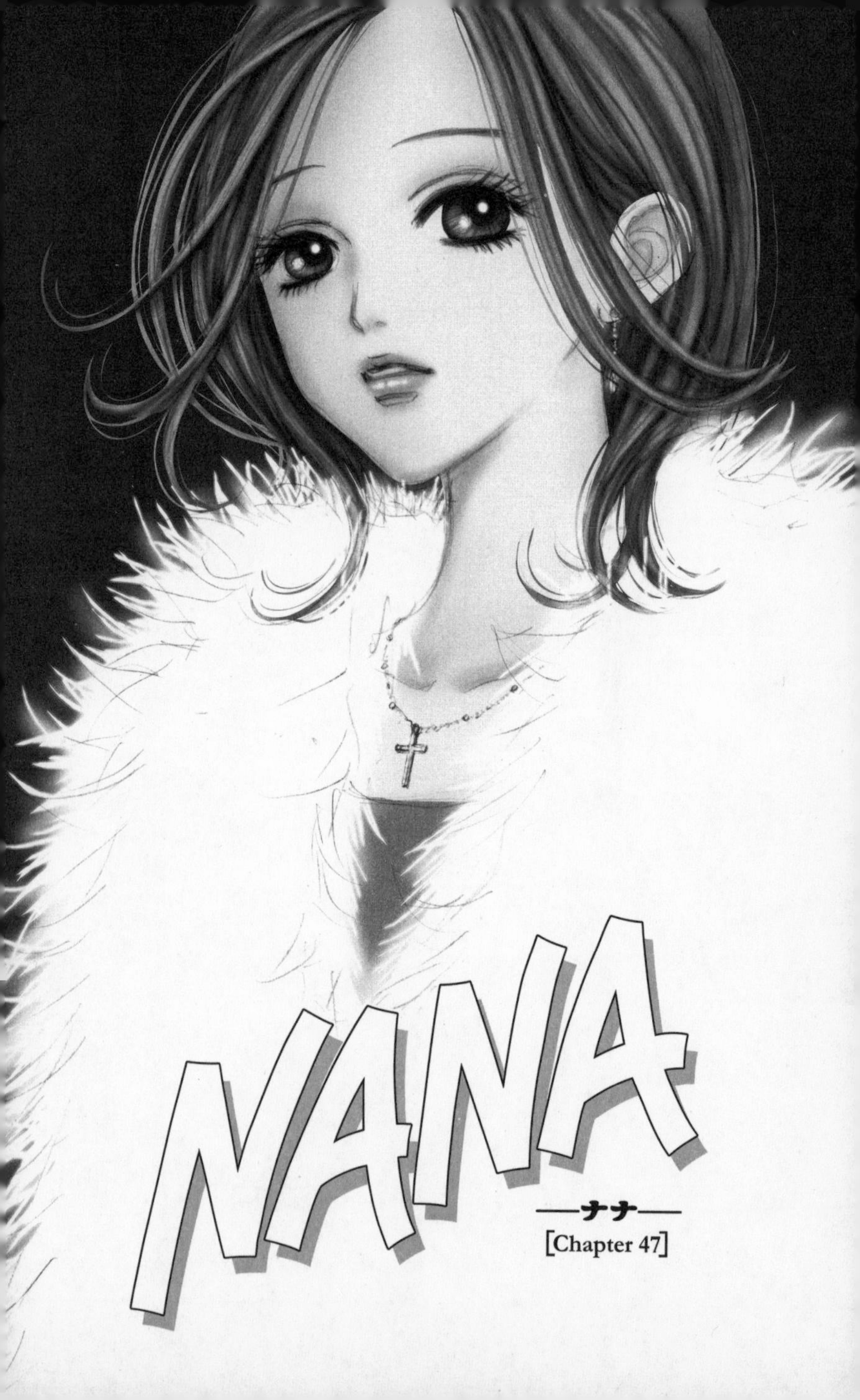
NANA
—ナナ—
[Chapter 47]

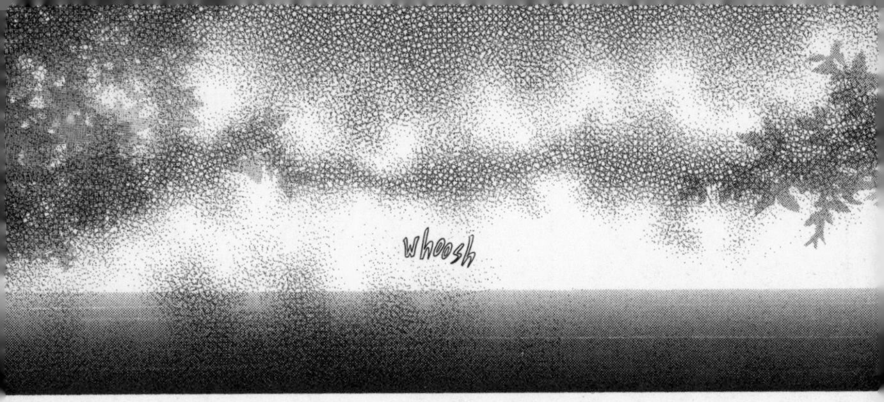
whoosh

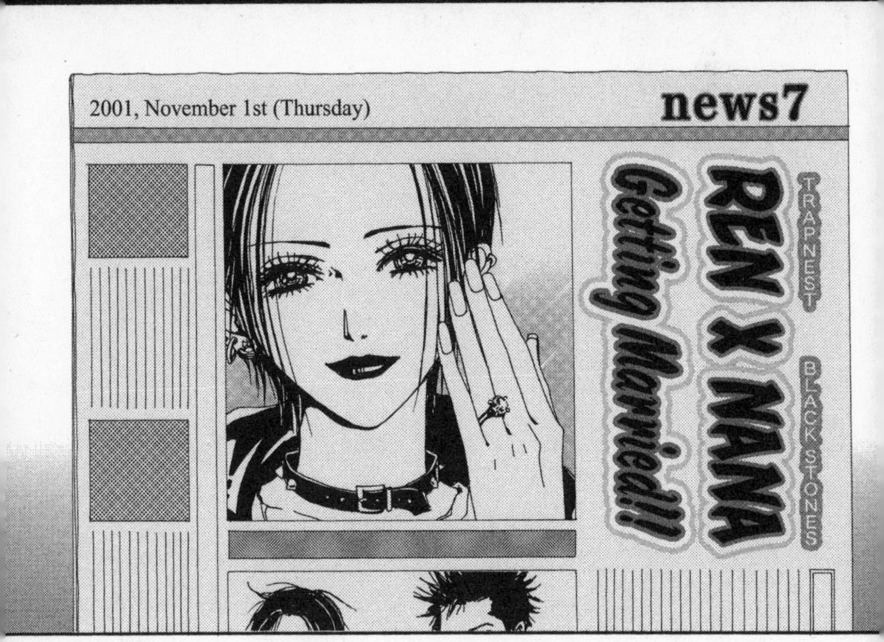
2001, November 1st (Thursday)
news7
TRAPNEST REN x BLACKSTONES NANA
Getting Married!!

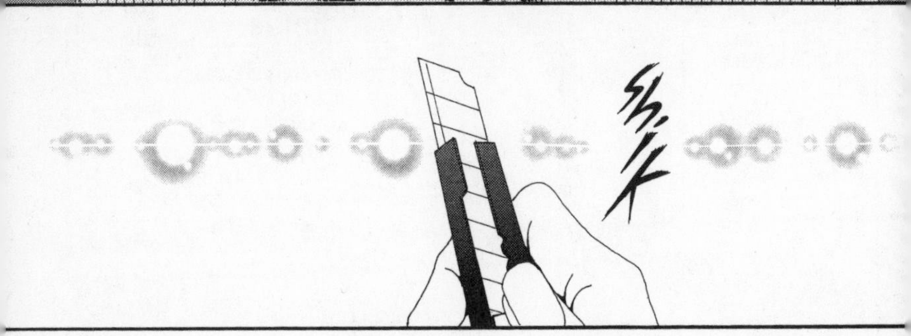
SHIK

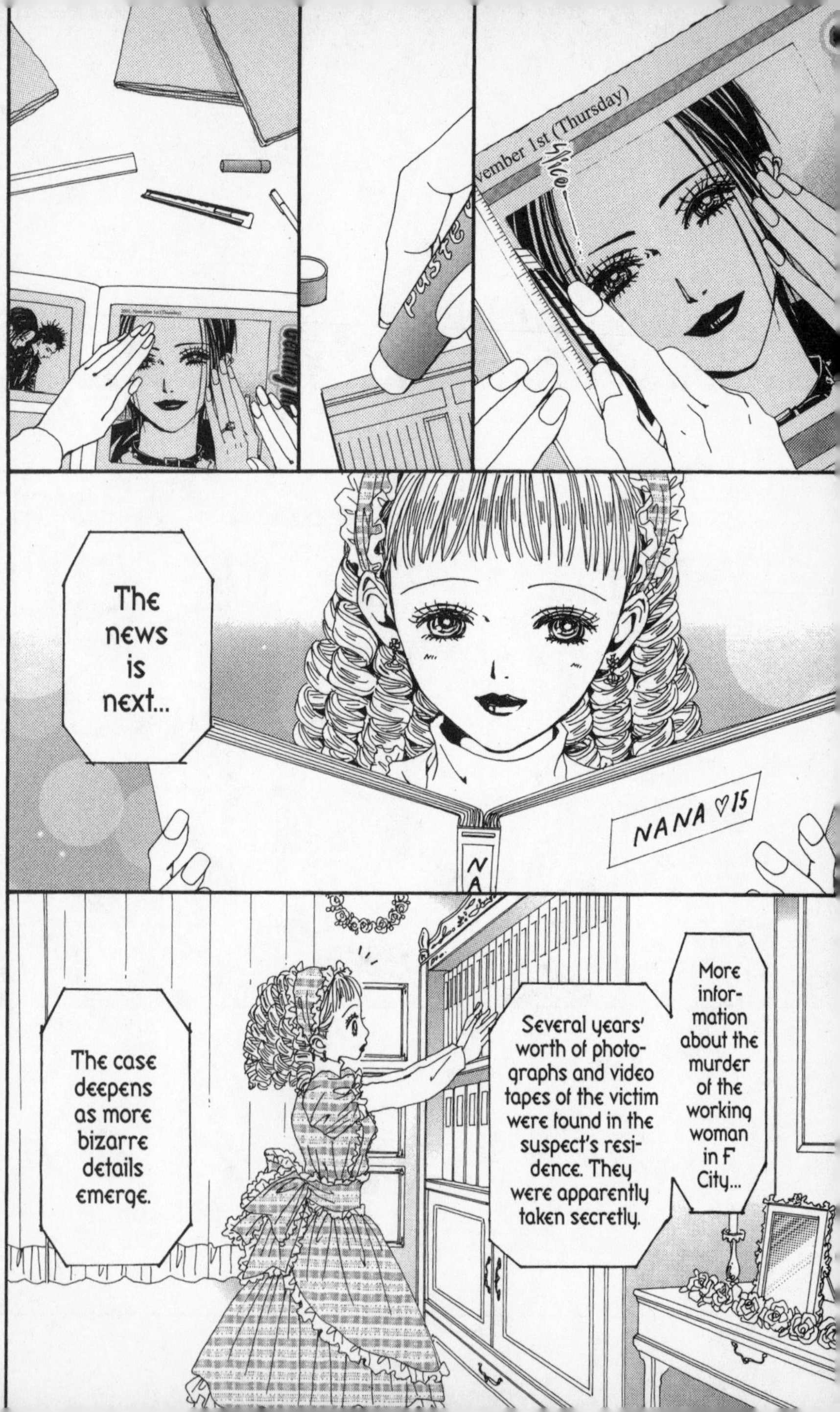
vember 1st (Thursday)
Slice
paste
The news is next...
NANA ♡15
NA
More information about the murder of the working woman in F City...
Several years' worth of photographs and video tapes of the victim were found in the suspect's residence. They were apparently taken secretly.
The case deepens as more bizarre details emerge.

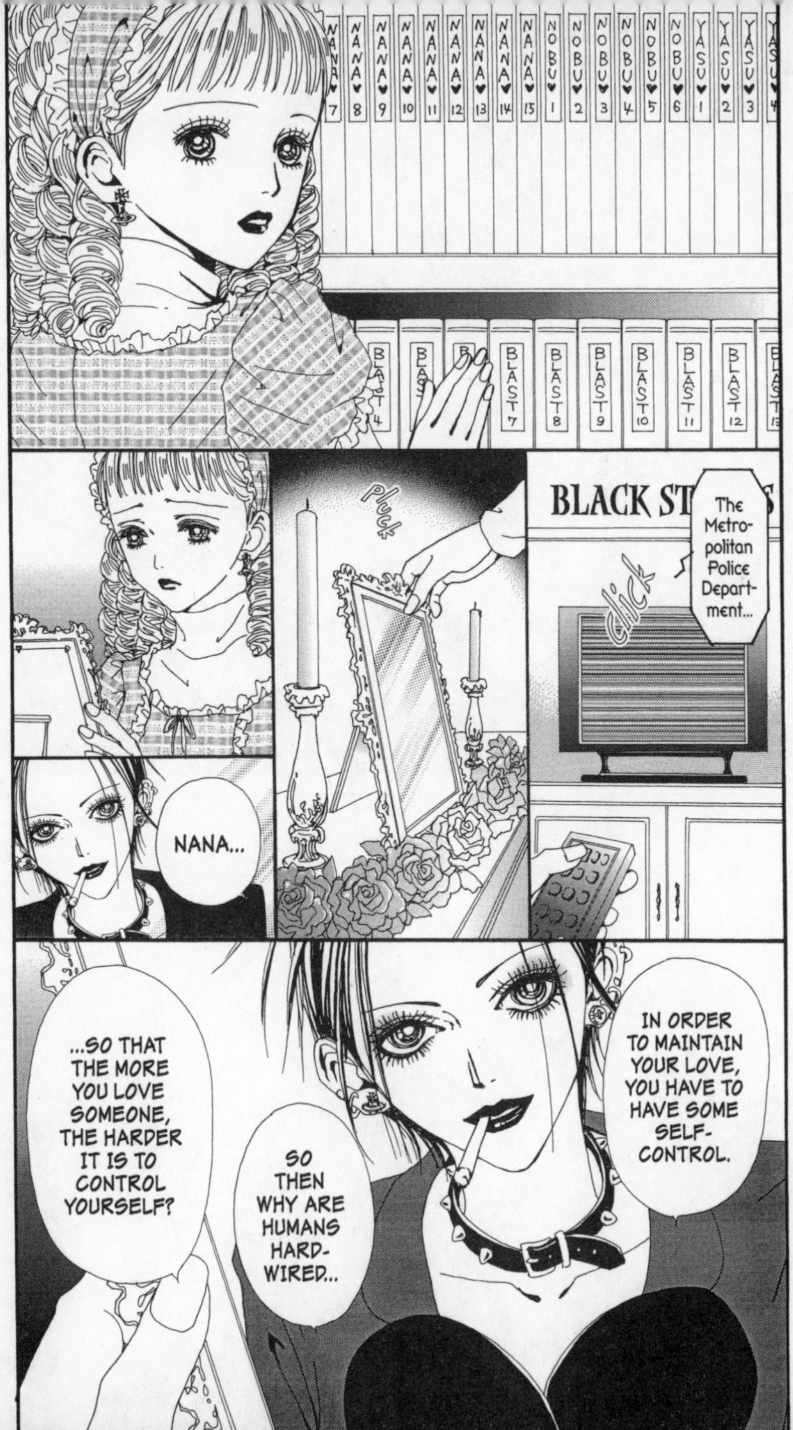

NANA♥7
NANA♥8
NANA♥9
NANA♥10
NANA♥11
NANA♥12
NANA♥13
NANA♥14
NANA♥15
NOBU♥1
NOBU♥2
NOBU♥3
NOBU♥4
NOBU♥5
NOBU♥6
YASU♥1
YASU♥2
YASU♥3
YASU♥4
BLAST 4
BLAST 7
BLAST 8
BLAST 9
BLAST 10
BLAST 11
BLAST 12
BLACK ST
The Metropolitan Police Department...
click
pluck
NANA...
IN ORDER TO MAINTAIN YOUR LOVE, YOU HAVE TO HAVE SOME SELF-CONTROL.
SO THEN WHY ARE HUMANS HARD-WIRED...
...SO THAT THE MORE YOU LOVE SOMEONE, THE HARDER IT IS TO CONTROL YOURSELF?

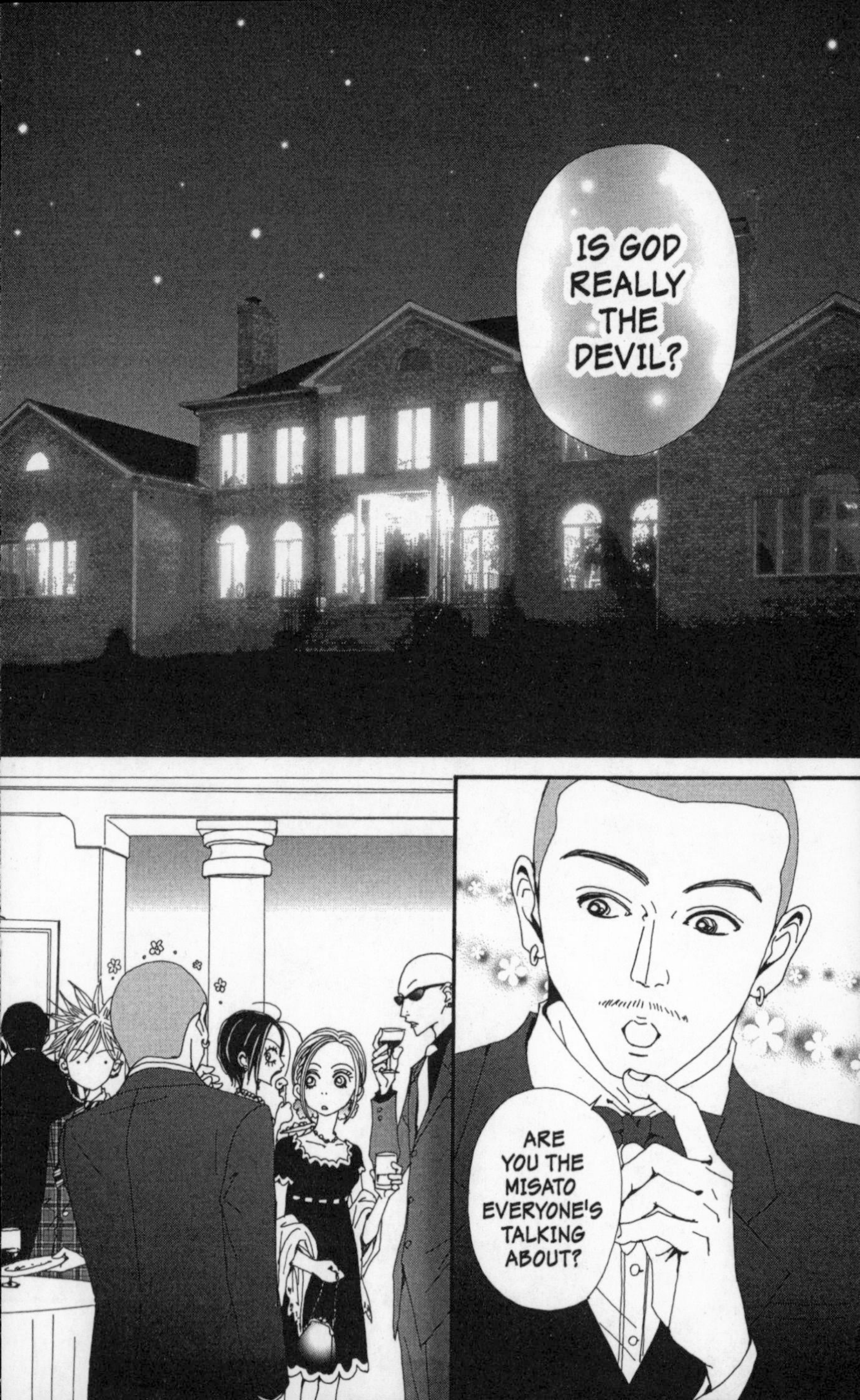
IS GOD REALLY THE DEVIL?
ARE YOU THE MISATO EVERYONE'S TALKING ABOUT?

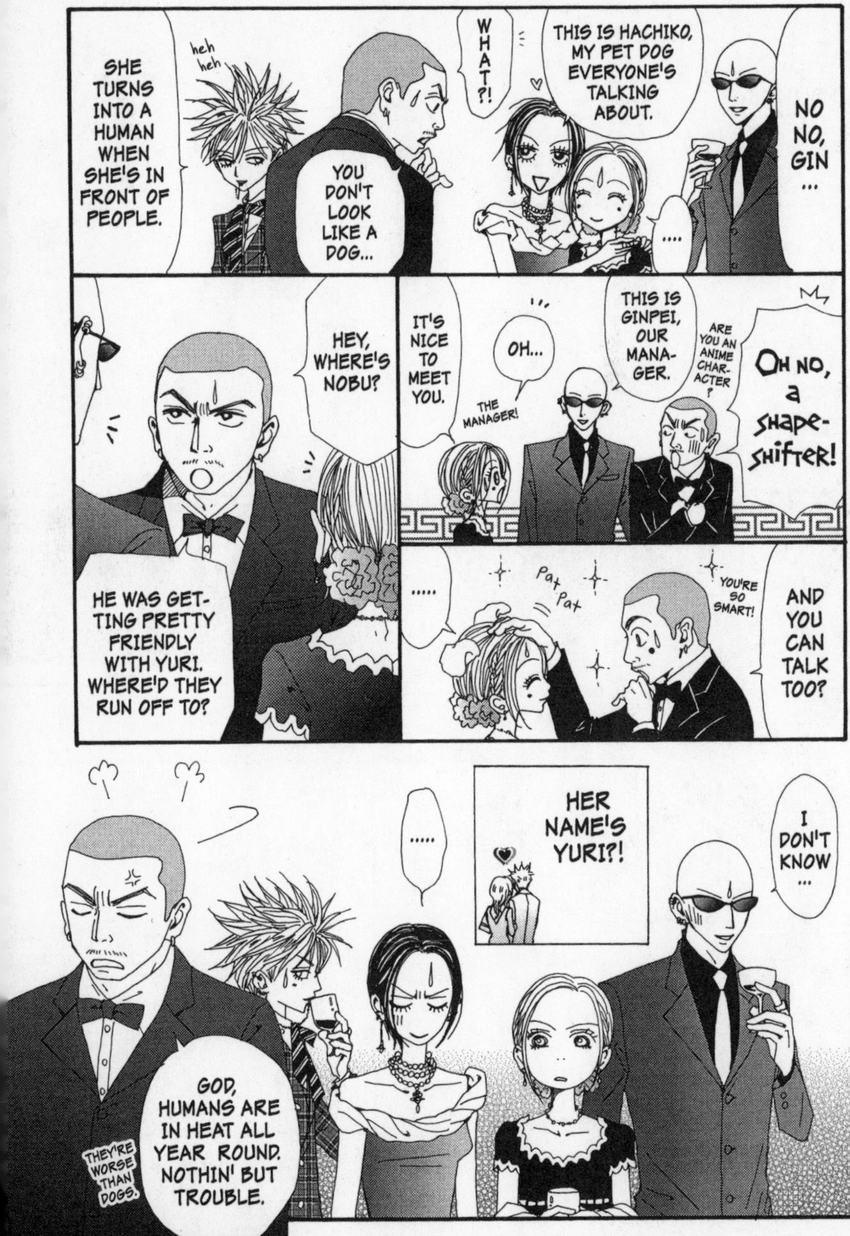
NO NO, GIN ...
....
THIS IS HACHIKO, MY PET DOG EVERYONE'S TALKING ABOUT.
WHAT?!
YOU DON'T LOOK LIKE A DOG...
heh heh
SHE TURNS INTO A HUMAN WHEN SHE'S IN FRONT OF PEOPLE.
OH NO, a SHAPE-SHIFTER!
ARE YOU AN ANIME CHARACTER?
THIS IS GINPEI, OUR MANAGER.
OH...
THE MANAGER!
IT'S NICE TO MEET YOU.
AND YOU CAN TALK TOO?
YOU'RE SO SMART!
Pat Pat
.....
HEY, WHERE'S NOBU?
HE WAS GETTING PRETTY FRIENDLY WITH YURI. WHERE'D THEY RUN OFF TO?
I DON'T KNOW ...
HER NAME'S YURI?!
.....
GOD, HUMANS ARE IN HEAT ALL YEAR ROUND. NOTHIN' BUT TROUBLE.
THEY'RE WORSE THAN DOGS.

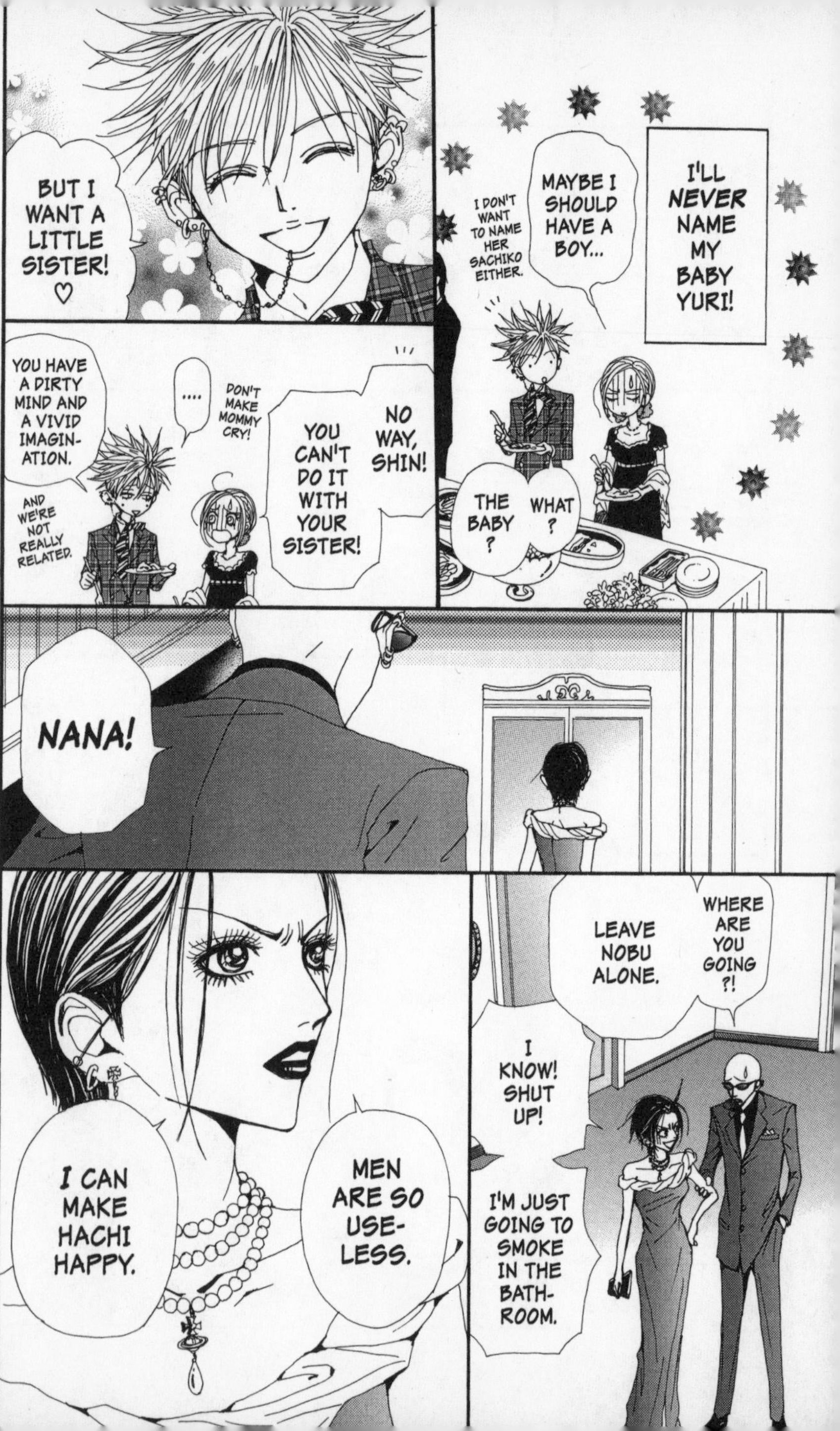
I'LL NEVER NAME MY BABY YURI!
MAYBE I SHOULD HAVE A BOY...
I DON'T WANT TO NAME HER SACHIKO EITHER.
WHAT?
THE BABY?
BUT I WANT A LITTLE SISTER! ♡
NO WAY, SHIN!
YOU CAN'T DO IT WITH YOUR SISTER!
DON'T MAKE MOMMY CRY!
....
YOU HAVE A DIRTY MIND AND A VIVID IMAGINATION.
AND WE'RE NOT REALLY RELATED.
NANA!
WHERE ARE YOU GOING?!
LEAVE NOBU ALONE.
I KNOW! SHUT UP!
I'M JUST GOING TO SMOKE IN THE BATHROOM.
MEN ARE SO USELESS.
I CAN MAKE HACHI HAPPY.

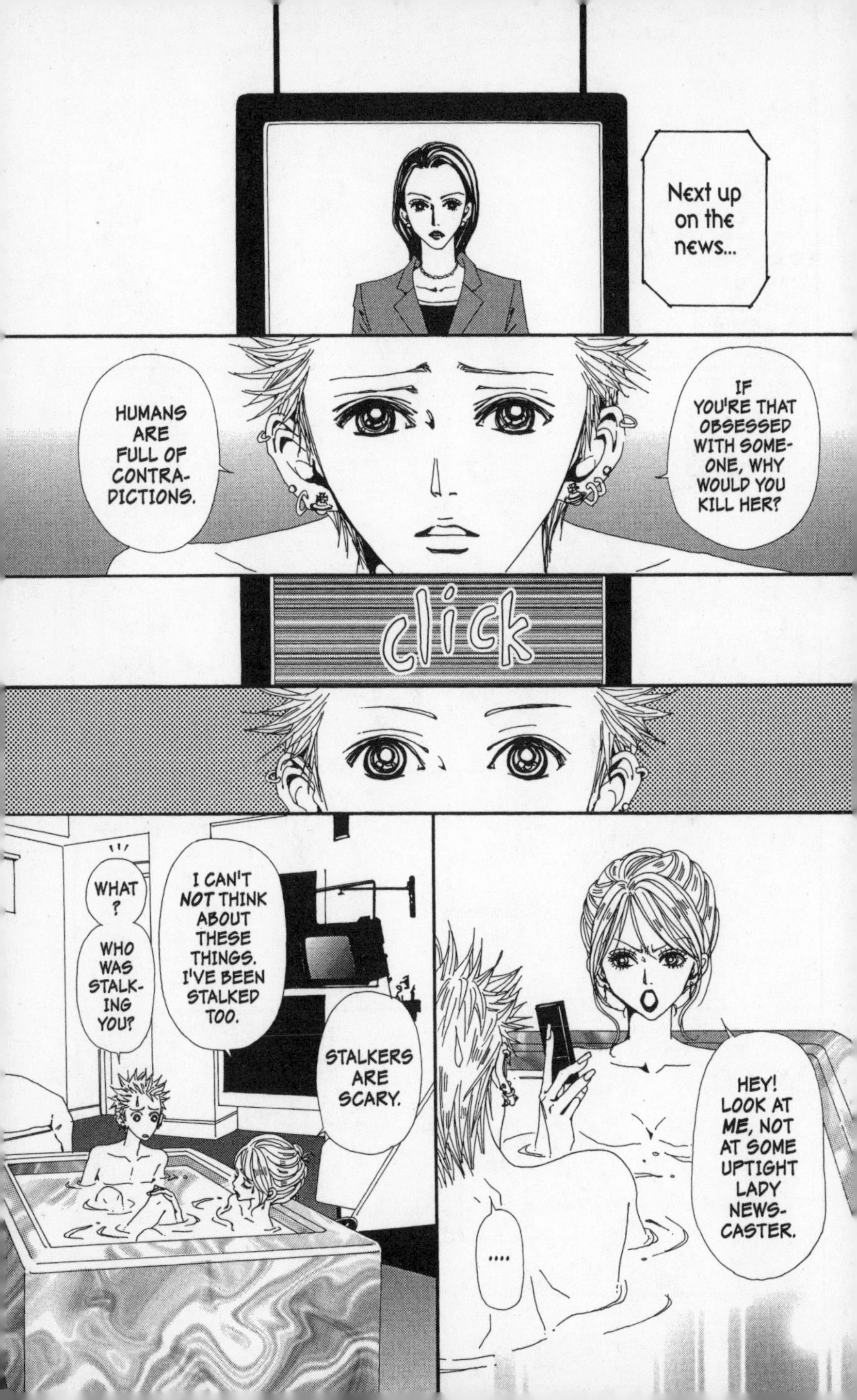
Next up on the news...
IF YOU'RE THAT OBSESSED WITH SOMEONE, WHY WOULD YOU KILL HER?
HUMANS ARE FULL OF CONTRADICTIONS.
click
HEY! LOOK AT *ME*, NOT AT SOME UPTIGHT LADY NEWSCASTER.
....
STALKERS ARE SCARY.
I CAN'T *NOT* THINK ABOUT THESE THINGS. I'VE BEEN STALKED TOO.
WHAT?
WHO WAS STALKING YOU?

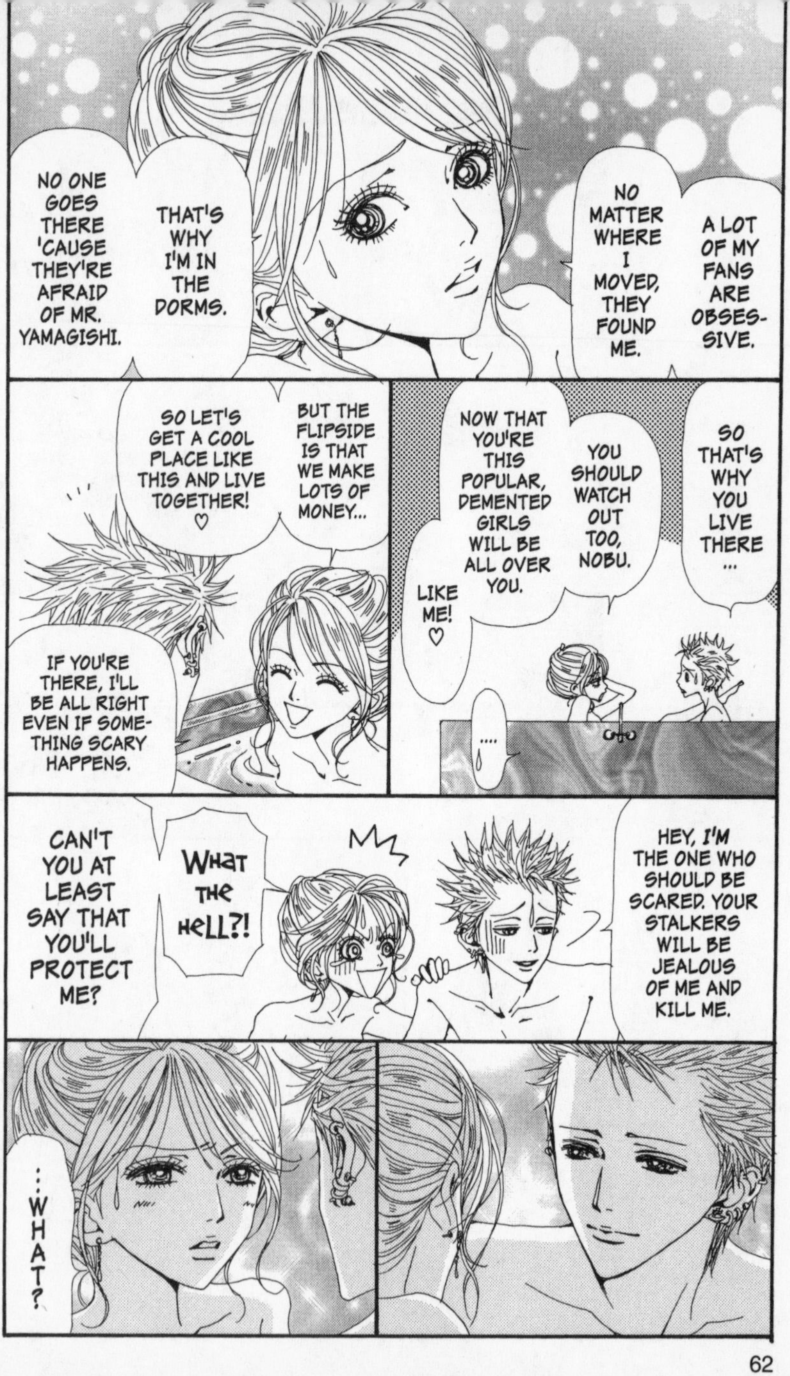
A LOT OF MY FANS ARE OBSESSIVE.
NO MATTER WHERE I MOVED, THEY FOUND ME.
THAT'S WHY I'M IN THE DORMS.
NO ONE GOES THERE 'CAUSE THEY'RE AFRAID OF MR. YAMAGISHI.
SO THAT'S WHY YOU LIVE THERE...
YOU SHOULD WATCH OUT TOO, NOBU.
NOW THAT YOU'RE THIS POPULAR, DEMENTED GIRLS WILL BE ALL OVER YOU.
LIKE ME! ♡
....
BUT THE FLIPSIDE IS THAT WE MAKE LOTS OF MONEY...
SO LET'S GET A COOL PLACE LIKE THIS AND LIVE TOGETHER! ♡
IF YOU'RE THERE, I'LL BE ALL RIGHT EVEN IF SOMETHING SCARY HAPPENS.
HEY, I'M THE ONE WHO SHOULD BE SCARED. YOUR STALKERS WILL BE JEALOUS OF ME AND KILL ME.
WHAT THE HELL?!
CAN'T YOU AT LEAST SAY THAT YOU'LL PROTECT ME?
...WHAT?

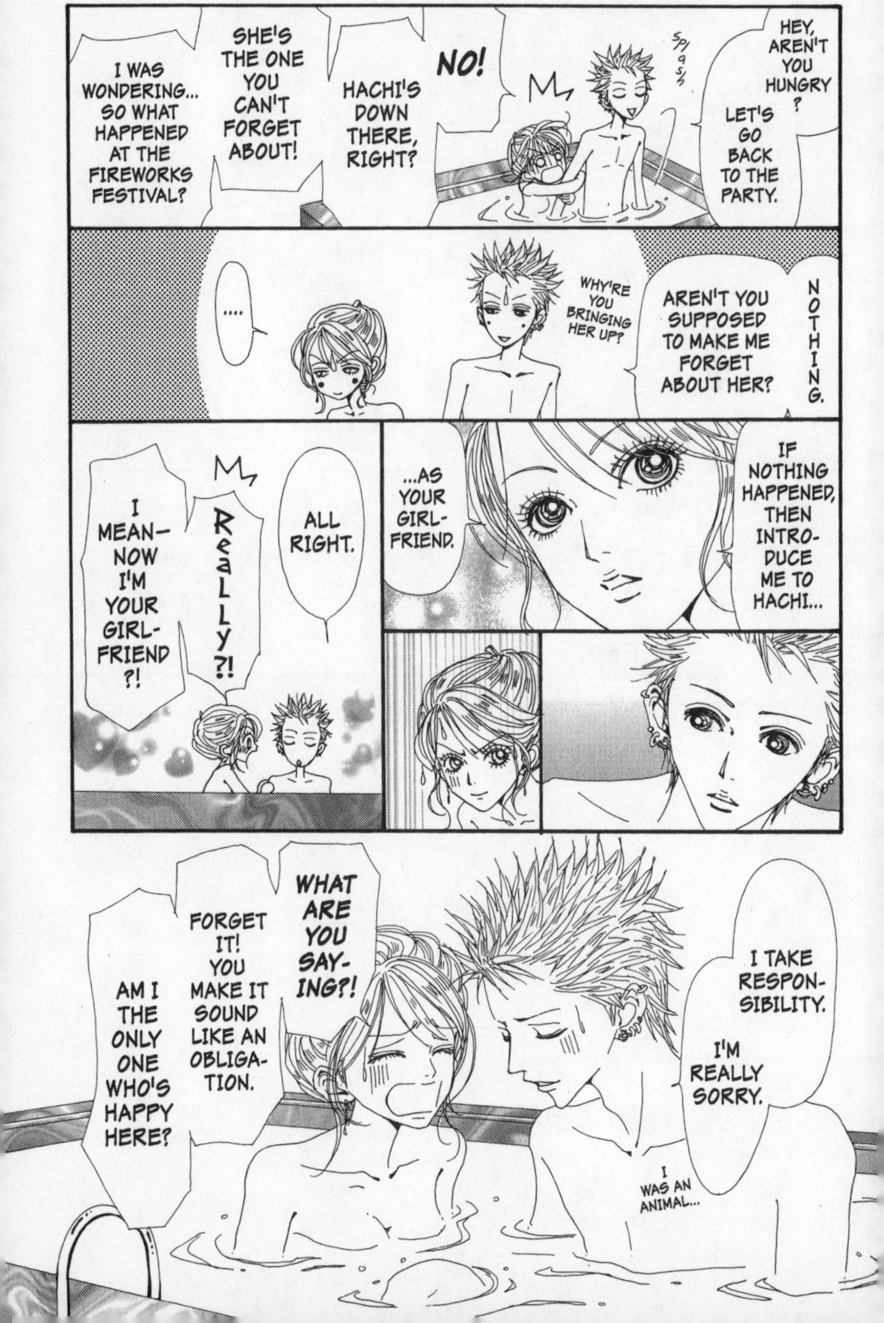
HEY, AREN'T YOU HUNGRY?
LET'S GO BACK TO THE PARTY.
SPLASH
NO!
HACHI'S DOWN THERE, RIGHT?
SHE'S THE ONE YOU CAN'T FORGET ABOUT!
I WAS WONDERING... SO WHAT HAPPENED AT THE FIREWORKS FESTIVAL?
NOTHING.
AREN'T YOU SUPPOSED TO MAKE ME FORGET ABOUT HER?
WHY'RE YOU BRINGING HER UP?
....
IF NOTHING HAPPENED, THEN INTRODUCE ME TO HACHI...
...AS YOUR GIRL-FRIEND.
ALL RIGHT.
Really?!
I MEAN—NOW I'M YOUR GIRL-FRIEND?!
I TAKE RESPON-SIBILITY.
I'M REALLY SORRY.
I WAS AN ANIMAL...
WHAT ARE YOU SAY-ING?!
FORGET IT! YOU MAKE IT SOUND LIKE AN OBLIGA-TION.
AM I THE ONLY ONE WHO'S HAPPY HERE?

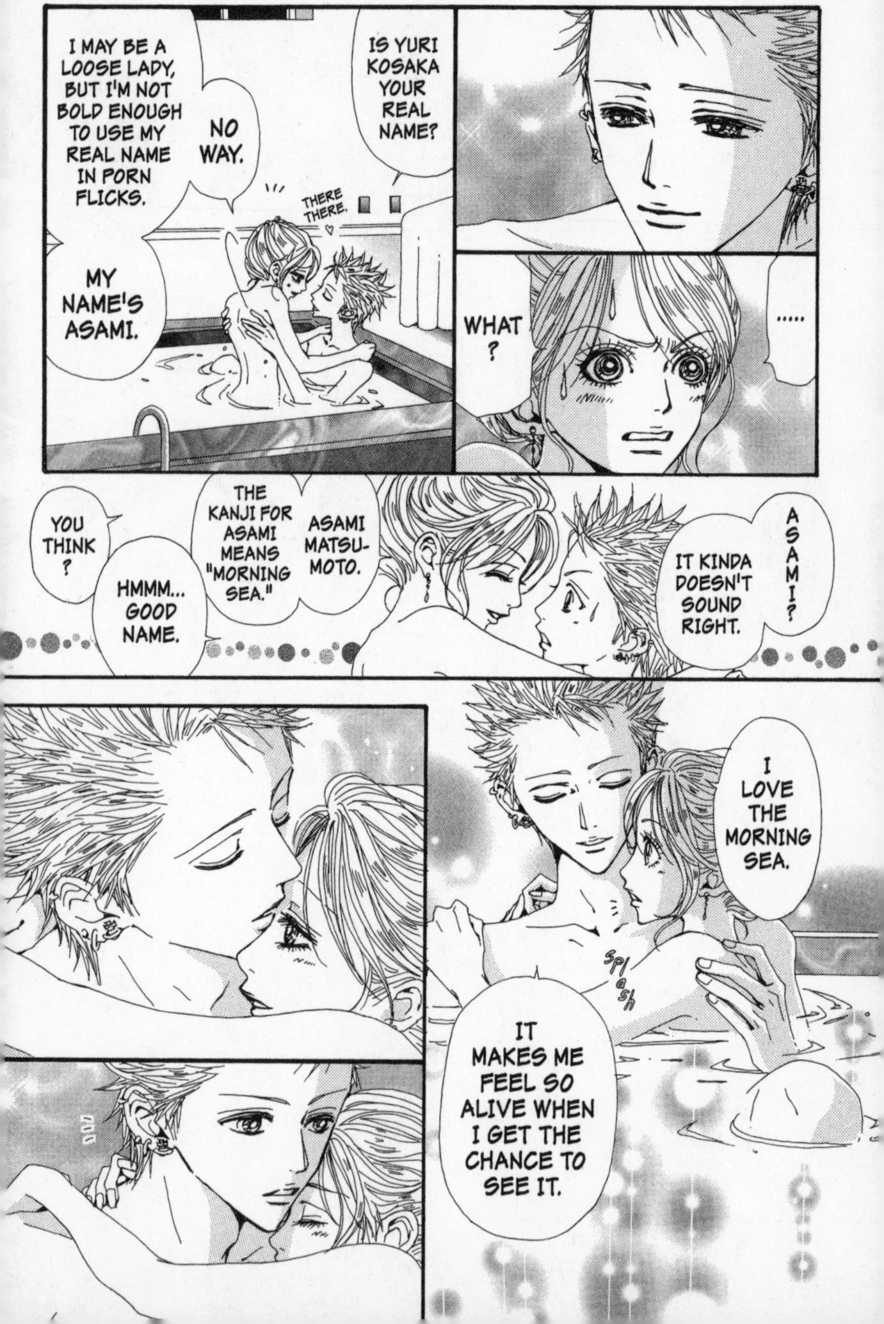
.....
WHAT?
IS YURI KOSAKA YOUR REAL NAME?
NO WAY.
I MAY BE A LOOSE LADY, BUT I'M NOT BOLD ENOUGH TO USE MY REAL NAME IN PORN FLICKS.
THERE THERE.
MY NAME'S ASAMI.
ASAMI?
IT KINDA DOESN'T SOUND RIGHT.
ASAMI MATSU-MOTO.
THE KANJI FOR ASAMI MEANS "MORNING SEA."
HMMM... GOOD NAME.
YOU THINK?
I LOVE THE MORNING SEA.
splash
IT MAKES ME FEEL SO ALIVE WHEN I GET THE CHANCE TO SEE IT.

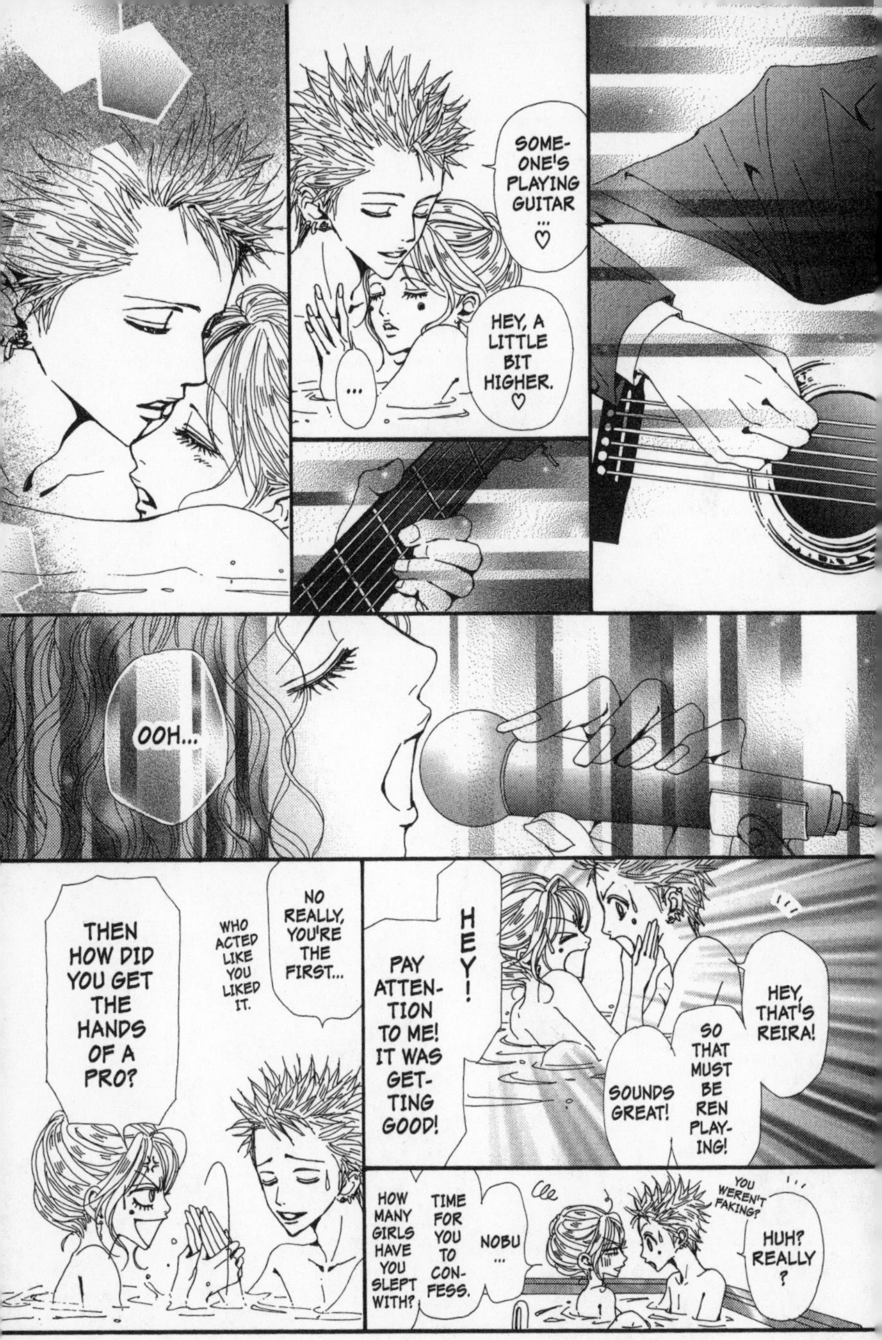
SOME-ONE'S PLAYING GUITAR ... ♡
HEY, A LITTLE BIT HIGHER. ♡
...
OOH...
HEY, THAT'S REIRA!
SO THAT MUST BE REN PLAYING!
SOUNDS GREAT!
HEY!
PAY ATTEN-TION TO ME! IT WAS GET-TING GOOD!
YOU WEREN'T FAKING?
HUH? REALLY?
NOBU...
TIME FOR YOU TO CON-FESS.
HOW MANY GIRLS HAVE YOU SLEPT WITH?
NO REALLY, YOU'RE THE FIRST...
WHO ACTED LIKE YOU LIKED IT.
THEN HOW DID YOU GET THE HANDS OF A PRO?

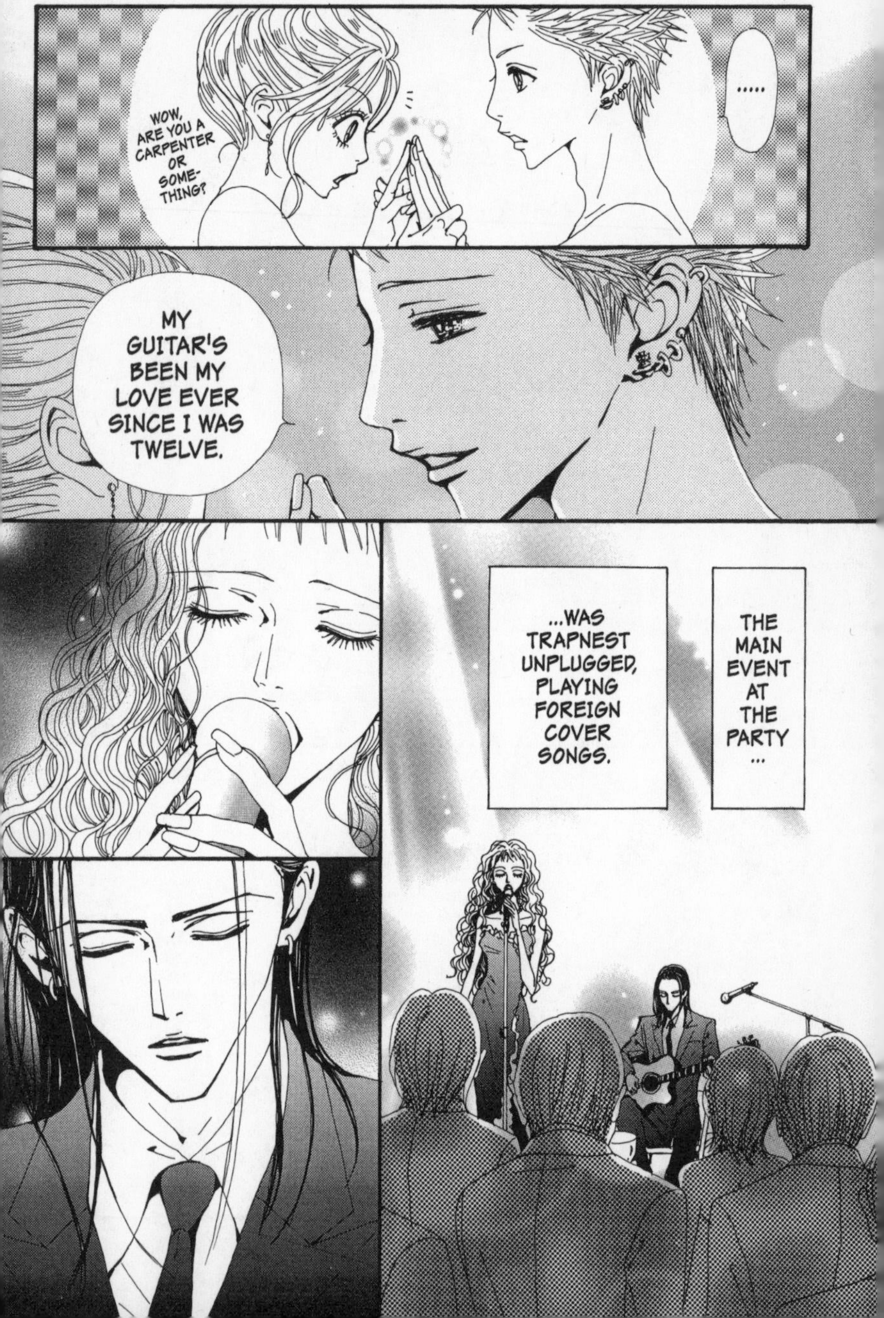
.....
WOW, ARE YOU A CARPENTER OR SOME-THING?
MY GUITAR'S BEEN MY LOVE EVER SINCE I WAS TWELVE.
THE MAIN EVENT AT THE PARTY...
...WAS TRAPNEST UNPLUGGED, PLAYING FOREIGN COVER SONGS.

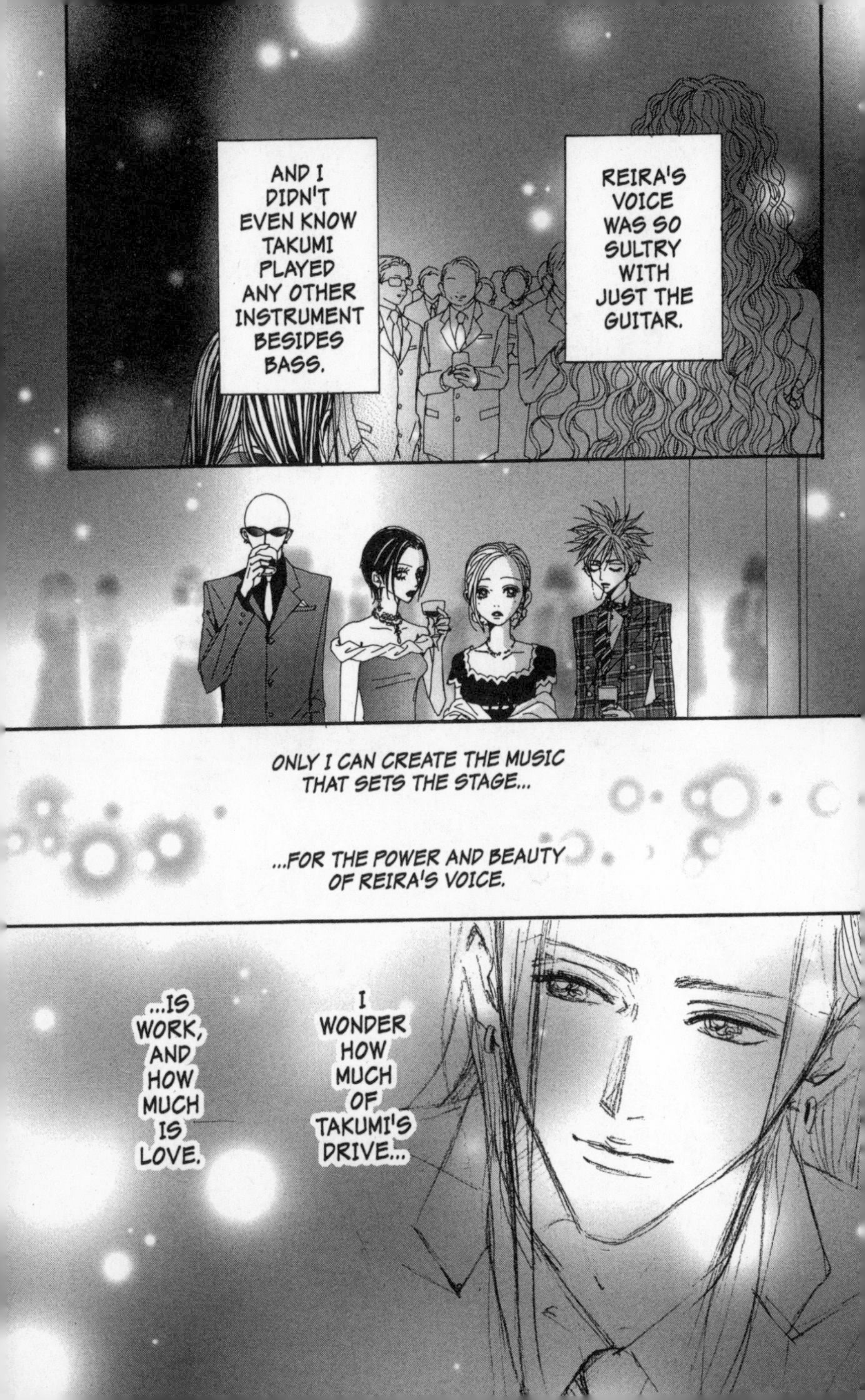
REIRA'S VOICE WAS SO SULTRY WITH JUST THE GUITAR.
AND I DIDN'T EVEN KNOW TAKUMI PLAYED ANY OTHER INSTRUMENT BESIDES BASS.
ONLY I CAN CREATE THE MUSIC THAT SETS THE STAGE...
...FOR THE POWER AND BEAUTY OF REIRA'S VOICE.
I WONDER HOW MUCH OF TAKUMI'S DRIVE...
...IS WORK, AND HOW MUCH IS LOVE.

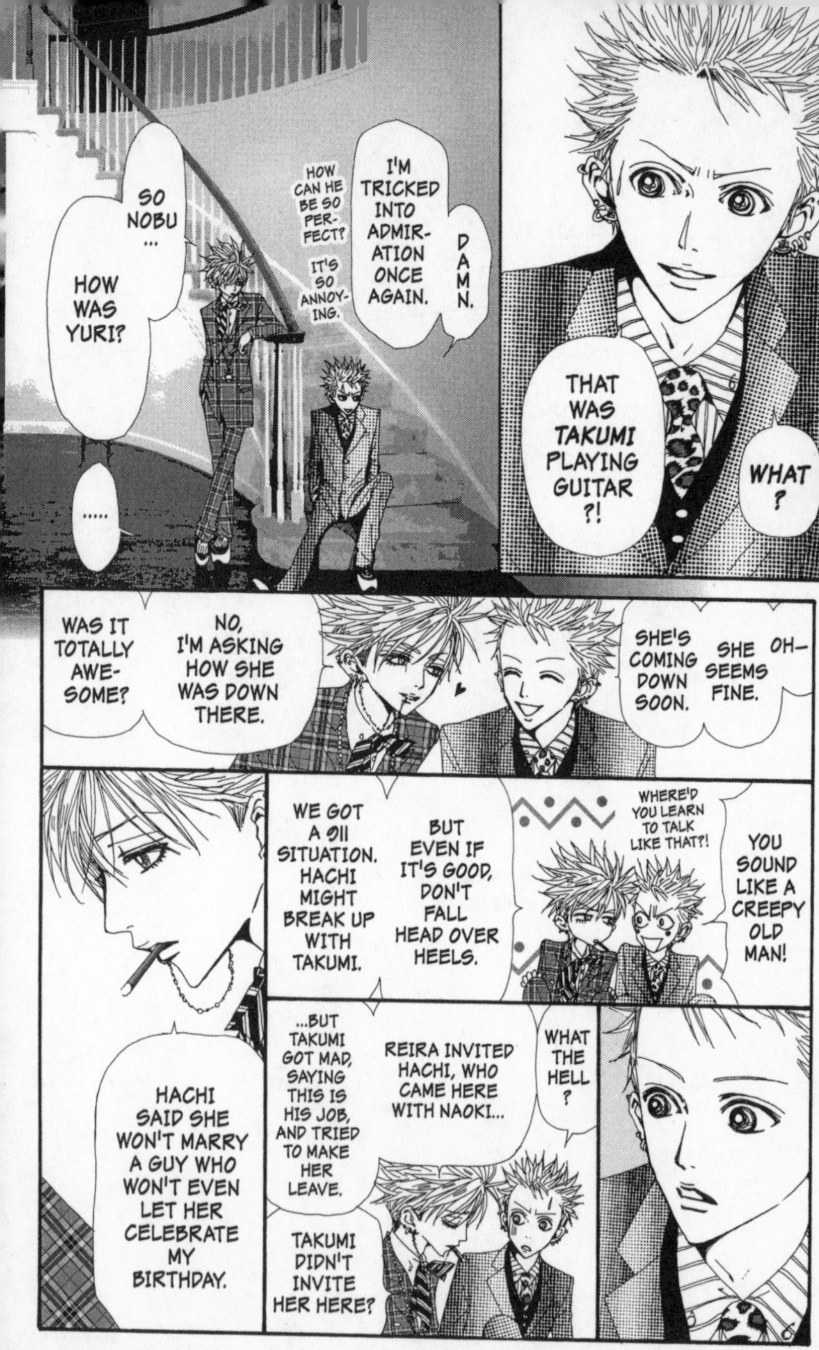
WHAT?
THAT WAS TAKUMI PLAYING GUITAR?!
DAMN.
I'M TRICKED INTO ADMIRATION ONCE AGAIN.
HOW CAN HE BE SO PERFECT? IT'S SO ANNOYING.
SO NOBU... HOW WAS YURI?
.....
OH— SHE SEEMS FINE.
SHE'S COMING DOWN SOON.
NO, I'M ASKING HOW SHE WAS DOWN THERE.
WAS IT TOTALLY AWESOME?
YOU SOUND LIKE A CREEPY OLD MAN!
WHERE'D YOU LEARN TO TALK LIKE THAT?!
BUT EVEN IF IT'S GOOD, DON'T FALL HEAD OVER HEELS.
WE GOT A 911 SITUATION. HACHI MIGHT BREAK UP WITH TAKUMI.
WHAT THE HELL?
REIRA INVITED HACHI, WHO CAME HERE WITH NAOKI...
...BUT TAKUMI GOT MAD, SAYING THIS IS HIS JOB, AND TRIED TO MAKE HER LEAVE.
TAKUMI DIDN'T INVITE HER HERE?
HACHI SAID SHE WON'T MARRY A GUY WHO WON'T EVEN LET HER CELEBRATE MY BIRTHDAY.

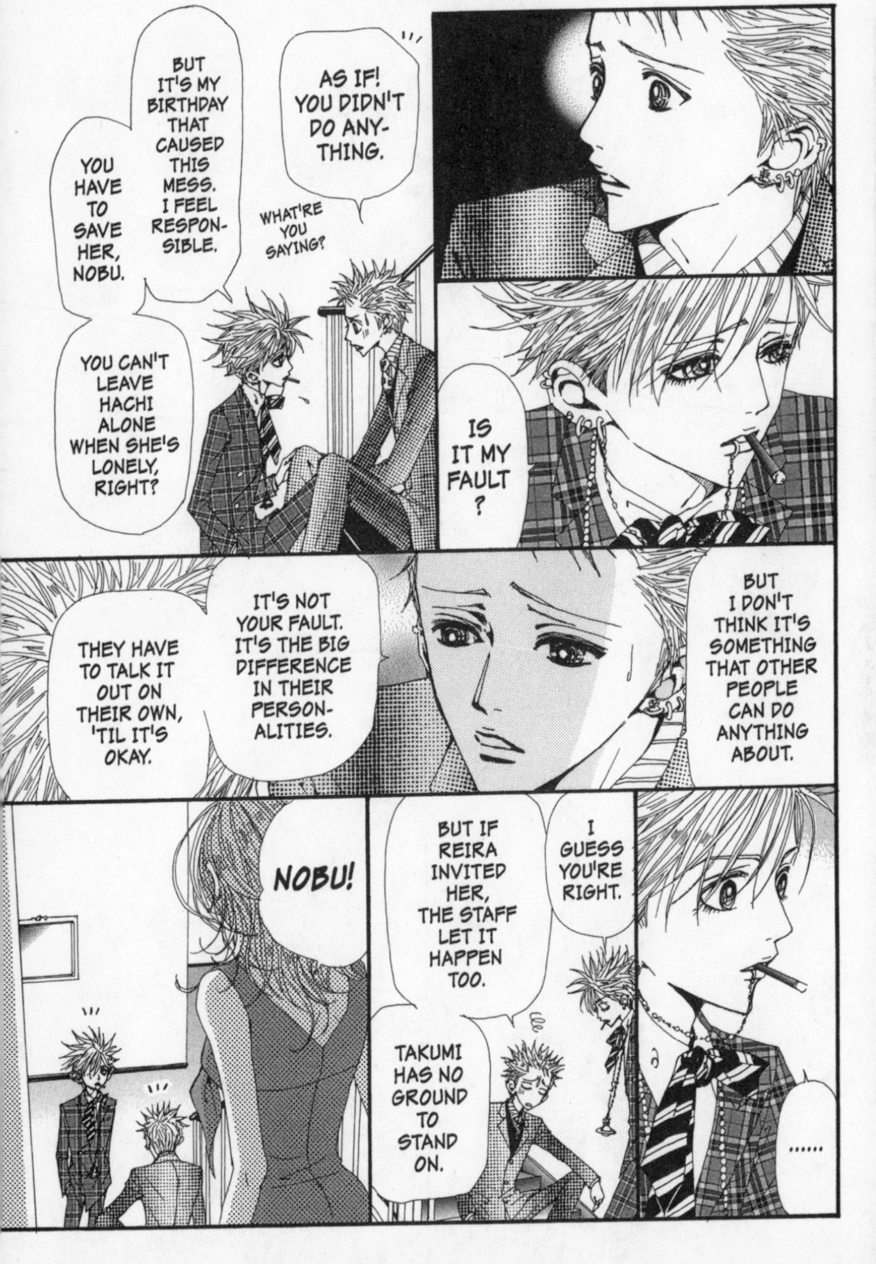
IS IT MY FAULT?
AS IF! YOU DIDN'T DO ANYTHING.
WHAT'RE YOU SAYING?
BUT IT'S MY BIRTHDAY THAT CAUSED THIS MESS. I FEEL RESPONSIBLE.
YOU HAVE TO SAVE HER, NOBU.
YOU CAN'T LEAVE HACHI ALONE WHEN SHE'S LONELY, RIGHT?
BUT I DON'T THINK IT'S SOMETHING THAT OTHER PEOPLE CAN DO ANYTHING ABOUT.
IT'S NOT YOUR FAULT. IT'S THE BIG DIFFERENCE IN THEIR PERSONALITIES.
THEY HAVE TO TALK IT OUT ON THEIR OWN, 'TIL IT'S OKAY.
......
I GUESS YOU'RE RIGHT.
BUT IF REIRA INVITED HER, THE STAFF LET IT HAPPEN TOO.
TAKUMI HAS NO GROUND TO STAND ON.
NOBU!

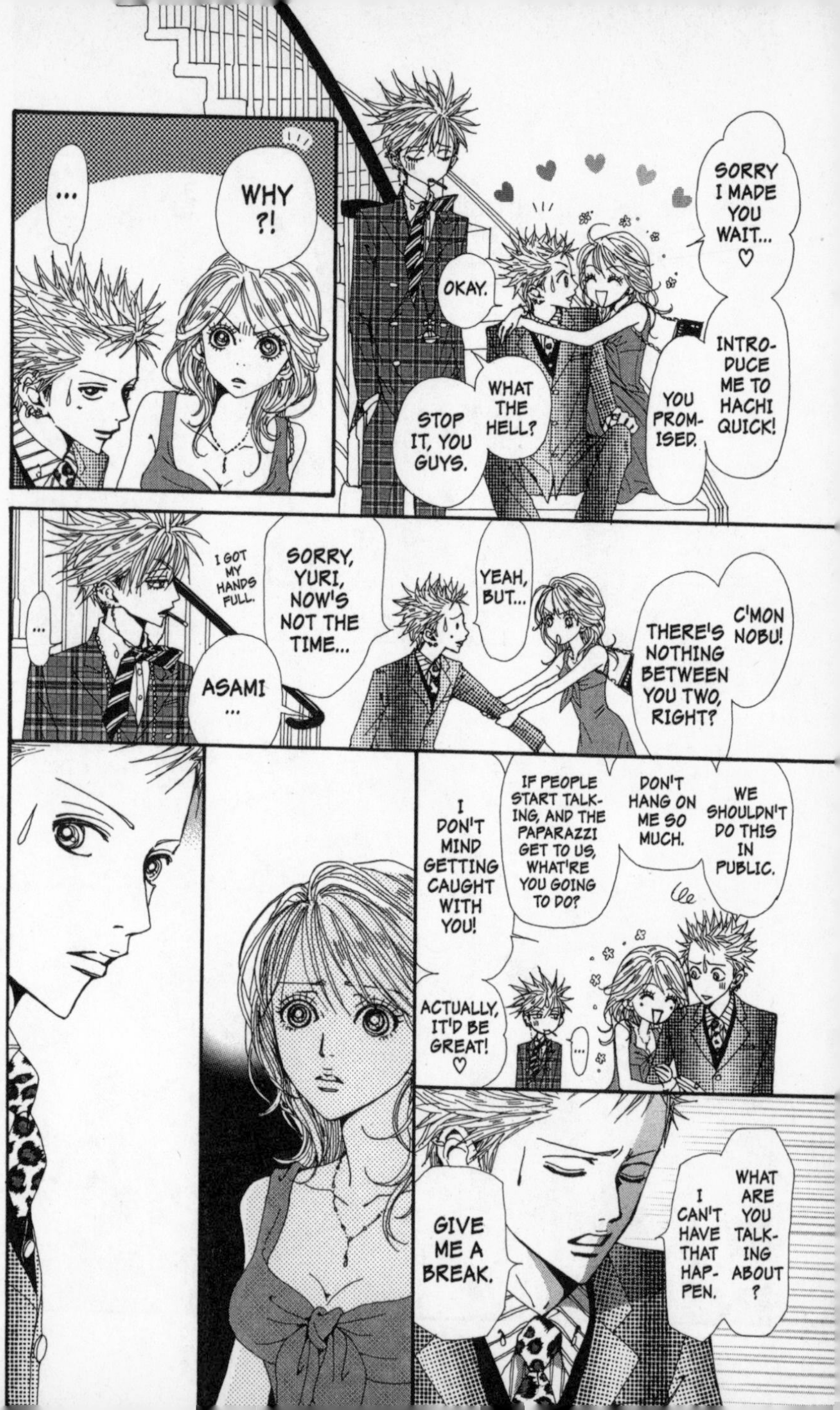
SORRY I MADE YOU WAIT... ♡
INTRODUCE ME TO HACHI QUICK!
YOU PROMISED.
OKAY.
WHAT THE HELL?
STOP IT, YOU GUYS.
WHY ?!
...
C'MON NOBU!
THERE'S NOTHING BETWEEN YOU TWO, RIGHT?
YEAH, BUT...
SORRY, YURI, NOW'S NOT THE TIME...
I GOT MY HANDS FULL.
ASAMI ...
...
WE SHOULDN'T DO THIS IN PUBLIC.
DON'T HANG ON ME SO MUCH.
IF PEOPLE START TALKING, AND THE PAPARAZZI GET TO US, WHAT'RE YOU GOING TO DO?
I DON'T MIND GETTING CAUGHT WITH YOU!
ACTUALLY, IT'D BE GREAT! ♡
...
WHAT ARE YOU TALKING ABOUT ?
I CAN'T HAVE THAT HAPPEN.
GIVE ME A BREAK.

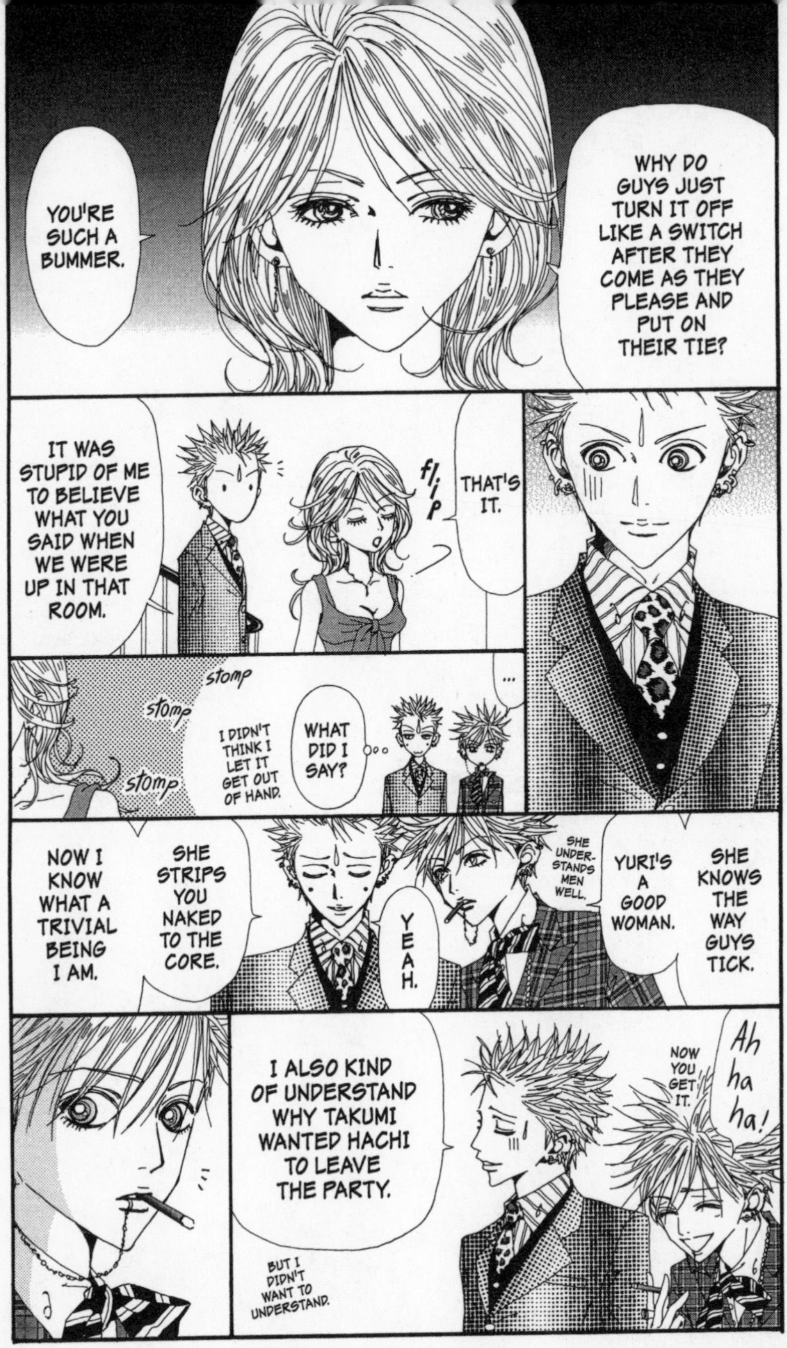
WHY DO GUYS JUST TURN IT OFF LIKE A SWITCH AFTER THEY COME AS THEY PLEASE AND PUT ON THEIR TIE?
YOU'RE SUCH A BUMMER.
THAT'S IT.
flip
IT WAS STUPID OF ME TO BELIEVE WHAT YOU SAID WHEN WE WERE UP IN THAT ROOM.
...
WHAT DID I SAY?
I DIDN'T THINK I LET IT GET OUT OF HAND.
stomp
stomp
stomp
SHE KNOWS THE WAY GUYS TICK.
YURI'S A GOOD WOMAN.
SHE UNDERSTANDS MEN WELL.
YEAH.
SHE STRIPS YOU NAKED TO THE CORE.
NOW I KNOW WHAT A TRIVIAL BEING I AM.
Ah ha ha!
NOW YOU GET IT.
I ALSO KIND OF UNDERSTAND WHY TAKUMI WANTED HACHI TO LEAVE THE PARTY.
BUT I DIDN'T WANT TO UNDERSTAND.

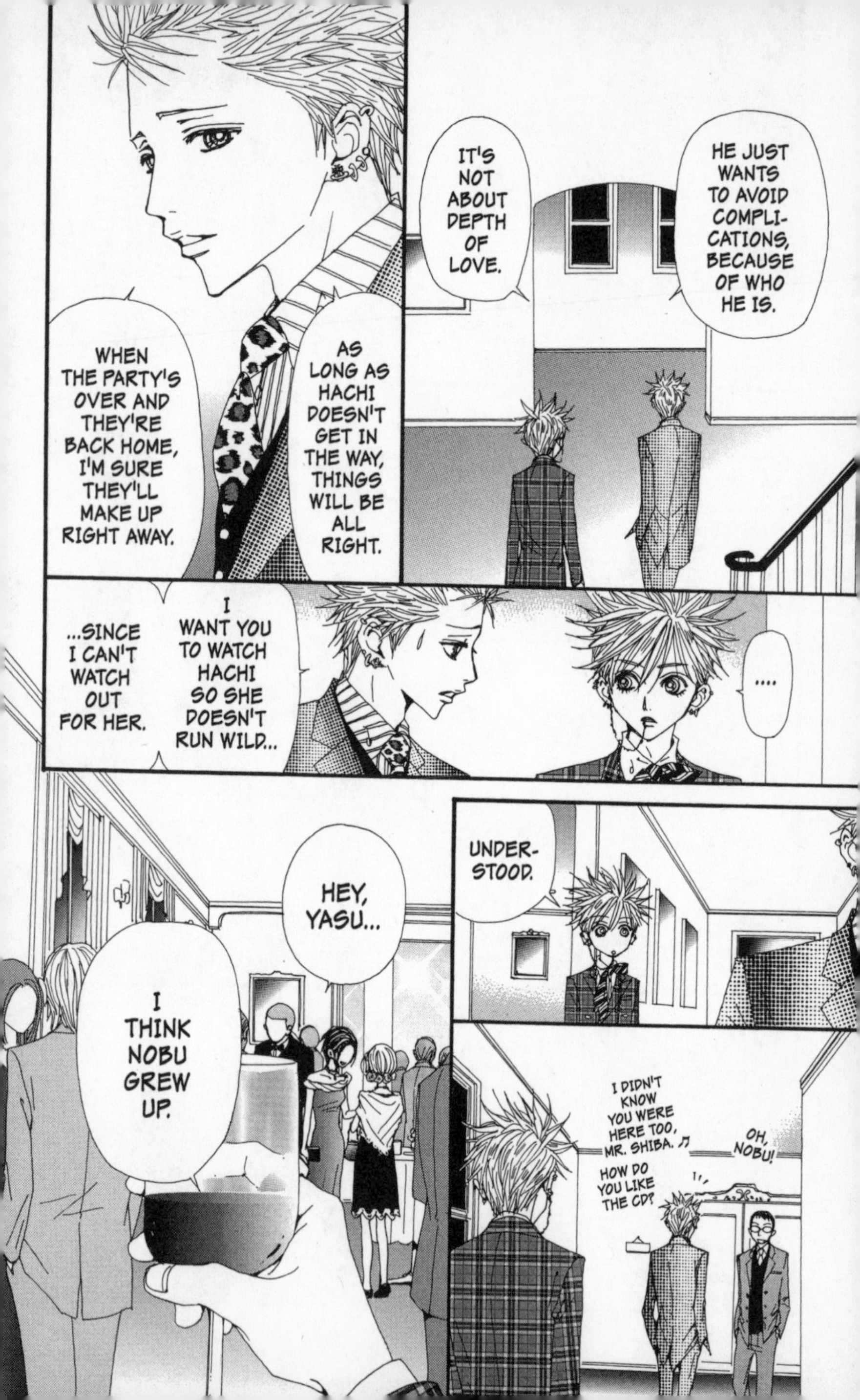
HE JUST WANTS TO AVOID COMPLI-CATIONS, BECAUSE OF WHO HE IS.
IT'S NOT ABOUT DEPTH OF LOVE.
AS LONG AS HACHI DOESN'T GET IN THE WAY, THINGS WILL BE ALL RIGHT.
WHEN THE PARTY'S OVER AND THEY'RE BACK HOME, I'M SURE THEY'LL MAKE UP RIGHT AWAY.
....
I WANT YOU TO WATCH HACHI SO SHE DOESN'T RUN WILD...
...SINCE I CAN'T WATCH OUT FOR HER.
UNDER-STOOD.
OH, NOBU!
I DIDN'T KNOW YOU WERE HERE TOO, MR. SHIBA. ♫
HOW DO YOU LIKE THE CD?
HEY, YASU...
I THINK NOBU GREW UP.

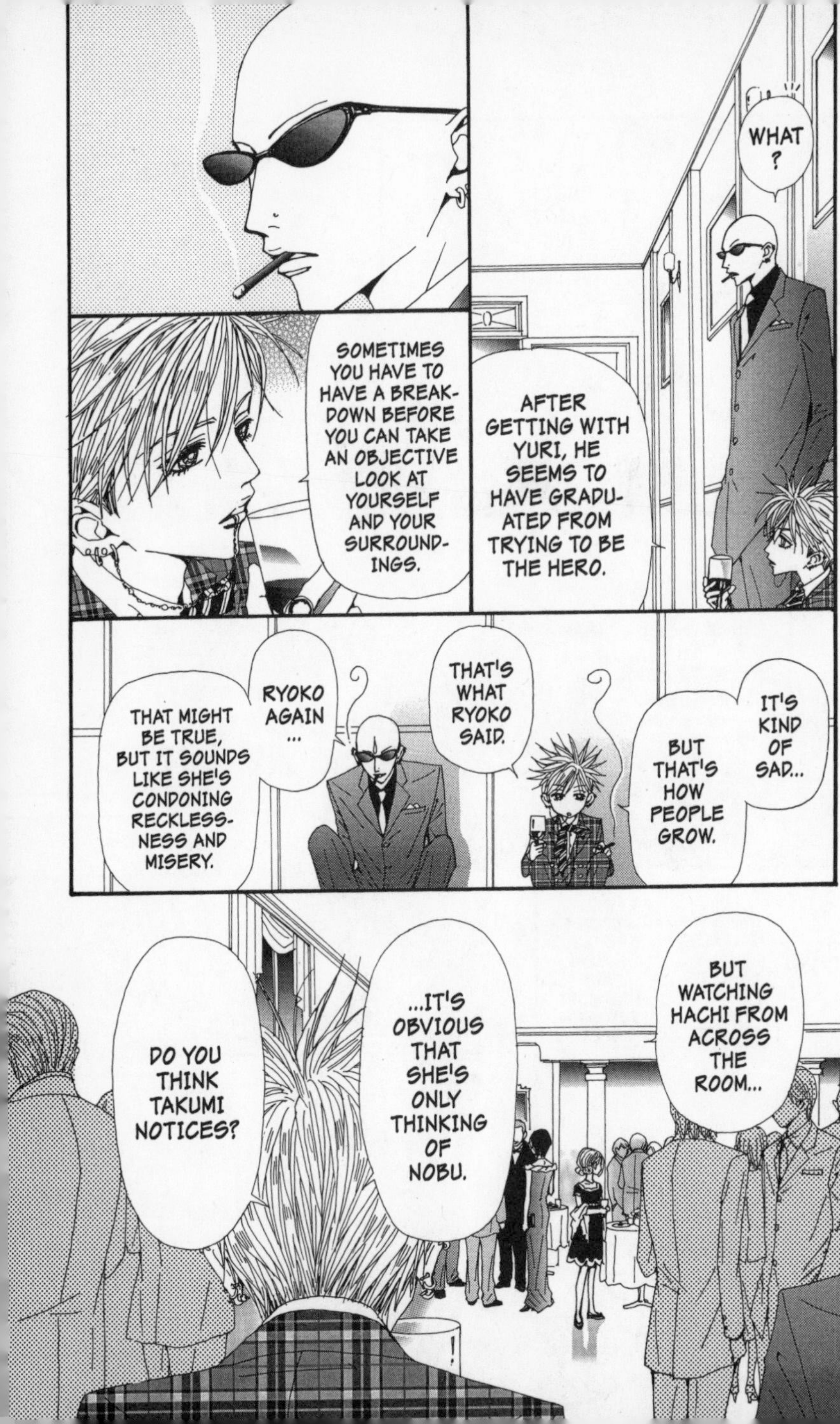
WHAT ?
AFTER GETTING WITH YURI, HE SEEMS TO HAVE GRADUATED FROM TRYING TO BE THE HERO.
SOMETIMES YOU HAVE TO HAVE A BREAKDOWN BEFORE YOU CAN TAKE AN OBJECTIVE LOOK AT YOURSELF AND YOUR SURROUNDINGS.
IT'S KIND OF SAD...
BUT THAT'S HOW PEOPLE GROW.
THAT'S WHAT RYOKO SAID.
RYOKO AGAIN ...
THAT MIGHT BE TRUE, BUT IT SOUNDS LIKE SHE'S CONDONING RECKLESSNESS AND MISERY.
BUT WATCHING HACHI FROM ACROSS THE ROOM...
...IT'S OBVIOUS THAT SHE'S ONLY THINKING OF NOBU.
DO YOU THINK TAKUMI NOTICES?
!

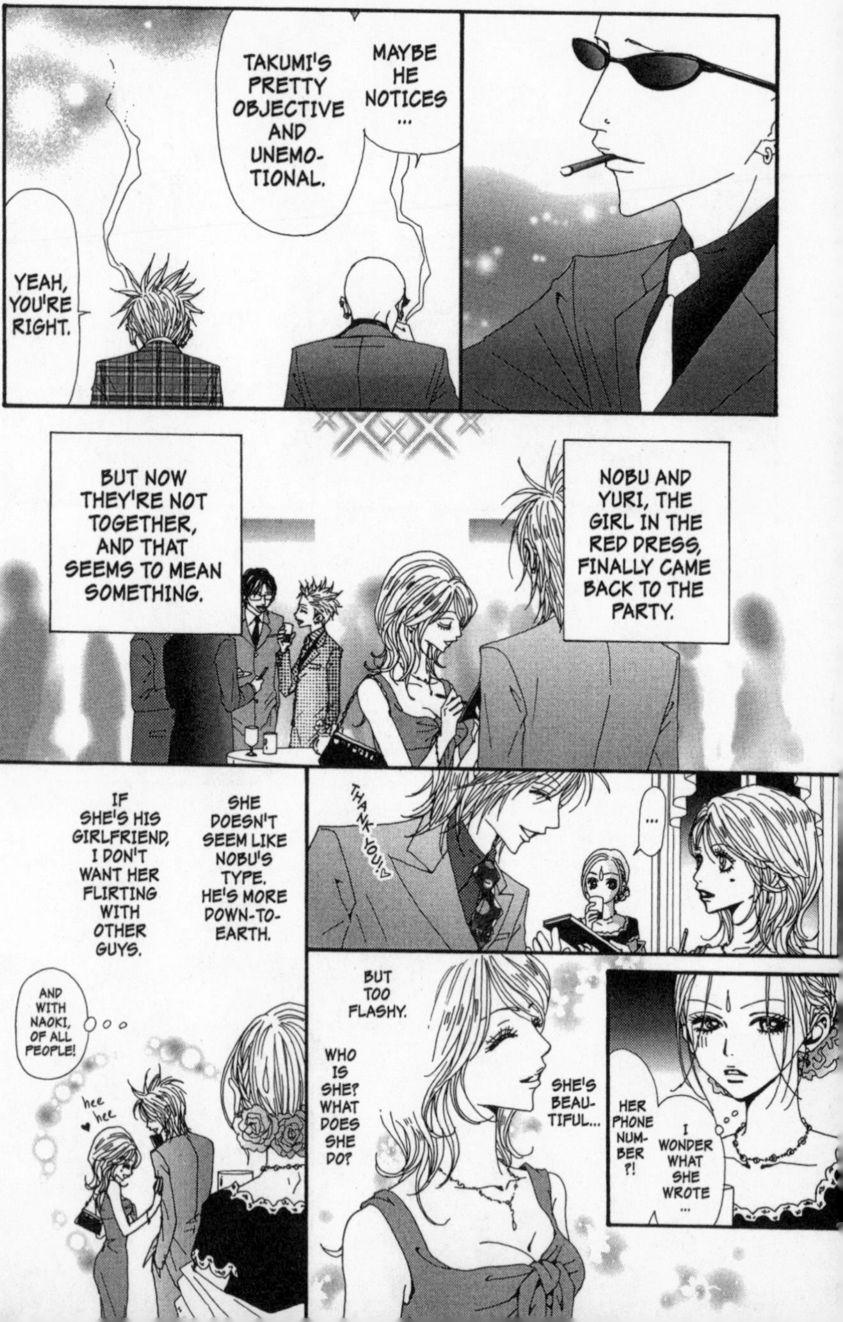
MAYBE HE NOTICES ...
TAKUMI'S PRETTY OBJECTIVE AND UNEMOTIONAL.
YEAH, YOU'RE RIGHT.
NOBU AND YURI, THE GIRL IN THE RED DRESS, FINALLY CAME BACK TO THE PARTY.
BUT NOW THEY'RE NOT TOGETHER, AND THAT SEEMS TO MEAN SOMETHING.
THANK YOU!♡
...
I WONDER WHAT SHE WROTE ...
HER PHONE NUMBER ?!
SHE'S BEAUTIFUL...
BUT TOO FLASHY.
WHO IS SHE? WHAT DOES SHE DO?
SHE DOESN'T SEEM LIKE NOBU'S TYPE. HE'S MORE DOWN-TO-EARTH.
IF SHE'S HIS GIRLFRIEND, I DON'T WANT HER FLIRTING WITH OTHER GUYS.
AND WITH NAOKI, OF ALL PEOPLE!
hee hee

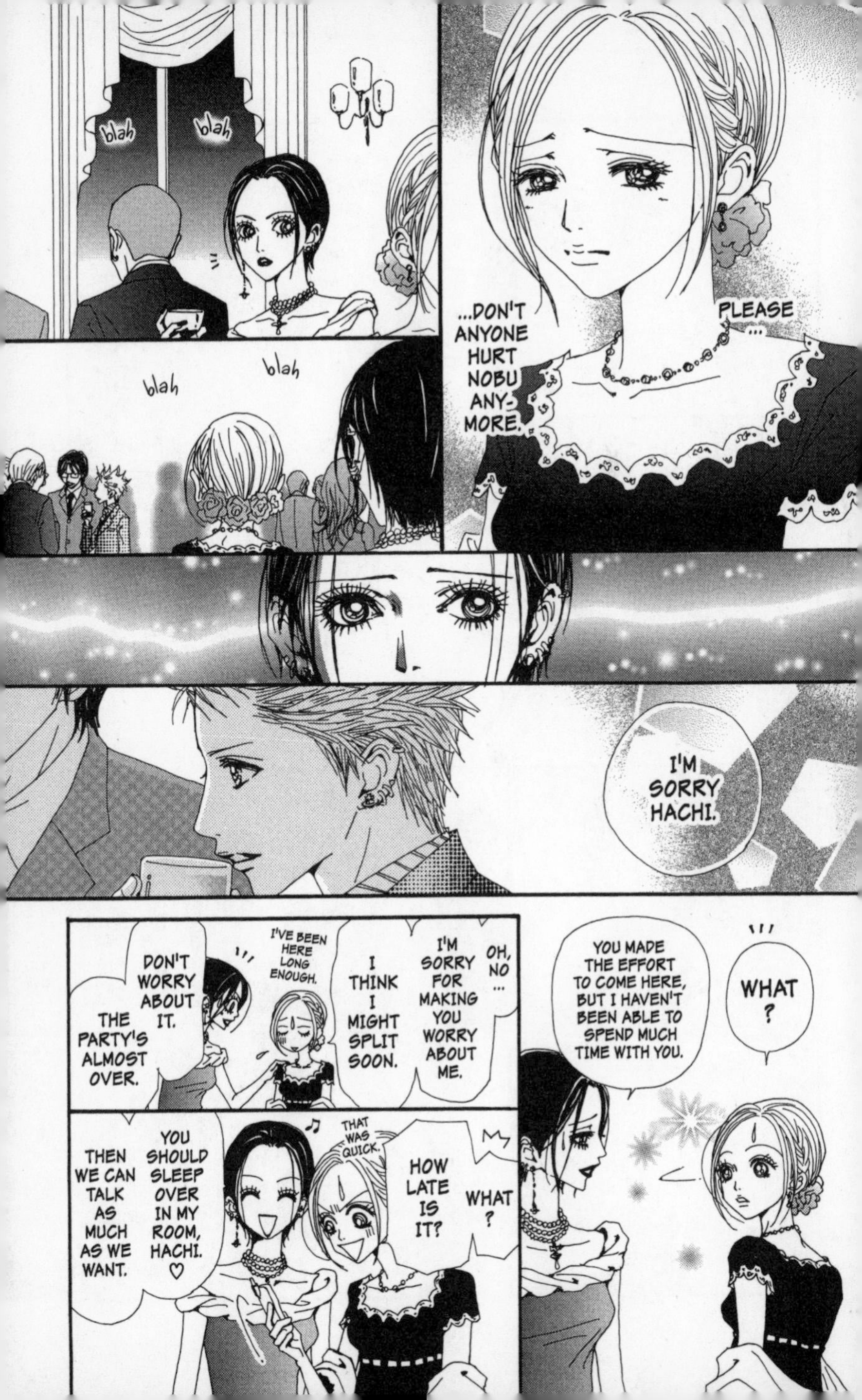
PLEASE...
...DON'T ANYONE HURT NOBU ANYMORE.
blah
blah
blah
blah
I'M SORRY HACHI.
WHAT?
YOU MADE THE EFFORT TO COME HERE, BUT I HAVEN'T BEEN ABLE TO SPEND MUCH TIME WITH YOU.
OH, NO...
I'M SORRY FOR MAKING YOU WORRY ABOUT ME.
I THINK I MIGHT SPLIT SOON.
I'VE BEEN HERE LONG ENOUGH.
DON'T WORRY ABOUT IT.
THE PARTY'S ALMOST OVER.
WHAT?
HOW LATE IS IT?
THAT WAS QUICK.
YOU SHOULD SLEEP OVER IN MY ROOM, HACHI. ♡
THEN WE CAN TALK AS MUCH AS WE WANT.

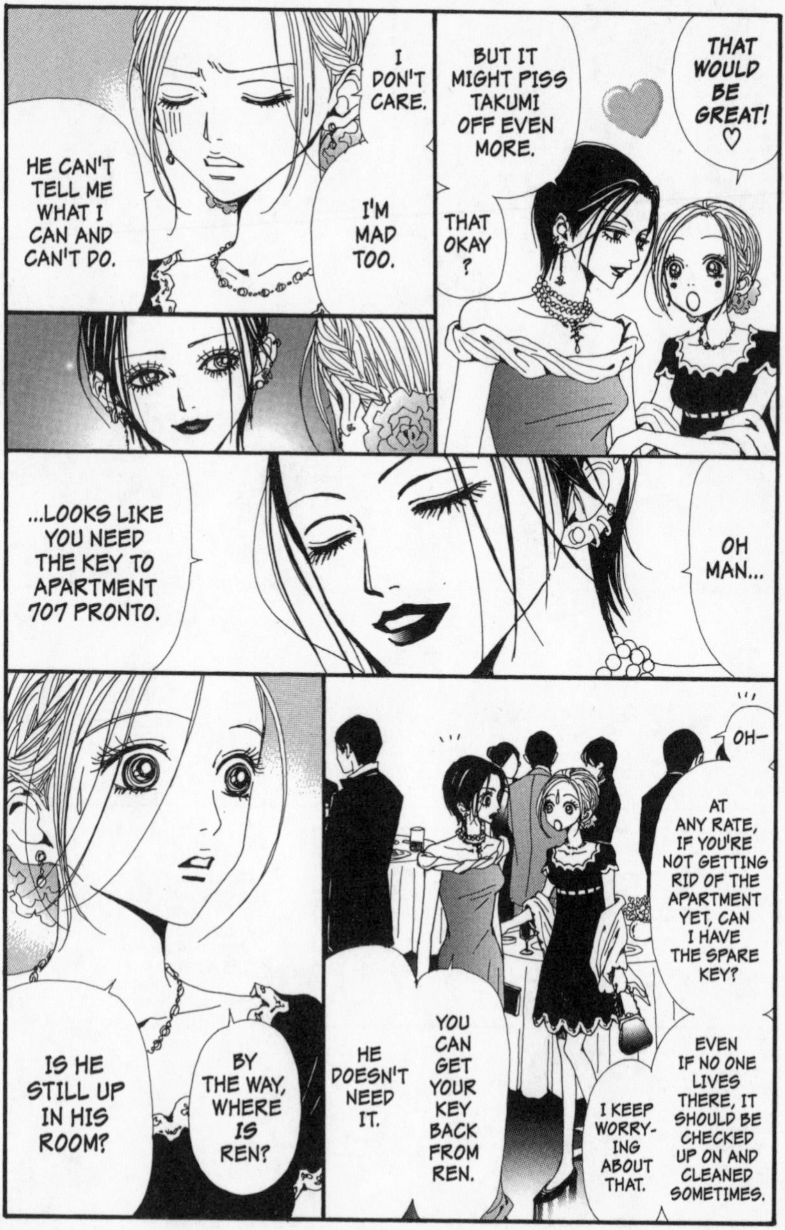

THAT WOULD BE GREAT! ♡
BUT IT MIGHT PISS TAKUMI OFF EVEN MORE.
THAT OKAY?
I DON'T CARE.
I'M MAD TOO.
HE CAN'T TELL ME WHAT I CAN AND CAN'T DO.
OH MAN...
...LOOKS LIKE YOU NEED THE KEY TO APARTMENT 707 PRONTO.
OH—
AT ANY RATE, IF YOU'RE NOT GETTING RID OF THE APARTMENT YET, CAN I HAVE THE SPARE KEY?
EVEN IF NO ONE LIVES THERE, IT SHOULD BE CHECKED UP ON AND CLEANED SOMETIMES.
I KEEP WORRYING ABOUT THAT.
YOU CAN GET YOUR KEY BACK FROM REN.
HE DOESN'T NEED IT.
BY THE WAY, WHERE IS REN?
IS HE STILL UP IN HIS ROOM?

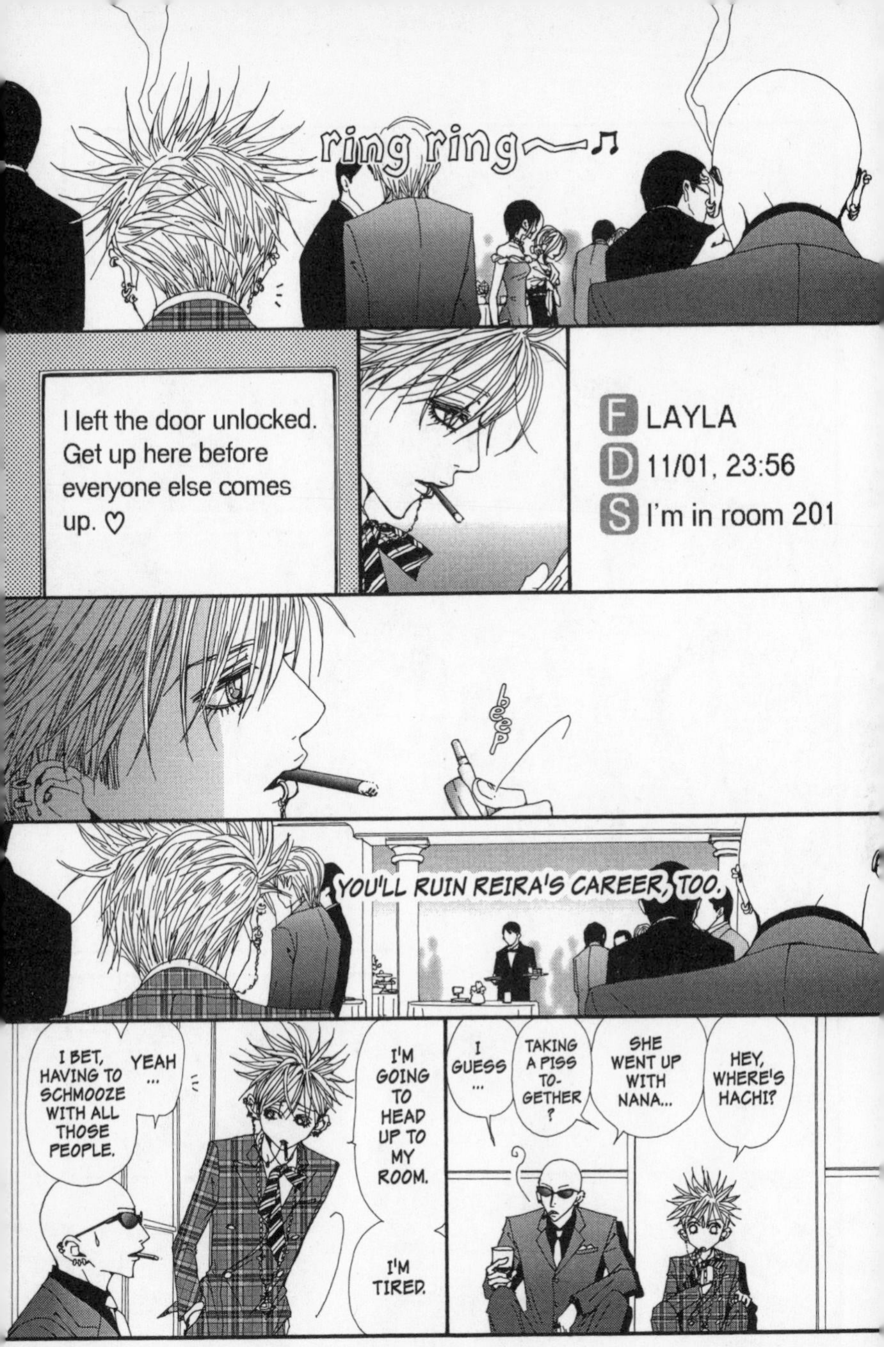

ring ring~♫
F LAYLA
D 11/01, 23:56
S I'm in room 201
I left the door unlocked. Get up here before everyone else comes up. ♡
beep
YOU'LL RUIN REIRA'S CAREER, TOO.
HEY, WHERE'S HACHI?
SHE WENT UP WITH NANA...
TAKING A PISS TO-GETHER?
I GUESS...
I'M GOING TO HEAD UP TO MY ROOM.
I'M TIRED.
YEAH...
I BET, HAVING TO SCHMOOZE WITH ALL THOSE PEOPLE.

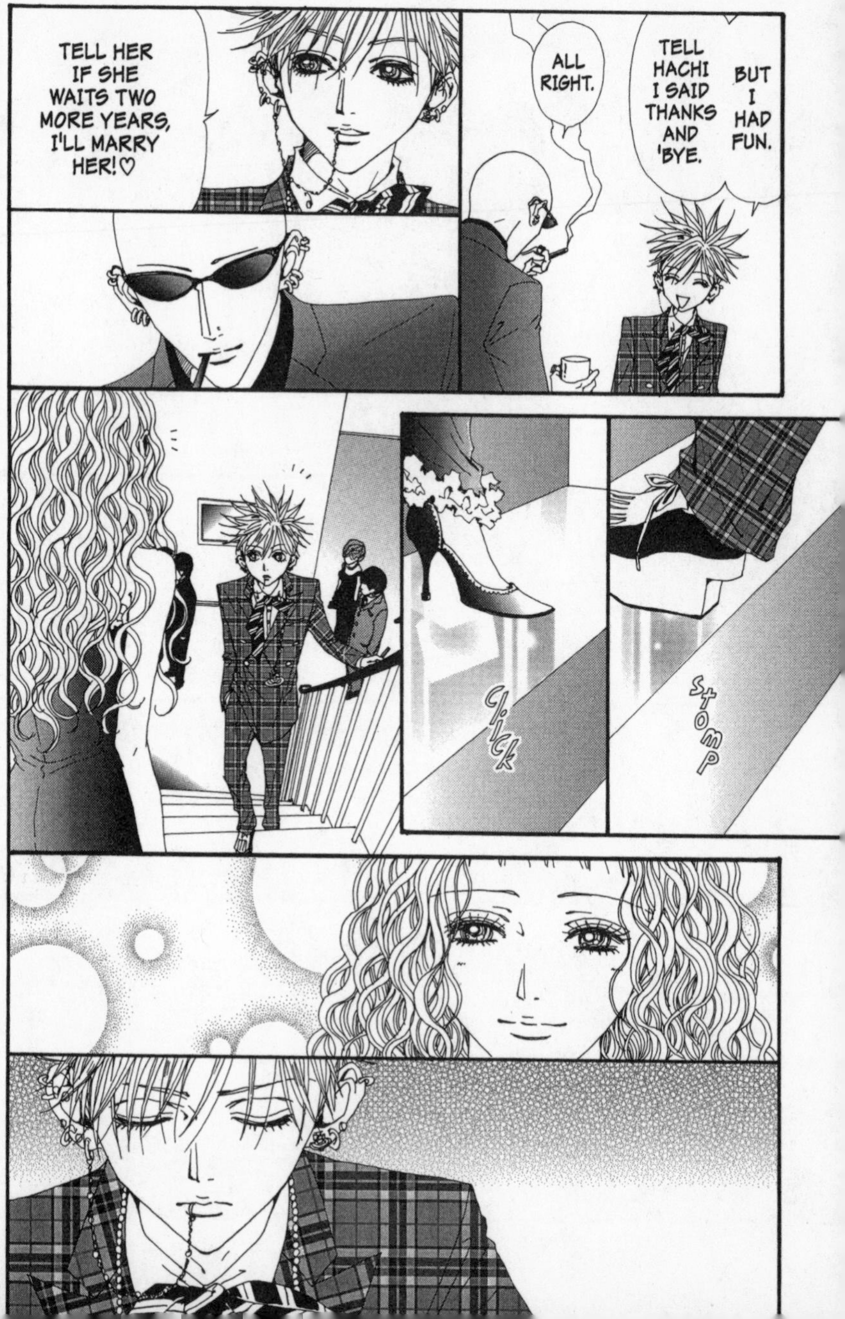
TELL HACHI I SAID THANKS AND 'BYE.
BUT I HAD FUN.
ALL RIGHT.
TELL HER IF SHE WAITS TWO MORE YEARS, I'LL MARRY HER!♡
STOMP
CLICK

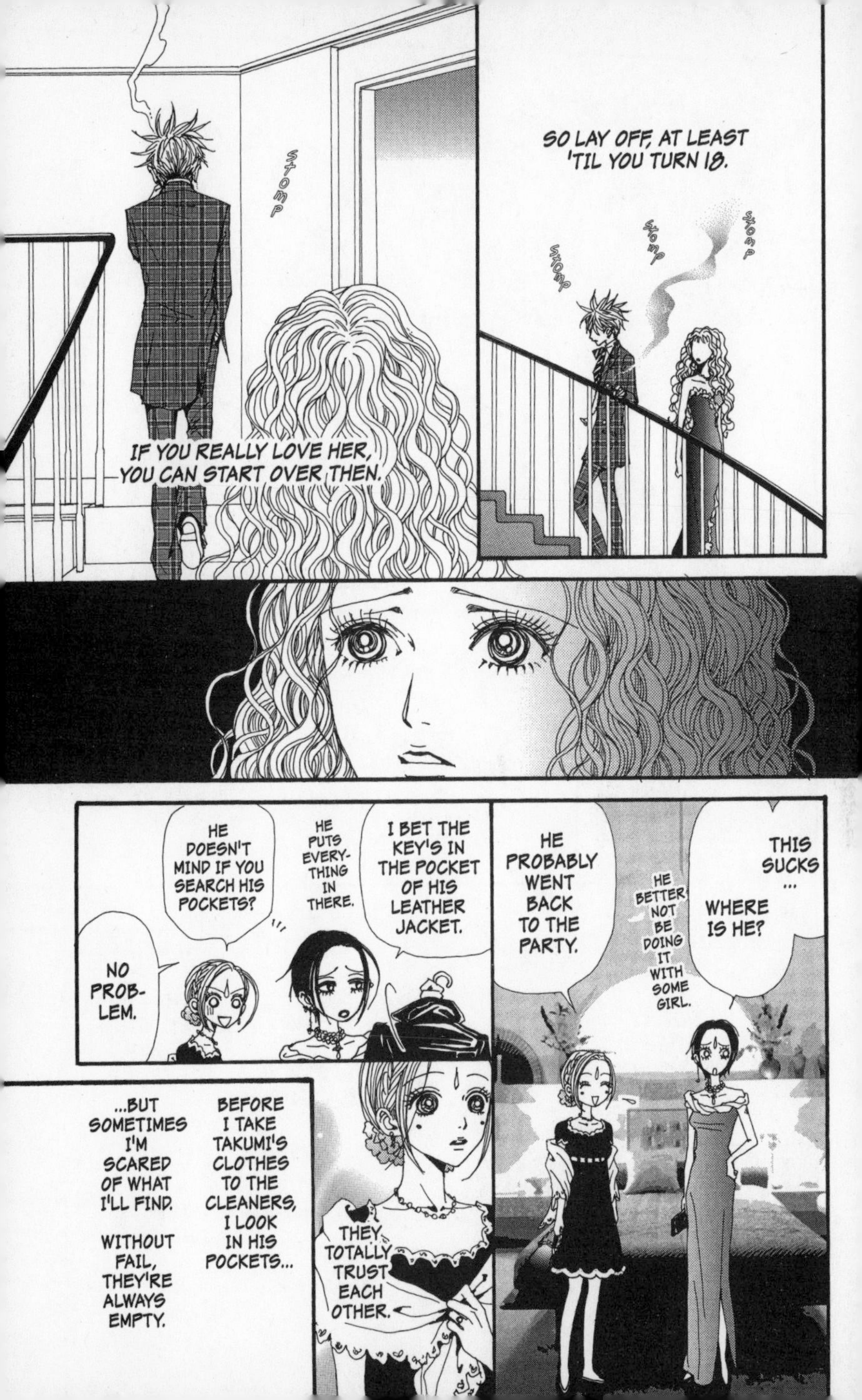
SO LAY OFF, AT LEAST 'TIL YOU TURN 18.
STOMP
STOMP
STOMP
STOMP
IF YOU REALLY LOVE HER, YOU CAN START OVER THEN.
THIS SUCKS... WHERE IS HE?
HE BETTER NOT BE DOING IT WITH SOME GIRL.
HE PROBABLY WENT BACK TO THE PARTY.
I BET THE KEY'S IN THE POCKET OF HIS LEATHER JACKET.
HE PUTS EVERY-THING IN THERE.
HE DOESN'T MIND IF YOU SEARCH HIS POCKETS?
NO PROB-LEM.
THEY TOTALLY TRUST EACH OTHER.
BEFORE I TAKE TAKUMI'S CLOTHES TO THE CLEANERS, I LOOK IN HIS POCKETS...
...BUT SOMETIMES I'M SCARED OF WHAT I'LL FIND.
WITHOUT FAIL, THEY'RE ALWAYS EMPTY.

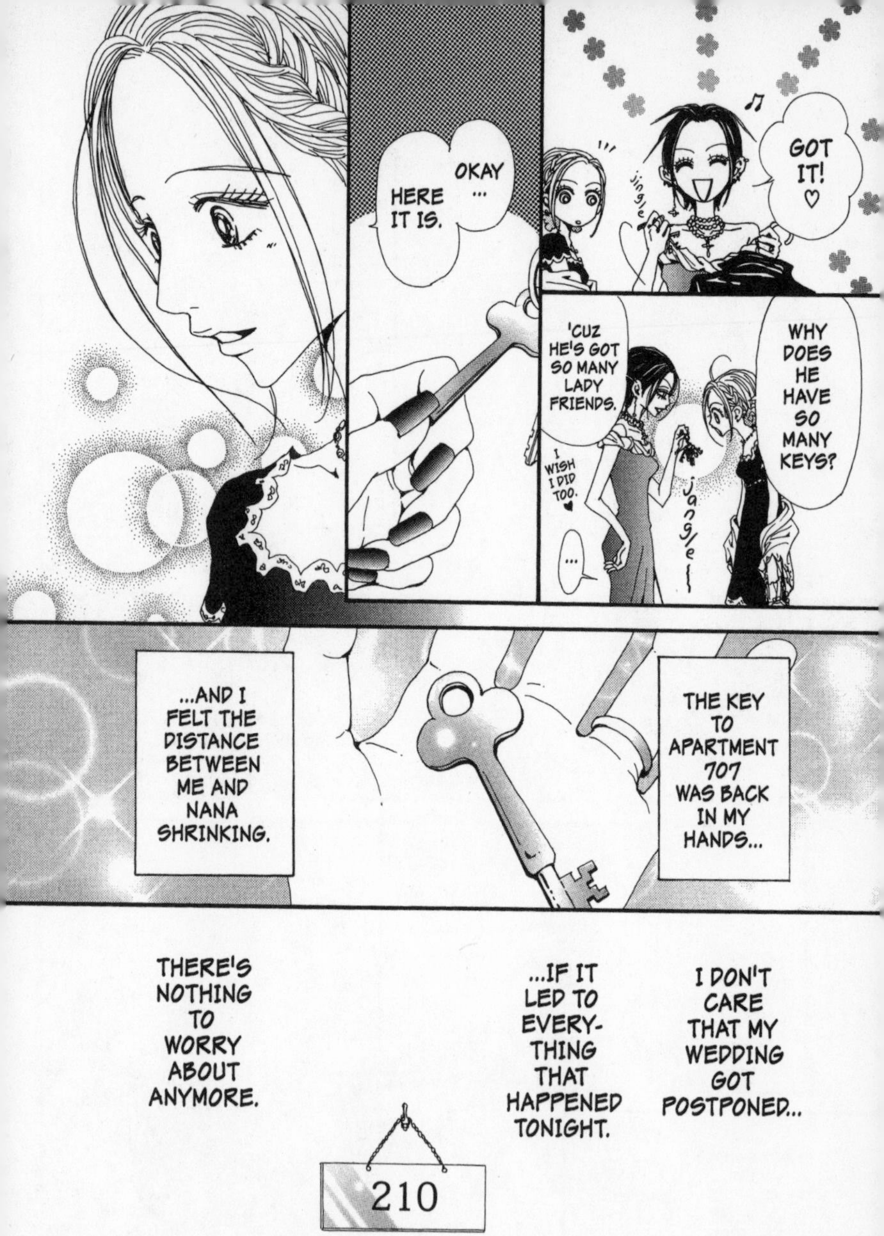
GOT IT! ♡
jingle
WHY DOES HE HAVE SO MANY KEYS?
jangle
'CUZ HE'S GOT SO MANY LADY FRIENDS.
I WISH I DID TOO. ♥
...
OKAY ...
HERE IT IS.
THE KEY TO APARTMENT 707 WAS BACK IN MY HANDS...
...AND I FELT THE DISTANCE BETWEEN ME AND NANA SHRINKING.
I DON'T CARE THAT MY WEDDING GOT POSTPONED...
...IF IT LED TO EVERY-THING THAT HAPPENED TONIGHT.
THERE'S NOTHING TO WORRY ABOUT ANYMORE.

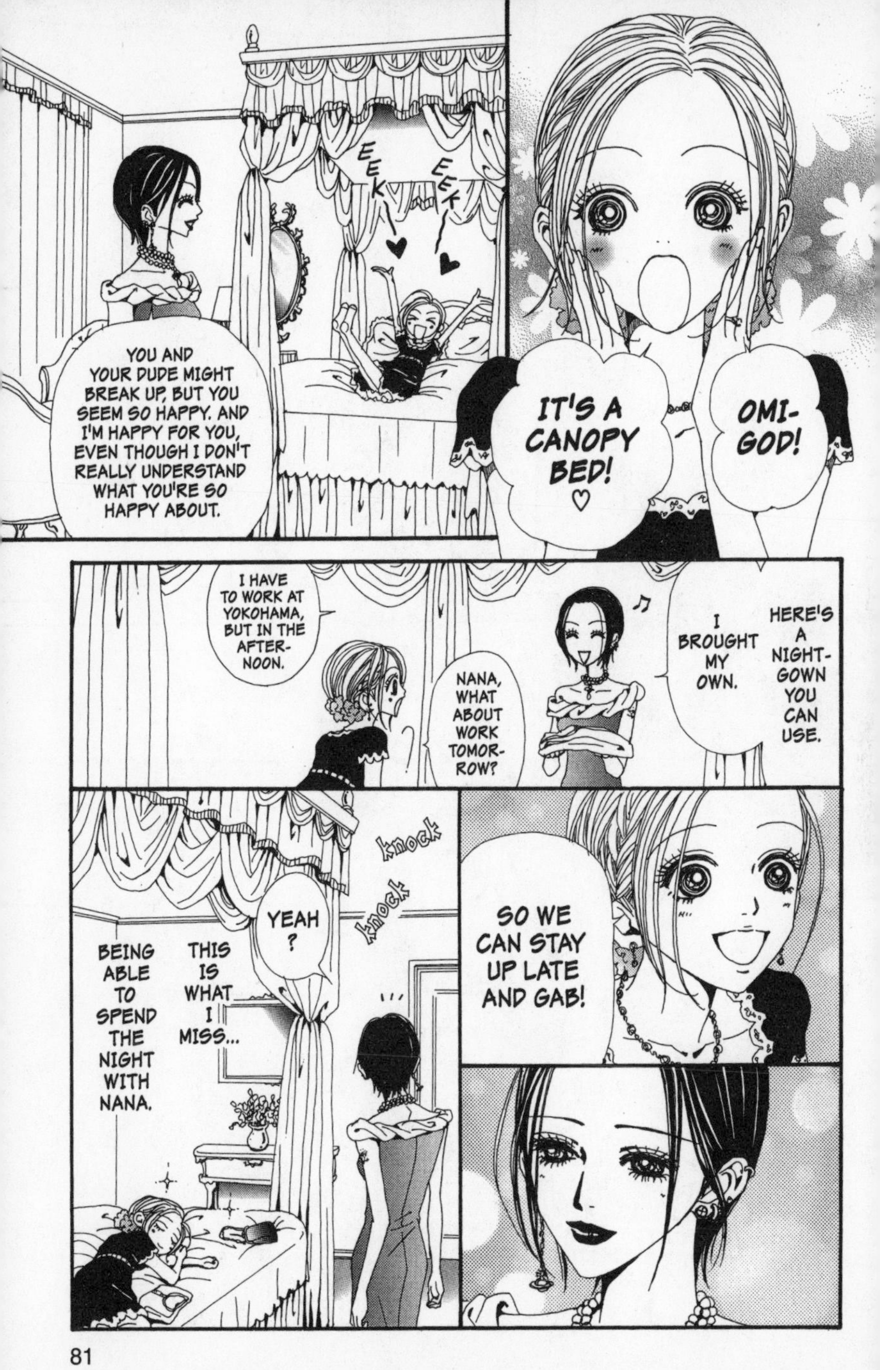
OMI-GOD!
IT'S A CANOPY BED! ♡
EEK EEK
YOU AND YOUR DUDE MIGHT BREAK UP, BUT YOU SEEM SO HAPPY. AND I'M HAPPY FOR YOU, EVEN THOUGH I DON'T REALLY UNDERSTAND WHAT YOU'RE SO HAPPY ABOUT.
HERE'S A NIGHT-GOWN YOU CAN USE.
I BROUGHT MY OWN.
NANA, WHAT ABOUT WORK TOMOR-ROW?
I HAVE TO WORK AT YOKOHAMA, BUT IN THE AFTER-NOON.
SO WE CAN STAY UP LATE AND GAB!
knock knock
YEAH?
THIS IS WHAT I MISS...
BEING ABLE TO SPEND THE NIGHT WITH NANA.

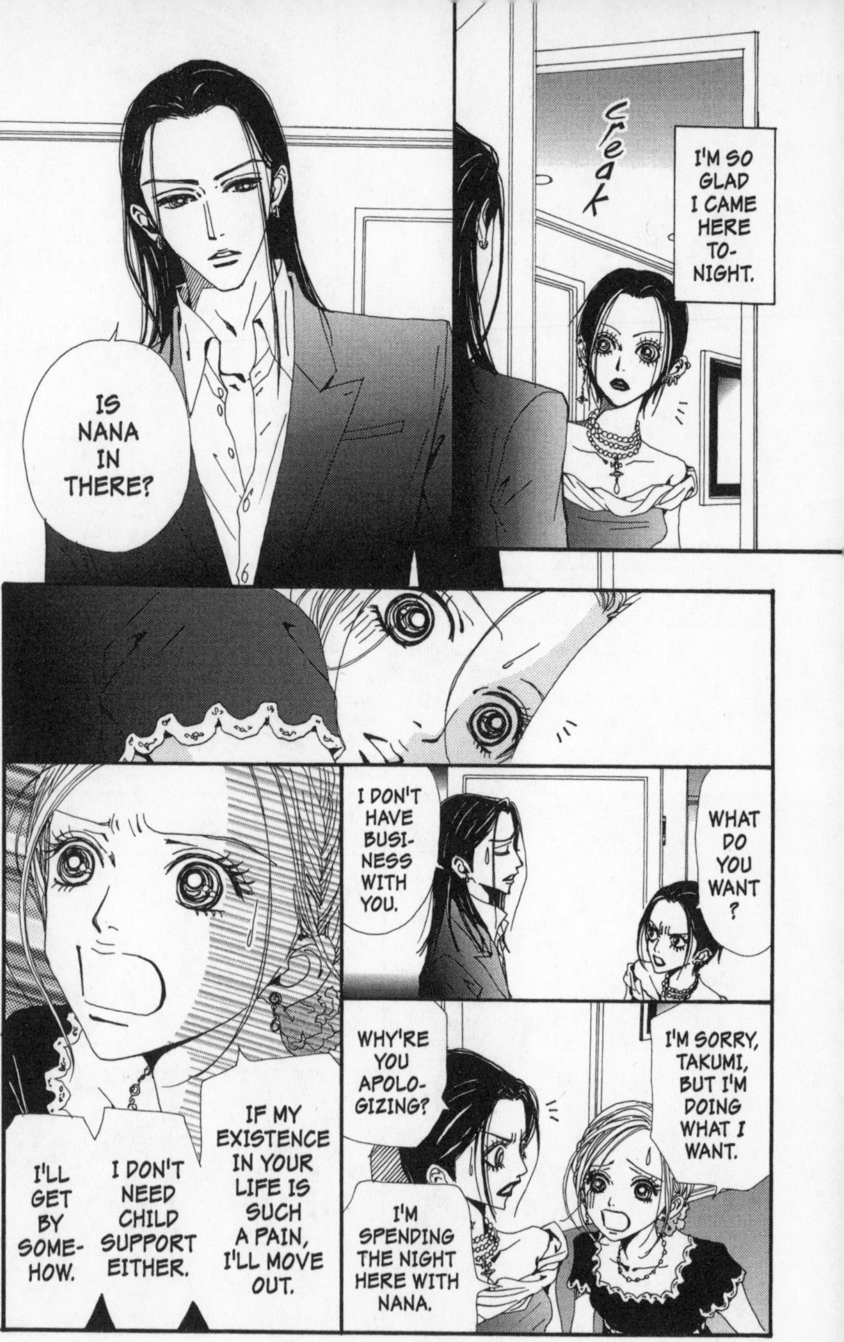
creak
I'M SO GLAD I CAME HERE TO-NIGHT.
IS NANA IN THERE?
WHAT DO YOU WANT?
I DON'T HAVE BUSI-NESS WITH YOU.
I'M SORRY, TAKUMI, BUT I'M DOING WHAT I WANT.
WHY'RE YOU APOLO-GIZING?
I'M SPENDING THE NIGHT HERE WITH NANA.
IF MY EXISTENCE IN YOUR LIFE IS SUCH A PAIN, I'LL MOVE OUT.
I DON'T NEED CHILD SUPPORT EITHER.
I'LL GET BY SOME-HOW.

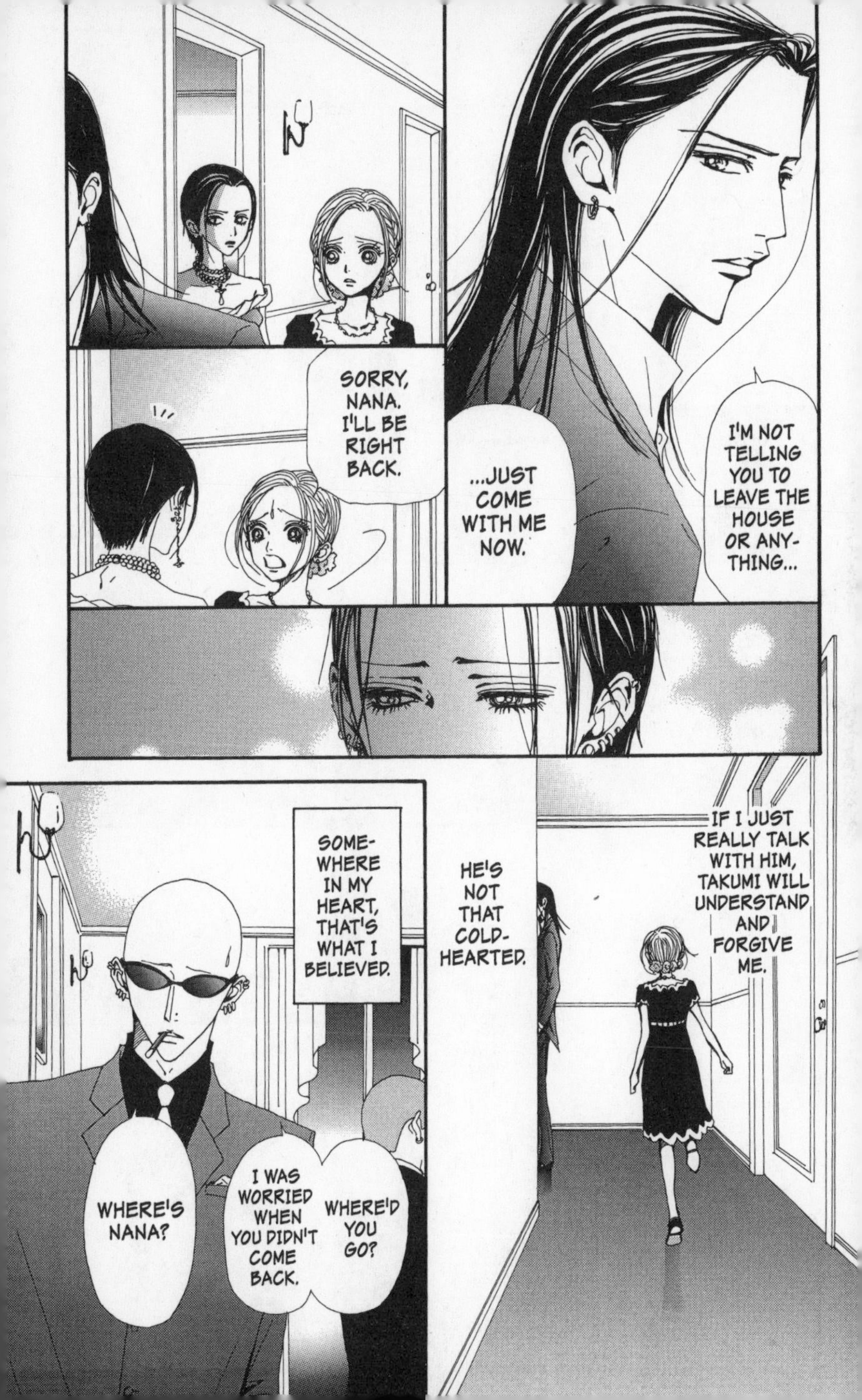
I'M NOT TELLING YOU TO LEAVE THE HOUSE OR ANY-THING...
...JUST COME WITH ME NOW.
SORRY, NANA. I'LL BE RIGHT BACK.
IF I JUST REALLY TALK WITH HIM, TAKUMI WILL UNDERSTAND AND FORGIVE ME.
HE'S NOT THAT COLD-HEARTED.
SOME-WHERE IN MY HEART, THAT'S WHAT I BELIEVED.
WHERE'D YOU GO?
I WAS WORRIED WHEN YOU DIDN'T COME BACK.
WHERE'S NANA?

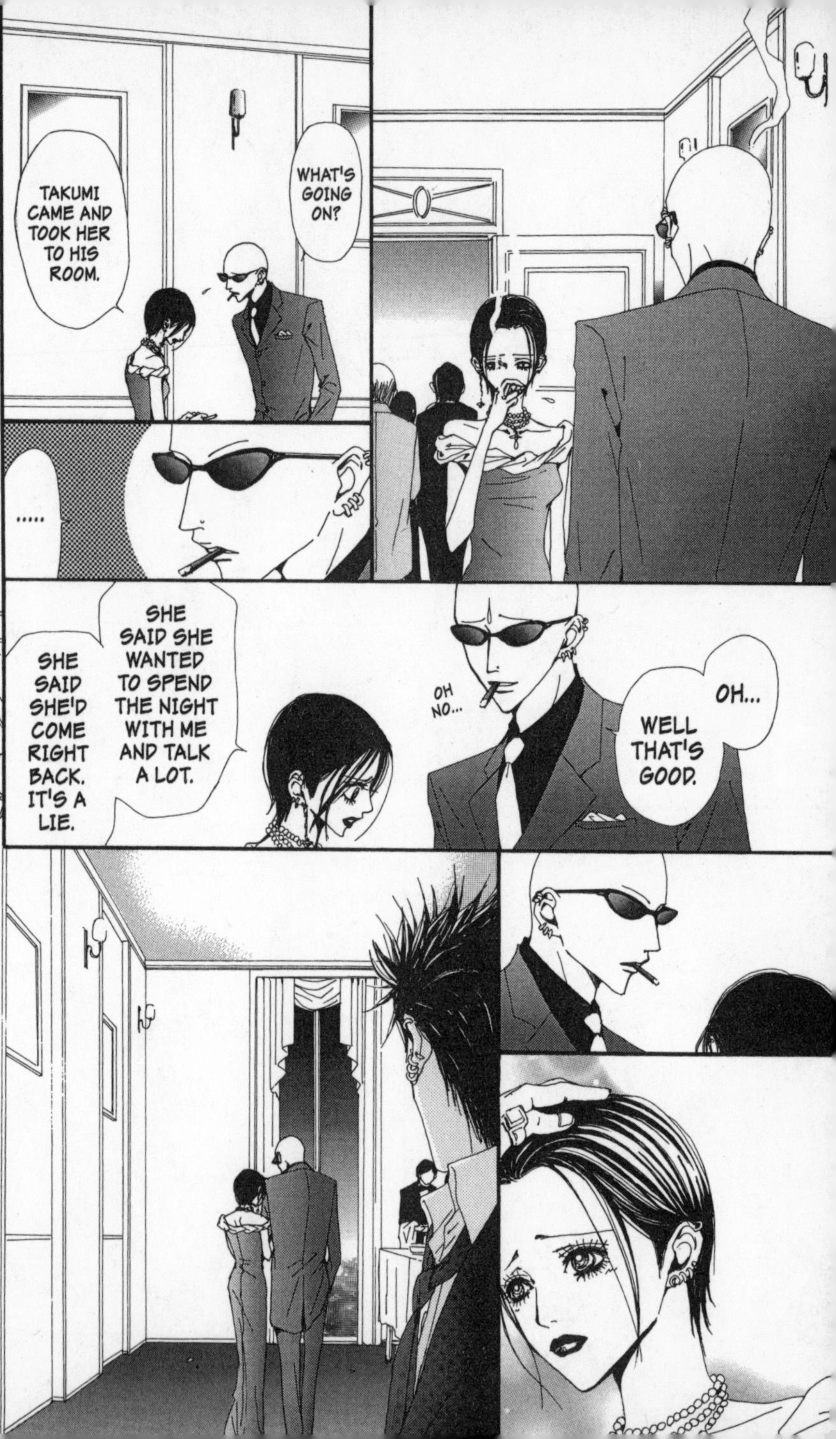
WHAT'S GOING ON?
TAKUMI CAME AND TOOK HER TO HIS ROOM.
.....
OH... WELL THAT'S GOOD.
OH NO...
SHE SAID SHE WANTED TO SPEND THE NIGHT WITH ME AND TALK A LOT.
SHE SAID SHE'D COME RIGHT BACK. IT'S A LIE.

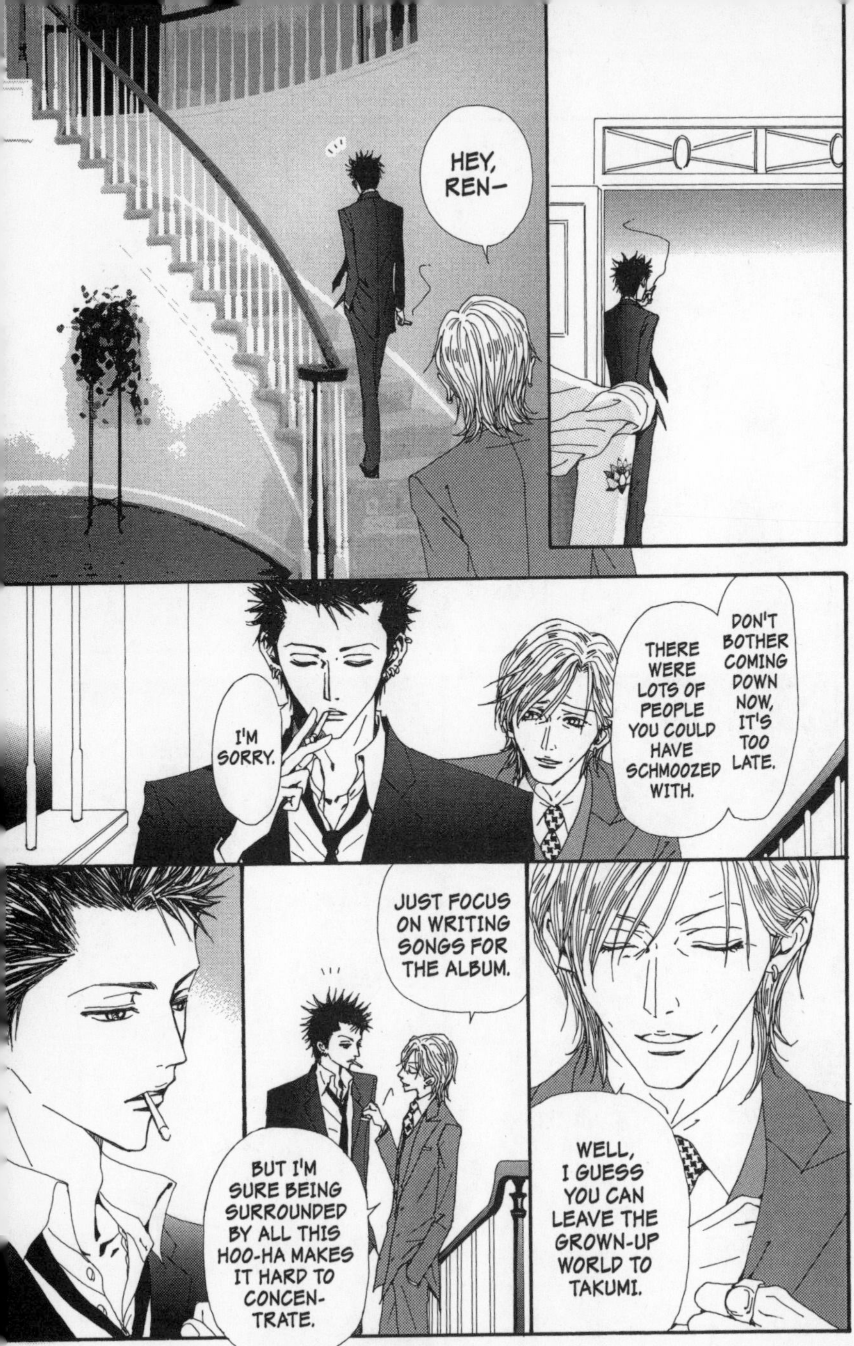
HEY, REN—
DON'T BOTHER COMING DOWN NOW, IT'S TOO LATE.
THERE WERE LOTS OF PEOPLE YOU COULD HAVE SCHMOOZED WITH.
I'M SORRY.
WELL, I GUESS YOU CAN LEAVE THE GROWN-UP WORLD TO TAKUMI.
JUST FOCUS ON WRITING SONGS FOR THE ALBUM.
BUT I'M SURE BEING SURROUNDED BY ALL THIS HOO-HA MAKES IT HARD TO CONCENTRATE.

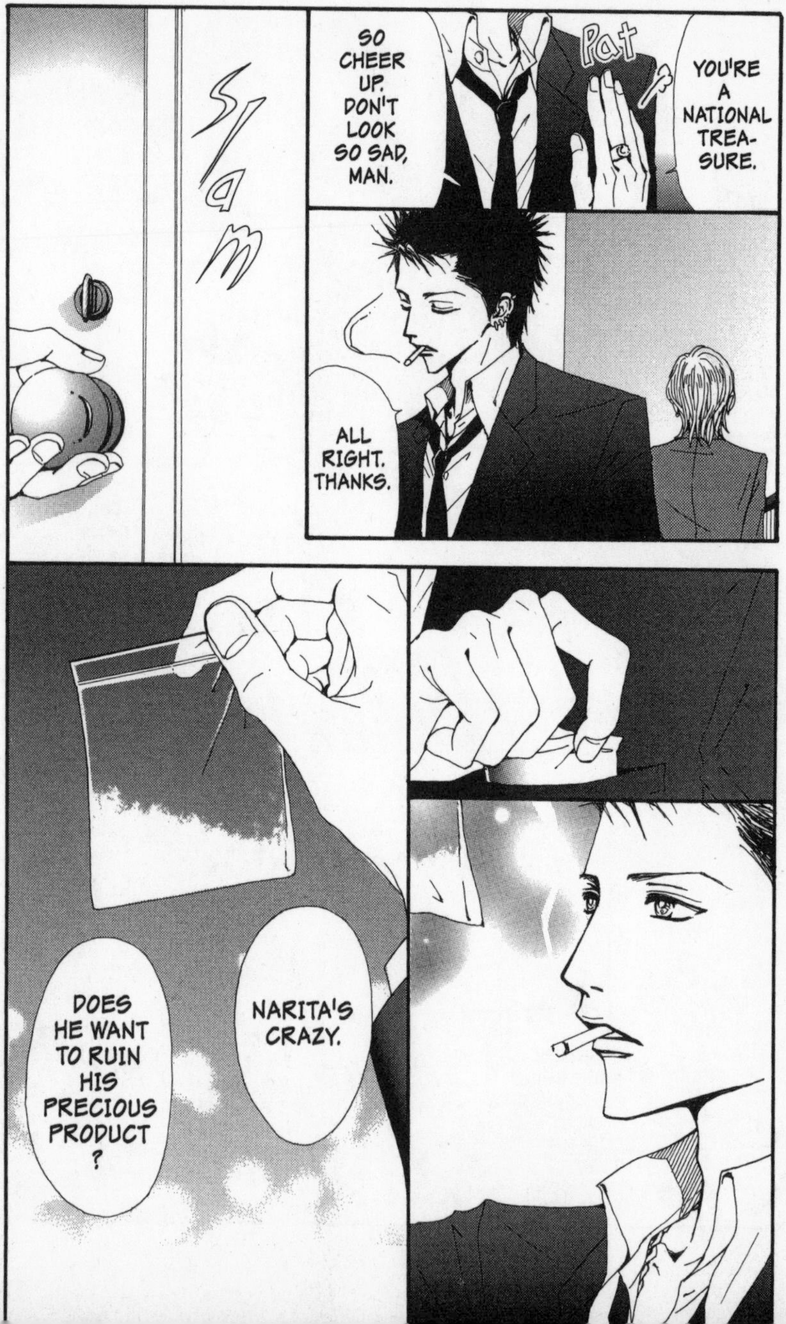

YOU'RE A NATIONAL TREA-SURE.
Pat
SO CHEER UP. DON'T LOOK SO SAD, MAN.
ALL RIGHT. THANKS.
Slam
NARITA'S CRAZY.
DOES HE WANT TO RUIN HIS PRECIOUS PRODUCT?

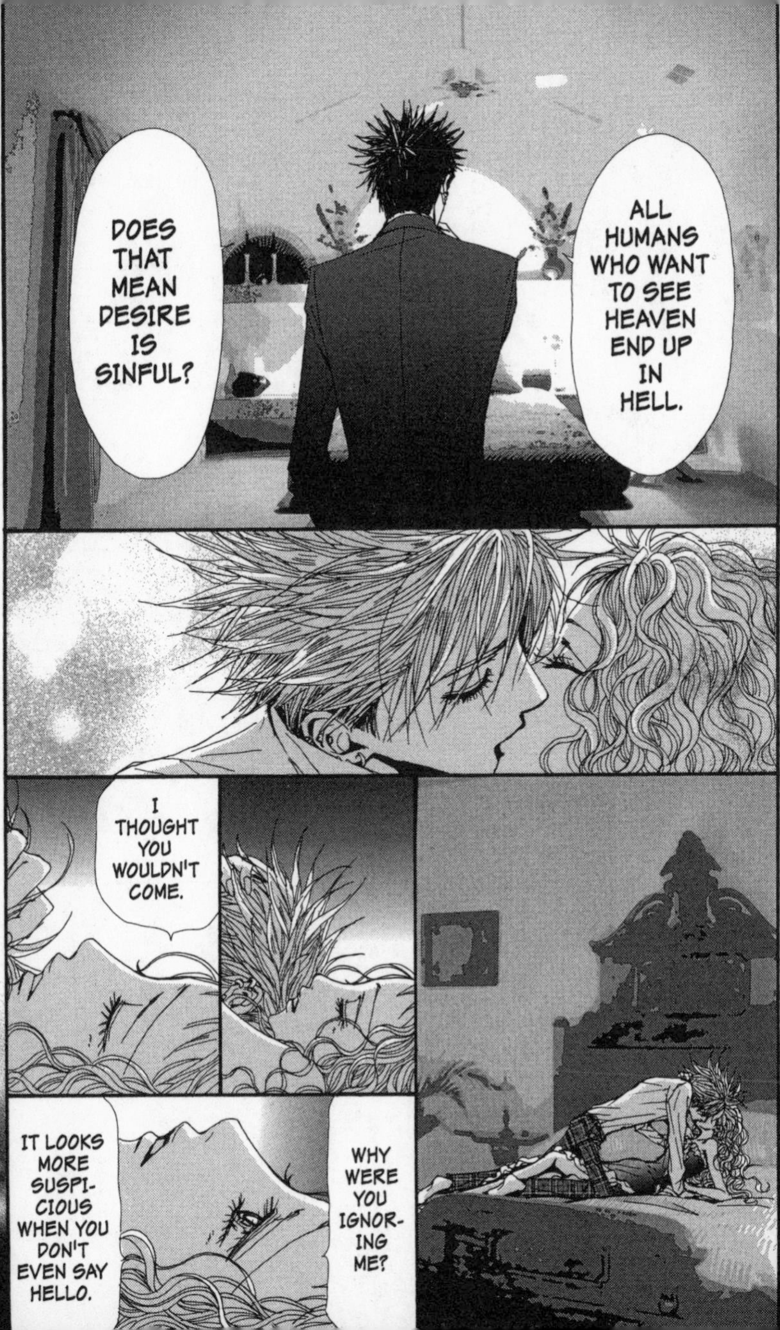
ALL HUMANS WHO WANT TO SEE HEAVEN END UP IN HELL.
DOES THAT MEAN DESIRE IS SINFUL?
I THOUGHT YOU WOULDN'T COME.
WHY WERE YOU IGNORING ME?
IT LOOKS MORE SUSPICIOUS WHEN YOU DON'T EVEN SAY HELLO.

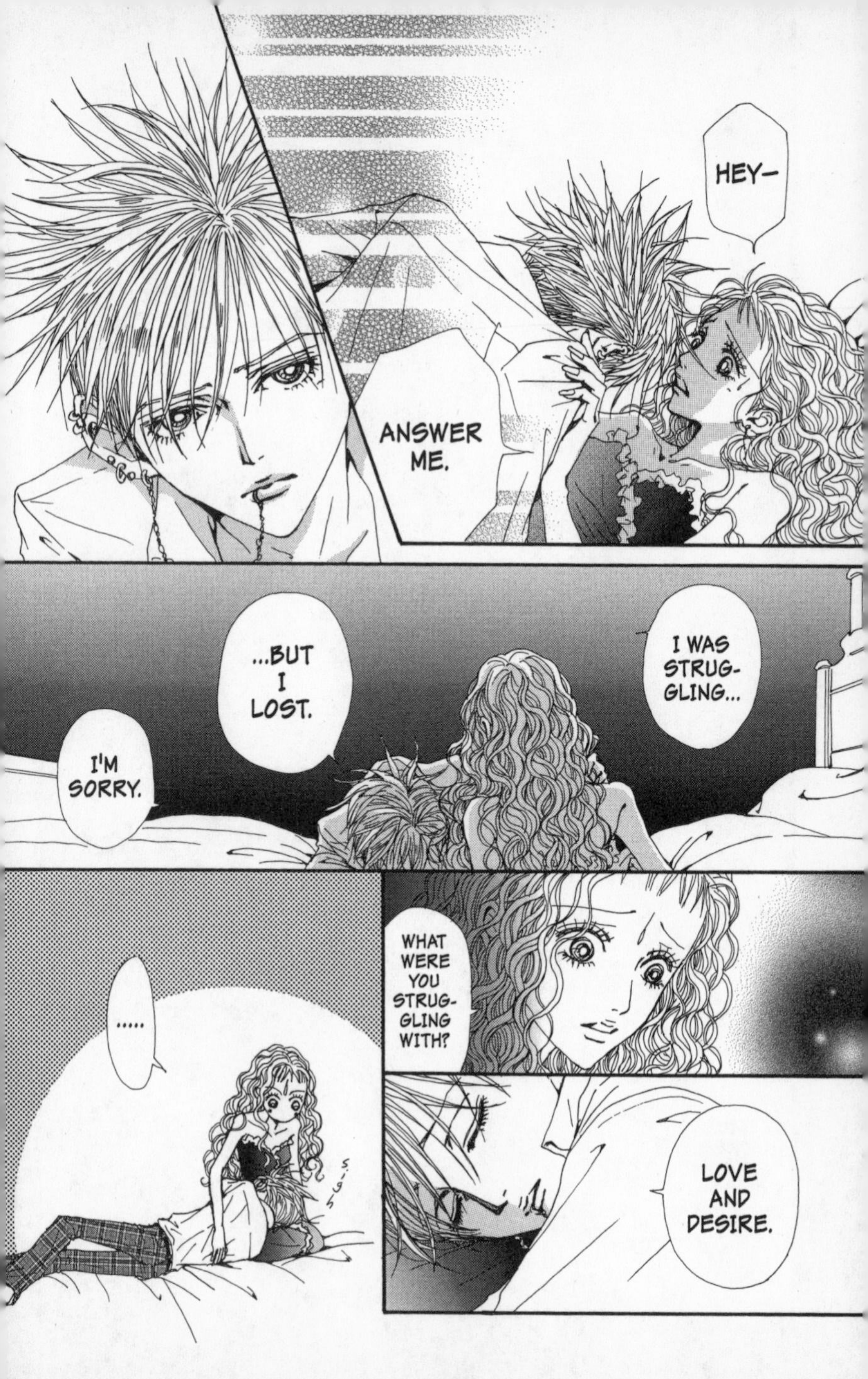
HEY—
ANSWER ME.
I WAS STRUGGLING...
...BUT I LOST.
I'M SORRY.
WHAT WERE YOU STRUGGLING WITH?
LOVE AND DESIRE.
.....
sigh

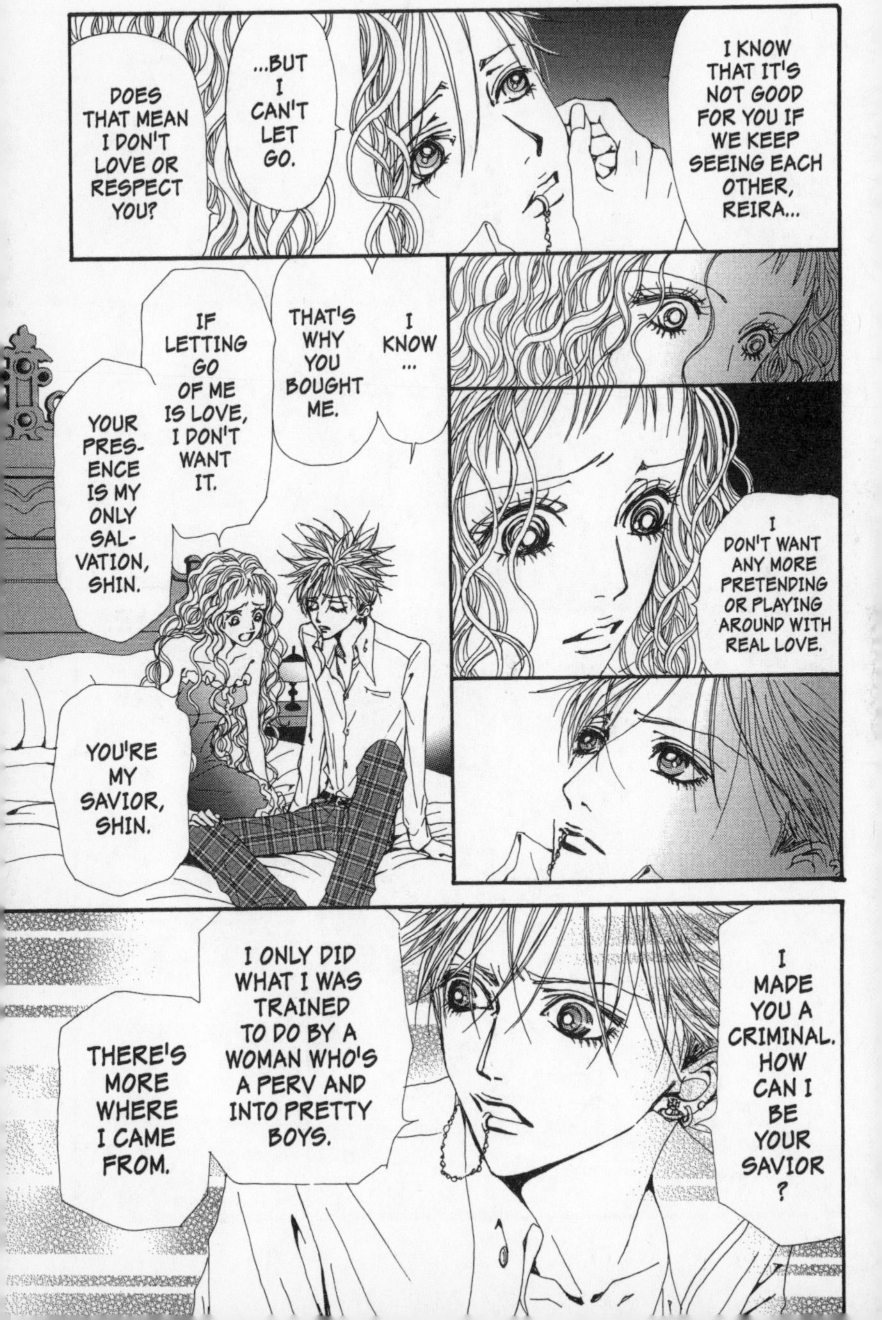
I KNOW THAT IT'S NOT GOOD FOR YOU IF WE KEEP SEEING EACH OTHER, REIRA...
...BUT I CAN'T LET GO.
DOES THAT MEAN I DON'T LOVE OR RESPECT YOU?
I DON'T WANT ANY MORE PRETENDING OR PLAYING AROUND WITH REAL LOVE.
I KNOW...
THAT'S WHY YOU BOUGHT ME.
IF LETTING GO OF ME IS LOVE, I DON'T WANT IT.
YOUR PRES-ENCE IS MY ONLY SAL-VATION, SHIN.
YOU'RE MY SAVIOR, SHIN.
I MADE YOU A CRIMINAL. HOW CAN I BE YOUR SAVIOR?
I ONLY DID WHAT I WAS TRAINED TO DO BY A WOMAN WHO'S A PERV AND INTO PRETTY BOYS.
THERE'S MORE WHERE I CAME FROM.

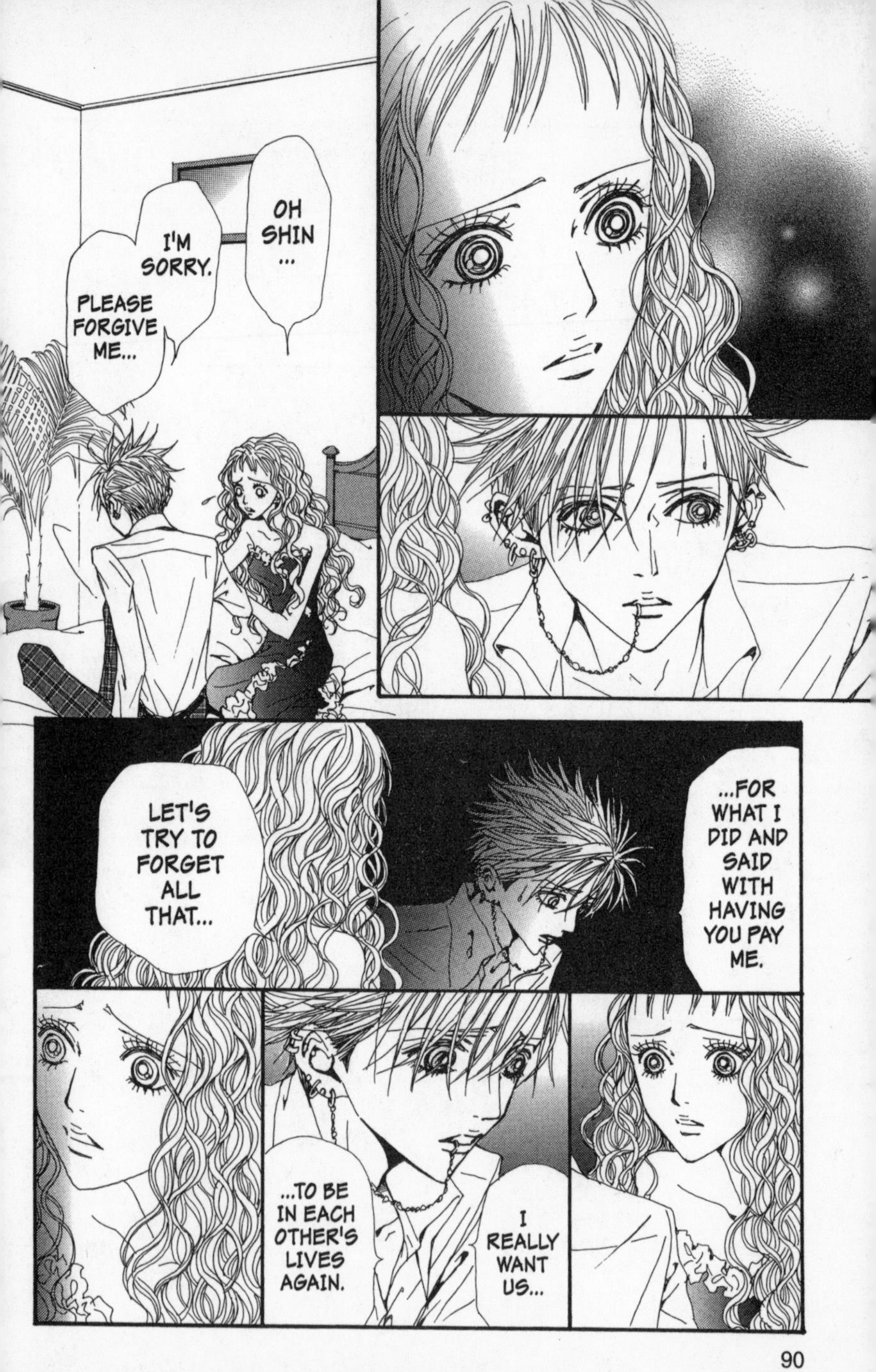
OH SHIN ...
I'M SORRY.
PLEASE FORGIVE ME...
...FOR WHAT I DID AND SAID WITH HAVING YOU PAY ME.
LET'S TRY TO FORGET ALL THAT...
I REALLY WANT US...
...TO BE IN EACH OTHER'S LIVES AGAIN.

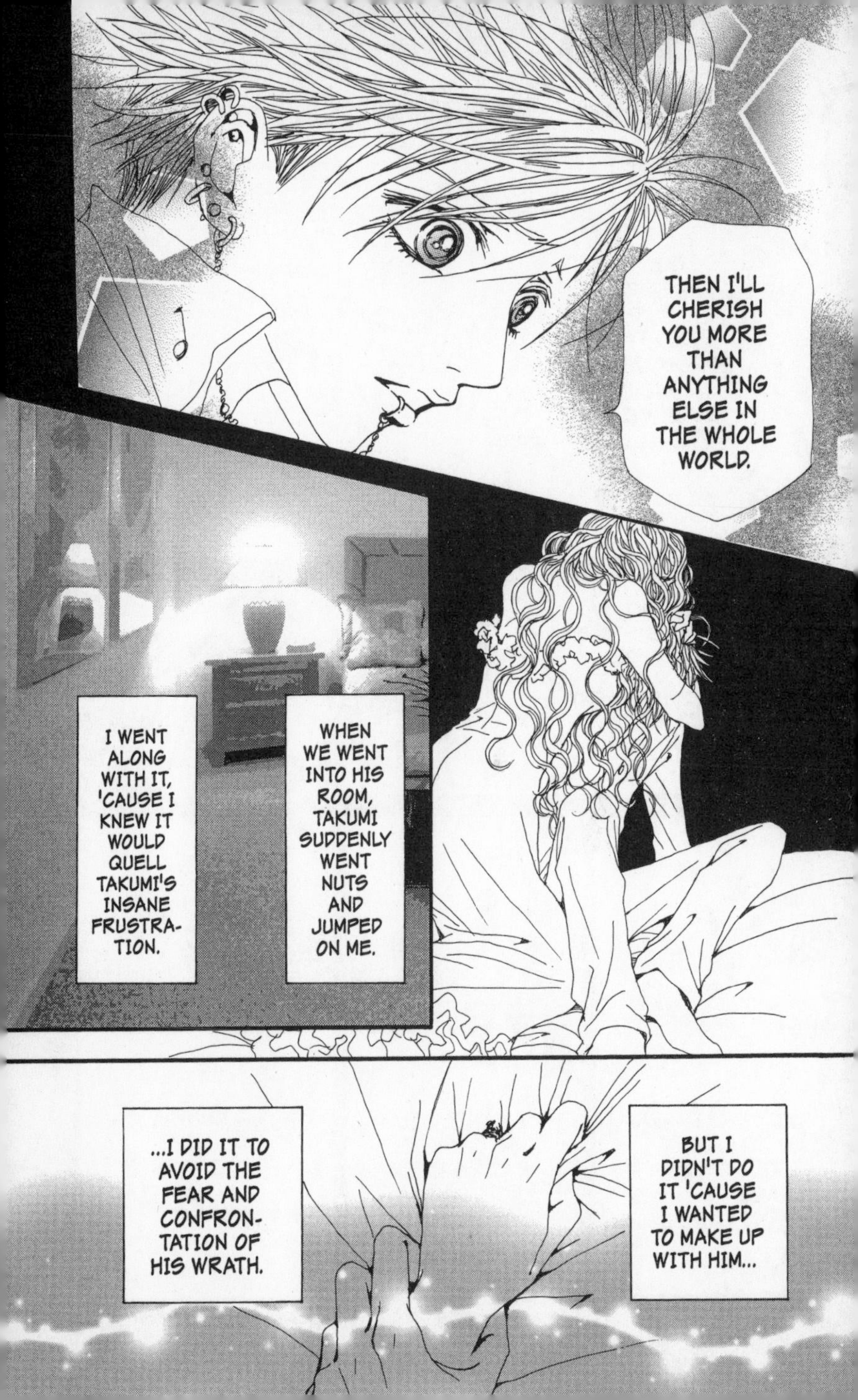
THEN I'LL CHERISH YOU MORE THAN ANYTHING ELSE IN THE WHOLE WORLD.
WHEN WE WENT INTO HIS ROOM, TAKUMI SUDDENLY WENT NUTS AND JUMPED ON ME.
I WENT ALONG WITH IT, 'CAUSE I KNEW IT WOULD QUELL TAKUMI'S INSANE FRUSTRA-TION.
BUT I DIDN'T DO IT 'CAUSE I WANTED TO MAKE UP WITH HIM...
...I DID IT TO AVOID THE FEAR AND CONFRON-TATION OF HIS WRATH.

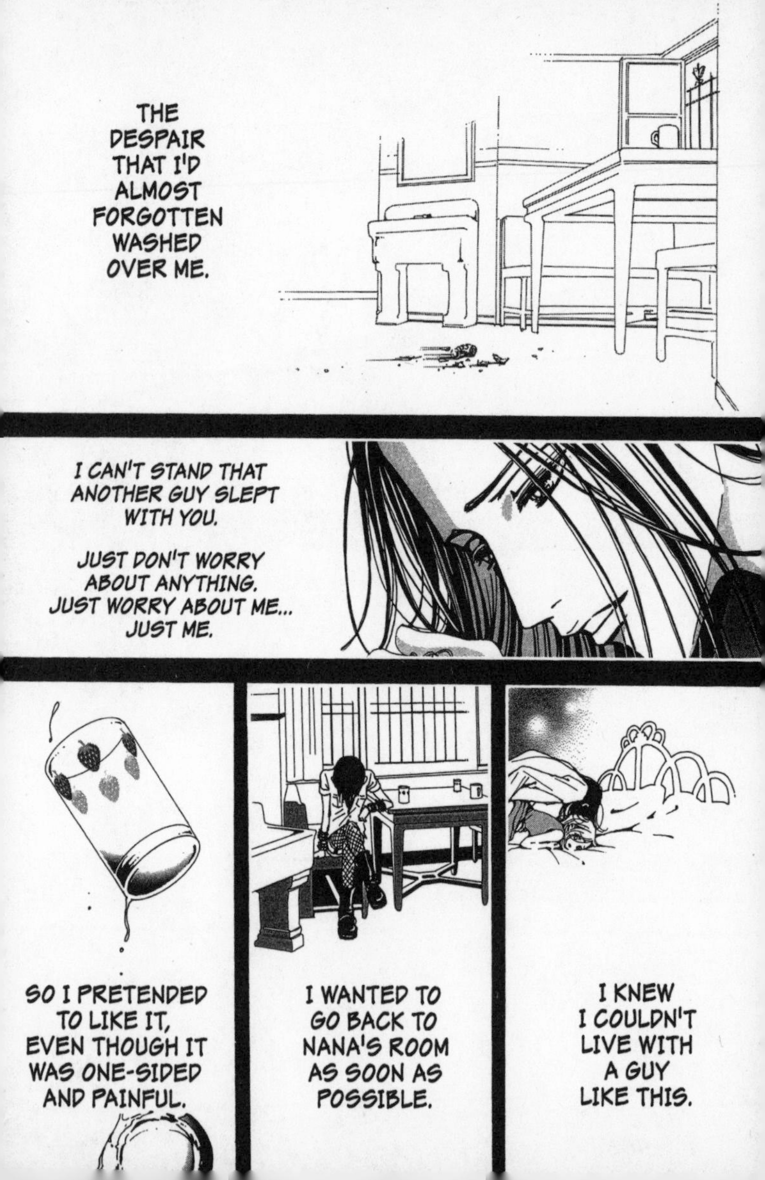
THE DESPAIR THAT I'D ALMOST FORGOTTEN WASHED OVER ME.
I CAN'T STAND THAT ANOTHER GUY SLEPT WITH YOU.
JUST DON'T WORRY ABOUT ANYTHING. JUST WORRY ABOUT ME... JUST ME.
I KNEW I COULDN'T LIVE WITH A GUY LIKE THIS.
I WANTED TO GO BACK TO NANA'S ROOM AS SOON AS POSSIBLE.
SO I PRETENDED TO LIKE IT, EVEN THOUGH IT WAS ONE-SIDED AND PAINFUL.

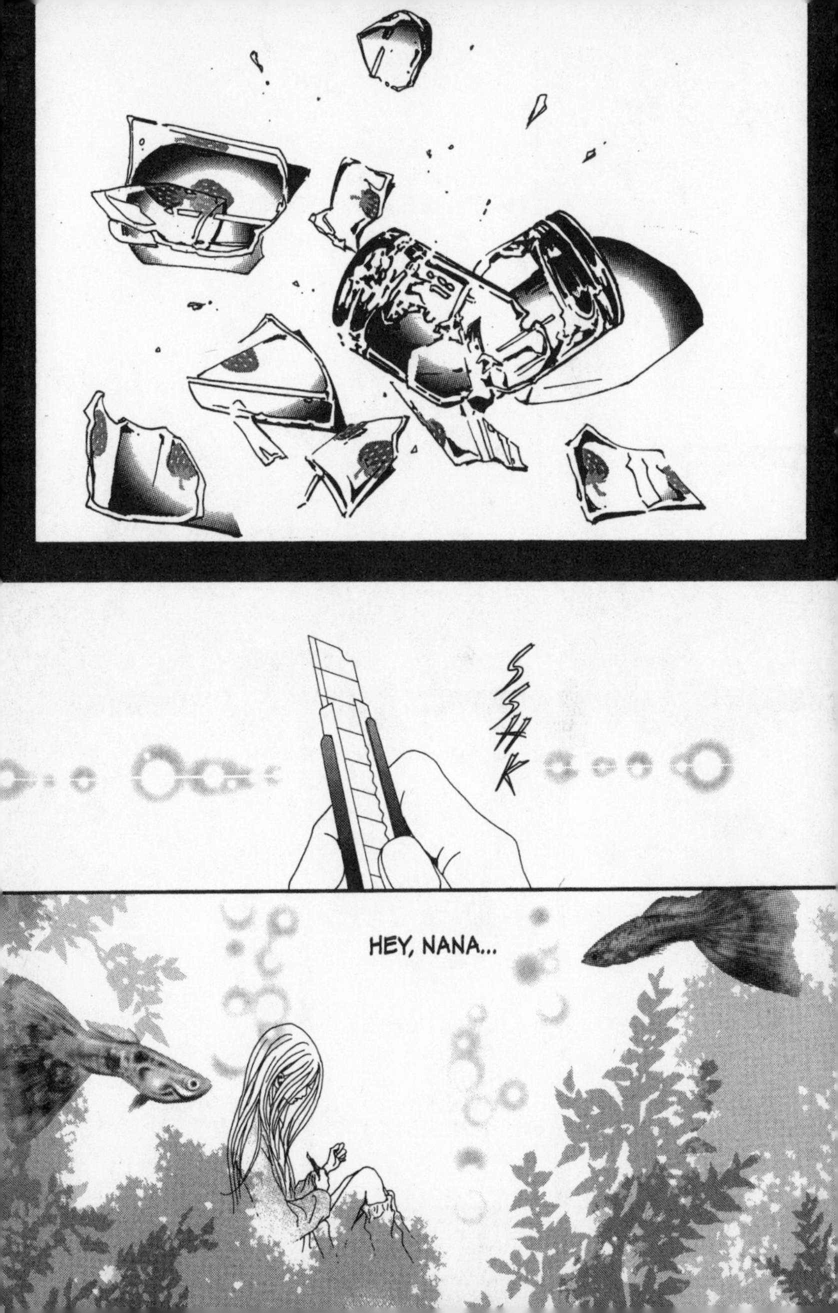
SSHK
HEY, NANA...

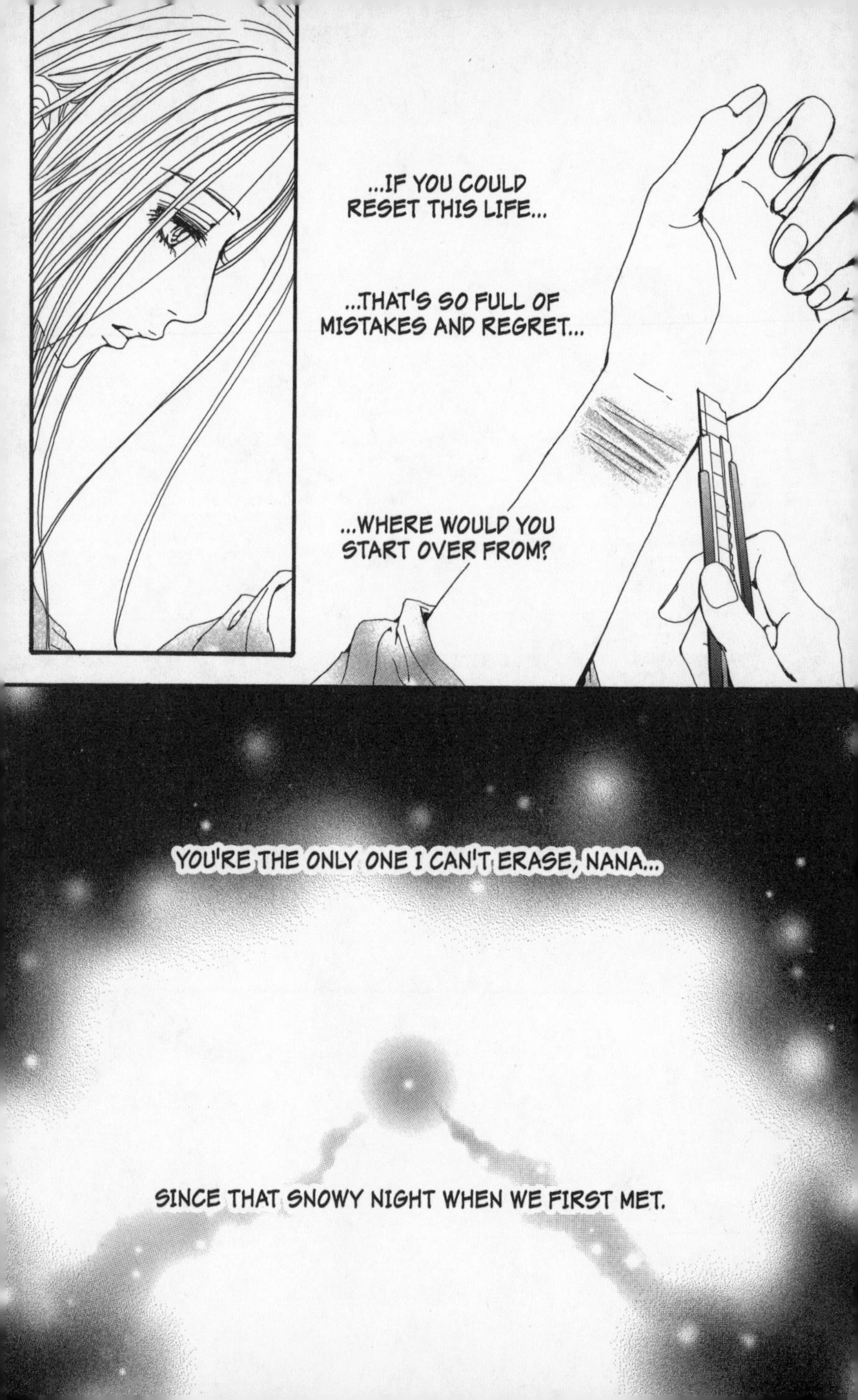
...IF YOU COULD RESET THIS LIFE...
...THAT'S SO FULL OF MISTAKES AND REGRET...
...WHERE WOULD YOU START OVER FROM?
YOU'RE THE ONLY ONE I CAN'T ERASE, NANA...
SINCE THAT SNOWY NIGHT WHEN WE FIRST MET.

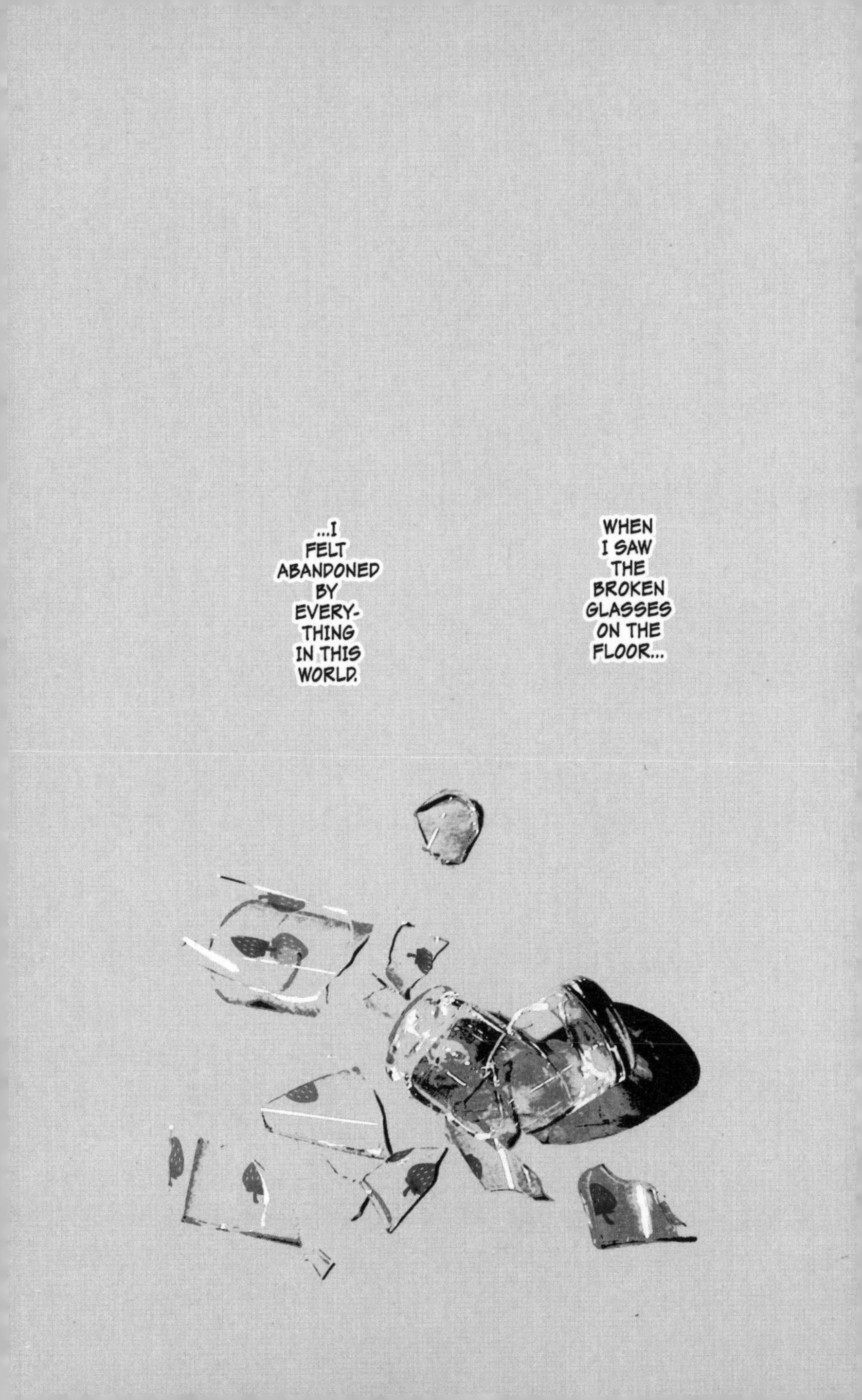
WHEN I SAW THE BROKEN GLASSES ON THE FLOOR...
...I FELT ABANDONED BY EVERY-THING IN THIS WORLD.

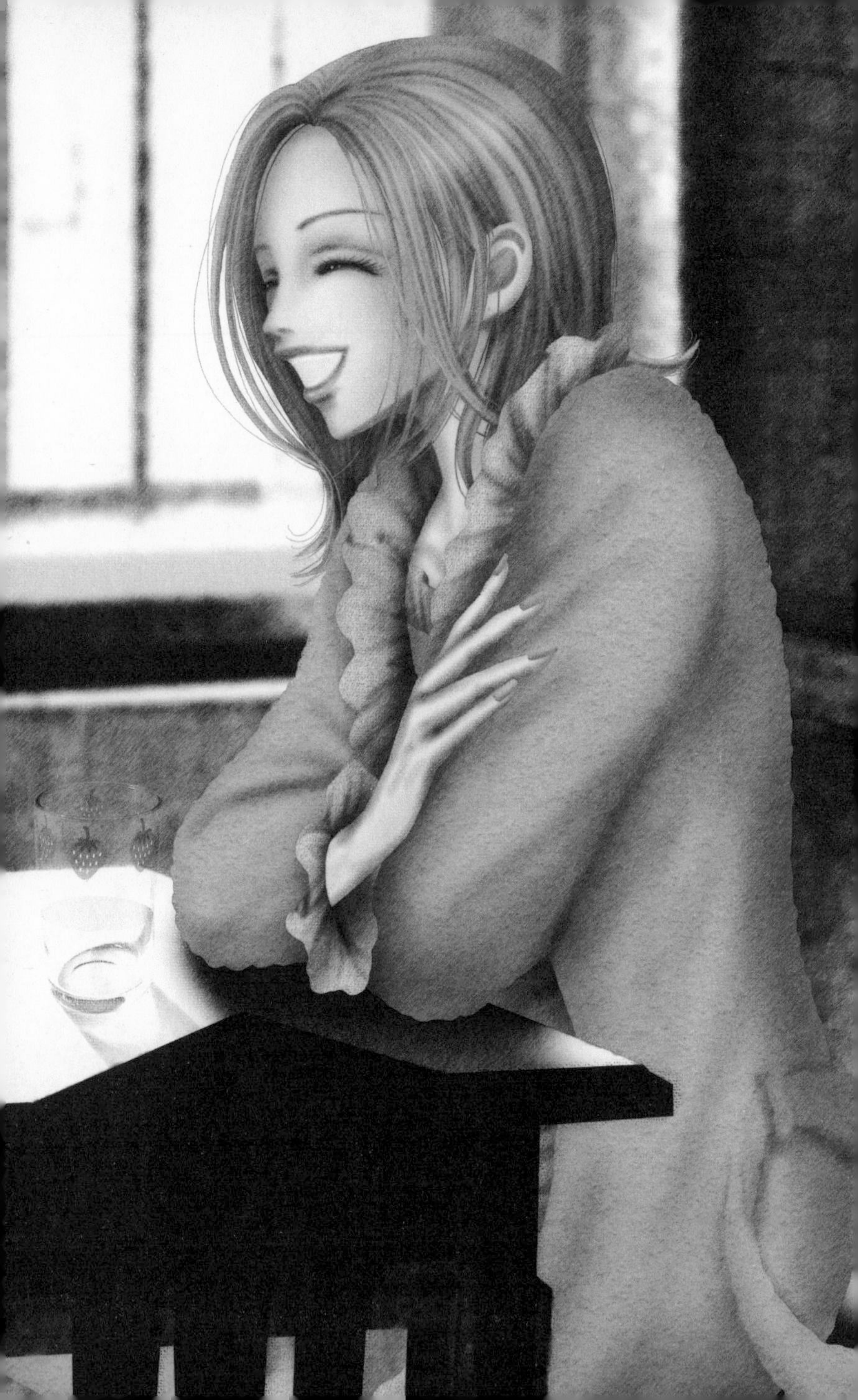

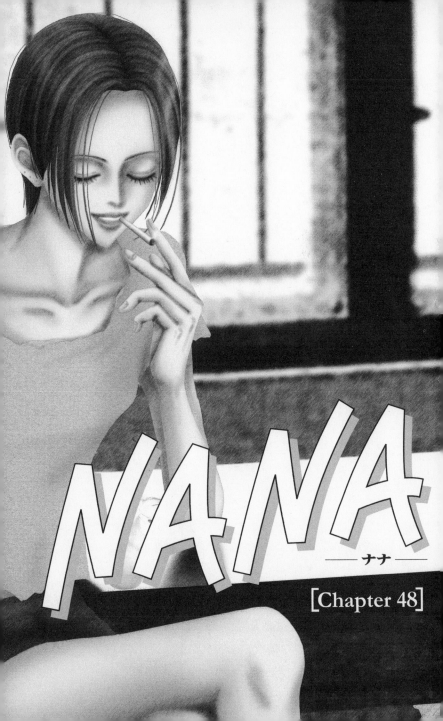

NANA —ナナ—

[Chapter 48]

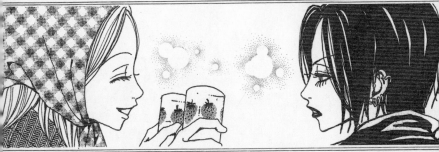

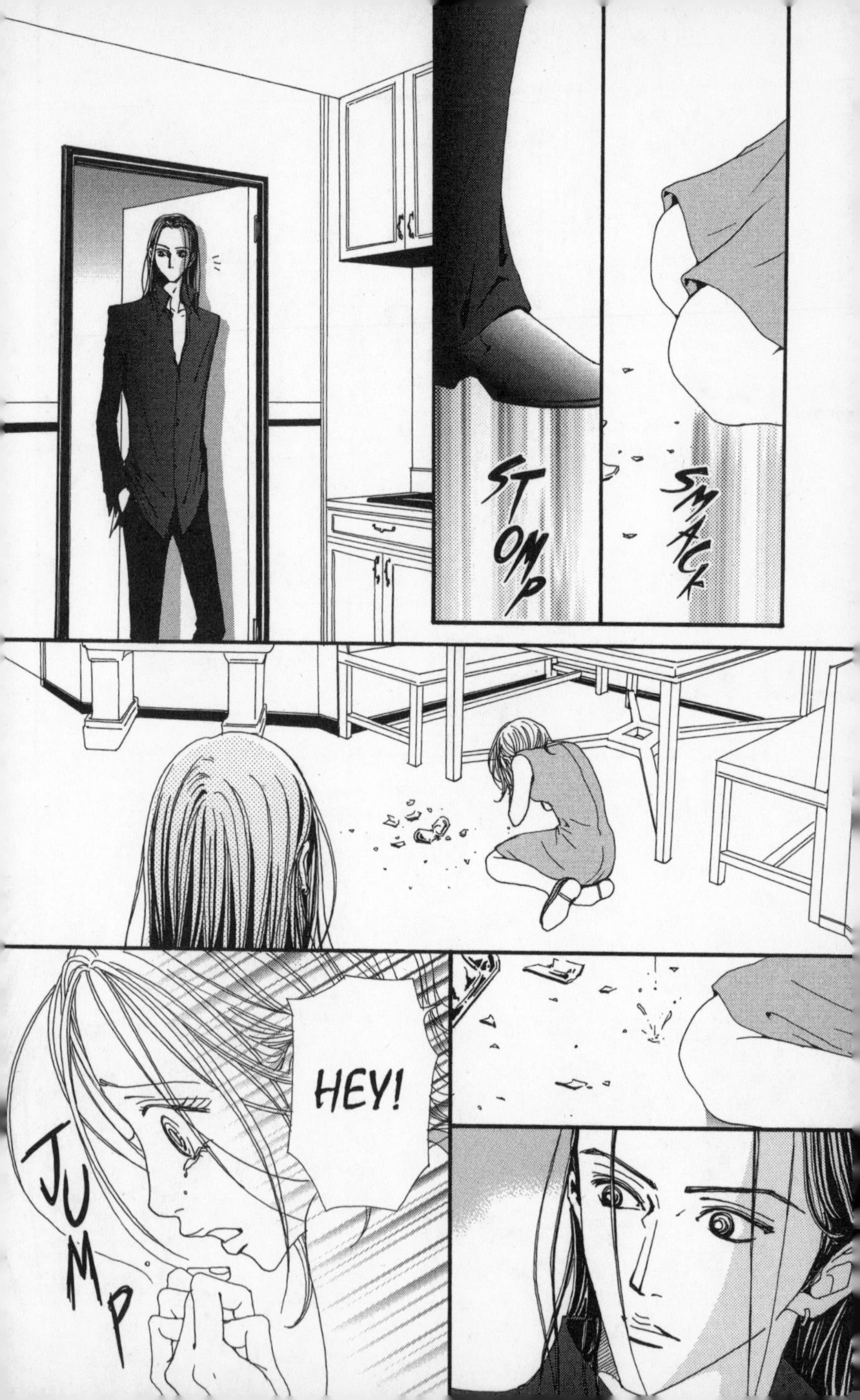
SMACK
STOMP
HEY!
JUMP

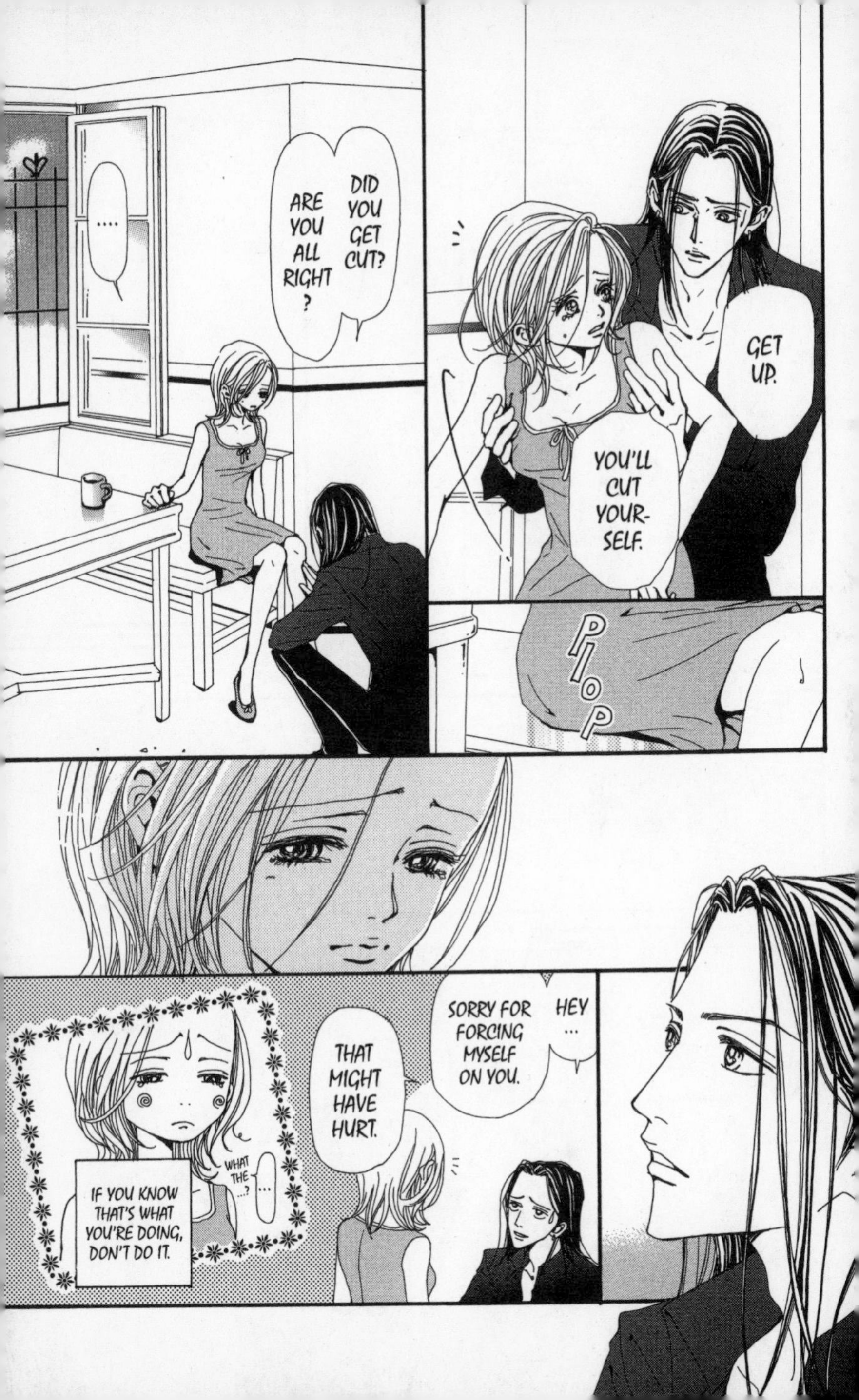
GET UP.
YOU'LL CUT YOURSELF.
POP
DID YOU GET CUT?
ARE YOU ALL RIGHT?
....
HEY ...
SORRY FOR FORCING MYSELF ON YOU.
THAT MIGHT HAVE HURT.
WHAT THE ...?
...
IF YOU KNOW THAT'S WHAT YOU'RE DOING, DON'T DO IT.

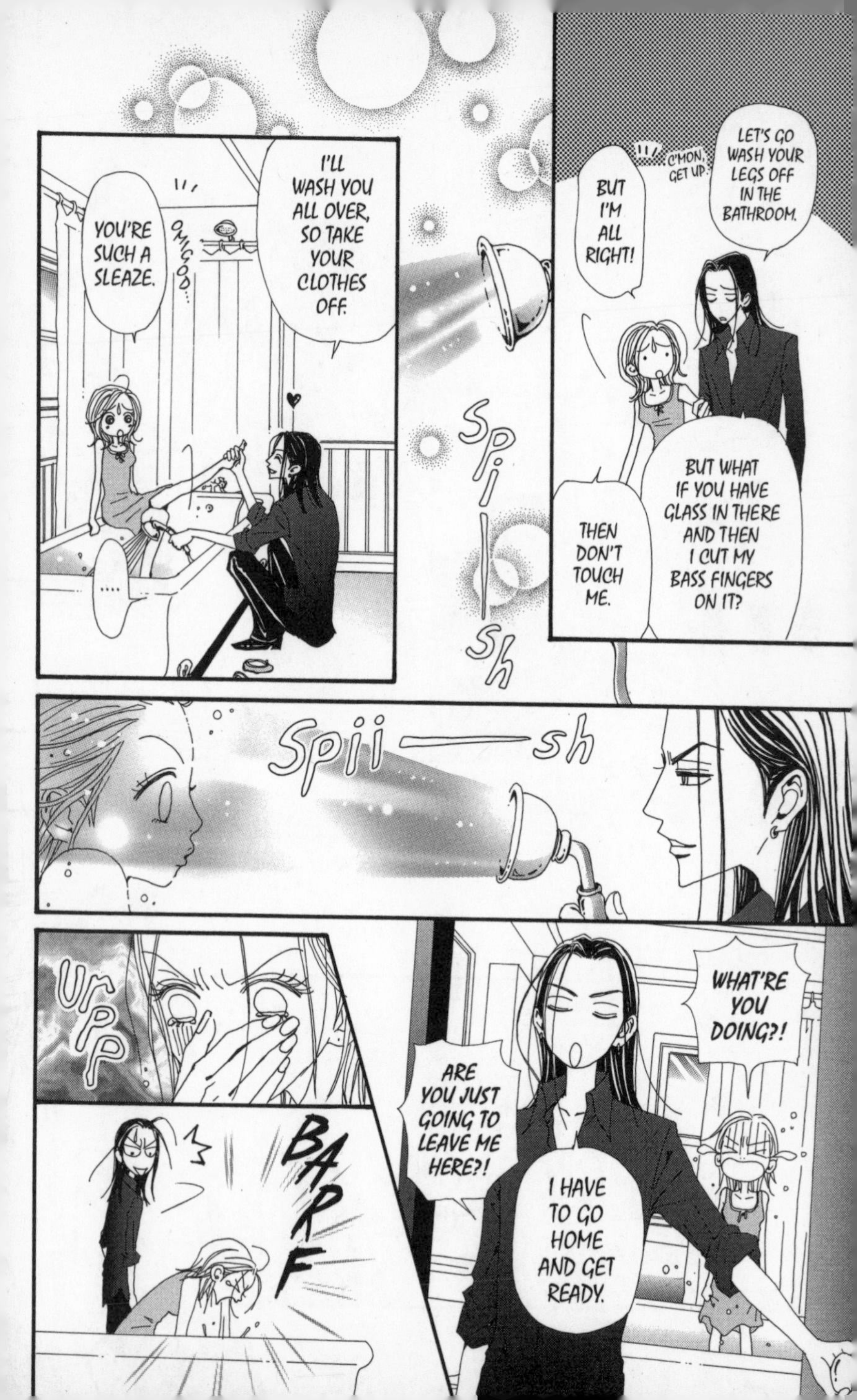
LET'S GO WASH YOUR LEGS OFF IN THE BATHROOM.
C'MON, GET UP.
BUT I'M ALL RIGHT!
BUT WHAT IF YOU HAVE GLASS IN THERE AND THEN I CUT MY BASS FINGERS ON IT?
THEN DON'T TOUCH ME.
Spii—sh
I'LL WASH YOU ALL OVER, SO TAKE YOUR CLOTHES OFF.
OMIGOD...
YOU'RE SUCH A SLEAZE.
.....
Spii—sh
WHAT'RE YOU DOING?!
ARE YOU JUST GOING TO LEAVE ME HERE?!
I HAVE TO GO HOME AND GET READY.
Urpp
BARF

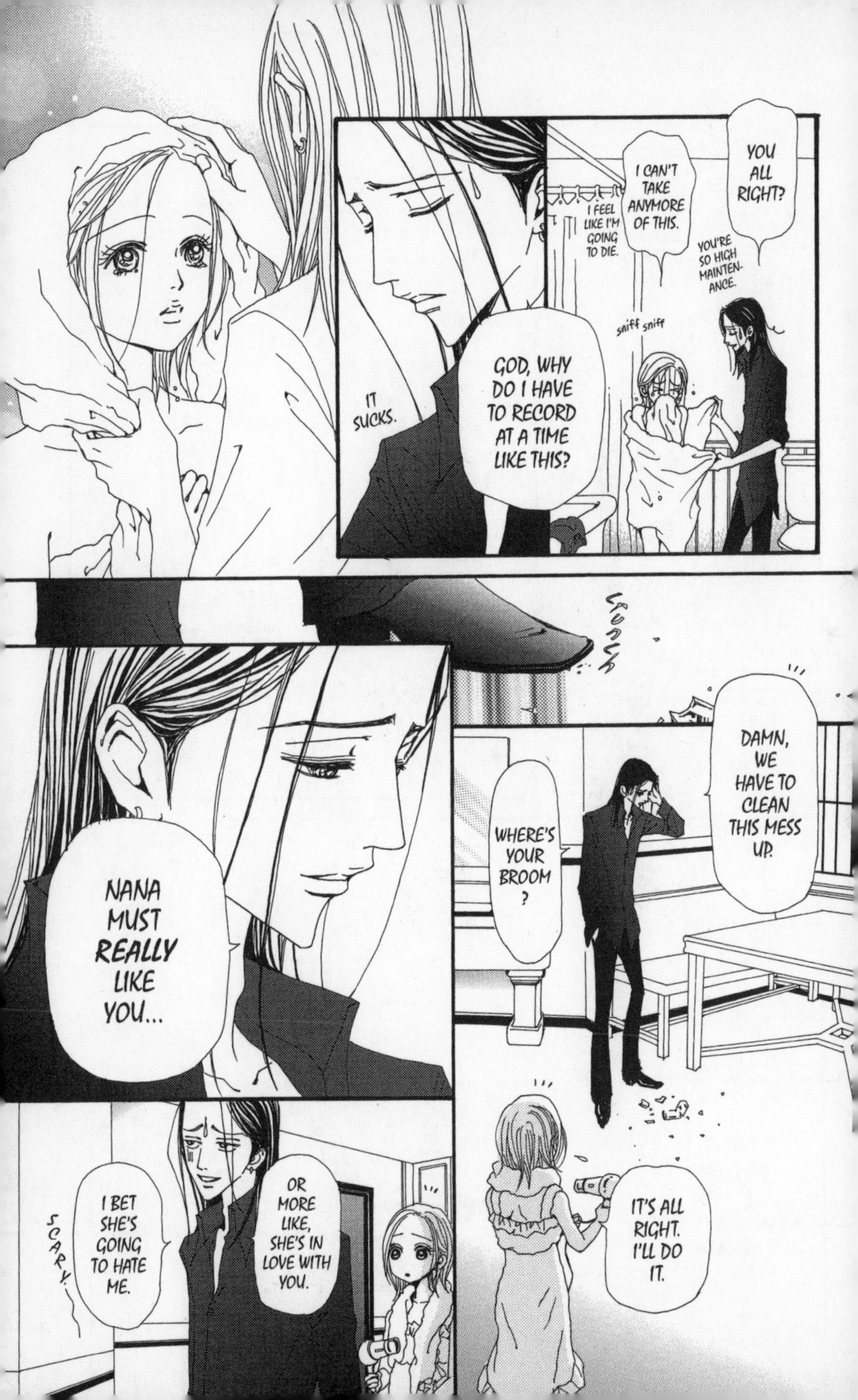
YOU ALL RIGHT?
YOU'RE SO HIGH MAINTENANCE.
I CAN'T TAKE ANYMORE OF THIS.
I FEEL LIKE I'M GOING TO DIE.
sniff sniff
GOD, WHY DO I HAVE TO RECORD AT A TIME LIKE THIS?
IT SUCKS.
DAMN, WE HAVE TO CLEAN THIS MESS UP.
WHERE'S YOUR BROOM?
IT'S ALL RIGHT. I'LL DO IT.
NANA MUST REALLY LIKE YOU...
OR MORE LIKE, SHE'S IN LOVE WITH YOU.
I BET SHE'S GOING TO HATE ME.
SCARY.

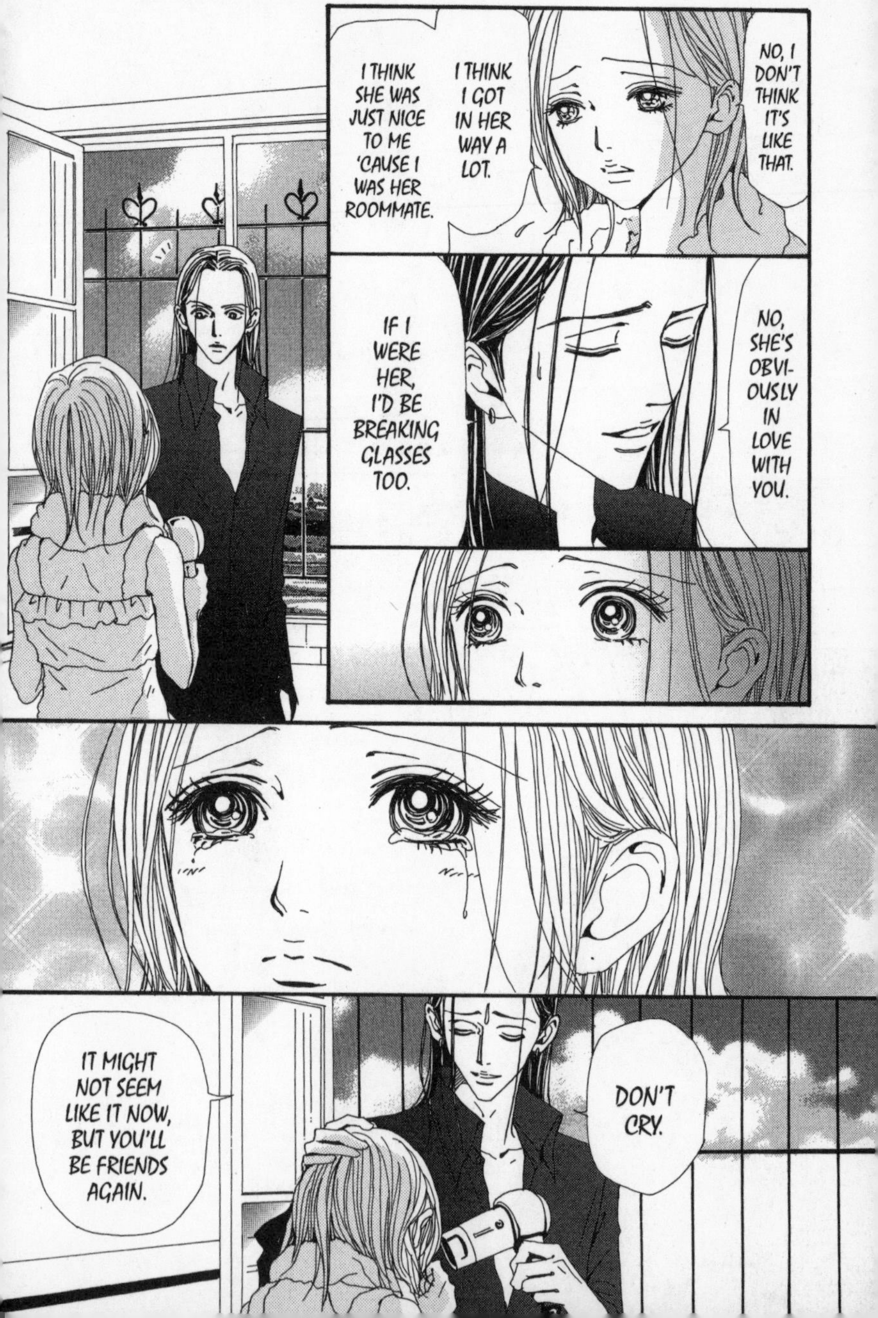
NO, I DON'T THINK IT'S LIKE THAT.
I THINK I GOT IN HER WAY A LOT.
I THINK SHE WAS JUST NICE TO ME 'CAUSE I WAS HER ROOMMATE.
NO, SHE'S OBVI-OUSLY IN LOVE WITH YOU.
IF I WERE HER, I'D BE BREAKING GLASSES TOO.
DON'T CRY.
IT MIGHT NOT SEEM LIKE IT NOW, BUT YOU'LL BE FRIENDS AGAIN.

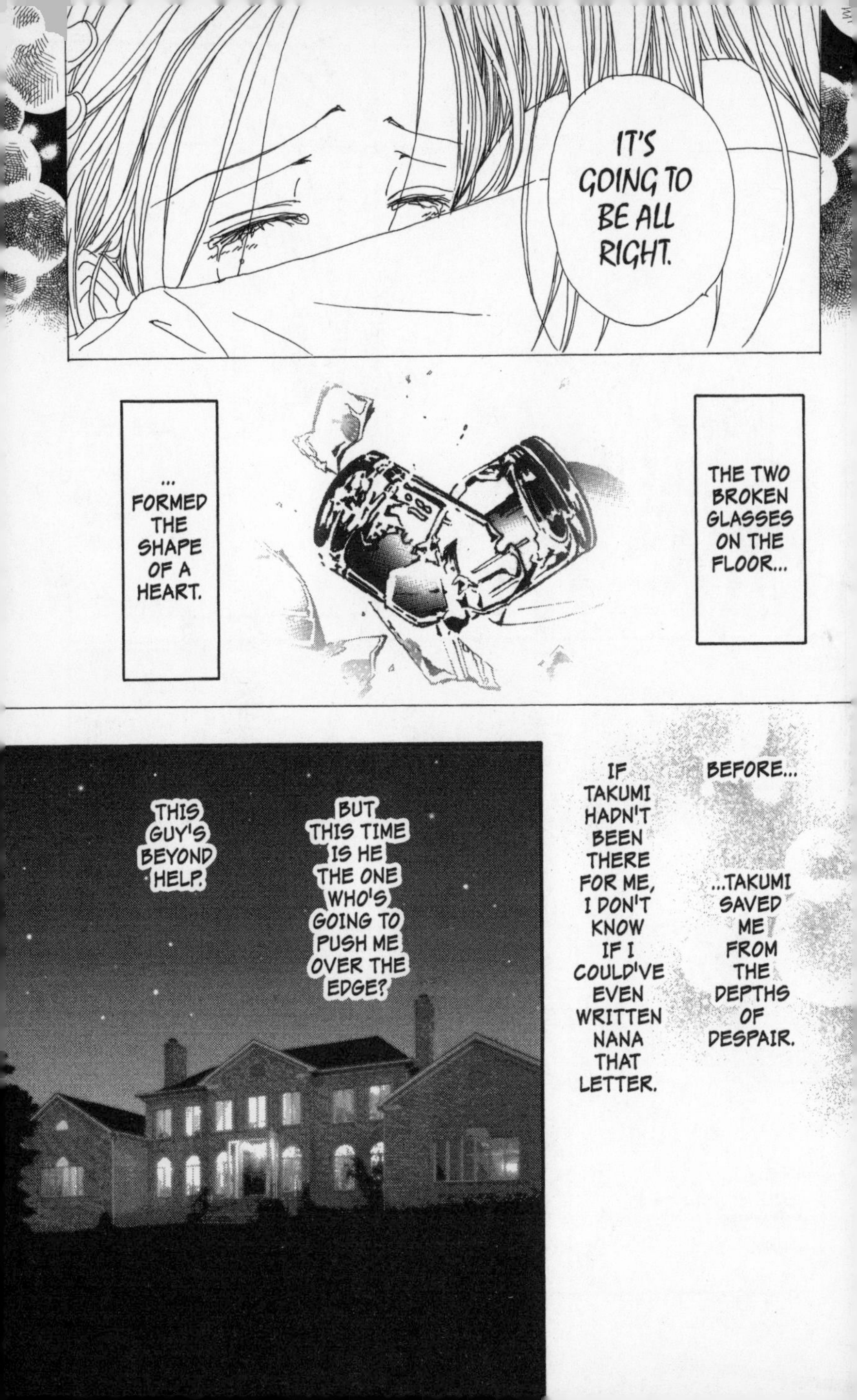
IT'S GOING TO BE ALL RIGHT.
THE TWO BROKEN GLASSES ON THE FLOOR...
...FORMED THE SHAPE OF A HEART.
BEFORE...
...TAKUMI SAVED ME FROM THE DEPTHS OF DESPAIR.
IF TAKUMI HADN'T BEEN THERE FOR ME, I DON'T KNOW IF I COULD'VE EVEN WRITTEN NANA THAT LETTER.
BUT THIS TIME IS HE THE ONE WHO'S GOING TO PUSH ME OVER THE EDGE?
THIS GUY'S BEYOND HELP.

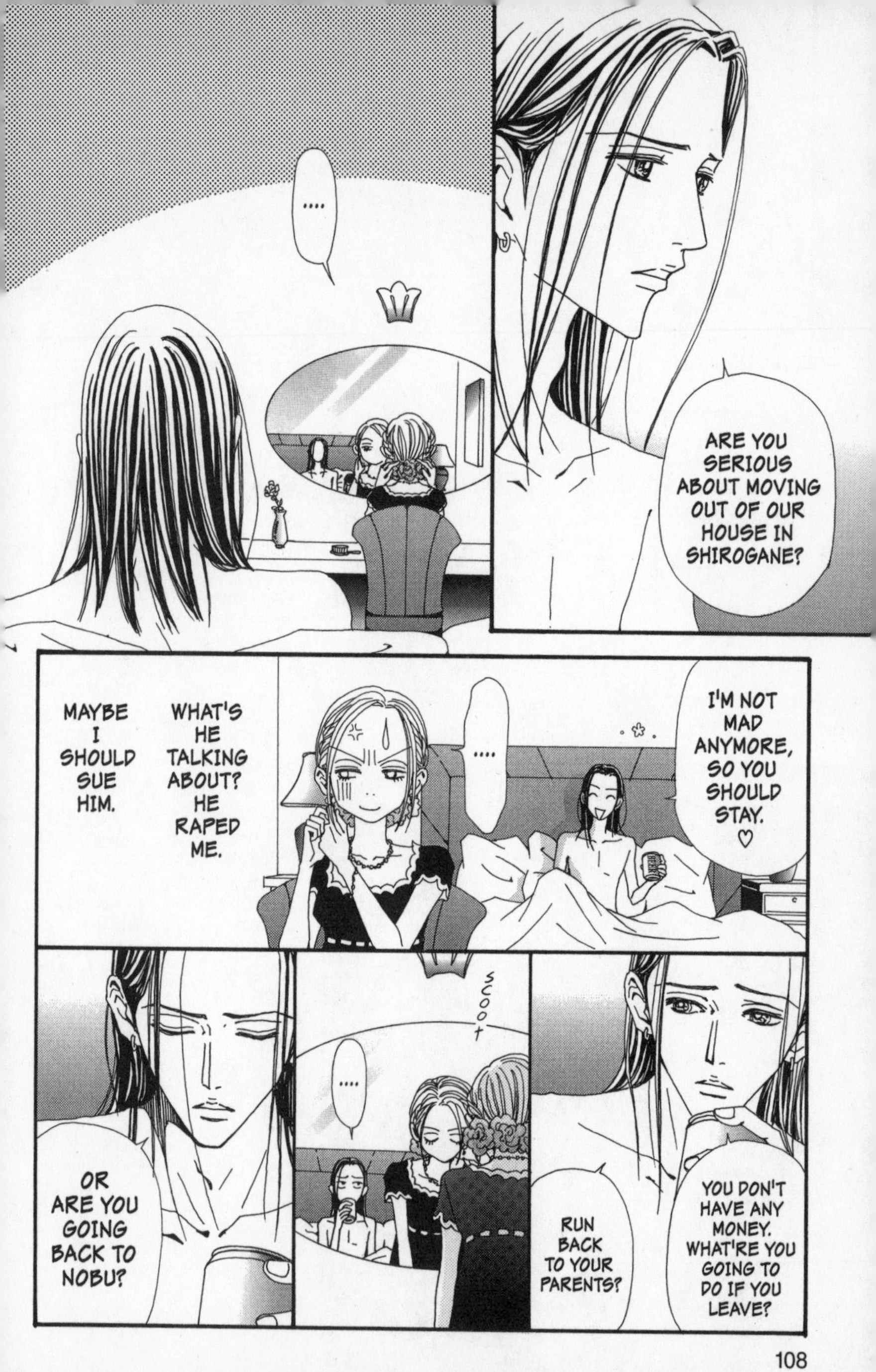
ARE YOU SERIOUS ABOUT MOVING OUT OF OUR HOUSE IN SHIROGANE?
....
I'M NOT MAD ANYMORE, SO YOU SHOULD STAY. ♡
....
WHAT'S HE TALKING ABOUT? HE RAPED ME.
MAYBE I SHOULD SUE HIM.
YOU DON'T HAVE ANY MONEY. WHAT'RE YOU GOING TO DO IF YOU LEAVE?
RUN BACK TO YOUR PARENTS?
SCOOT
....
OR ARE YOU GOING BACK TO NOBU?

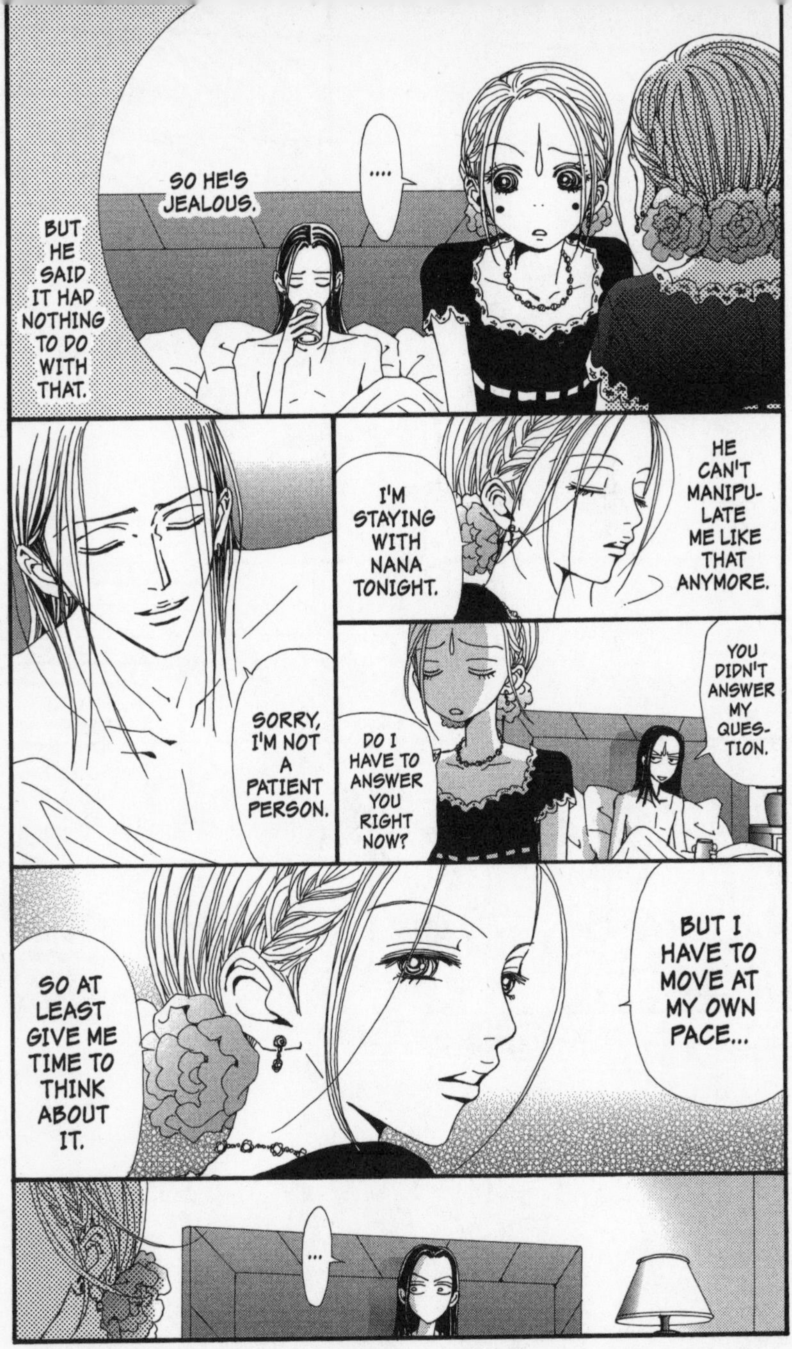

.....
SO HE'S JEALOUS.
BUT HE SAID IT HAD NOTHING TO DO WITH THAT.
HE CAN'T MANIPU-LATE ME LIKE THAT ANYMORE.
I'M STAYING WITH NANA TONIGHT.
YOU DIDN'T ANSWER MY QUES-TION.
DO I HAVE TO ANSWER YOU RIGHT NOW?
SORRY, I'M NOT A PATIENT PERSON.
BUT I HAVE TO MOVE AT MY OWN PACE...
SO AT LEAST GIVE ME TIME TO THINK ABOUT IT.
...

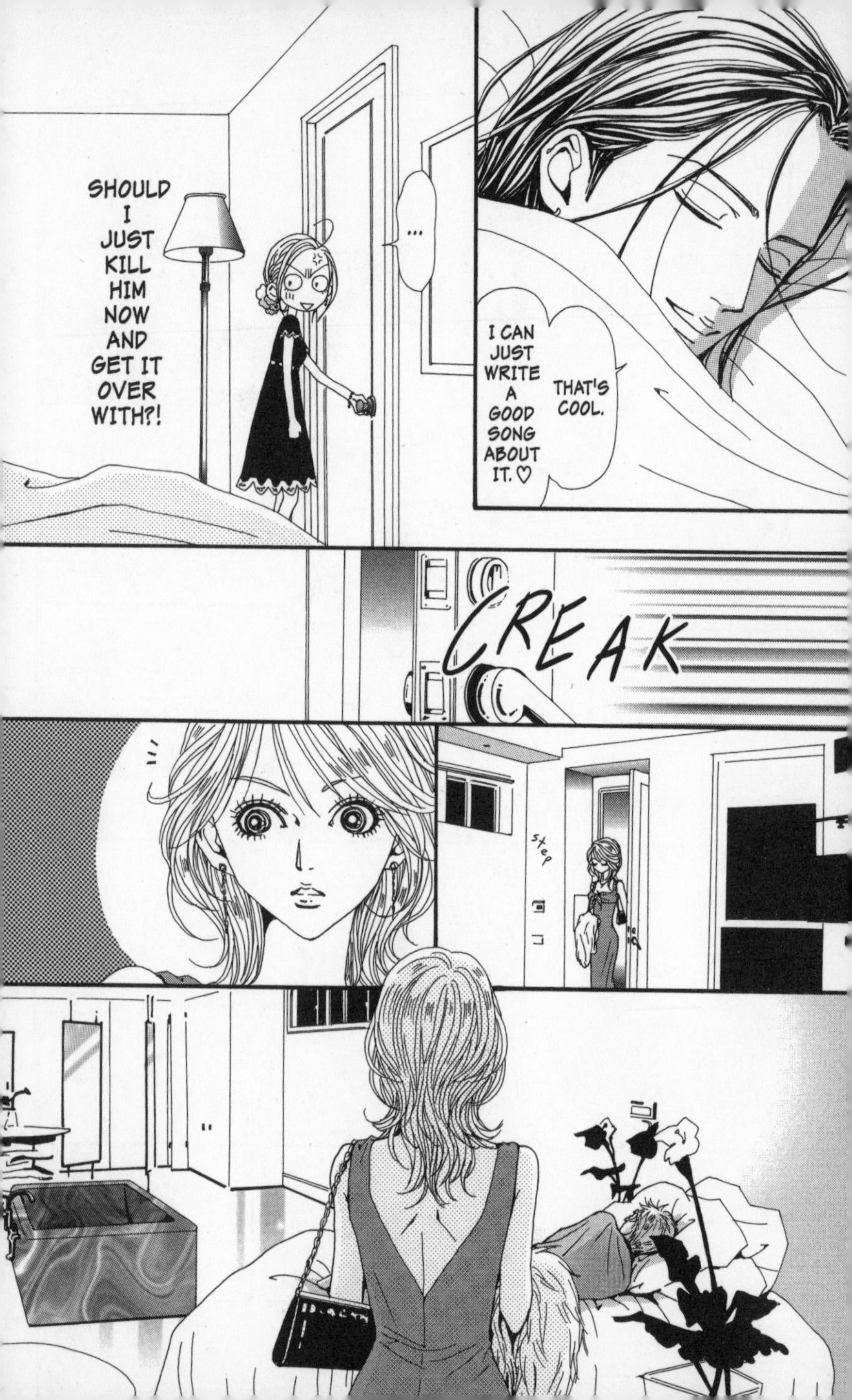
THAT'S COOL.
I CAN JUST WRITE A GOOD SONG ABOUT IT. ♡
...
SHOULD I JUST KILL HIM NOW AND GET IT OVER WITH?!
CREAK
step
!

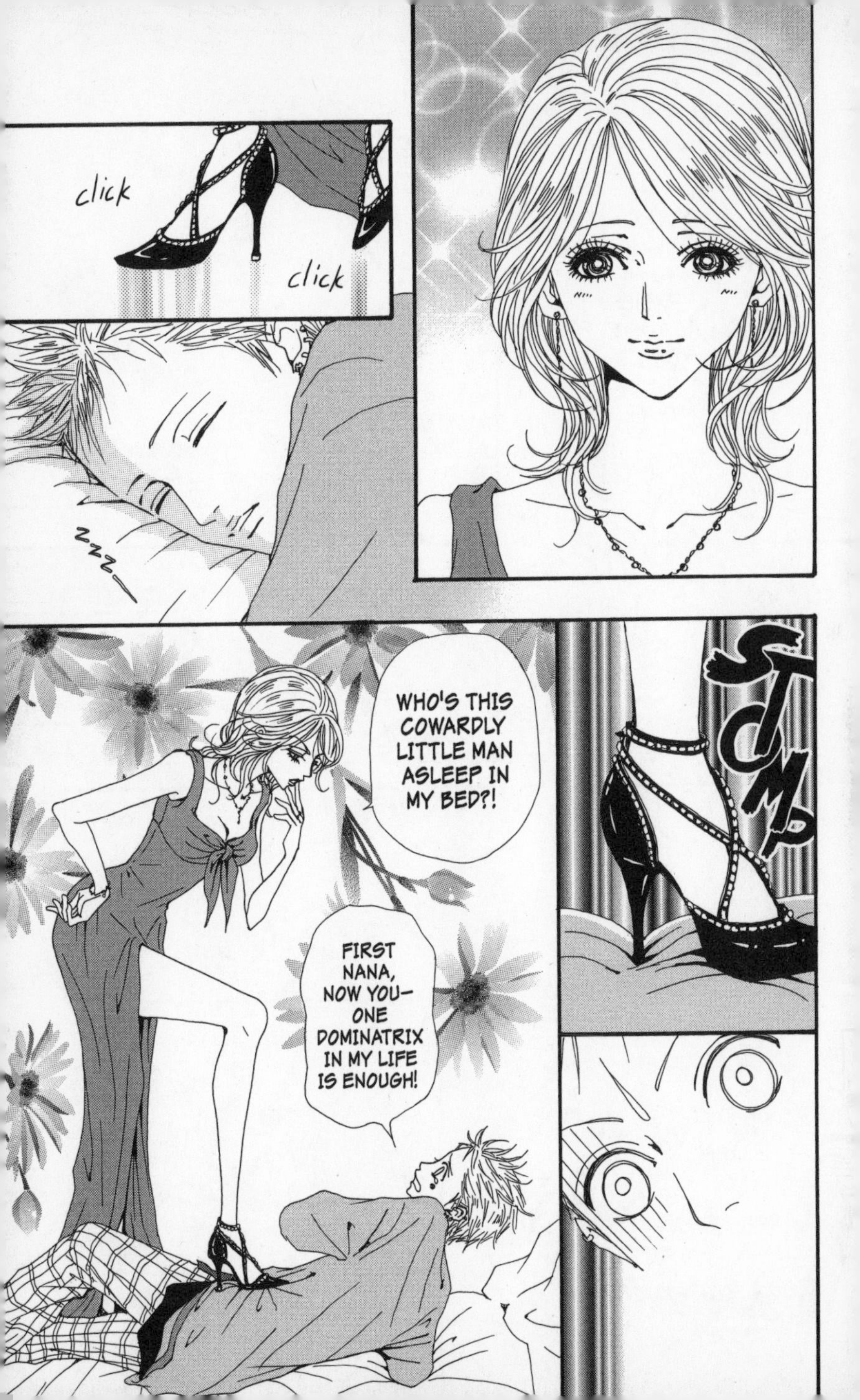
click
click
ZZZ
STOMP
WHO'S THIS COWARDLY LITTLE MAN ASLEEP IN MY BED?!
FIRST NANA, NOW YOU— ONE DOMINATRIX IN MY LIFE IS ENOUGH!

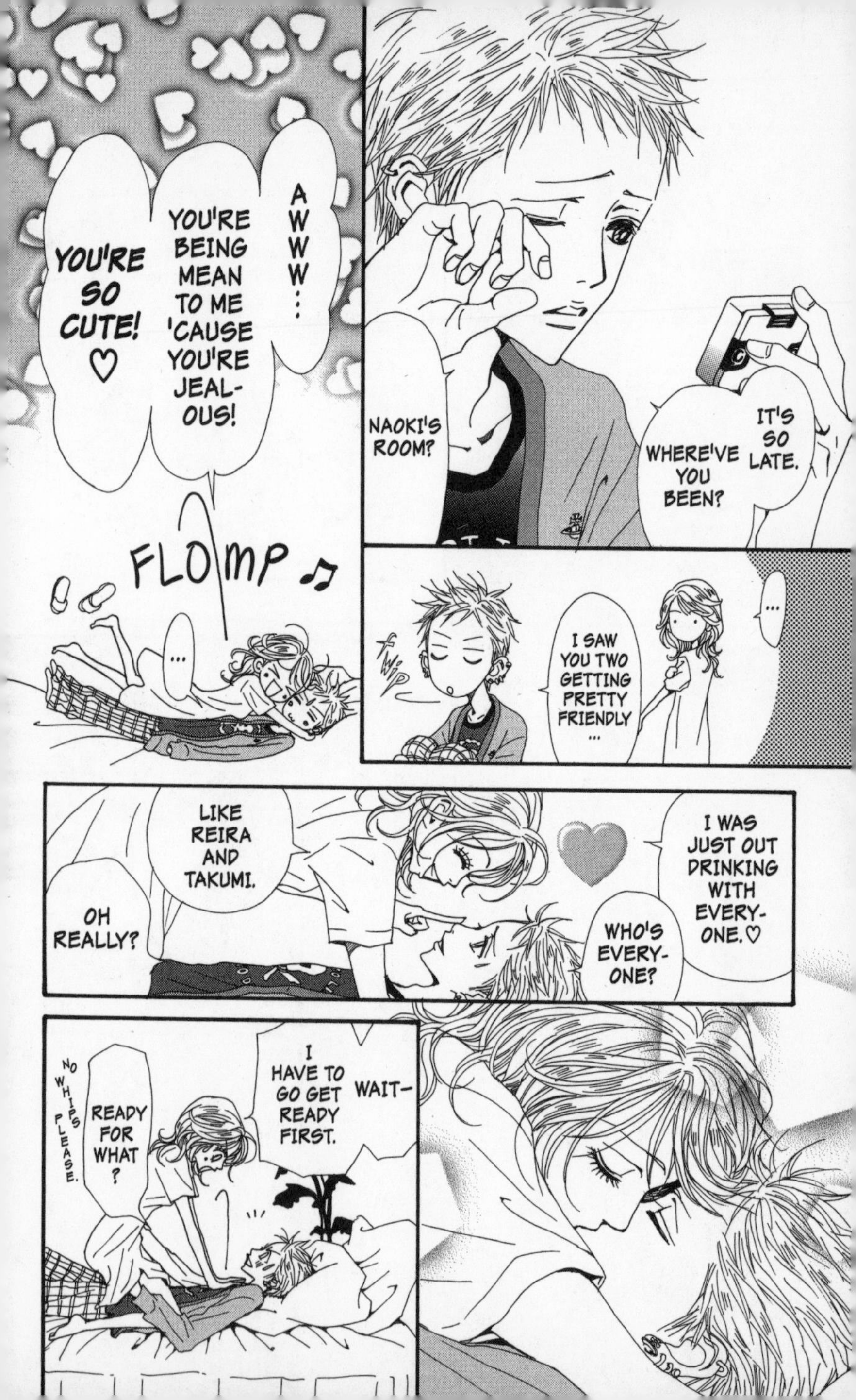
IT'S SO LATE.
WHERE'VE YOU BEEN?
NAOKI'S ROOM?
...
I SAW YOU TWO GETTING PRETTY FRIENDLY ...
FWIP
AWWW...
YOU'RE BEING MEAN TO ME 'CAUSE YOU'RE JEAL-OUS!
YOU'RE SO CUTE! ♡
FLOMP ♫
...
I WAS JUST OUT DRINKING WITH EVERY-ONE. ♡
WHO'S EVERY-ONE?
LIKE REIRA AND TAKUMI.
OH REALLY?
WAIT-
I HAVE TO GO GET READY FIRST.
READY FOR WHAT?
NO WHIPS PLEASE.

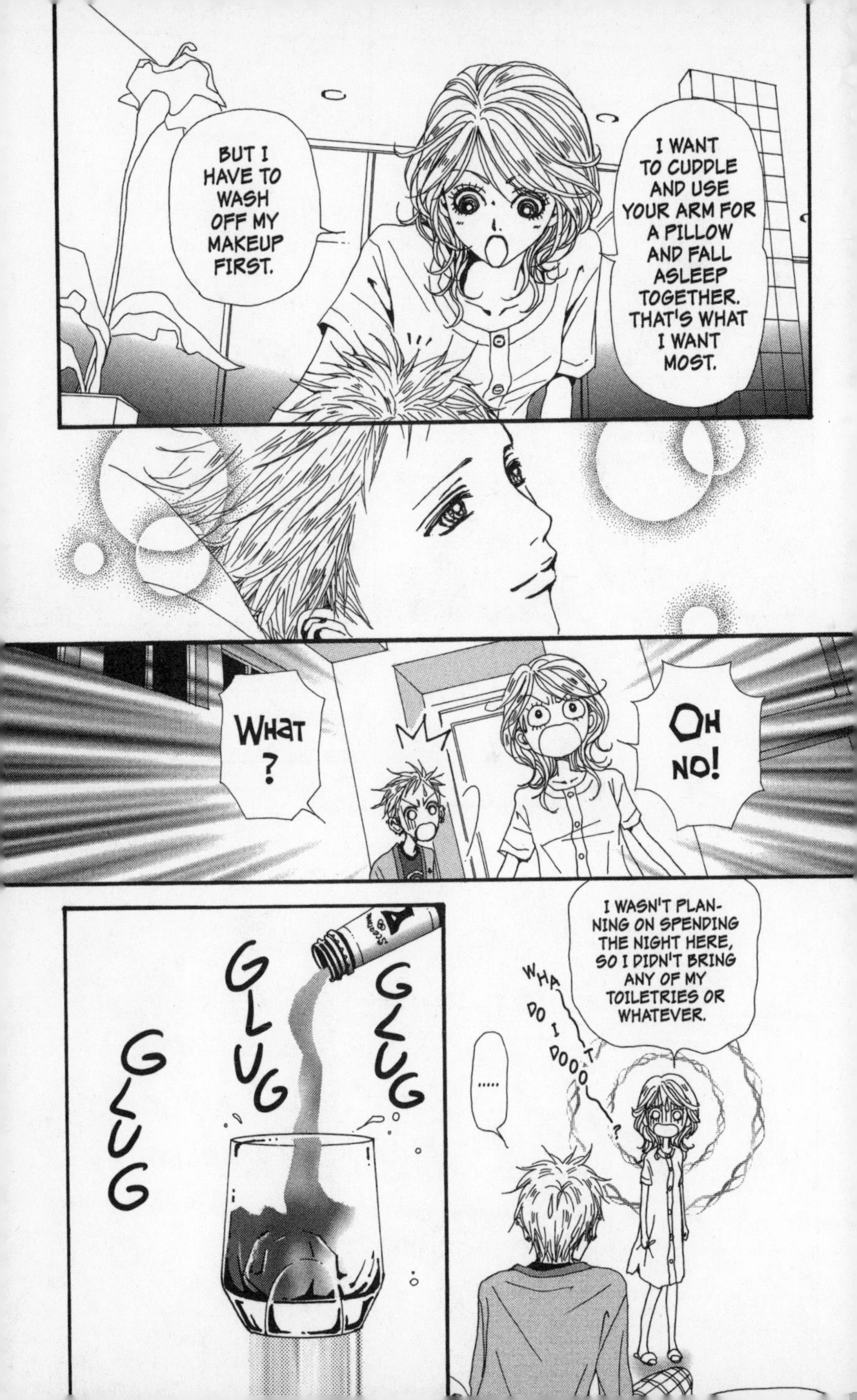
I WANT TO CUDDLE AND USE YOUR ARM FOR A PILLOW AND FALL ASLEEP TOGETHER. THAT'S WHAT I WANT MOST.
BUT I HAVE TO WASH OFF MY MAKEUP FIRST.
OH NO!
WHAT?
I WASN'T PLAN-NING ON SPENDING THE NIGHT HERE, SO I DIDN'T BRING ANY OF MY TOILETRIES OR WHATEVER.
WHAT DO I DOOOO?
......
GLUG
GLUG
GLUG

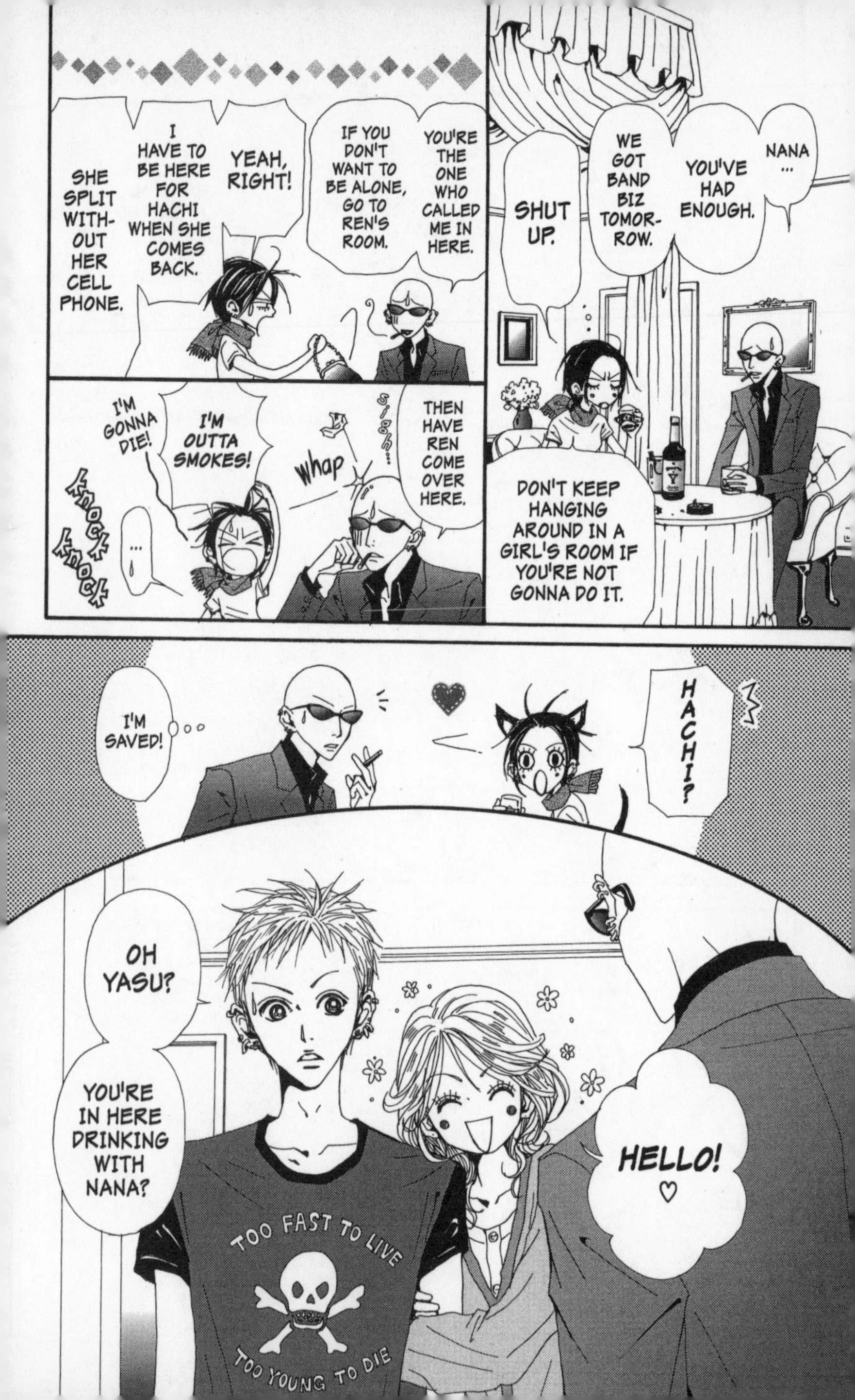
NANA ...
YOU'VE HAD ENOUGH.
WE GOT BAND BIZ TOMOR-ROW.
SHUT UP.
DON'T KEEP HANGING AROUND IN A GIRL'S ROOM IF YOU'RE NOT GONNA DO IT.
YOU'RE THE ONE WHO CALLED ME IN HERE.
IF YOU DON'T WANT TO BE ALONE, GO TO REN'S ROOM.
YEAH, RIGHT!
I HAVE TO BE HERE FOR HACHI WHEN SHE COMES BACK.
SHE SPLIT WITH-OUT HER CELL PHONE.
THEN HAVE REN COME OVER HERE.
sigh...
whap
I'M OUTTA SMOKES!
I'M GONNA DIE!
...
knock knock
HACHI?
I'M SAVED!
HELLO! ♡
OH YASU?
YOU'RE IN HERE DRINKING WITH NANA?
TOO FAST TO LIVE
TOO YOUNG TO DIE

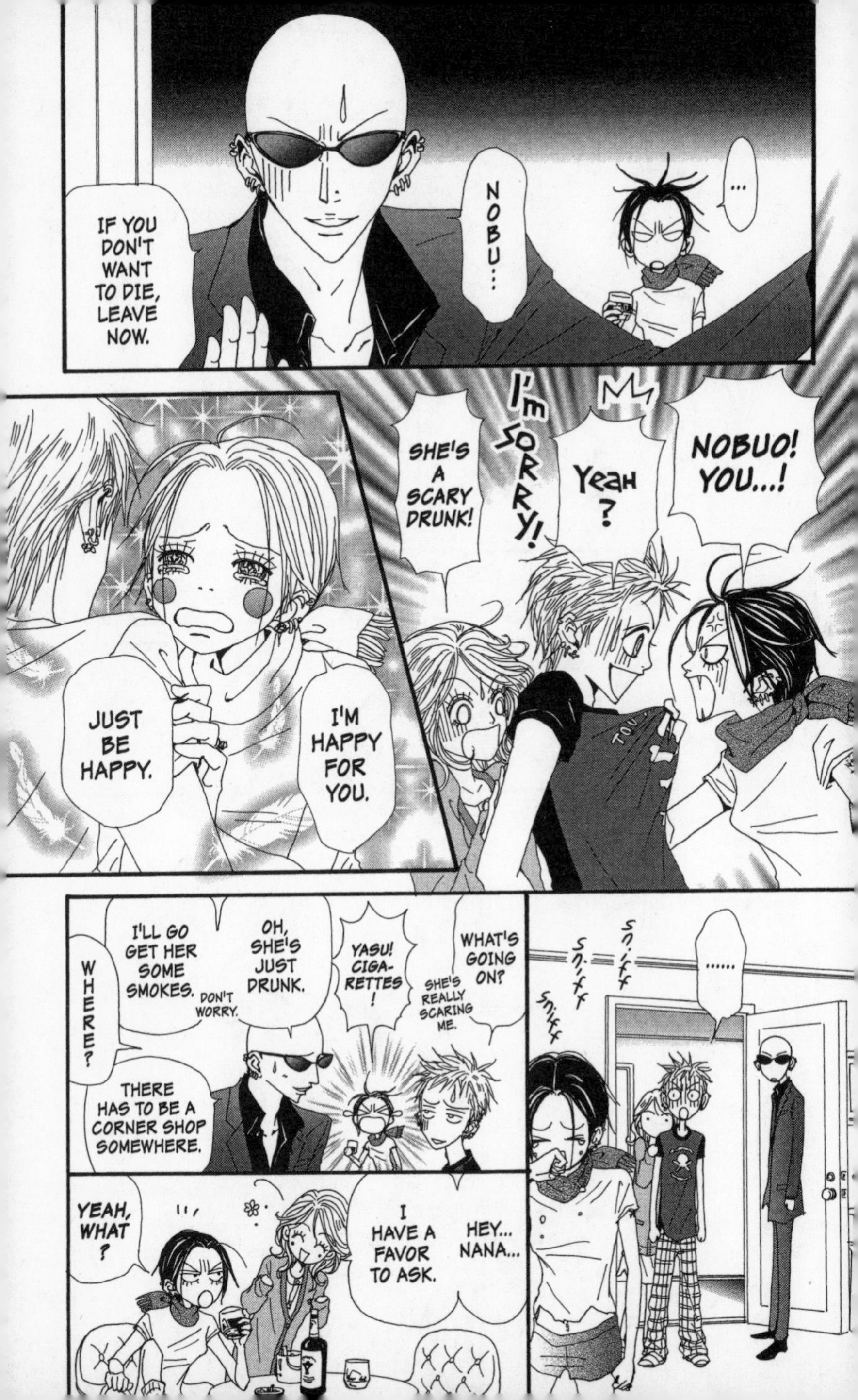
...
NOBU...
IF YOU DON'T WANT TO DIE, LEAVE NOW.
NOBUO! YOU...!
Yeah?
I'm SORRY!
SHE'S A SCARY DRUNK!
I'M HAPPY FOR YOU.
JUST BE HAPPY.
sniff
sniff
sniff
......
WHAT'S GOING ON?
SHE'S REALLY SCARING ME.
YASU! CIGARETTES!
OH, SHE'S JUST DRUNK.
DON'T WORRY.
I'LL GO GET HER SOME SMOKES.
WHERE?
THERE HAS TO BE A CORNER SHOP SOMEWHERE.
HEY... NANA...
I HAVE A FAVOR TO ASK.
YEAH, WHAT?

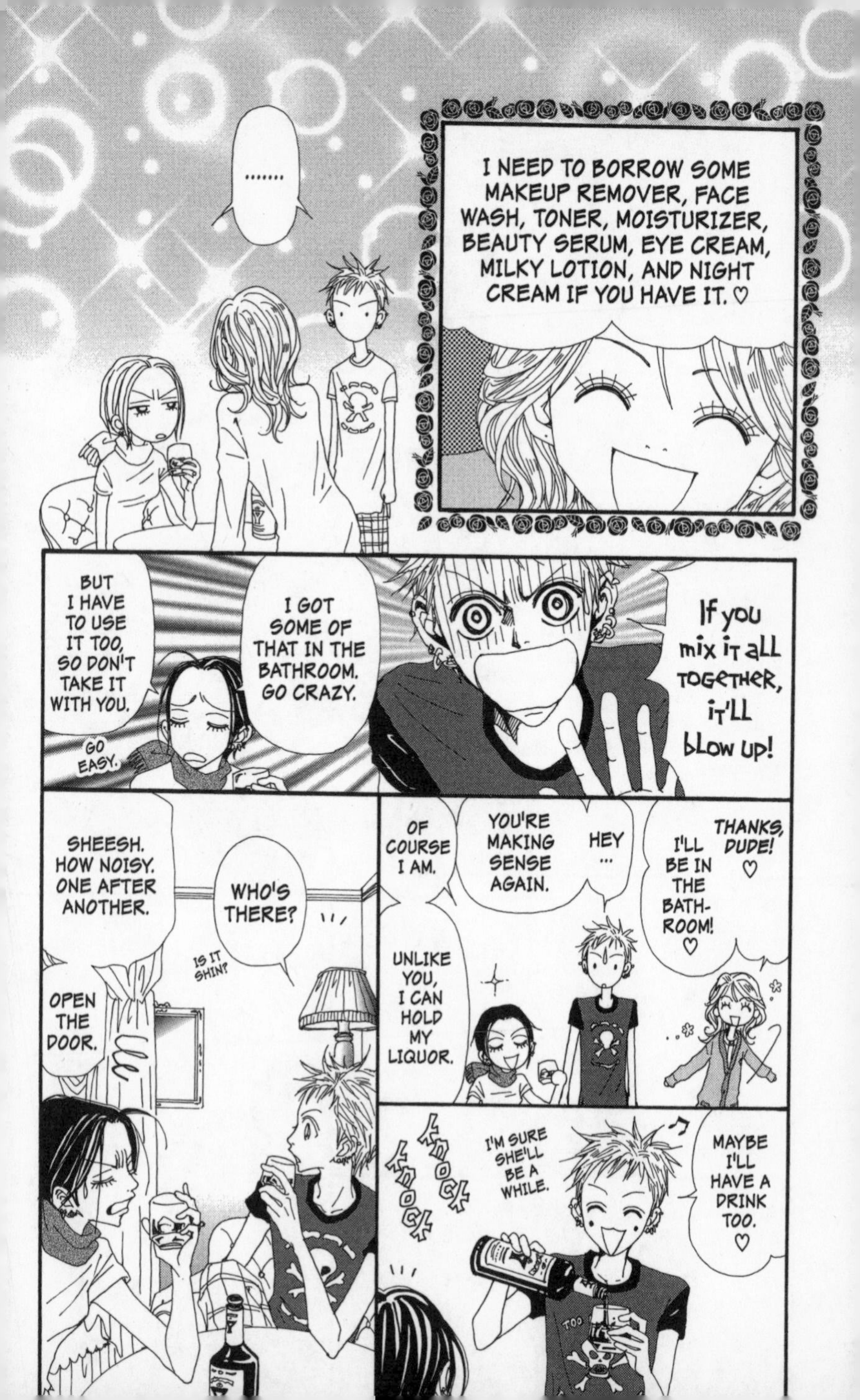
I NEED TO BORROW SOME MAKEUP REMOVER, FACE WASH, TONER, MOISTURIZER, BEAUTY SERUM, EYE CREAM, MILKY LOTION, AND NIGHT CREAM IF YOU HAVE IT. ♡
......
If you mix it all together, it'll blow up!
I GOT SOME OF THAT IN THE BATHROOM. GO CRAZY.
BUT I HAVE TO USE IT TOO, SO DON'T TAKE IT WITH YOU.
GO EASY.
THANKS, DUDE! ♡
I'LL BE IN THE BATHROOM! ♡
HEY ...
YOU'RE MAKING SENSE AGAIN.
OF COURSE I AM.
UNLIKE YOU, I CAN HOLD MY LIQUOR.
MAYBE I'LL HAVE A DRINK TOO. ♡
I'M SURE SHE'LL BE A WHILE.
KNOCK
KNOCK
WHO'S THERE?
SHEESH. HOW NOISY. ONE AFTER ANOTHER.
IS IT SHIN?
OPEN THE DOOR.

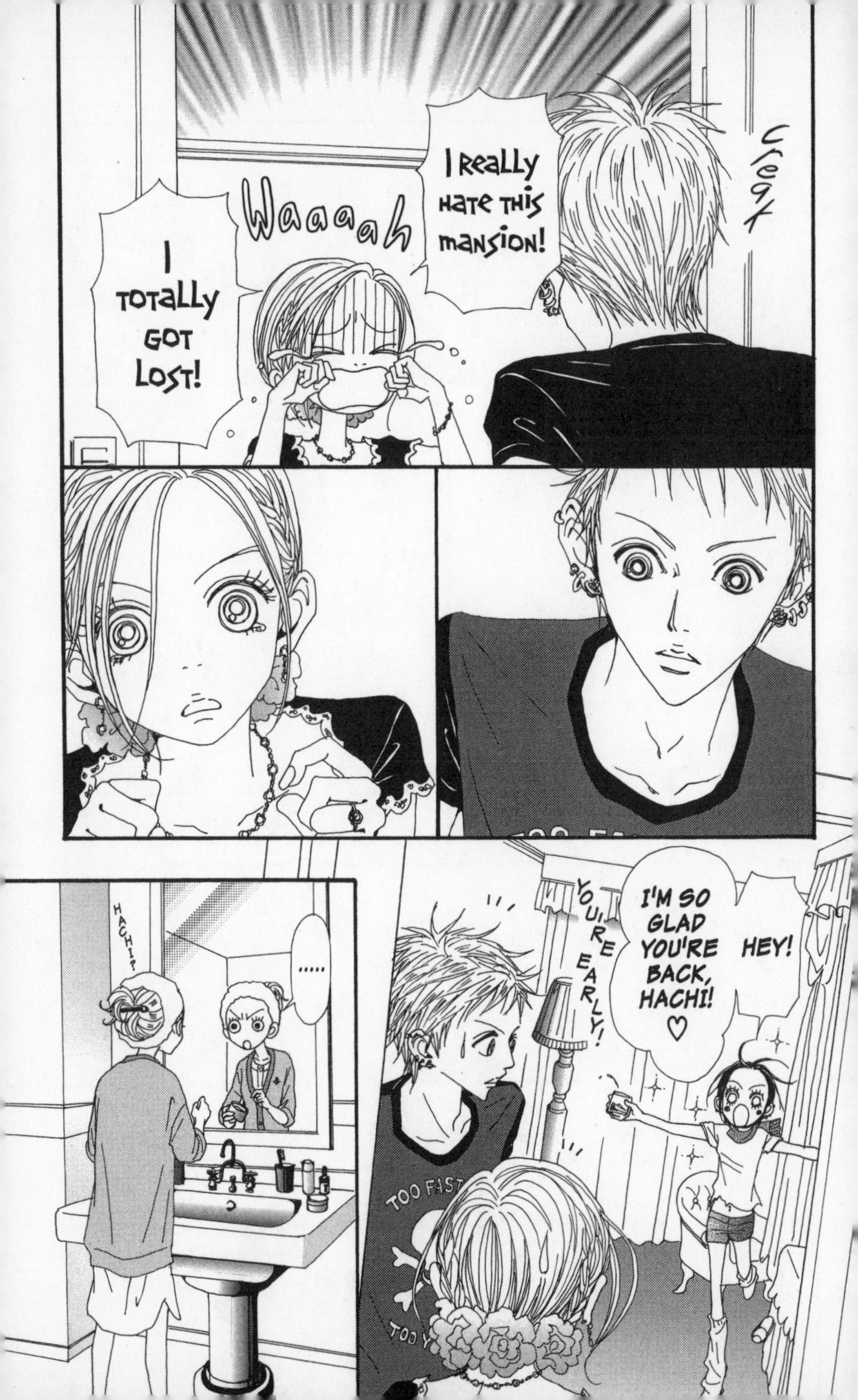
Creak
I really hate this mansion!
Waaaah
I totally got lost!
HEY!
I'M SO GLAD YOU'RE BACK, HACHI! ♡
YOU'RE EARLY!
HACHI!?
......

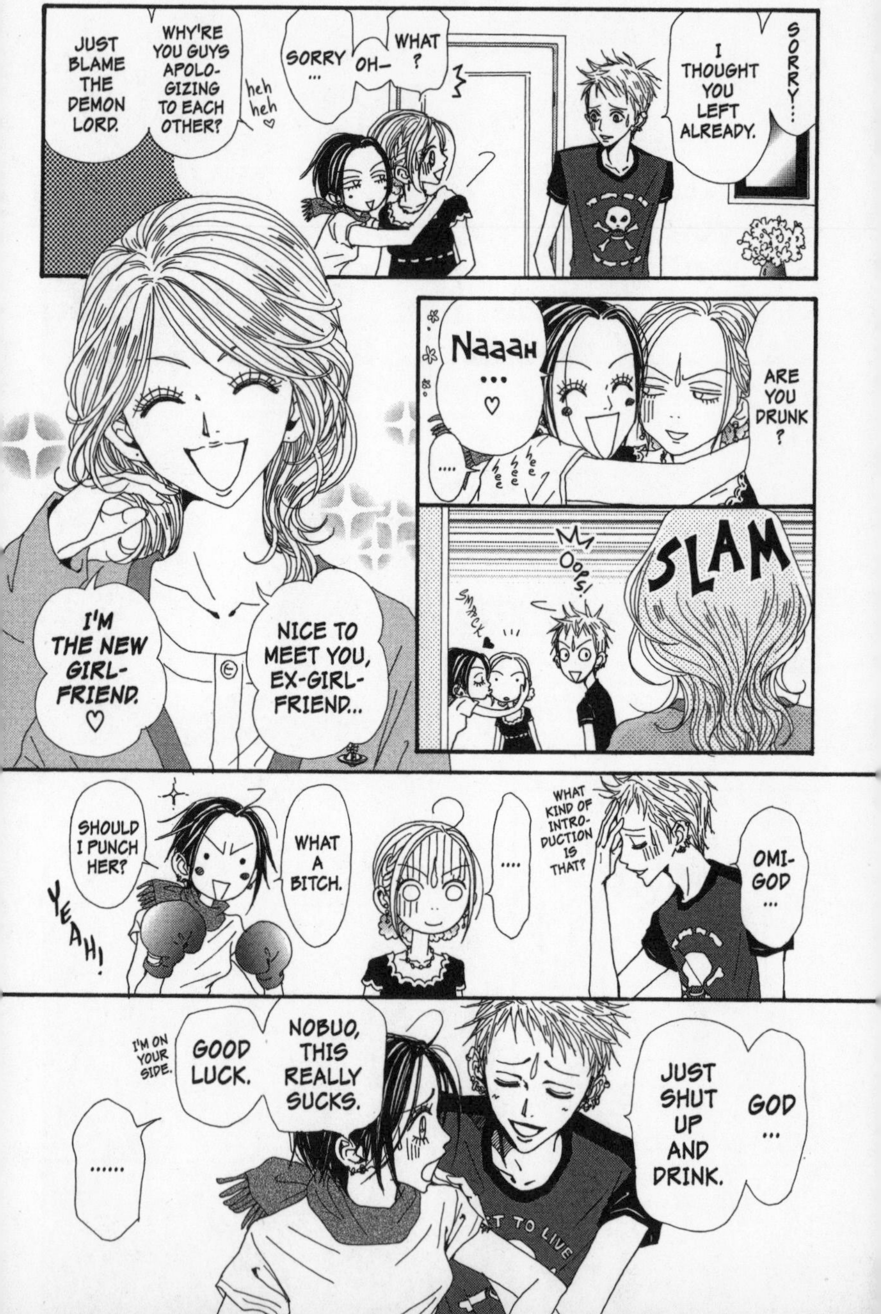
SORRY...
I THOUGHT YOU LEFT ALREADY.
WHAT?
OH—
SORRY...
WHY'RE YOU GUYS APOLOGIZING TO EACH OTHER?
heh heh ♡
JUST BLAME THE DEMON LORD.
ARE YOU DRUNK?
Naaah... ♡
hee hee hee
....
SLAM
OOPS!
SMACK
NICE TO MEET YOU, EX-GIRLFRIEND...
I'M THE NEW GIRLFRIEND. ♡
OMIGOD...
WHAT KIND OF INTRODUCTION IS THAT?
....
WHAT A BITCH.
SHOULD I PUNCH HER?
YEAH!
GOD...
JUST SHUT UP AND DRINK.
NOBUO, THIS REALLY SUCKS.
GOOD LUCK.
I'M ON YOUR SIDE.
......

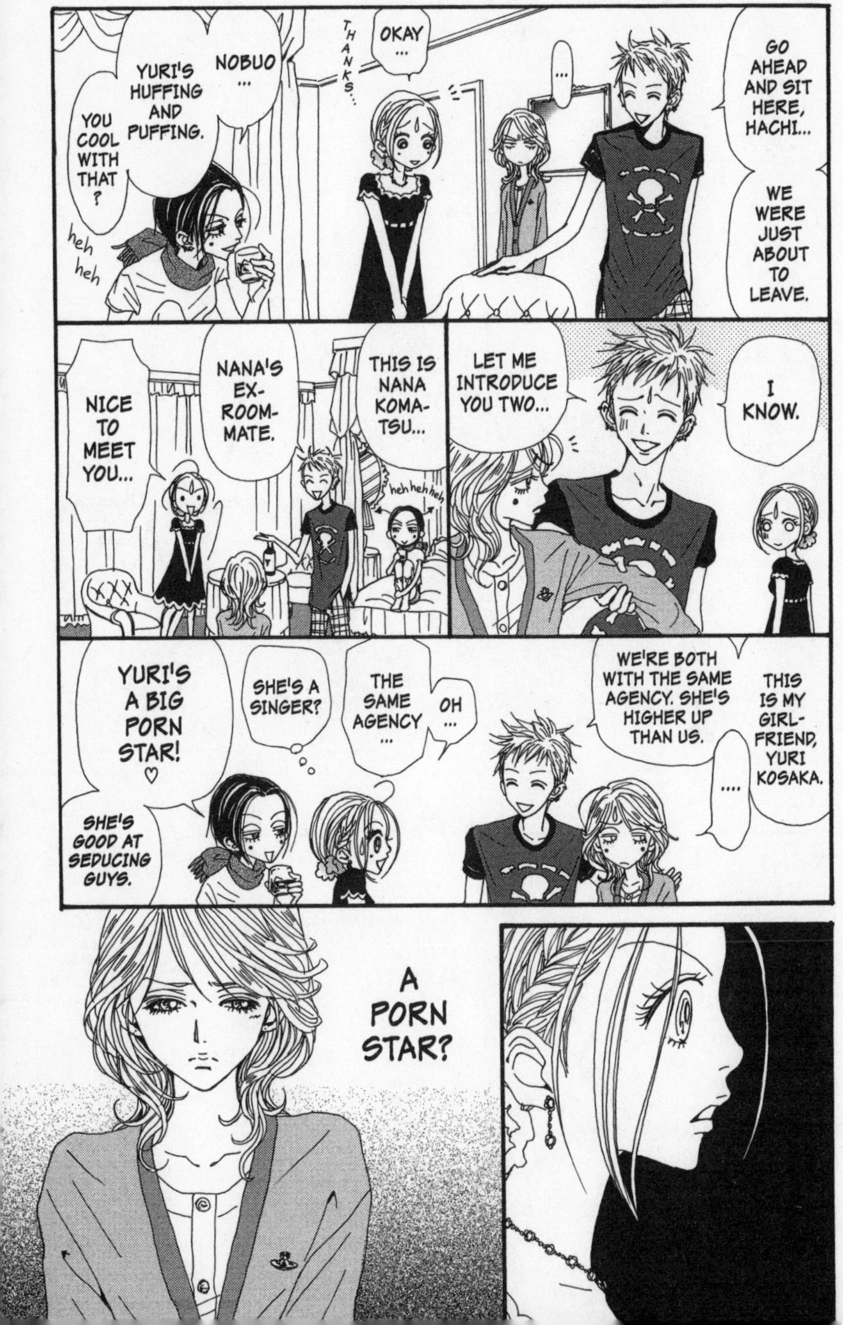
GO AHEAD AND SIT HERE, HACHI...
WE WERE JUST ABOUT TO LEAVE.
...
OKAY ...
THANKS...
NOBUO ...
YURI'S HUFFING AND PUFFING.
YOU COOL WITH THAT?
heh heh
I KNOW.
LET ME INTRODUCE YOU TWO...
THIS IS NANA KOMATSU...
NANA'S EX-ROOMMATE.
heh heh heh
NICE TO MEET YOU...
THIS IS MY GIRLFRIEND, YURI KOSAKA.
WE'RE BOTH WITH THE SAME AGENCY. SHE'S HIGHER UP THAN US.
....
OH ...
THE SAME AGENCY ...
SHE'S A SINGER?
YURI'S A BIG PORN STAR! ♡
SHE'S GOOD AT SEDUCING GUYS.
A PORN STAR?

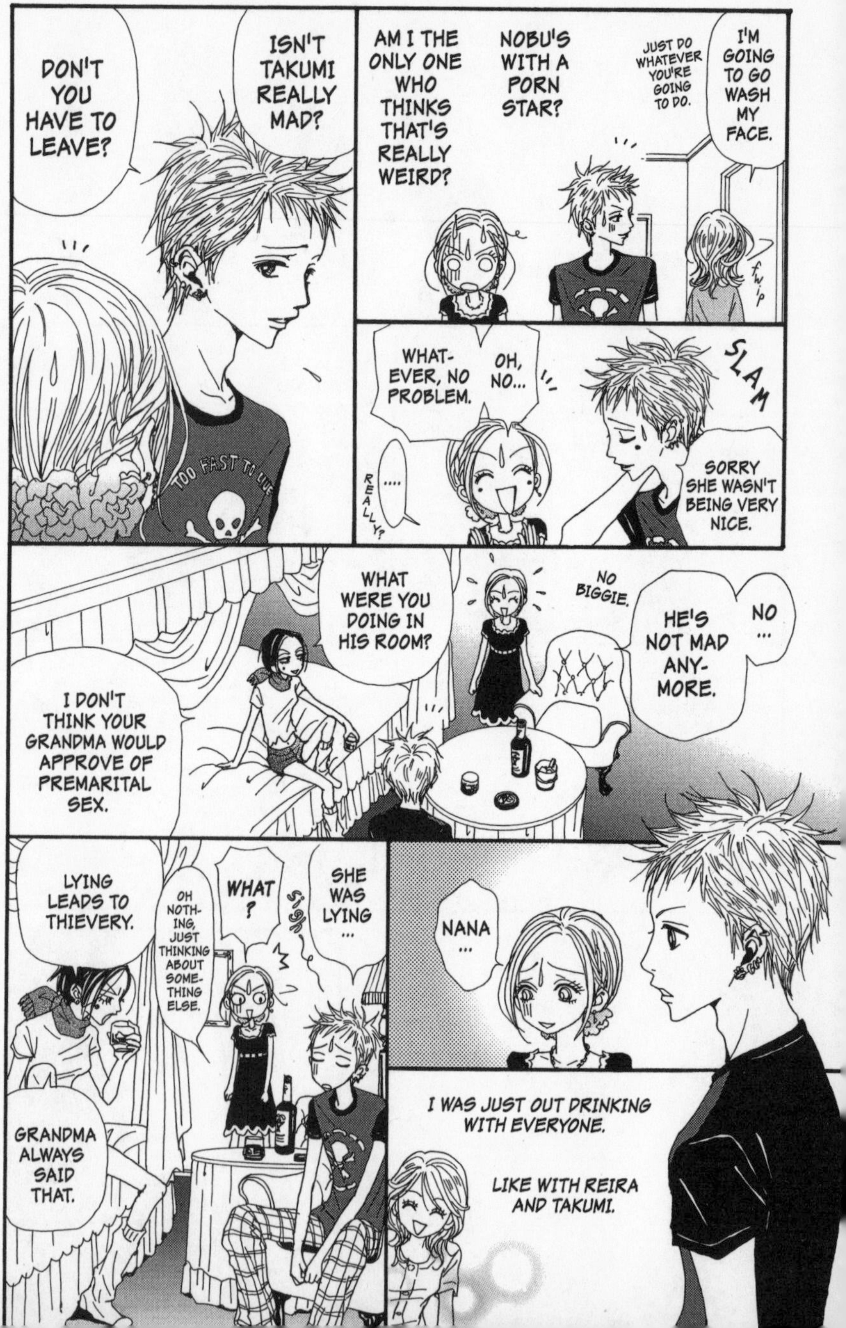
I'M GOING TO GO WASH MY FACE.
JUST DO WHATEVER YOU'RE GOING TO DO.
NOBU'S WITH A PORN STAR?
AM I THE ONLY ONE WHO THINKS THAT'S REALLY WEIRD?
fwip
SLAM
SORRY SHE WASN'T BEING VERY NICE.
OH, NO...
WHAT-EVER, NO PROBLEM.
....
REALLY?
ISN'T TAKUMI REALLY MAD?
DON'T YOU HAVE TO LEAVE?
TOO FAST TO LIVE
NO ...
HE'S NOT MAD ANY-MORE.
NO BIGGIE.
WHAT WERE YOU DOING IN HIS ROOM?
I DON'T THINK YOUR GRANDMA WOULD APPROVE OF PREMARITAL SEX.
NANA ...
I WAS JUST OUT DRINKING WITH EVERYONE.
LIKE WITH REIRA AND TAKUMI.
SHE WAS LYING ...
sigh
WHAT?
OH NOTH-ING, JUST THINKING ABOUT SOME-THING ELSE.
LYING LEADS TO THIEVERY.
GRANDMA ALWAYS SAID THAT.

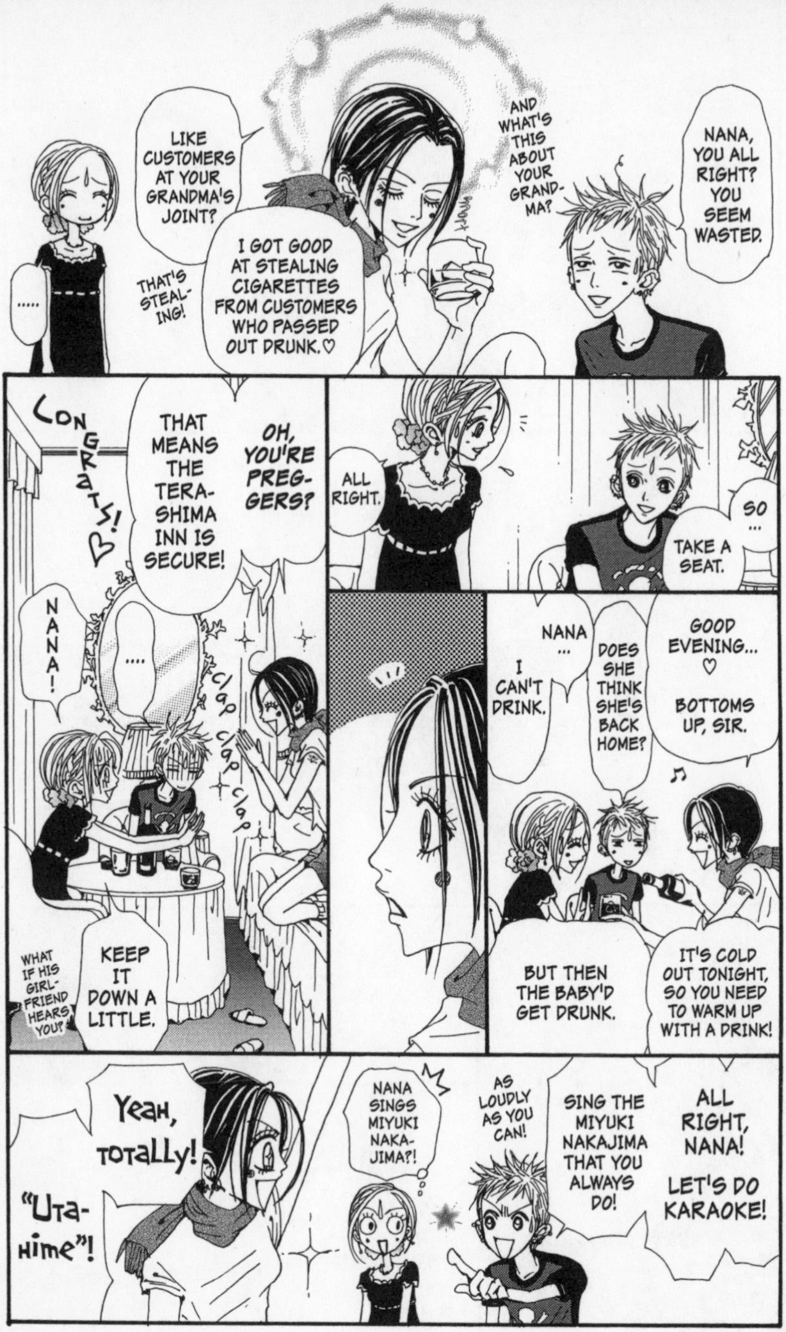
NANA, YOU ALL RIGHT? YOU SEEM WASTED.
AND WHAT'S THIS ABOUT YOUR GRANDMA?
LIKE CUSTOMERS AT YOUR GRANDMA'S JOINT?
I GOT GOOD AT STEALING CIGARETTES FROM CUSTOMERS WHO PASSED OUT DRUNK.♡
THAT'S STEAL-ING!
......
SO ...
TAKE A SEAT.
ALL RIGHT.
GOOD EVENING...♡
BOTTOMS UP, SIR.
DOES SHE THINK SHE'S BACK HOME?
NANA ...
I CAN'T DRINK.
IT'S COLD OUT TONIGHT, SO YOU NEED TO WARM UP WITH A DRINK!
BUT THEN THE BABY'D GET DRUNK.
OH, YOU'RE PREG-GERS?
THAT MEANS THE TERA-SHIMA INN IS SECURE!
CONGRATS!♡
....
NANA!
clap clap clap clap
KEEP IT DOWN A LITTLE.
WHAT IF HIS GIRL-FRIEND HEARS YOU?
ALL RIGHT, NANA!
LET'S DO KARAOKE!
SING THE MIYUKI NAKAJIMA THAT YOU ALWAYS DO!
AS LOUDLY AS YOU CAN!
NANA SINGS MIYUKI NAKAJIMA?!
Yeah, totally!
"Uta-hime"!

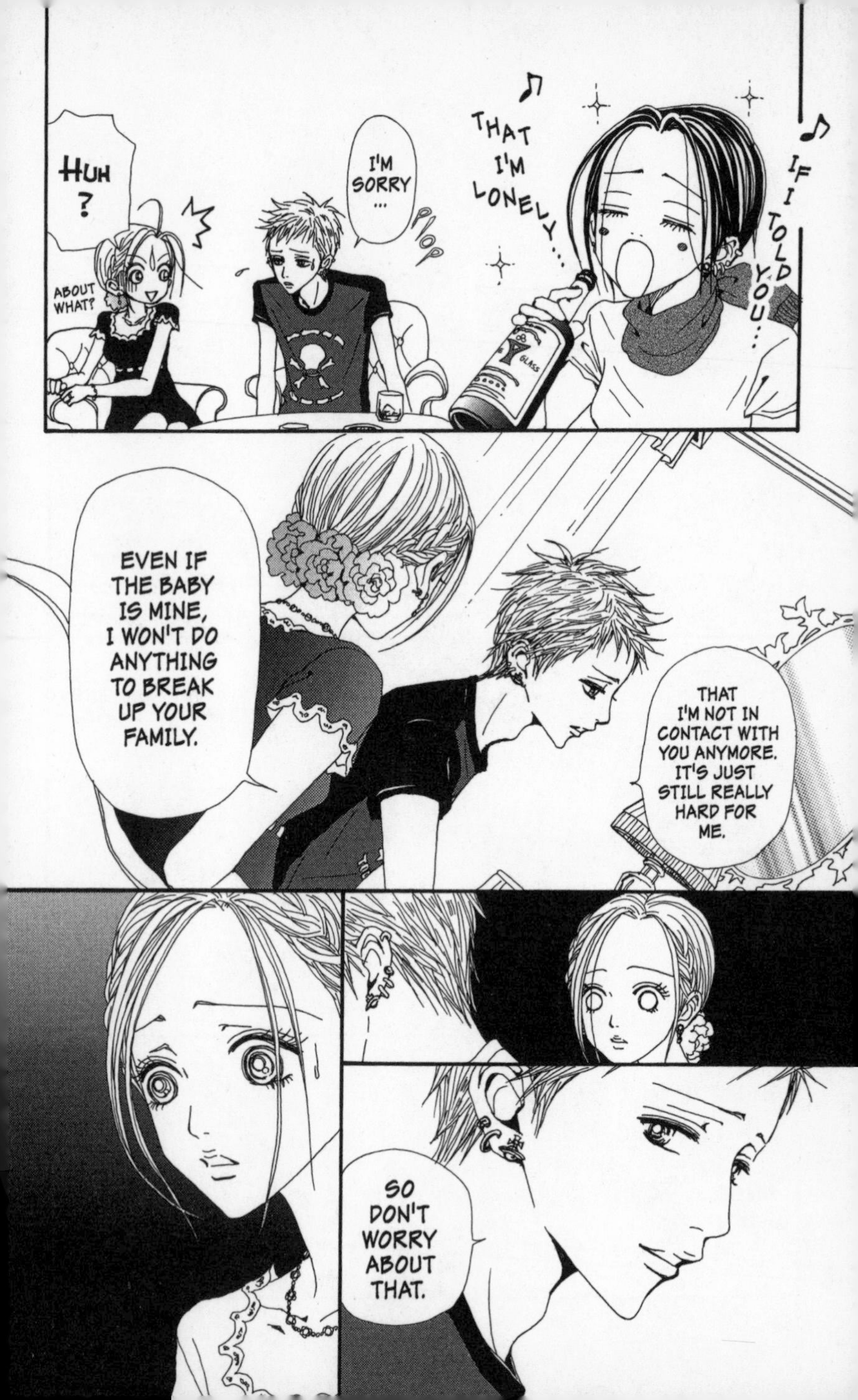
IF I TOLD YOU...
THAT I'M LONELY...
I'M SORRY...
PLOP
HUH?
ABOUT WHAT?
THAT I'M NOT IN CONTACT WITH YOU ANYMORE. IT'S JUST STILL REALLY HARD FOR ME.
EVEN IF THE BABY IS MINE, I WON'T DO ANYTHING TO BREAK UP YOUR FAMILY.
SO DON'T WORRY ABOUT THAT.

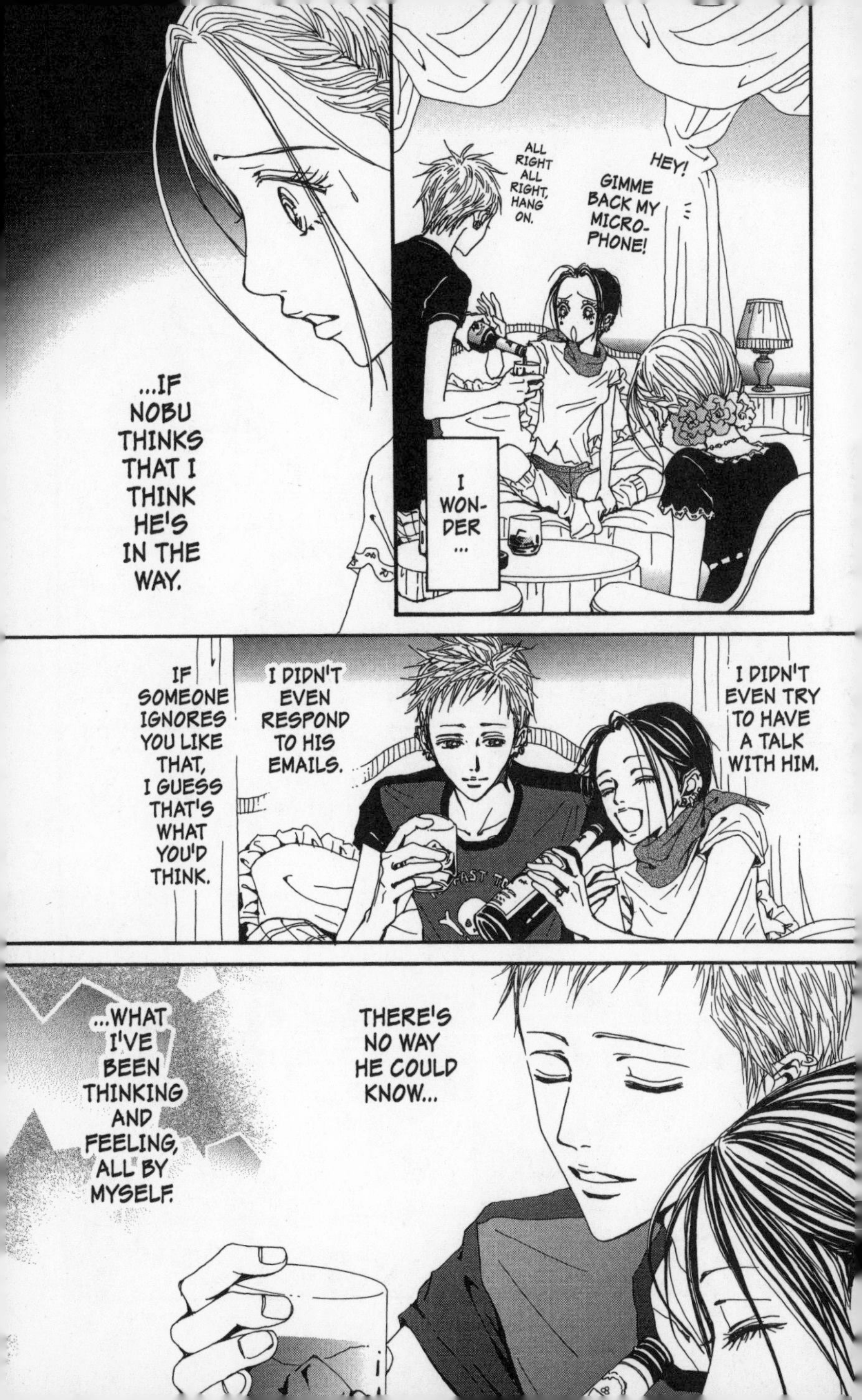
HEY! GIMME BACK MY MICROPHONE!
ALL RIGHT ALL RIGHT, HANG ON.
I WONDER...
...IF NOBU THINKS THAT I THINK HE'S IN THE WAY.
I DIDN'T EVEN TRY TO HAVE A TALK WITH HIM.
I DIDN'T EVEN RESPOND TO HIS EMAILS.
IF SOMEONE IGNORES YOU LIKE THAT, I GUESS THAT'S WHAT YOU'D THINK.
THERE'S NO WAY HE COULD KNOW...
...WHAT I'VE BEEN THINKING AND FEELING, ALL BY MYSELF.

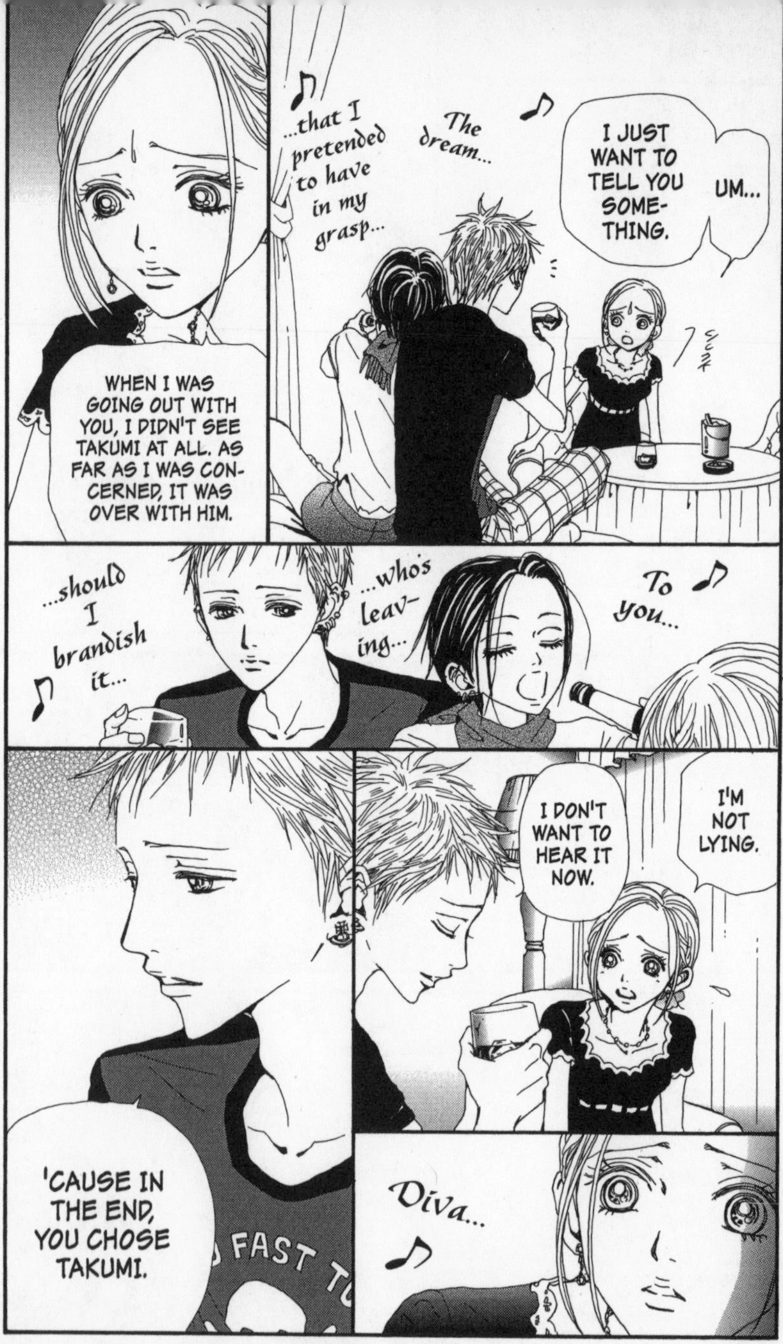
UM...
I JUST WANT TO TELL YOU SOMETHING.
The dream...
...that I pretended to have in my grasp...
GULK
WHEN I WAS GOING OUT WITH YOU, I DIDN'T SEE TAKUMI AT ALL. AS FAR AS I WAS CONCERNED, IT WAS OVER WITH HIM.
To you...
...who's leaving...
...should I brandish it...
I'M NOT LYING.
I DON'T WANT TO HEAR IT NOW.
Diva...
'CAUSE IN THE END, YOU CHOSE TAKUMI.

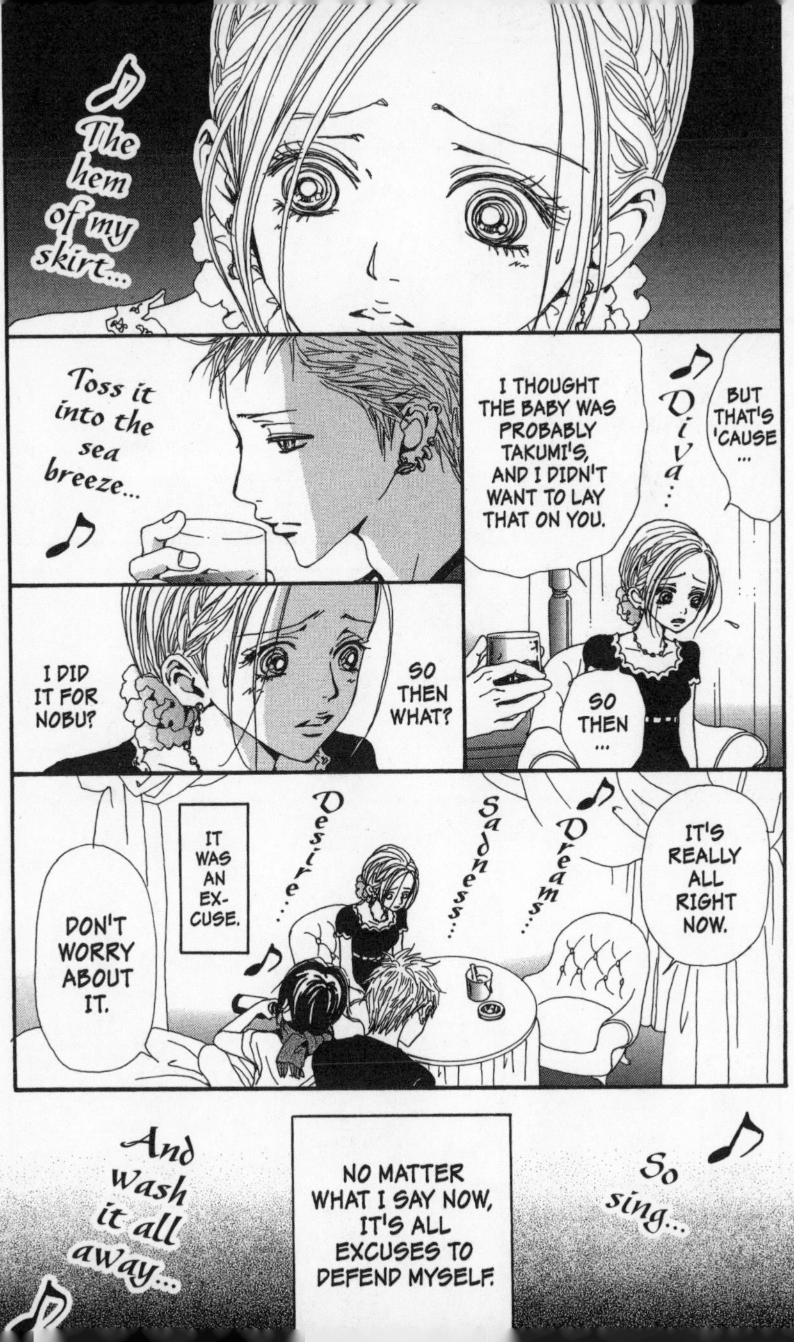
The hem of my skirt...
But that's 'cause ...
Diva...
I thought the baby was probably Takumi's, and I didn't want to lay that on you.
So then ...
Toss it into the sea breeze...
So then what?
I did it for Nobu?
It's really all right now.
Dreams...
Sadness...
Desire...
It was an excuse.
Don't worry about it.
So sing...
No matter what I say now, it's all excuses to defend myself.
And wash it all away...

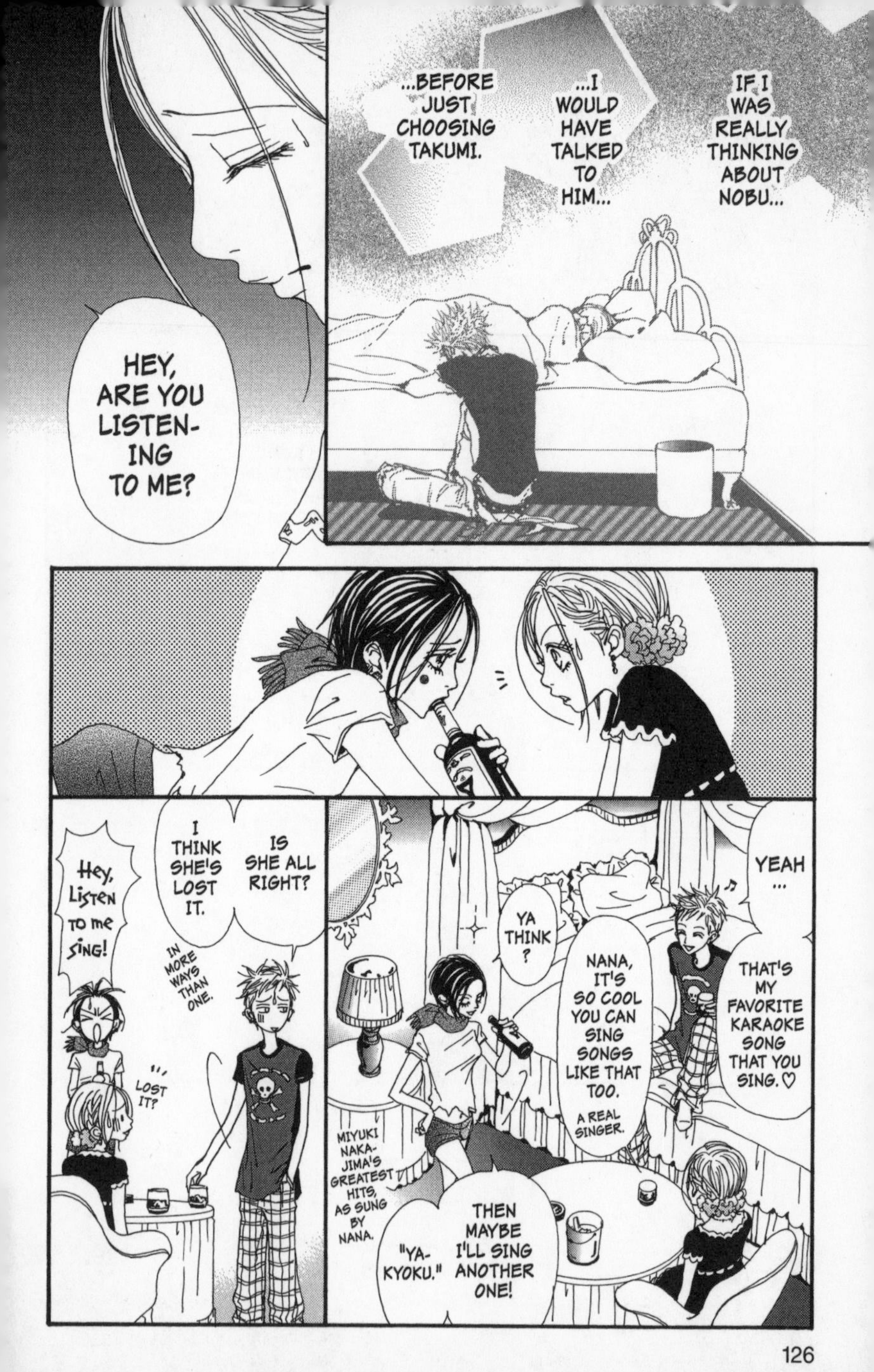
IF I WAS REALLY THINKING ABOUT NOBU...
...I WOULD HAVE TALKED TO HIM...
...BEFORE JUST CHOOSING TAKUMI.
HEY, ARE YOU LISTEN-ING TO ME?
YEAH ...
THAT'S MY FAVORITE KARAOKE SONG THAT YOU SING.♡
NANA, IT'S SO COOL YOU CAN SING SONGS LIKE THAT TOO.
A REAL SINGER.
YA THINK?
MIYUKI NAKA-JIMA'S GREATEST HITS, AS SUNG BY NANA.
THEN MAYBE I'LL SING ANOTHER ONE!
"YA-KYOKU."
IS SHE ALL RIGHT?
I THINK SHE'S LOST IT.
IN MORE WAYS THAN ONE.
Hey, Listen to me sing!
LOST IT?

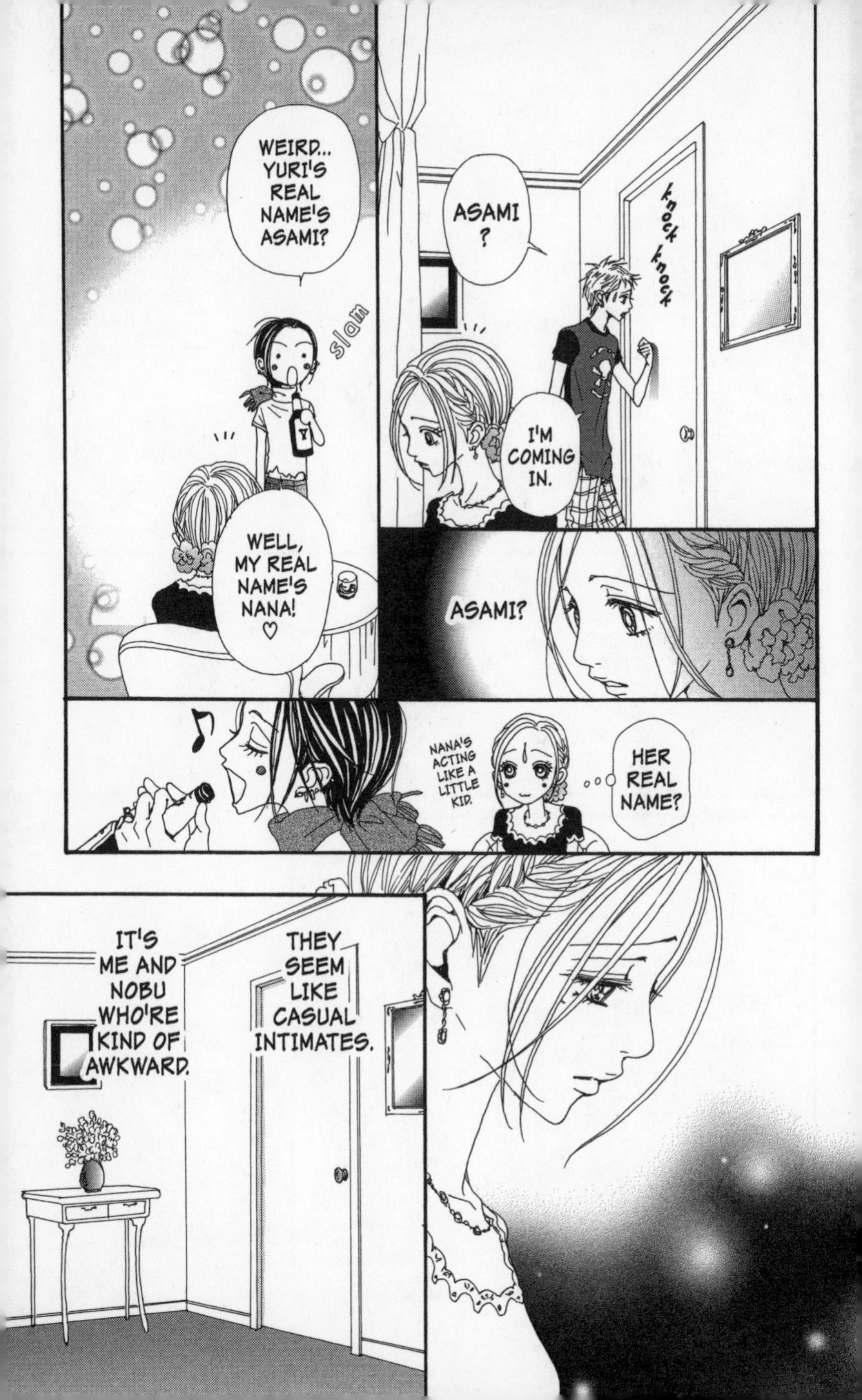

knock knock
ASAMI ?
I'M COMING IN.
ASAMI?
WEIRD... YURI'S REAL NAME'S ASAMI?
slam
WELL, MY REAL NAME'S NANA! ♡
HER REAL NAME?
NANA'S ACTING LIKE A LITTLE KID.
THEY SEEM LIKE CASUAL INTIMATES.
IT'S ME AND NOBU WHO'RE KIND OF AWKWARD.

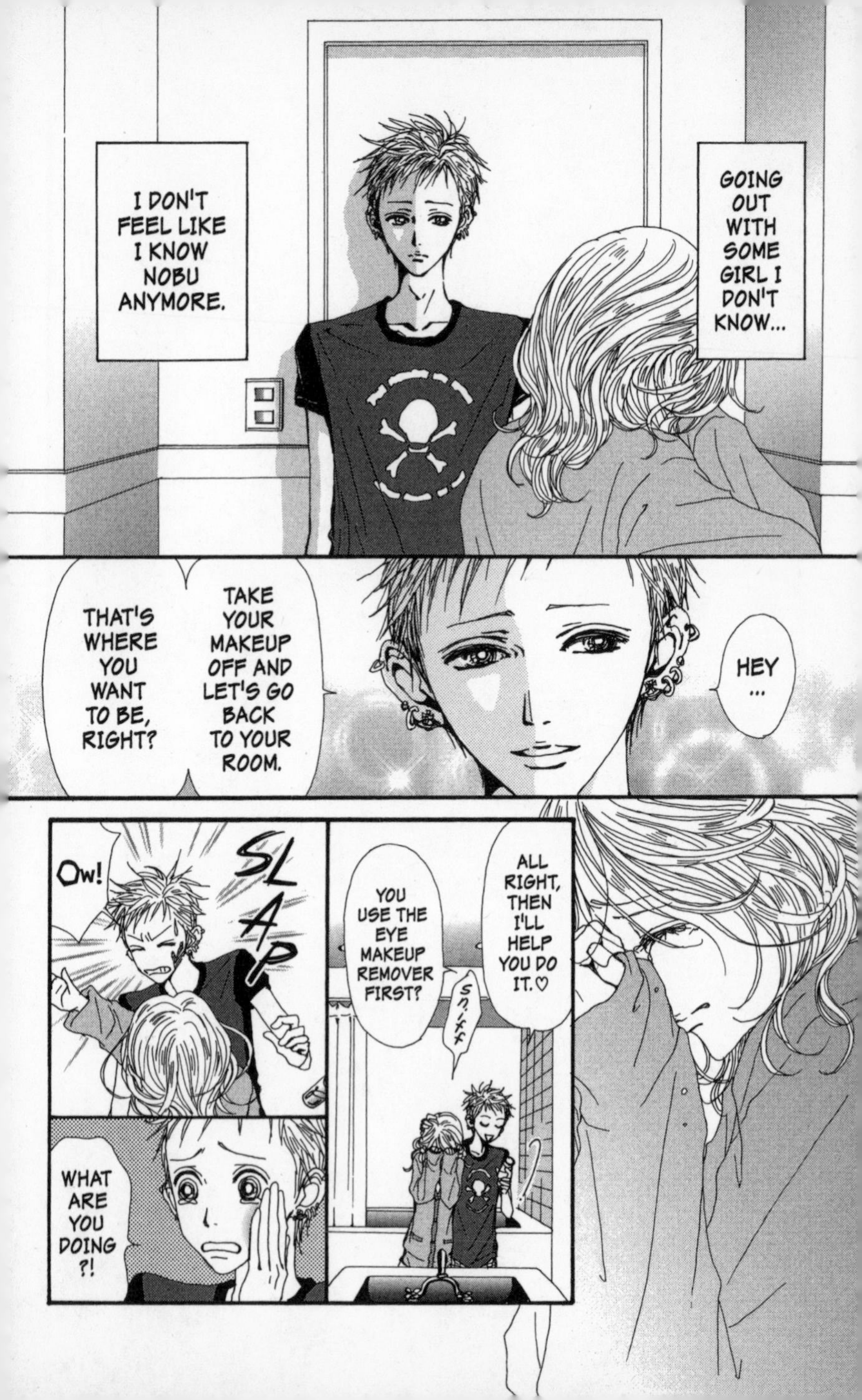
GOING OUT WITH SOME GIRL I DON'T KNOW...
I DON'T FEEL LIKE I KNOW NOBU ANYMORE.
HEY ...
TAKE YOUR MAKEUP OFF AND LET'S GO BACK TO YOUR ROOM.
THAT'S WHERE YOU WANT TO BE, RIGHT?
ALL RIGHT, THEN I'LL HELP YOU DO IT.♡
YOU USE THE EYE MAKEUP REMOVER FIRST?
sniff
SLAP
Ow!
WHAT ARE YOU DOING?!

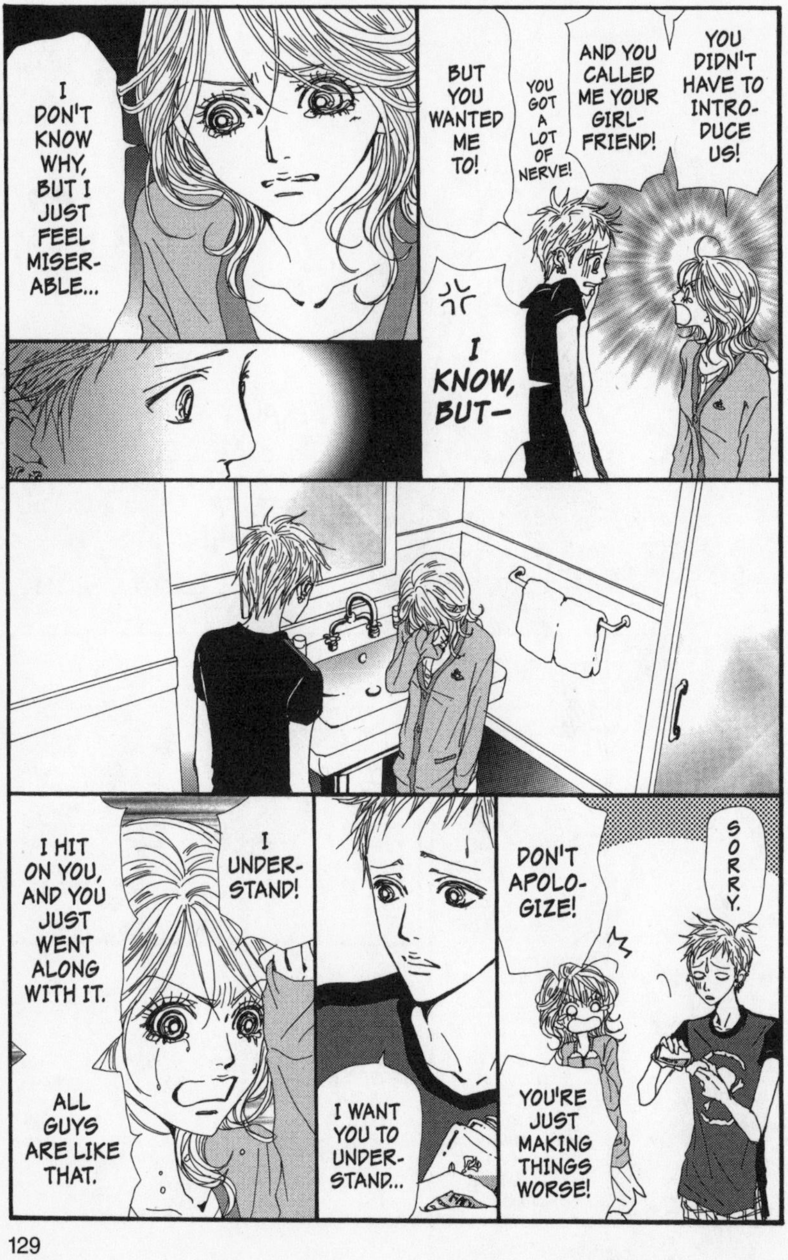
YOU DIDN'T HAVE TO INTRODUCE US!
AND YOU CALLED ME YOUR GIRLFRIEND!
YOU GOT A LOT OF NERVE!
BUT YOU WANTED ME TO!
I KNOW, BUT—
I DON'T KNOW WHY, BUT I JUST FEEL MISERABLE...
SORRY.
DON'T APOLOGIZE!
YOU'RE JUST MAKING THINGS WORSE!
I WANT YOU TO UNDERSTAND...
I UNDERSTAND!
I HIT ON YOU, AND YOU JUST WENT ALONG WITH IT.
ALL GUYS ARE LIKE THAT.

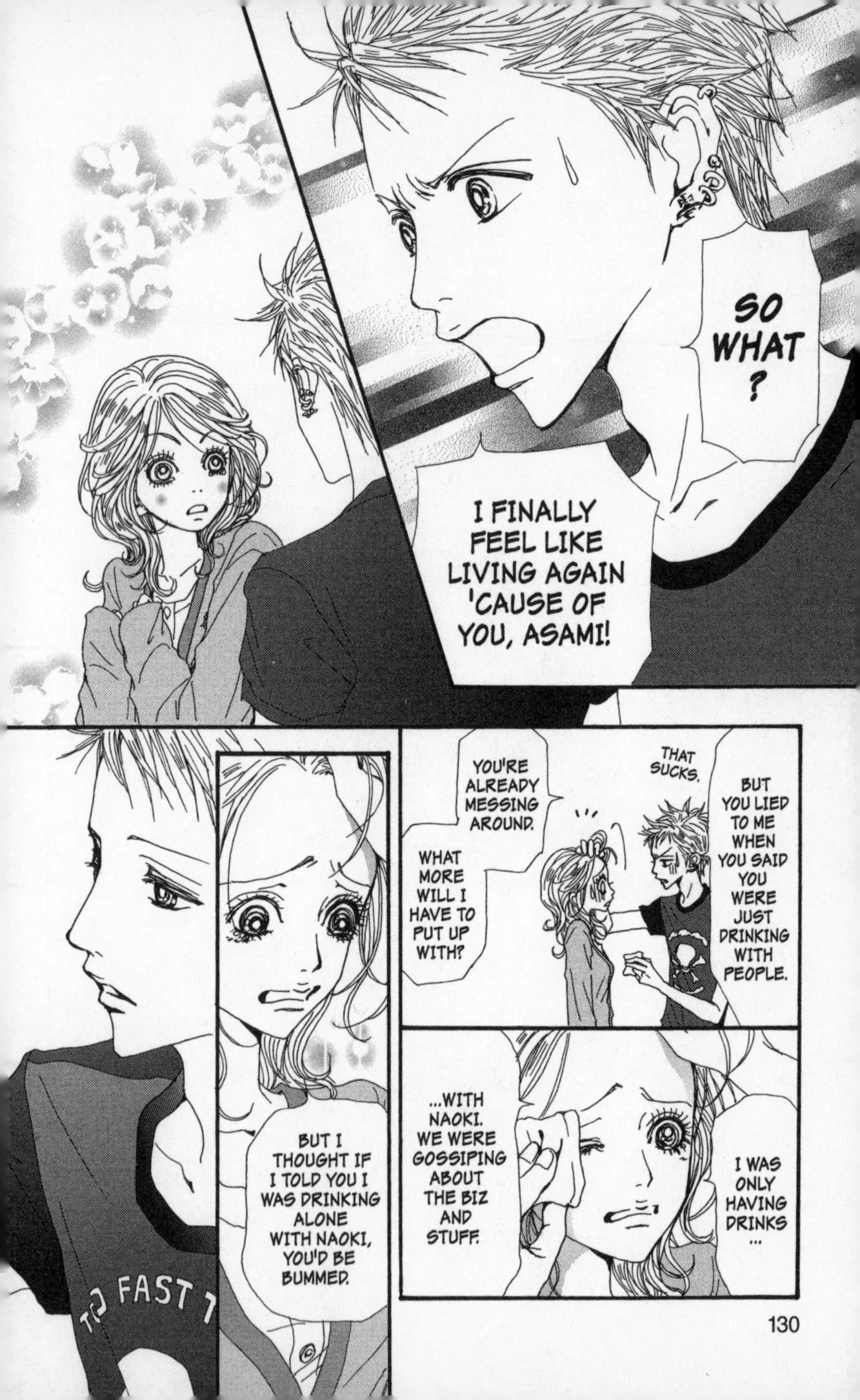
SO WHAT?
I FINALLY FEEL LIKE LIVING AGAIN 'CAUSE OF YOU, ASAMI!
THAT SUCKS.
BUT YOU LIED TO ME WHEN YOU SAID YOU WERE JUST DRINKING WITH PEOPLE.
YOU'RE ALREADY MESSING AROUND.
WHAT MORE WILL I HAVE TO PUT UP WITH?
I WAS ONLY HAVING DRINKS...
...WITH NAOKI. WE WERE GOSSIPING ABOUT THE BIZ AND STUFF.
BUT I THOUGHT IF I TOLD YOU I WAS DRINKING ALONE WITH NAOKI, YOU'D BE BUMMED.

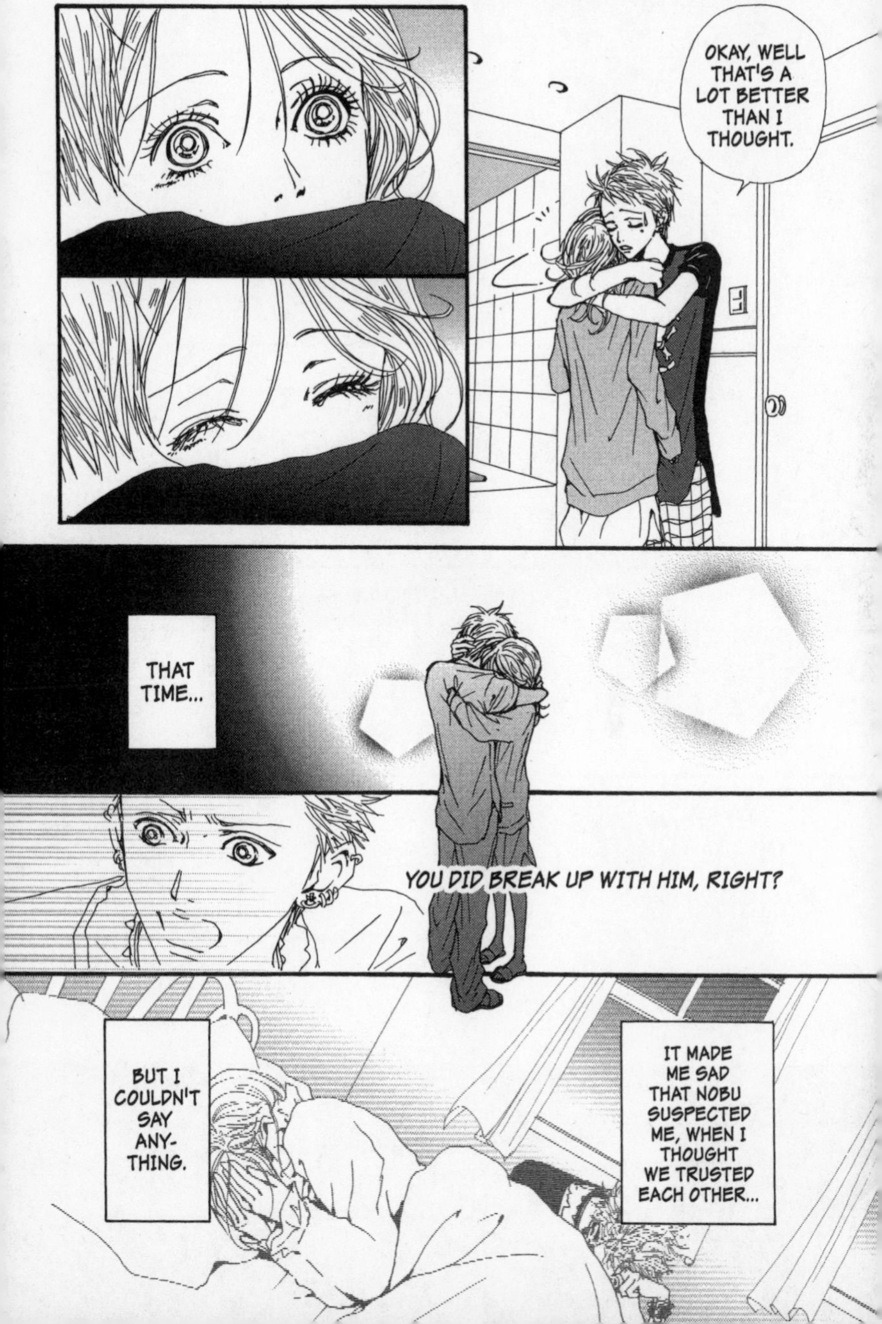
OKAY, WELL THAT'S A LOT BETTER THAN I THOUGHT.
THAT TIME...
YOU DID BREAK UP WITH HIM, RIGHT?
IT MADE ME SAD THAT NOBU SUSPECTED ME, WHEN I THOUGHT WE TRUSTED EACH OTHER...
BUT I COULDN'T SAY ANY-THING.

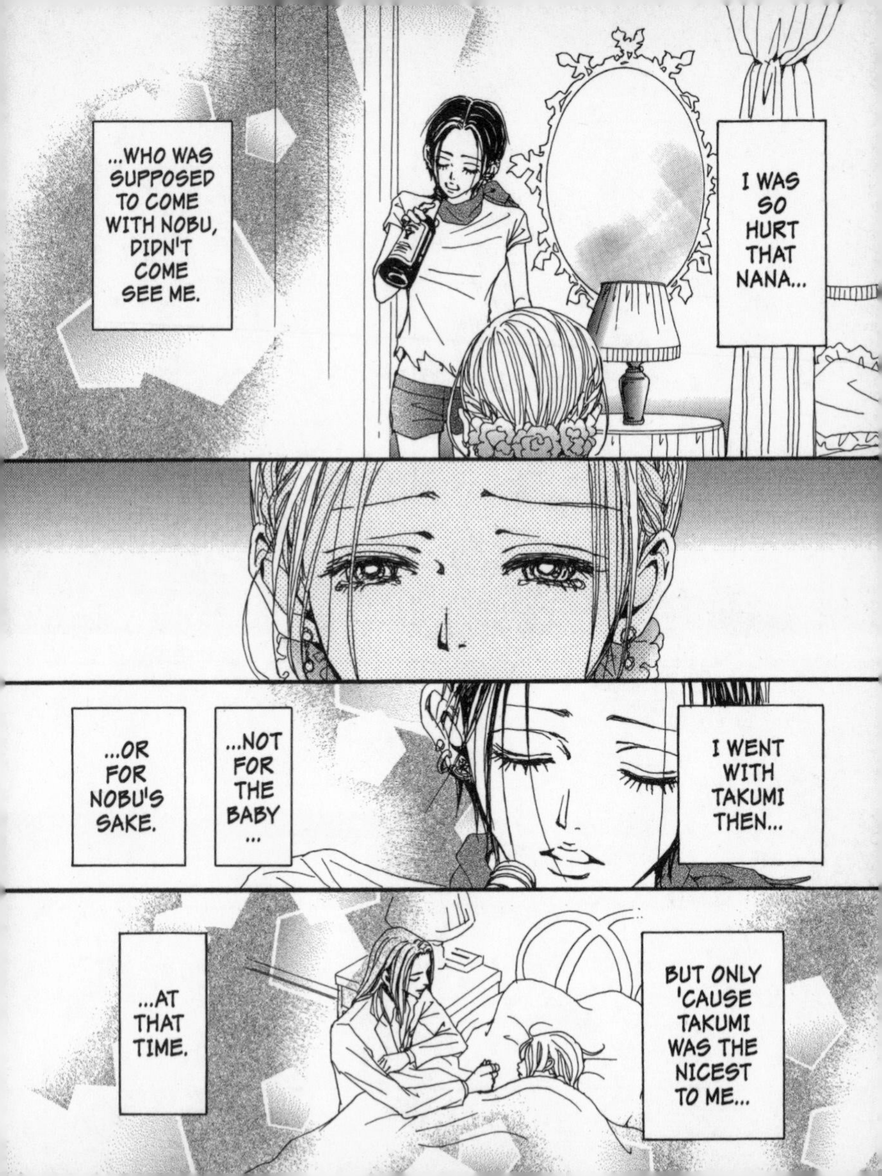
I WAS SO HURT THAT NANA...
...WHO WAS SUPPOSED TO COME WITH NOBU, DIDN'T COME SEE ME.
I WENT WITH TAKUMI THEN...
...NOT FOR THE BABY...
...OR FOR NOBU'S SAKE.
BUT ONLY 'CAUSE TAKUMI WAS THE NICEST TO ME...
...AT THAT TIME.

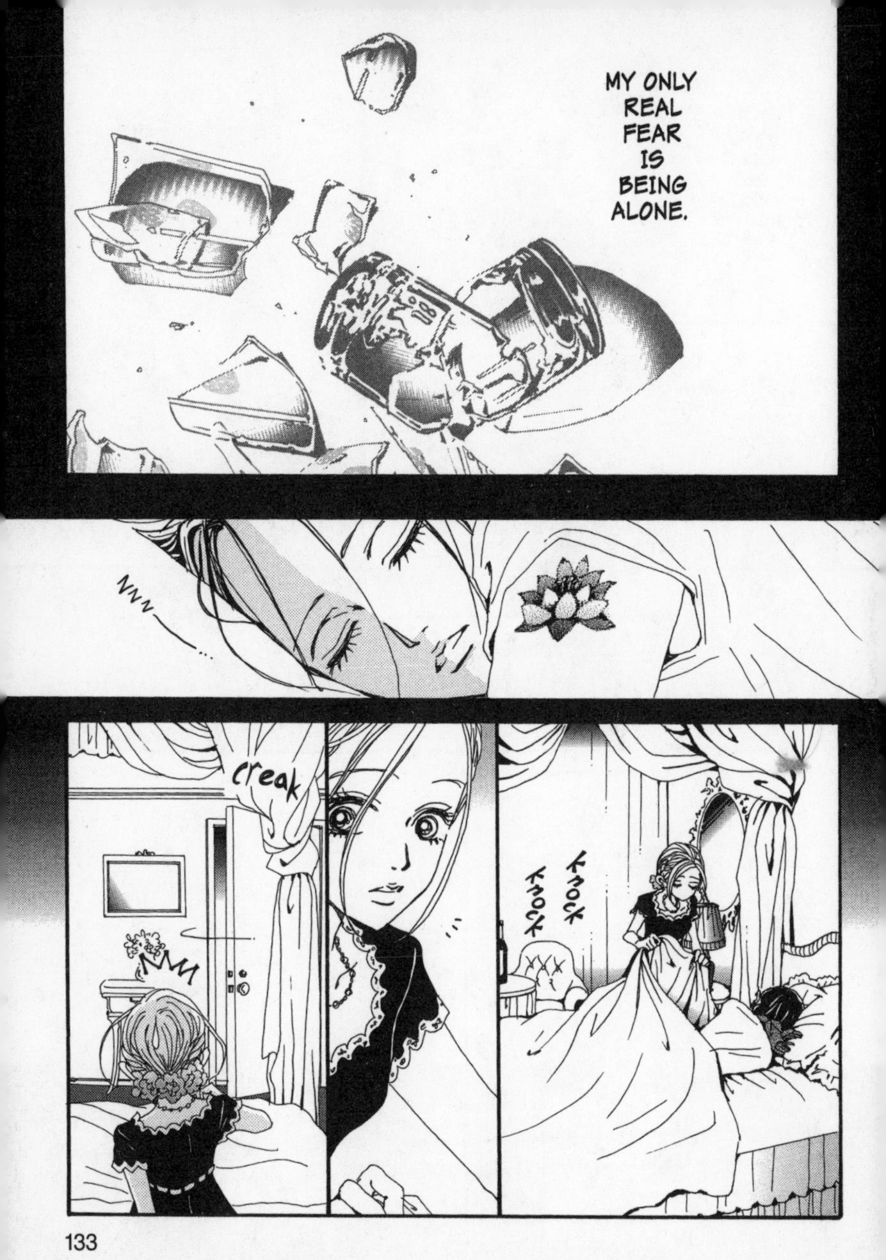
MY ONLY REAL FEAR IS BEING ALONE.
Nnn...
knock knock
creak

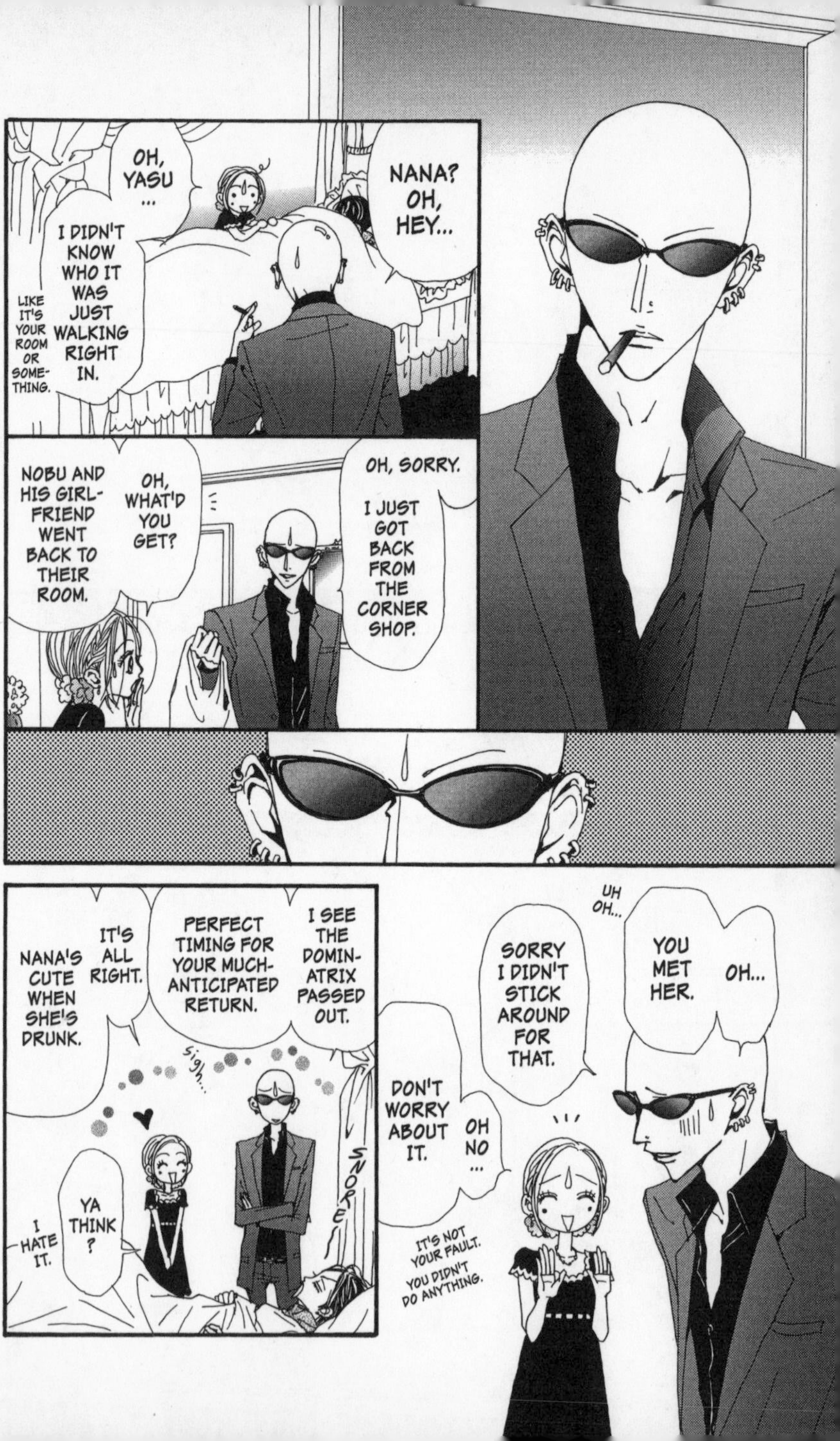
NANA? OH, HEY...
OH, YASU...
I DIDN'T KNOW WHO IT WAS JUST WALKING RIGHT IN.
LIKE IT'S YOUR ROOM OR SOME-THING.
OH, SORRY.
I JUST GOT BACK FROM THE CORNER SHOP.
OH, WHAT'D YOU GET?
NOBU AND HIS GIRL-FRIEND WENT BACK TO THEIR ROOM.
OH...
YOU MET HER.
UH OH...
SORRY I DIDN'T STICK AROUND FOR THAT.
DON'T WORRY ABOUT IT.
OH NO...
IT'S NOT YOUR FAULT. YOU DIDN'T DO ANYTHING.
I SEE THE DOMIN-ATRIX PASSED OUT.
PERFECT TIMING FOR YOUR MUCH-ANTICIPATED RETURN.
IT'S ALL RIGHT.
NANA'S CUTE WHEN SHE'S DRUNK.
sigh...
SNORE
YA THINK?
I HATE IT.

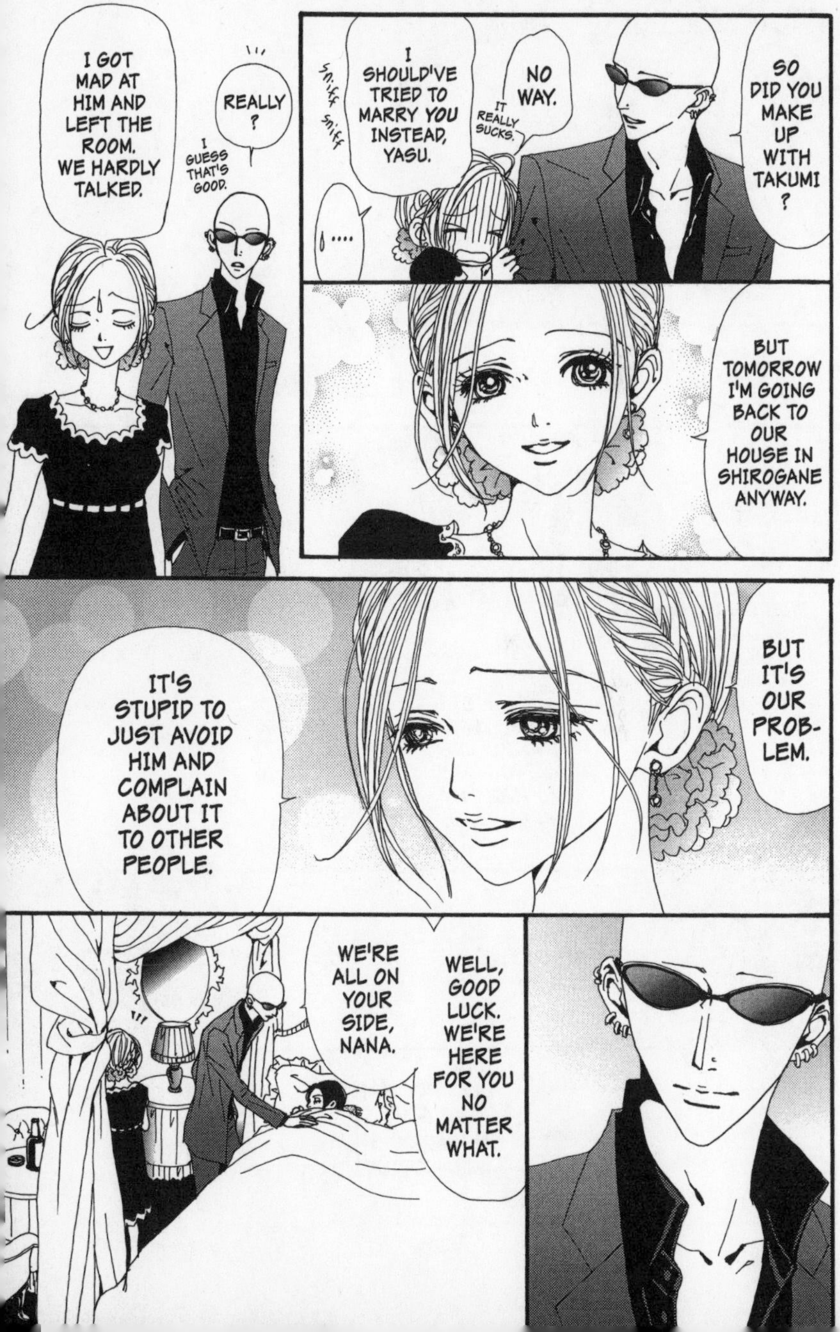
SO DID YOU MAKE UP WITH TAKUMI?
NO WAY.
IT REALLY SUCKS.
I SHOULD'VE TRIED TO MARRY YOU INSTEAD, YASU.
sniff sniff
I....
BUT TOMORROW I'M GOING BACK TO OUR HOUSE IN SHIROGANE ANYWAY.
I GOT MAD AT HIM AND LEFT THE ROOM. WE HARDLY TALKED.
REALLY?
I GUESS THAT'S GOOD.
BUT IT'S OUR PROB-LEM.
IT'S STUPID TO JUST AVOID HIM AND COMPLAIN ABOUT IT TO OTHER PEOPLE.
WELL, GOOD LUCK. WE'RE HERE FOR YOU NO MATTER WHAT.
WE'RE ALL ON YOUR SIDE, NANA.

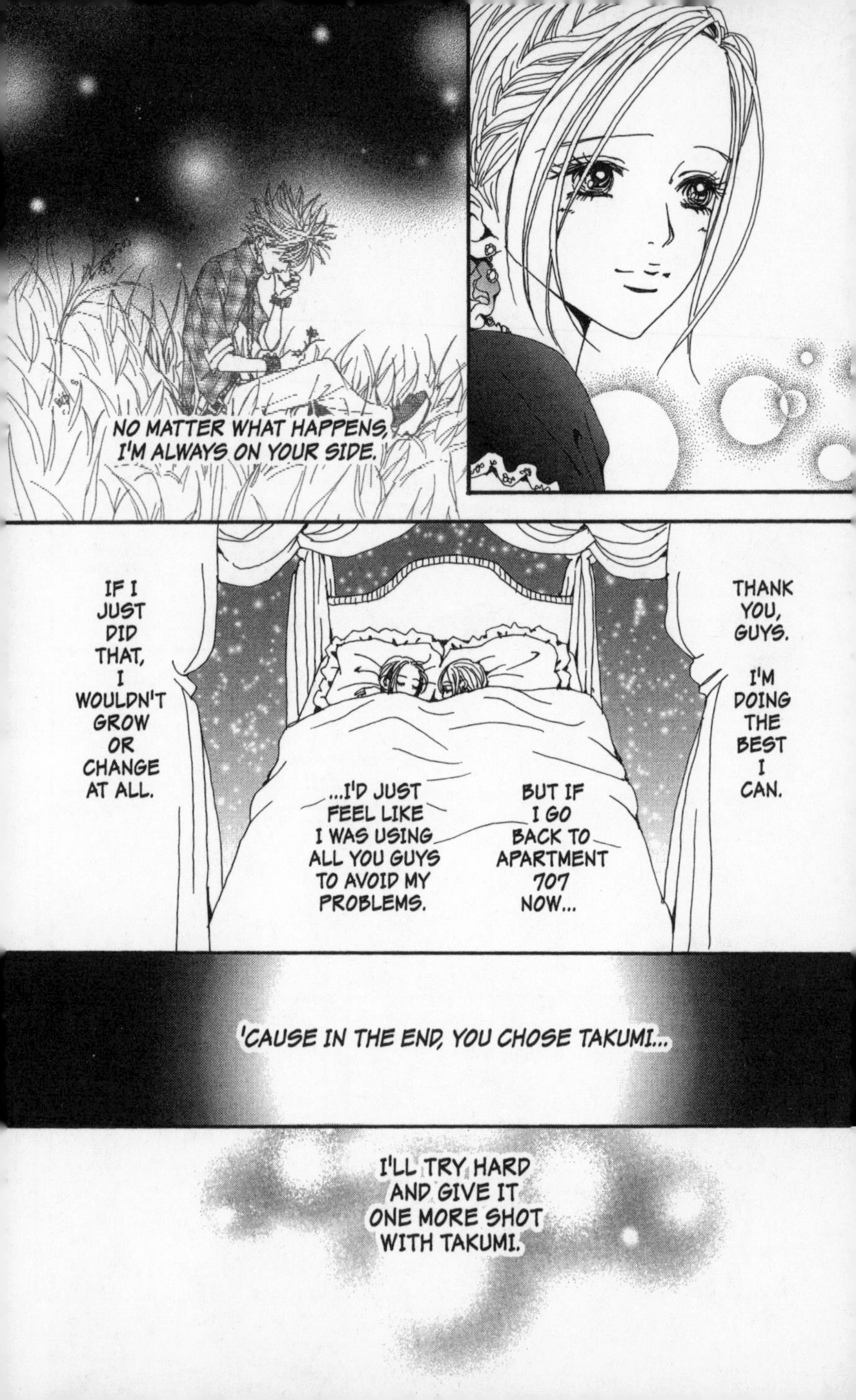
NO MATTER WHAT HAPPENS, I'M ALWAYS ON YOUR SIDE.
THANK YOU, GUYS.
I'M DOING THE BEST I CAN.
BUT IF I GO BACK TO APARTMENT 707 NOW...
...I'D JUST FEEL LIKE I WAS USING ALL YOU GUYS TO AVOID MY PROBLEMS.
IF I JUST DID THAT, I WOULDN'T GROW OR CHANGE AT ALL.
'CAUSE IN THE END, YOU CHOSE TAKUMI...
I'LL TRY HARD AND GIVE IT ONE MORE SHOT WITH TAKUMI.

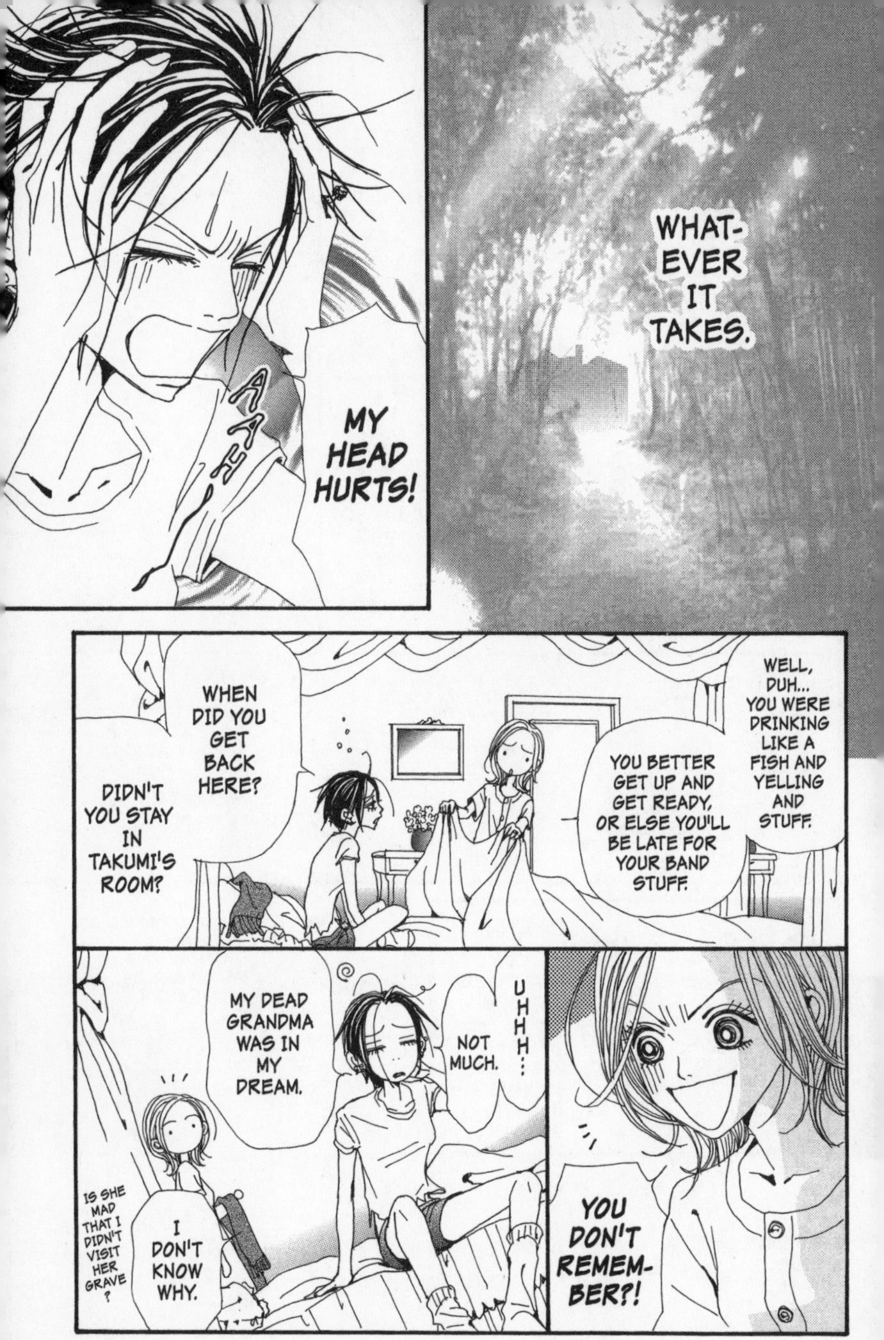
WHAT-EVER IT TAKES.
AAAH
MY HEAD HURTS!
WELL, DUH... YOU WERE DRINKING LIKE A FISH AND YELLING AND STUFF.
YOU BETTER GET UP AND GET READY, OR ELSE YOU'LL BE LATE FOR YOUR BAND STUFF.
WHEN DID YOU GET BACK HERE?
DIDN'T YOU STAY IN TAKUMI'S ROOM?
YOU DON'T REMEMBER?!
UHHH...
NOT MUCH.
MY DEAD GRANDMA WAS IN MY DREAM.
I DON'T KNOW WHY.
IS SHE MAD THAT I DIDN'T VISIT HER GRAVE?

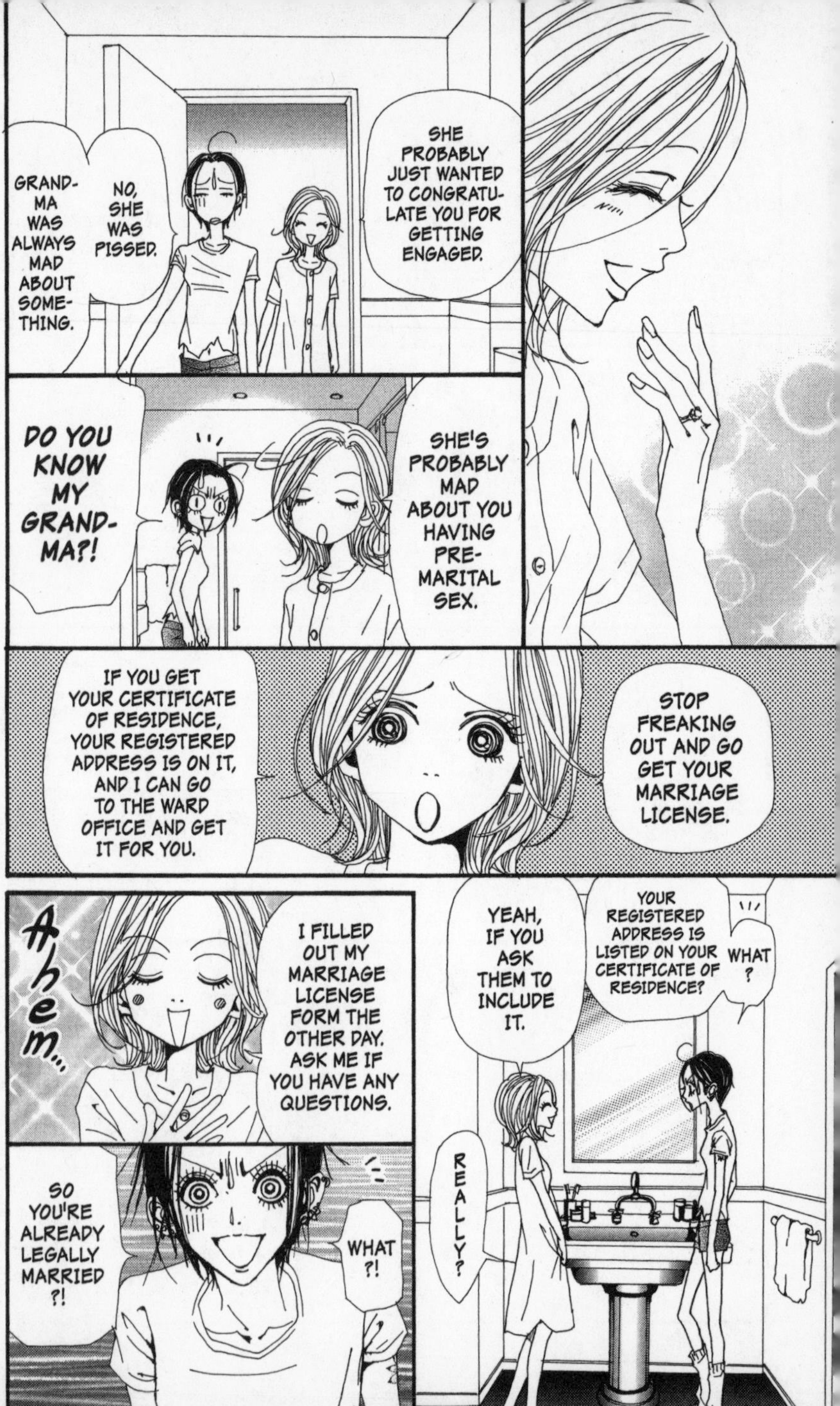
SHE PROBABLY JUST WANTED TO CONGRATULATE YOU FOR GETTING ENGAGED.
NO, SHE WAS PISSED.
GRANDMA WAS ALWAYS MAD ABOUT SOMETHING.
SHE'S PROBABLY MAD ABOUT YOU HAVING PREMARITAL SEX.
DO YOU KNOW MY GRANDMA?!
STOP FREAKING OUT AND GO GET YOUR MARRIAGE LICENSE.
IF YOU GET YOUR CERTIFICATE OF RESIDENCE, YOUR REGISTERED ADDRESS IS ON IT, AND I CAN GO TO THE WARD OFFICE AND GET IT FOR YOU.
WHAT?
YOUR REGISTERED ADDRESS IS LISTED ON YOUR CERTIFICATE OF RESIDENCE?
YEAH, IF YOU ASK THEM TO INCLUDE IT.
REALLY?
I FILLED OUT MY MARRIAGE LICENSE FORM THE OTHER DAY. ASK ME IF YOU HAVE ANY QUESTIONS.
Ahem...
WHAT?!
SO YOU'RE ALREADY LEGALLY MARRIED?!

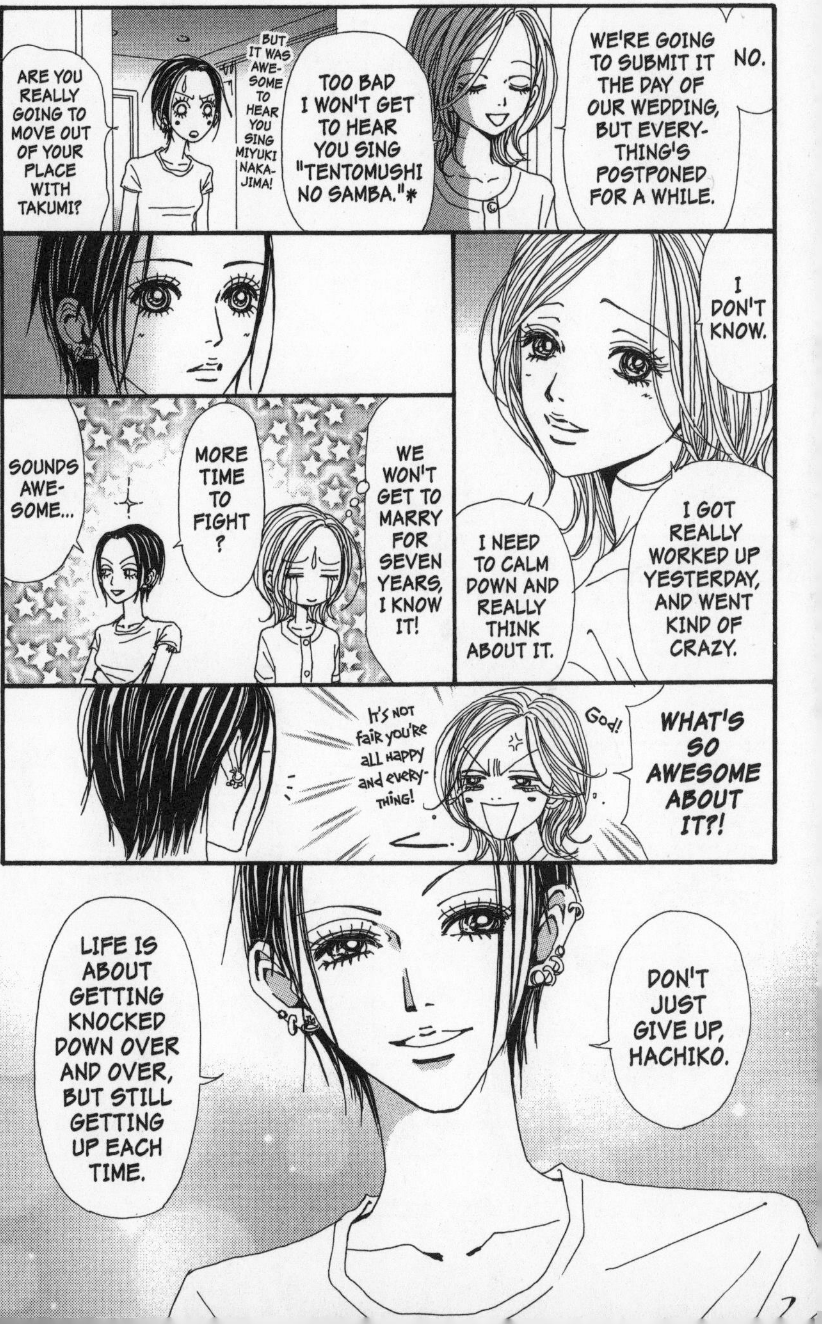
NO.
WE'RE GOING TO SUBMIT IT THE DAY OF OUR WEDDING, BUT EVERYTHING'S POSTPONED FOR A WHILE.
TOO BAD I WON'T GET TO HEAR YOU SING "TENTOMUSHI NO SAMBA."*
BUT IT WAS AWESOME TO HEAR YOU SING MIYUKI NAKAJIMA!
ARE YOU REALLY GOING TO MOVE OUT OF YOUR PLACE WITH TAKUMI?
I DON'T KNOW.
I GOT REALLY WORKED UP YESTERDAY, AND WENT KIND OF CRAZY.
I NEED TO CALM DOWN AND REALLY THINK ABOUT IT.
WE WON'T GET TO MARRY FOR SEVEN YEARS, I KNOW IT!
MORE TIME TO FIGHT?
SOUNDS AWESOME...
WHAT'S SO AWESOME ABOUT IT?!
God!
It's not fair you're all happy and everything!
DON'T JUST GIVE UP, HACHIKO.
LIFE IS ABOUT GETTING KNOCKED DOWN OVER AND OVER, BUT STILL GETTING UP EACH TIME.

* A popular song at weddings.

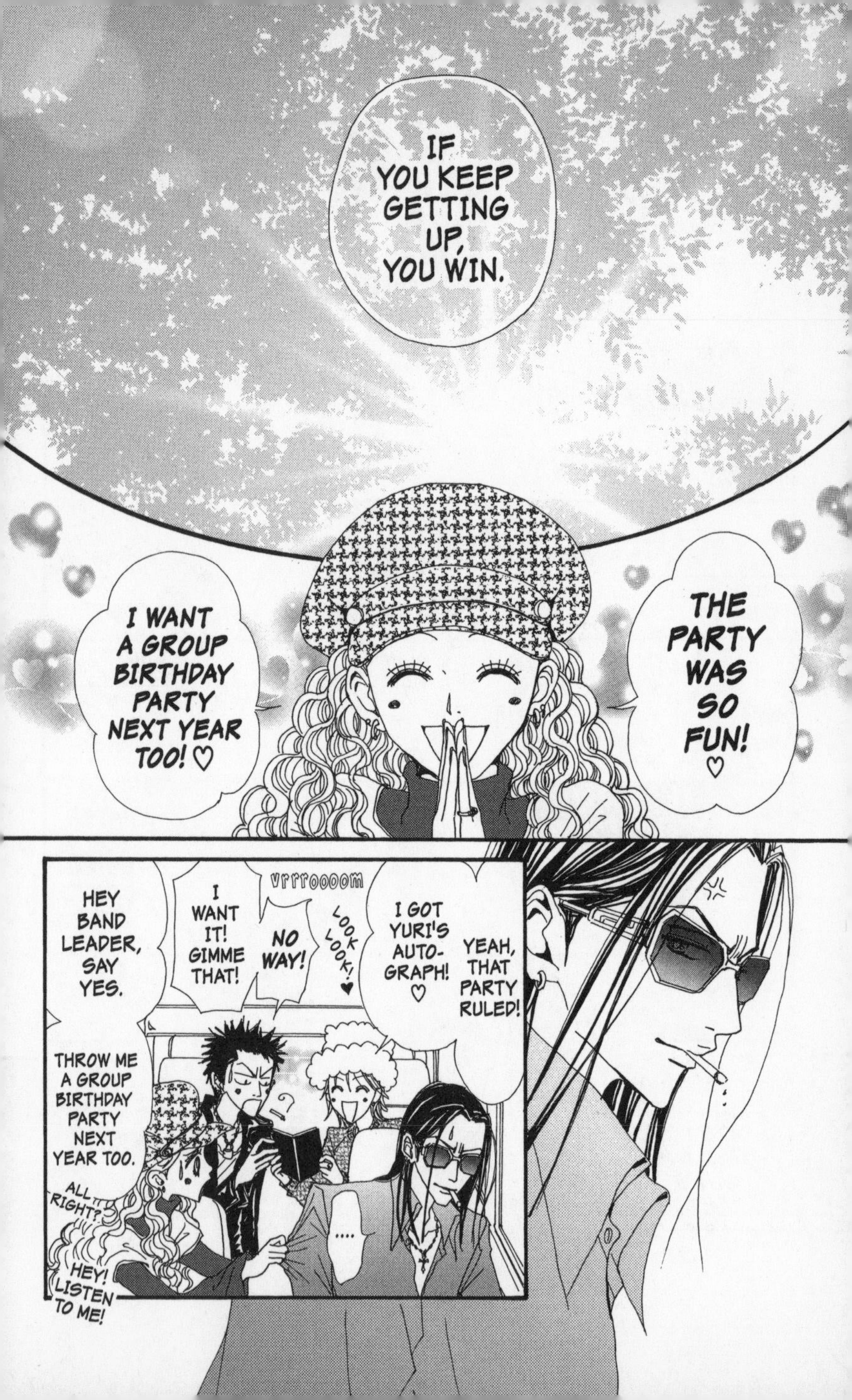
IF YOU KEEP GETTING UP, YOU WIN.
THE PARTY WAS SO FUN! ♡
I WANT A GROUP BIRTHDAY PARTY NEXT YEAR TOO! ♡
YEAH, THAT PARTY RULED!
I GOT YURI'S AUTO-GRAPH! ♡
LOOK LOOK! ♥
vrrroooom
NO WAY!
I WANT IT! GIMME THAT!
HEY BAND LEADER, SAY YES.
THROW ME A GROUP BIRTHDAY PARTY NEXT YEAR TOO.
ALL RIGHT?
....
HEY! LISTEN TO ME!

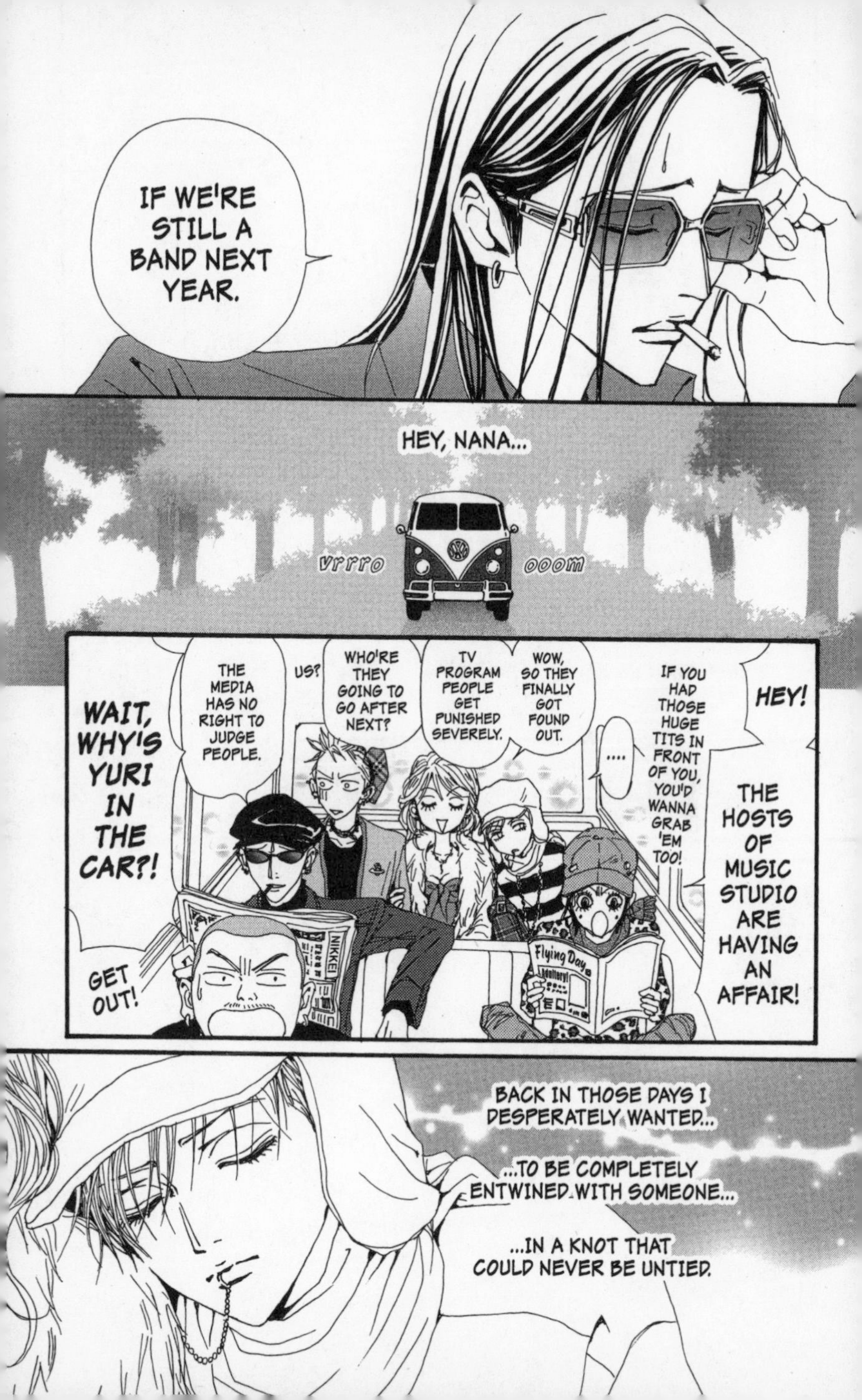
IF WE'RE STILL A BAND NEXT YEAR.
HEY, NANA...
vrrro ooom
HEY!
THE HOSTS OF MUSIC STUDIO ARE HAVING AN AFFAIR!
IF YOU HAD THOSE HUGE TITS IN FRONT OF YOU, YOU'D WANNA GRAB 'EM TOO!
....
WOW, SO THEY FINALLY GOT FOUND OUT.
TV PROGRAM PEOPLE GET PUNISHED SEVERELY.
WHO'RE THEY GOING TO GO AFTER NEXT?
US?
THE MEDIA HAS NO RIGHT TO JUDGE PEOPLE.
Flying Day
NIKKEI
WAIT, WHY'S YURI IN THE CAR?!
GET OUT!
BACK IN THOSE DAYS I DESPERATELY WANTED...
...TO BE COMPLETELY ENTWINED WITH SOMEONE...
...IN A KNOT THAT COULD NEVER BE UNTIED.

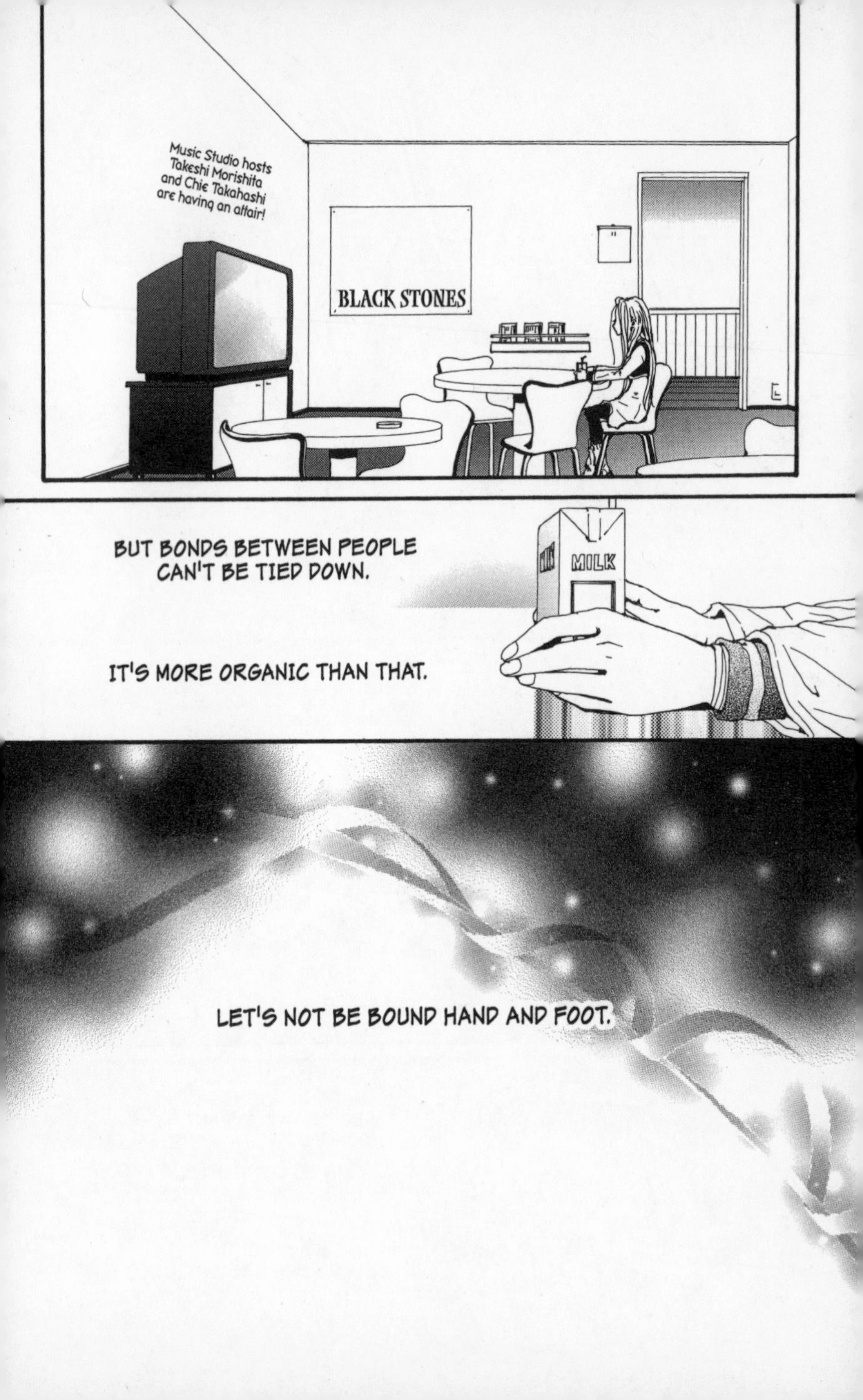
Music Studio hosts Takeshi Morishita and Chie Takahashi are having an affair!
BLACK STONES
MILK
BUT BONDS BETWEEN PEOPLE CAN'T BE TIED DOWN.
IT'S MORE ORGANIC THAN THAT.
LET'S NOT BE BOUND HAND AND FOOT.

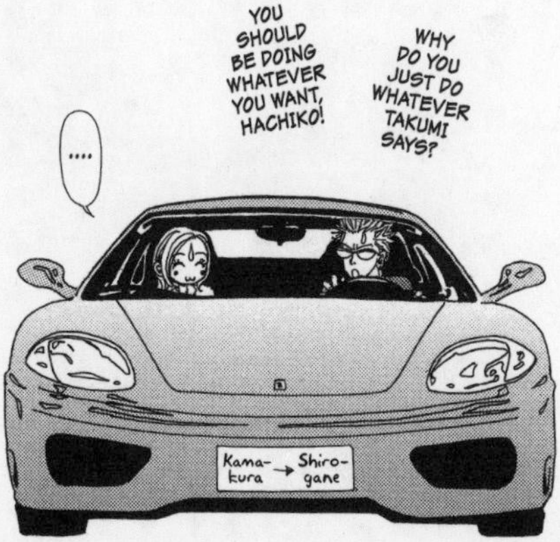
WHY DO YOU JUST DO WHATEVER TAKUMI SAYS?
YOU SHOULD BE DOING WHATEVER YOU WANT, HACHIKO!
....
Kama-kura → Shiro-gane

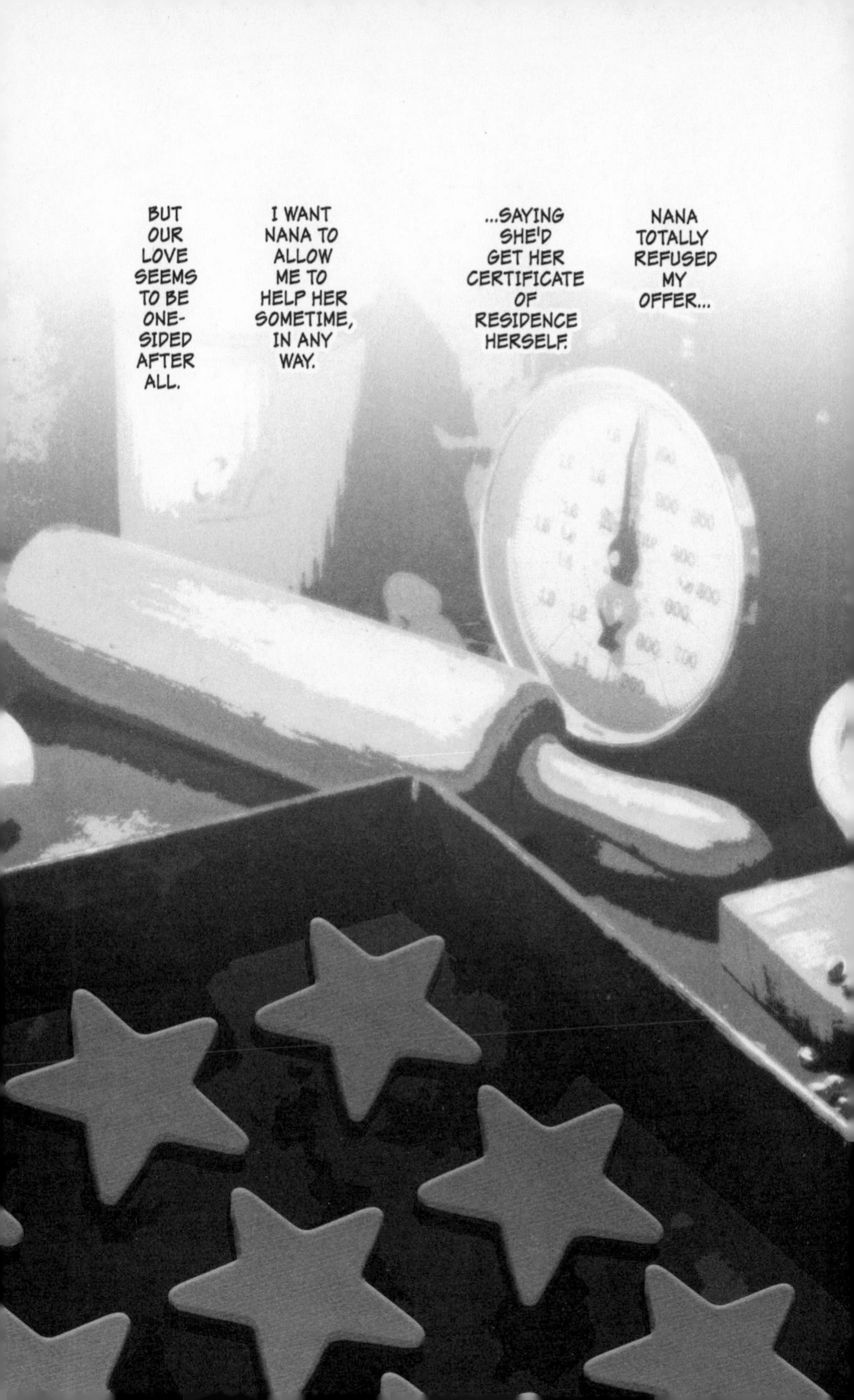
NANA TOTALLY REFUSED MY OFFER...
...SAYING SHE'D GET HER CERTIFICATE OF RESIDENCE HERSELF.
I WANT NANA TO ALLOW ME TO HELP HER SOMETIME, IN ANY WAY.
BUT OUR LOVE SEEMS TO BE ONE-SIDED AFTER ALL.

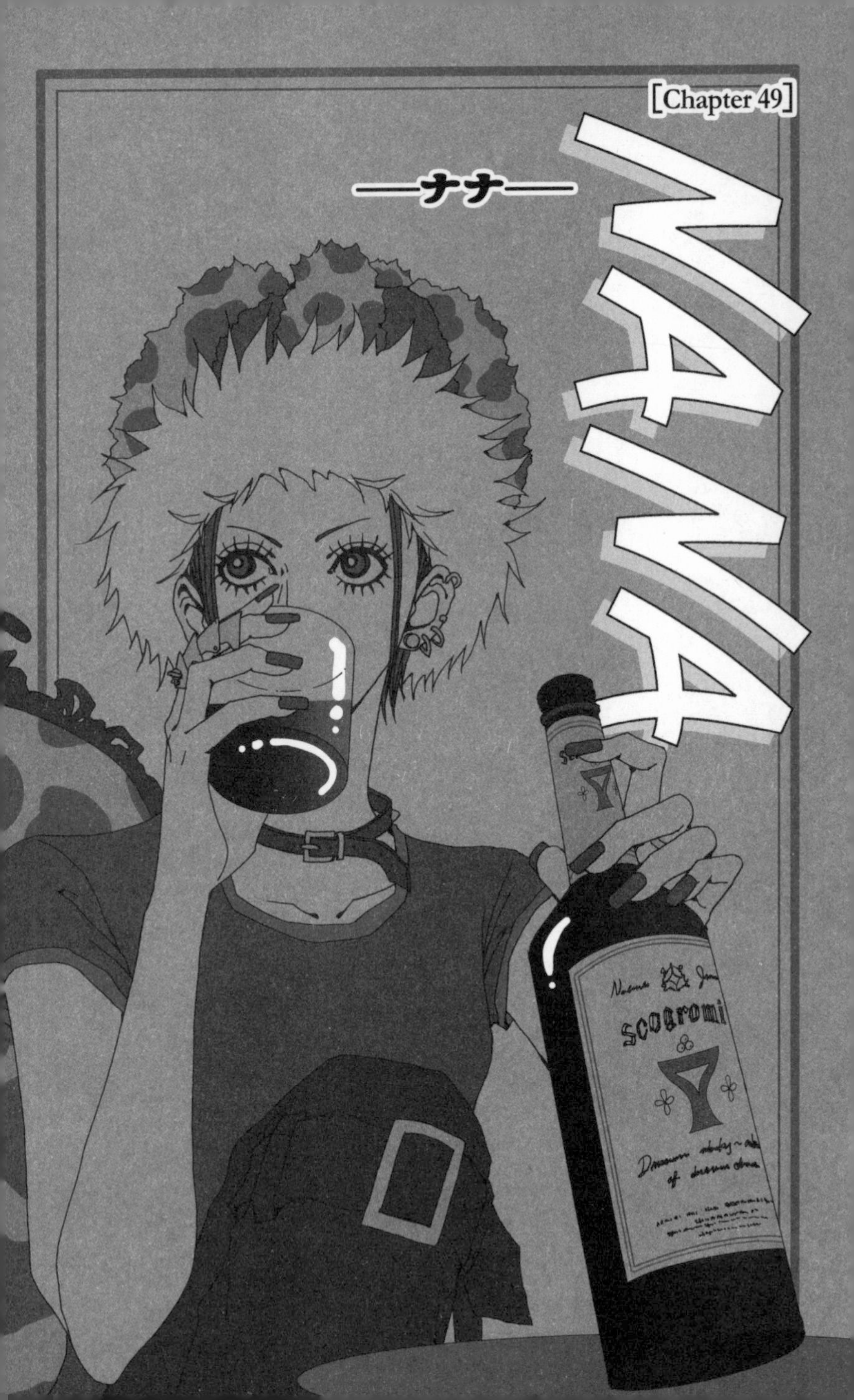
[Chapter 49]
NANA
—ナナ—

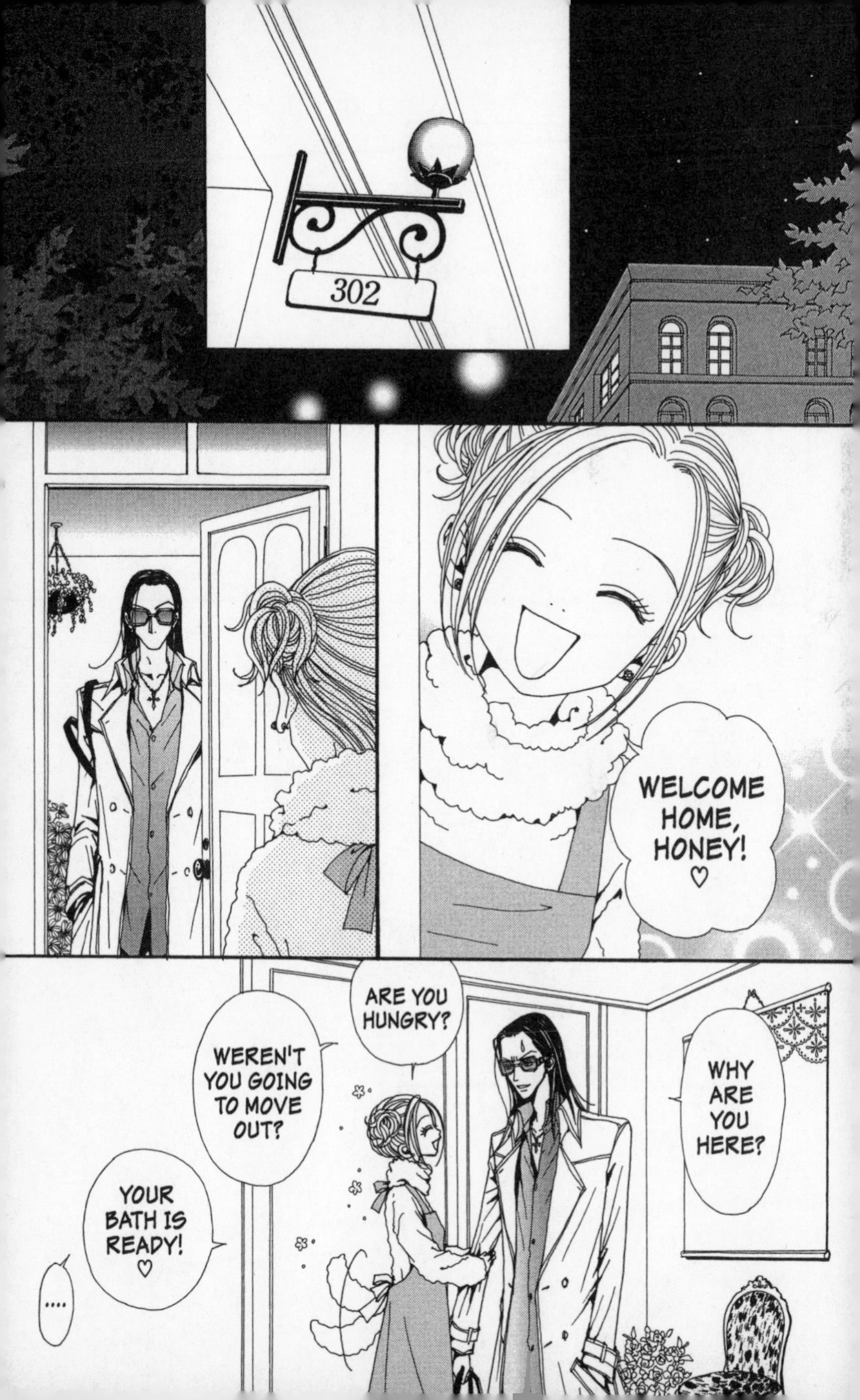
302
WELCOME HOME, HONEY! ♡
WHY ARE YOU HERE?
ARE YOU HUNGRY?
WEREN'T YOU GOING TO MOVE OUT?
YOUR BATH IS READY! ♡
....

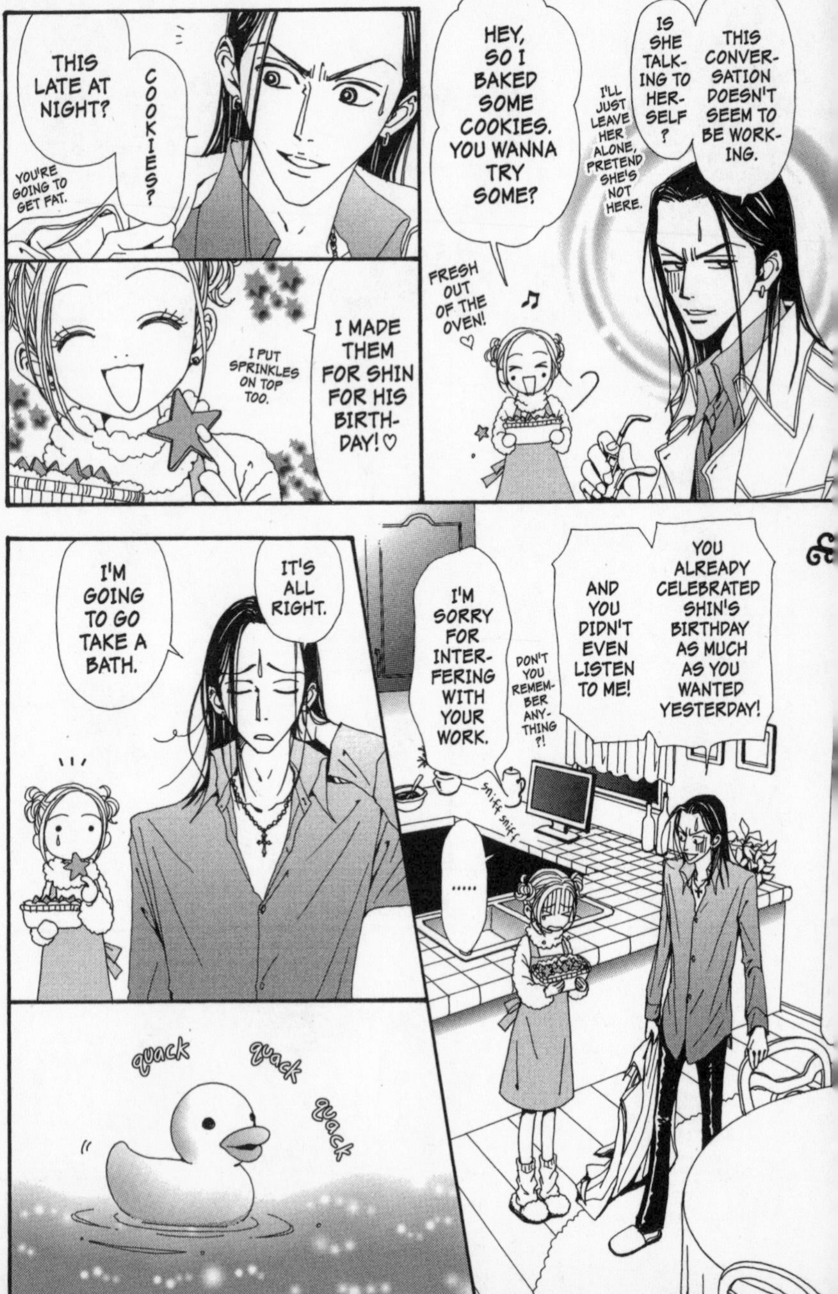
THIS CONVER-SATION DOESN'T SEEM TO BE WORK-ING.
IS SHE TALK-ING TO HER-SELF?
I'LL JUST LEAVE HER ALONE, PRETEND SHE'S NOT HERE.
HEY, SO I BAKED SOME COOKIES. YOU WANNA TRY SOME?
FRESH OUT OF THE OVEN! ♡
COOKIES?
THIS LATE AT NIGHT?
YOU'RE GOING TO GET FAT.
I MADE THEM FOR SHIN FOR HIS BIRTH-DAY! ♡
I PUT SPRINKLES ON TOP TOO.
YOU ALREADY CELEBRATED SHIN'S BIRTHDAY AS MUCH AS YOU WANTED YESTERDAY!
AND YOU DIDN'T EVEN LISTEN TO ME!
DON'T YOU REMEM-BER ANY-THING?!
I'M SORRY FOR INTER-FERING WITH YOUR WORK.
sniff sniff
......
IT'S ALL RIGHT.
I'M GOING TO GO TAKE A BATH.
quack
quack
quack

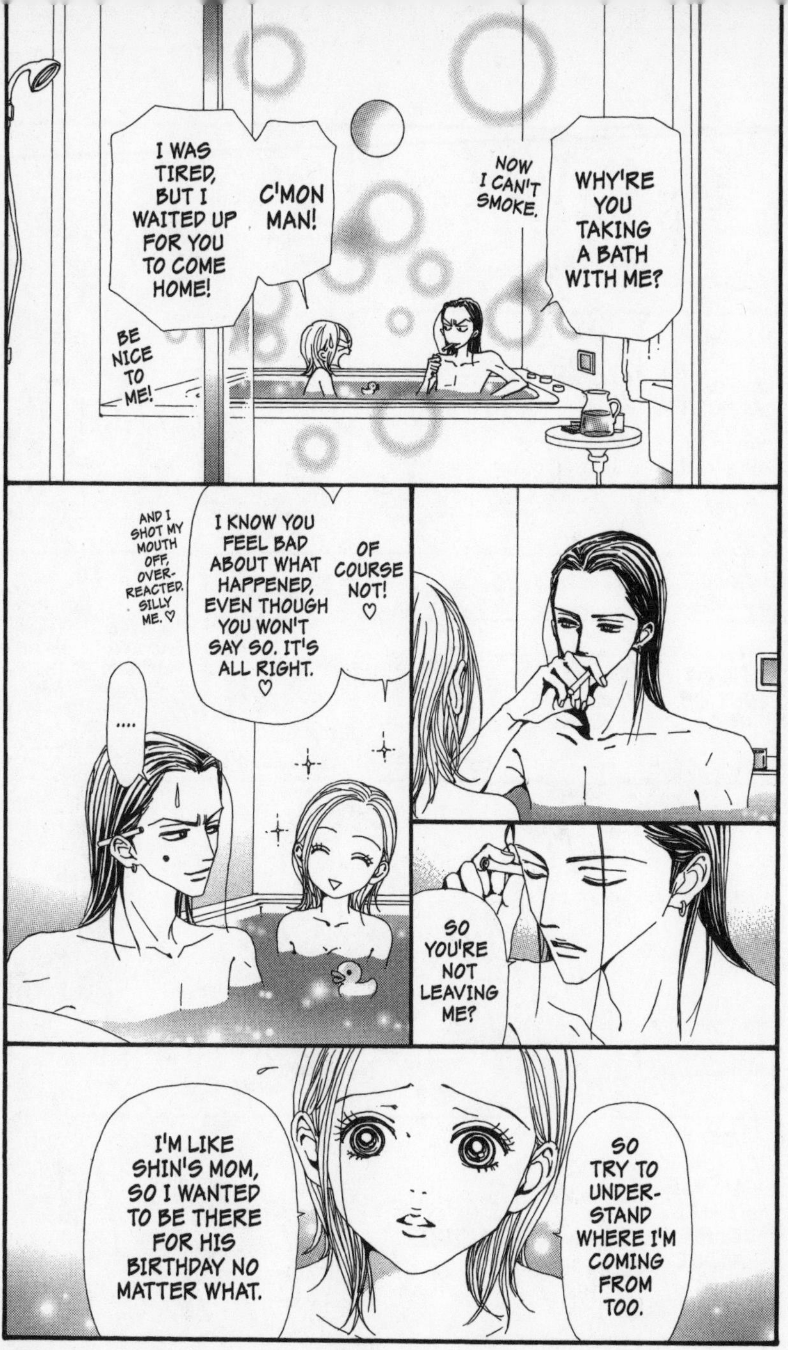
WHY'RE YOU TAKING A BATH WITH ME?
NOW I CAN'T SMOKE.
C'MON MAN!
I WAS TIRED, BUT I WAITED UP FOR YOU TO COME HOME!
BE NICE TO ME!
SO YOU'RE NOT LEAVING ME?
OF COURSE NOT! ♡
I KNOW YOU FEEL BAD ABOUT WHAT HAPPENED, EVEN THOUGH YOU WON'T SAY SO. IT'S ALL RIGHT. ♡
AND I SHOT MY MOUTH OFF, OVER-REACTED. SILLY ME. ♡
....
I'M LIKE SHIN'S MOM, SO I WANTED TO BE THERE FOR HIS BIRTHDAY NO MATTER WHAT.
SO TRY TO UNDER-STAND WHERE I'M COMING FROM TOO.

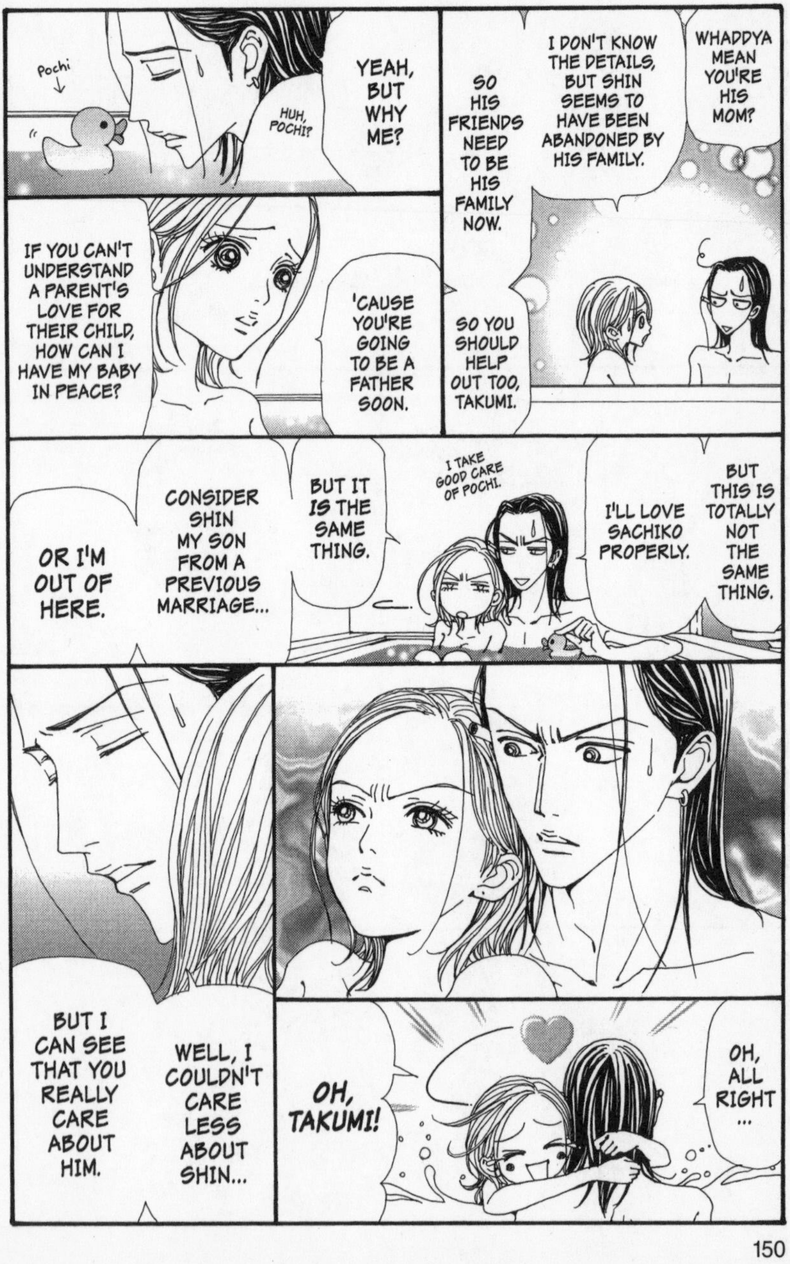
WHADDYA MEAN YOU'RE HIS MOM?
I DON'T KNOW THE DETAILS, BUT SHIN SEEMS TO HAVE BEEN ABANDONED BY HIS FAMILY.
SO HIS FRIENDS NEED TO BE HIS FAMILY NOW.
SO YOU SHOULD HELP OUT TOO, TAKUMI.
YEAH, BUT WHY ME?
HUH, POCHI?
Pochi
'CAUSE YOU'RE GOING TO BE A FATHER SOON.
IF YOU CAN'T UNDERSTAND A PARENT'S LOVE FOR THEIR CHILD, HOW CAN I HAVE MY BABY IN PEACE?
BUT THIS IS TOTALLY NOT THE SAME THING.
I'LL LOVE SACHIKO PROPERLY.
I TAKE GOOD CARE OF POCHI.
BUT IT IS THE SAME THING.
CONSIDER SHIN MY SON FROM A PREVIOUS MARRIAGE...
OR I'M OUT OF HERE.
OH, ALL RIGHT...
OH, TAKUMI!
WELL, I COULDN'T CARE LESS ABOUT SHIN...
BUT I CAN SEE THAT YOU REALLY CARE ABOUT HIM.

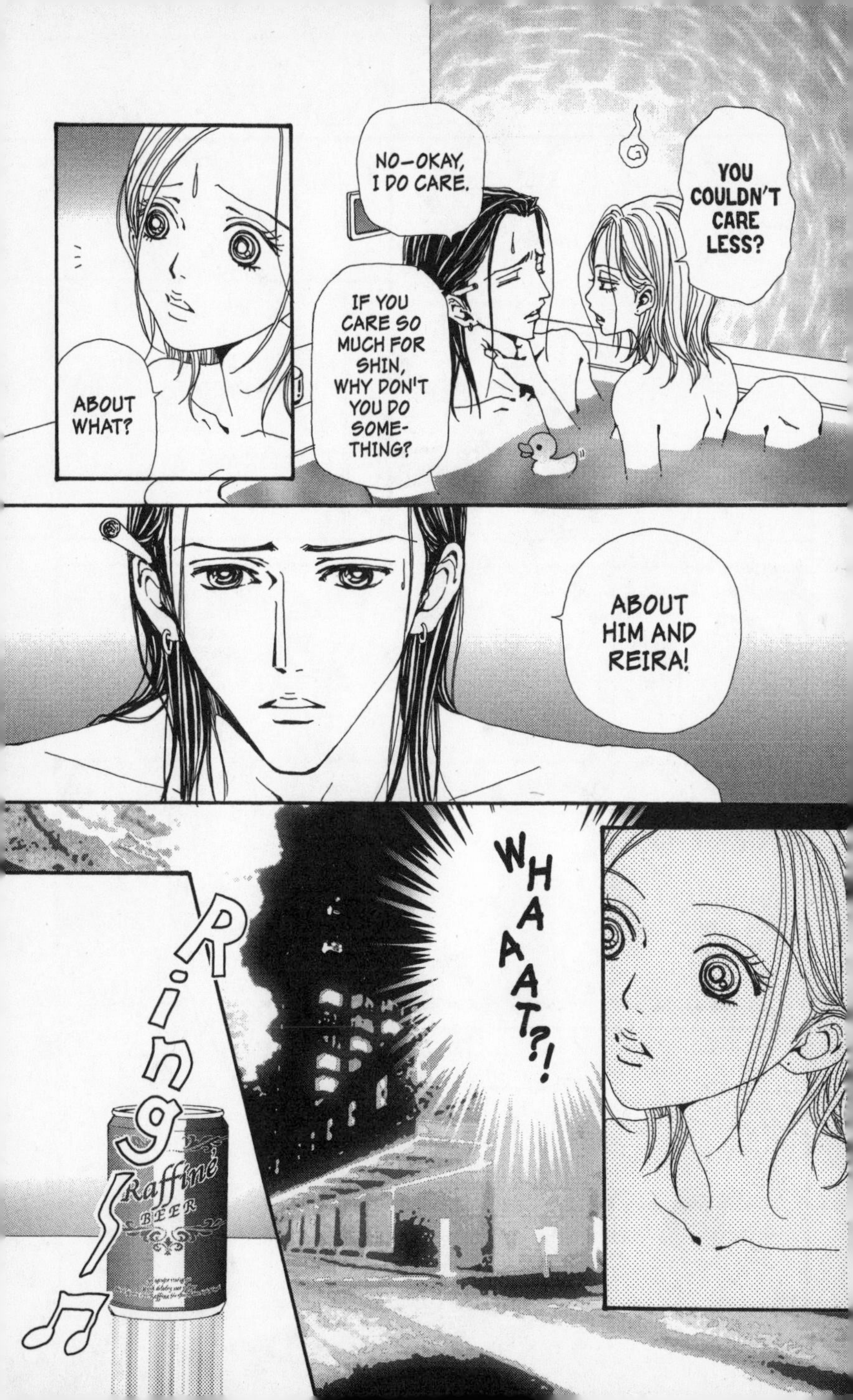
YOU COULDN'T CARE LESS?
NO—OKAY, I DO CARE.
IF YOU CARE SO MUCH FOR SHIN, WHY DON'T YOU DO SOMETHING?
ABOUT WHAT?
ABOUT HIM AND REIRA!
WHAAAT?!
Ring
Raffiné
BEER

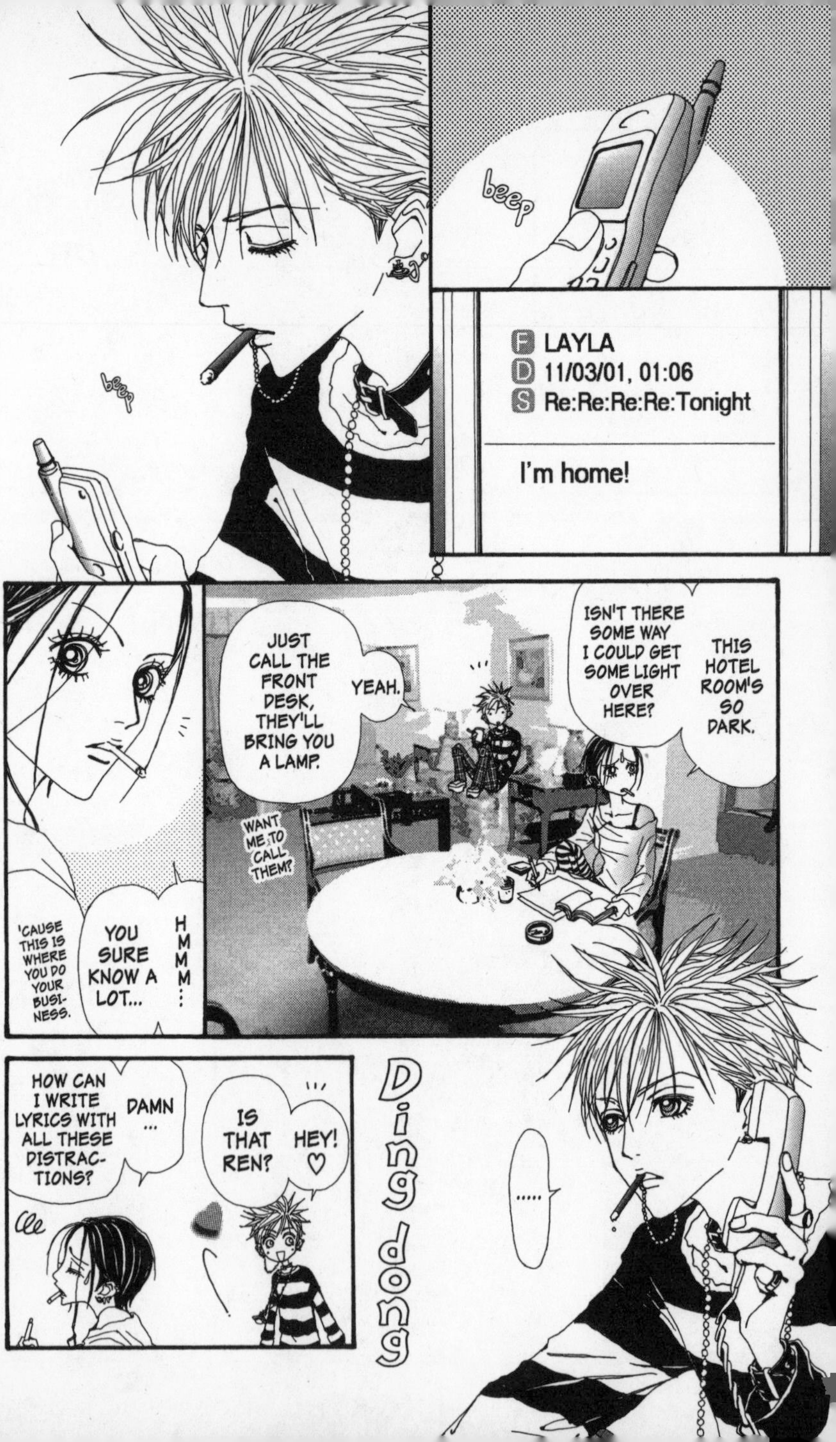
beep
F LAYLA
D 11/03/01, 01:06
S Re:Re:Re:Re:Tonight
I'm home!
beep
THIS HOTEL ROOM'S SO DARK.
ISN'T THERE SOME WAY I COULD GET SOME LIGHT OVER HERE?
YEAH.
JUST CALL THE FRONT DESK, THEY'LL BRING YOU A LAMP.
WANT ME TO CALL THEM?
HMMM...
YOU SURE KNOW A LOT...
'CAUSE THIS IS WHERE YOU DO YOUR BUSINESS.
......
Ding dong
HEY! ♡
IS THAT REN?
DAMN ...
HOW CAN I WRITE LYRICS WITH ALL THESE DISTRACTIONS?

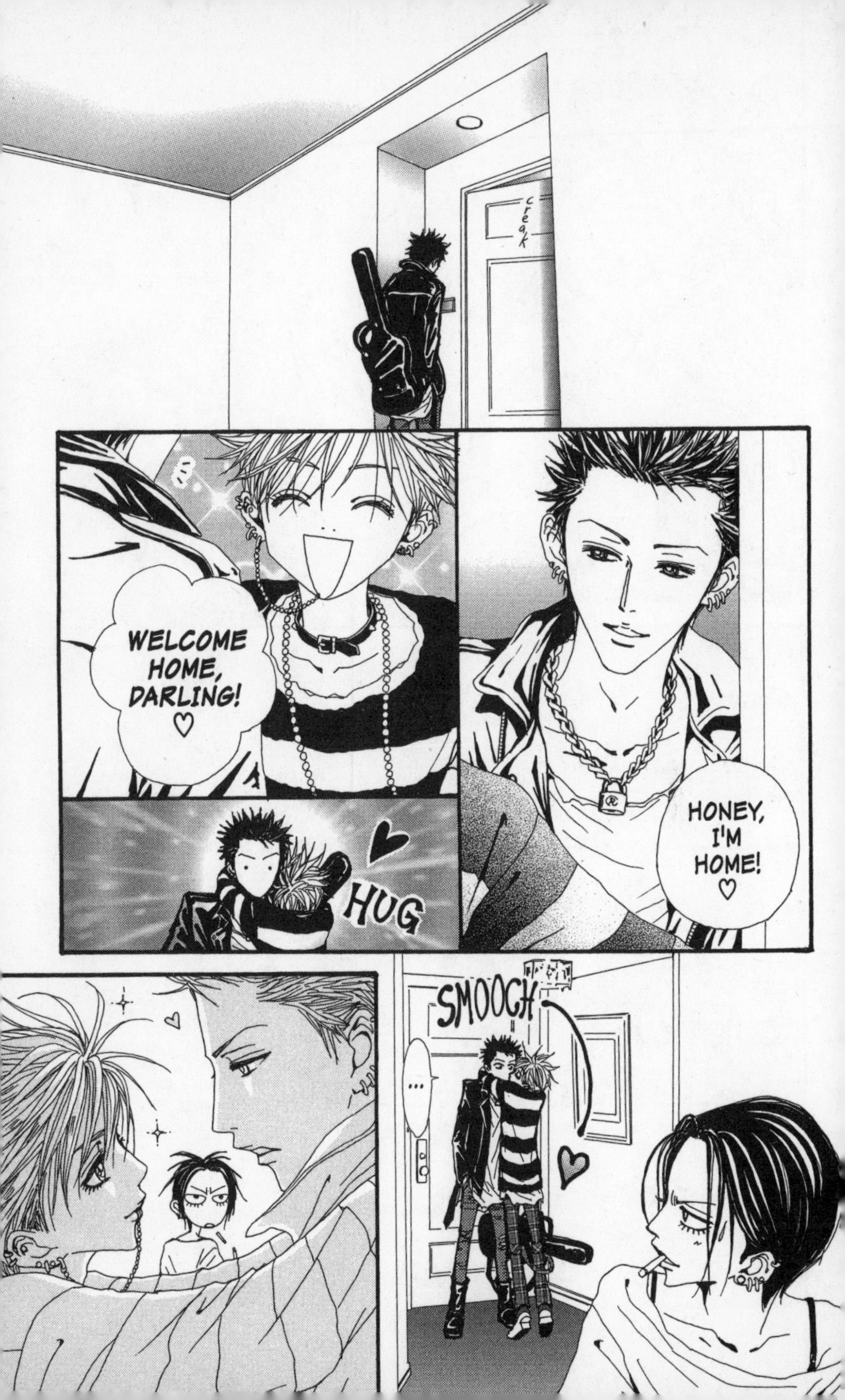
creak
HONEY, I'M HOME! ♡
WELCOME HOME, DARLING! ♡
HUG
SMOOCH
...

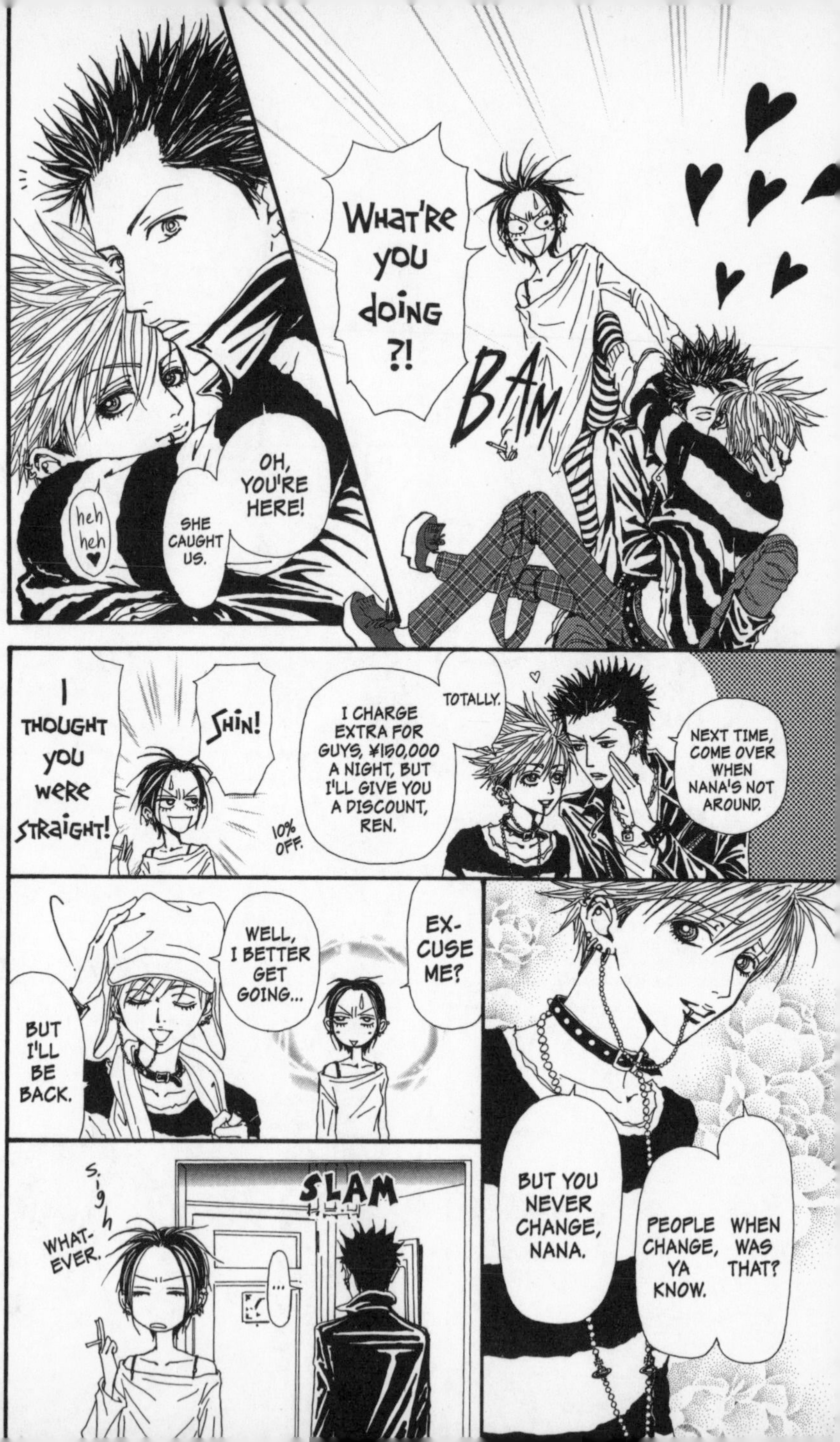
WHAT'RE YOU DOING ?!
BAM
OH, YOU'RE HERE!
SHE CAUGHT US.
heh heh ♥
NEXT TIME, COME OVER WHEN NANA'S NOT AROUND.
TOTALLY.
I CHARGE EXTRA FOR GUYS, ¥150,000 A NIGHT, BUT I'LL GIVE YOU A DISCOUNT, REN.
10% OFF.
SHIN!
I THOUGHT YOU WERE STRAIGHT!
WHEN WAS THAT?
PEOPLE CHANGE, YA KNOW.
BUT YOU NEVER CHANGE, NANA.
EX-CUSE ME?
WELL, I BETTER GET GOING...
BUT I'LL BE BACK.
SLAM
...
Sigh
WHAT-EVER.

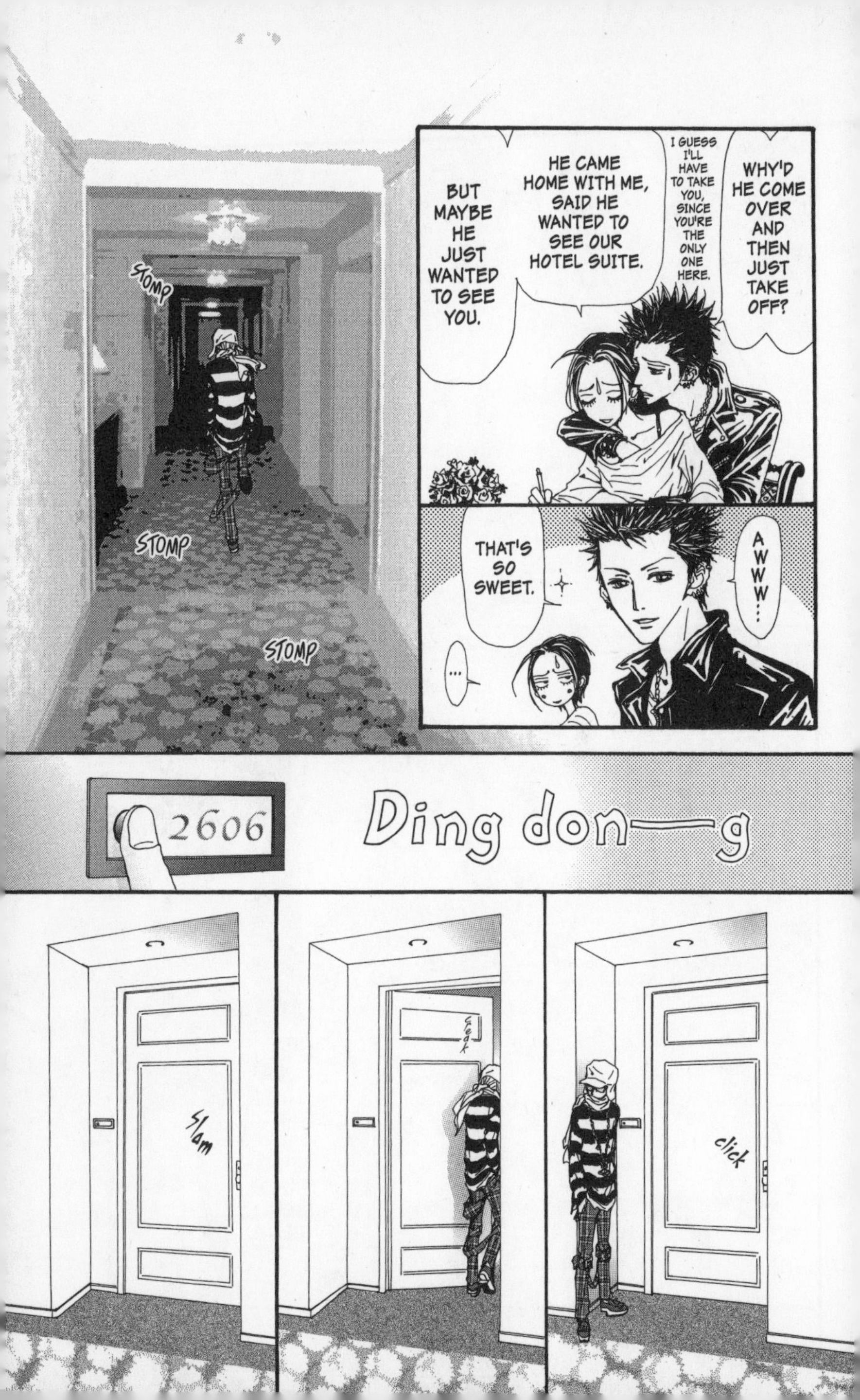
WHY'D HE COME OVER AND THEN JUST TAKE OFF?
I GUESS I'LL HAVE TO TAKE YOU, SINCE YOU'RE THE ONLY ONE HERE.
HE CAME HOME WITH ME, SAID HE WANTED TO SEE OUR HOTEL SUITE.
BUT MAYBE HE JUST WANTED TO SEE YOU.
AWWW...
THAT'S SO SWEET.
...
STOMP
STOMP
STOMP
2606
Ding don—g
click
creak
slam

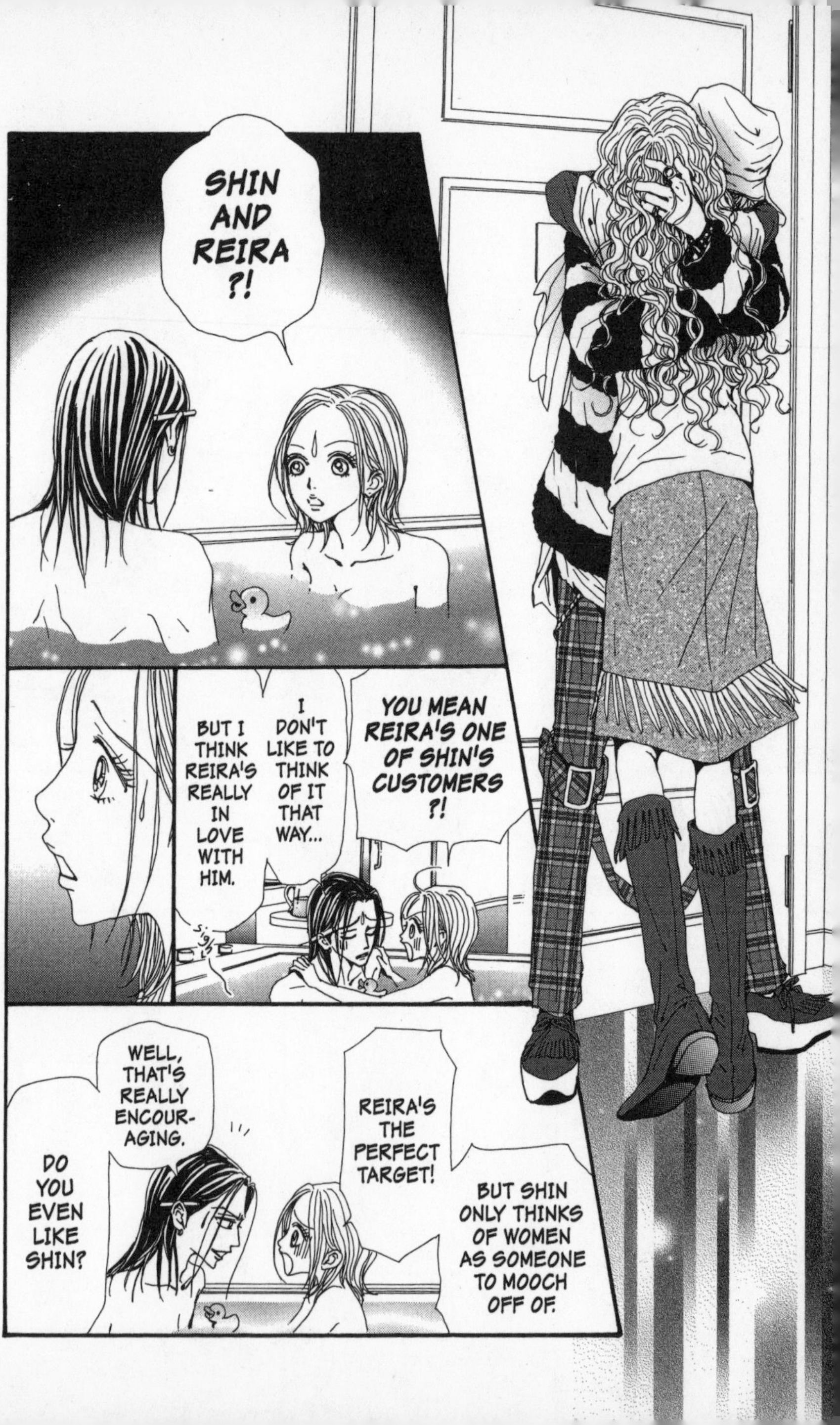
SHIN AND REIRA ?!
YOU MEAN REIRA'S ONE OF SHIN'S CUSTOMERS ?!
I DON'T LIKE TO THINK OF IT THAT WAY...
BUT I THINK REIRA'S REALLY IN LOVE WITH HIM.
sigh
REIRA'S THE PERFECT TARGET!
BUT SHIN ONLY THINKS OF WOMEN AS SOMEONE TO MOOCH OFF OF.
WELL, THAT'S REALLY ENCOURAGING.
DO YOU EVEN LIKE SHIN?

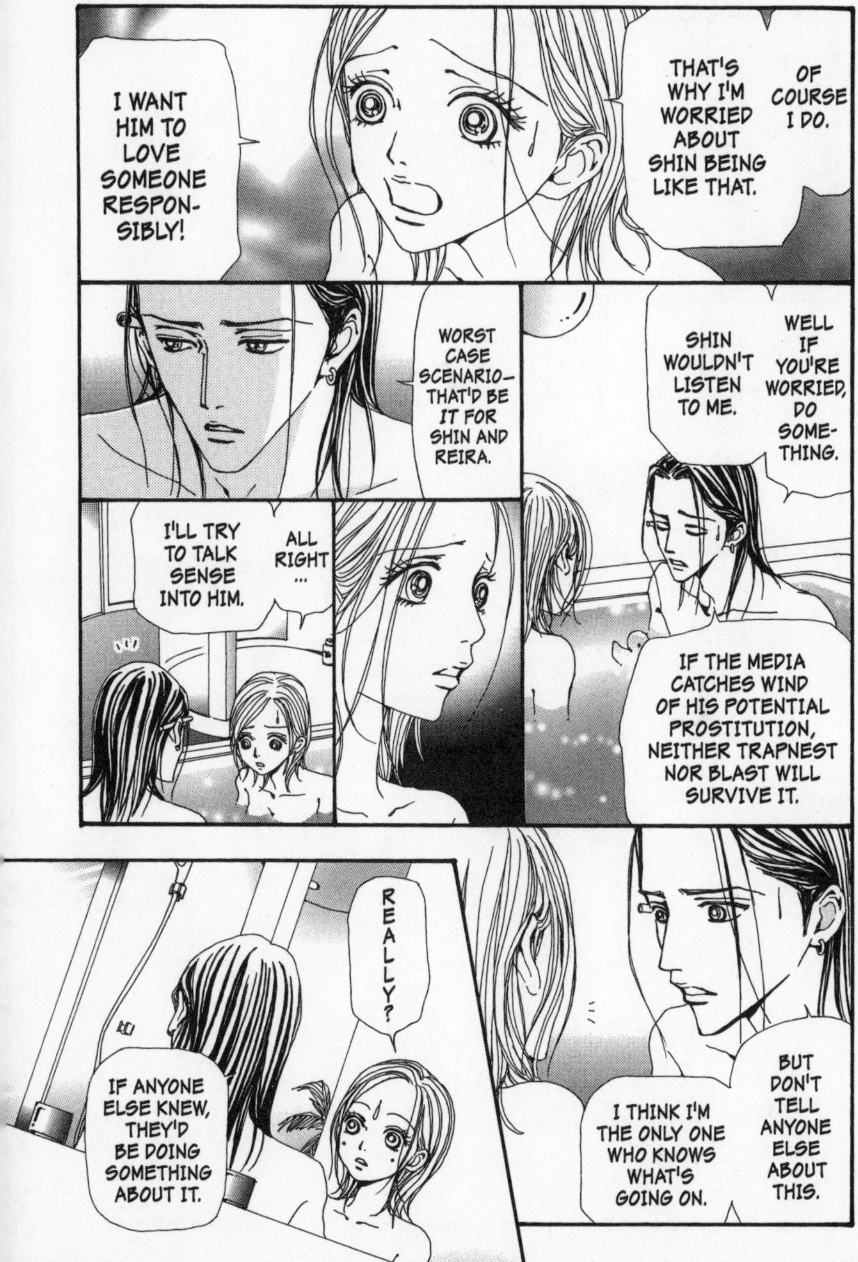
OF COURSE I DO.
THAT'S WHY I'M WORRIED ABOUT SHIN BEING LIKE THAT.
I WANT HIM TO LOVE SOMEONE RESPONSIBLY!
WELL IF YOU'RE WORRIED, DO SOMETHING.
SHIN WOULDN'T LISTEN TO ME.
IF THE MEDIA CATCHES WIND OF HIS POTENTIAL PROSTITUTION, NEITHER TRAPNEST NOR BLAST WILL SURVIVE IT.
WORST CASE SCENARIO—THAT'D BE IT FOR SHIN AND REIRA.
ALL RIGHT...
I'LL TRY TO TALK SENSE INTO HIM.
BUT DON'T TELL ANYONE ELSE ABOUT THIS.
I THINK I'M THE ONLY ONE WHO KNOWS WHAT'S GOING ON.
REALLY?
IF ANYONE ELSE KNEW, THEY'D BE DOING SOMETHING ABOUT IT.

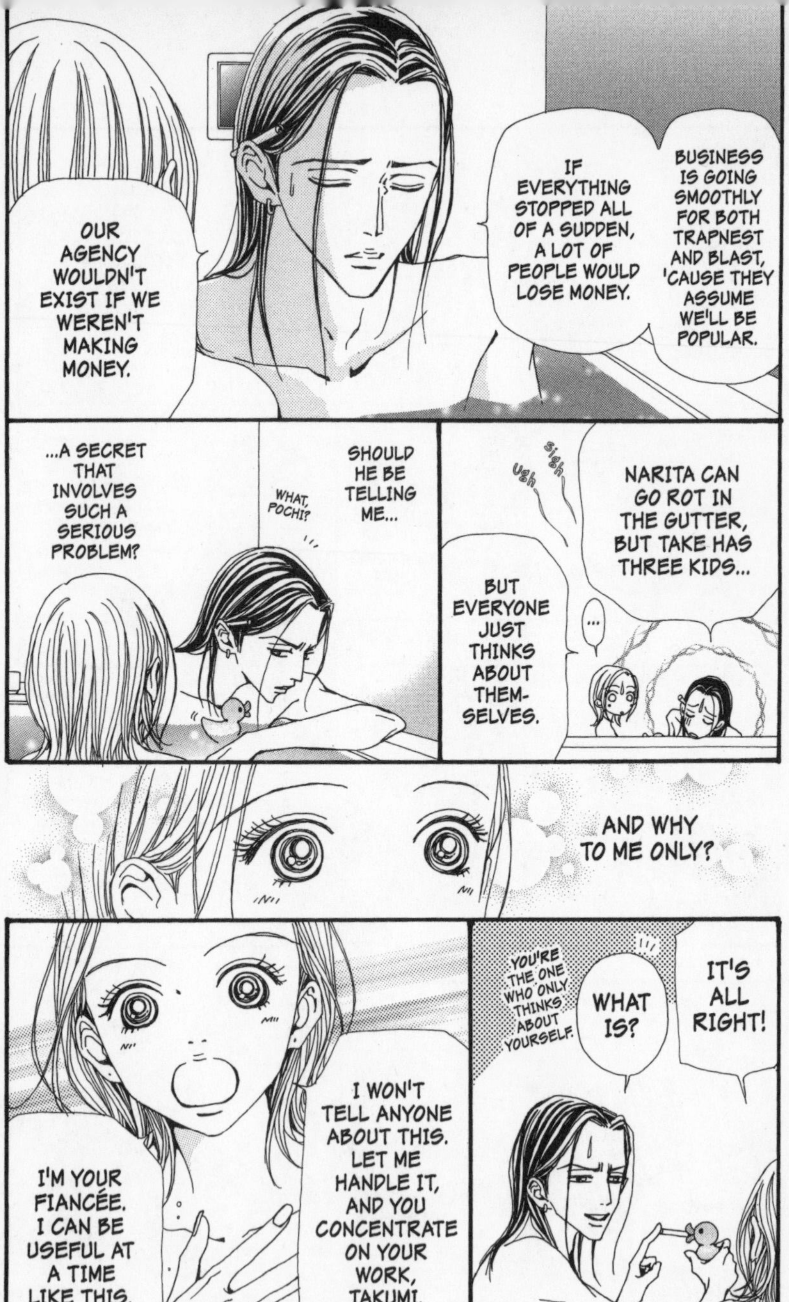
BUSINESS IS GOING SMOOTHLY FOR BOTH TRAPNEST AND BLAST, 'CAUSE THEY ASSUME WE'LL BE POPULAR.
IF EVERYTHING STOPPED ALL OF A SUDDEN, A LOT OF PEOPLE WOULD LOSE MONEY.
OUR AGENCY WOULDN'T EXIST IF WE WEREN'T MAKING MONEY.
sigh
Ugh
NARITA CAN GO ROT IN THE GUTTER, BUT TAKE HAS THREE KIDS...
BUT EVERYONE JUST THINKS ABOUT THEM-SELVES.
...
SHOULD HE BE TELLING ME...
WHAT, POCHI?
...A SECRET THAT INVOLVES SUCH A SERIOUS PROBLEM?
AND WHY TO ME ONLY?
IT'S ALL RIGHT!
WHAT IS?
YOU'RE THE ONE WHO ONLY THINKS ABOUT YOURSELF.
I WON'T TELL ANYONE ABOUT THIS. LET ME HANDLE IT, AND YOU CONCENTRATE ON YOUR WORK, TAKUMI.
I'M YOUR FIANCÉE. I CAN BE USEFUL AT A TIME LIKE THIS.

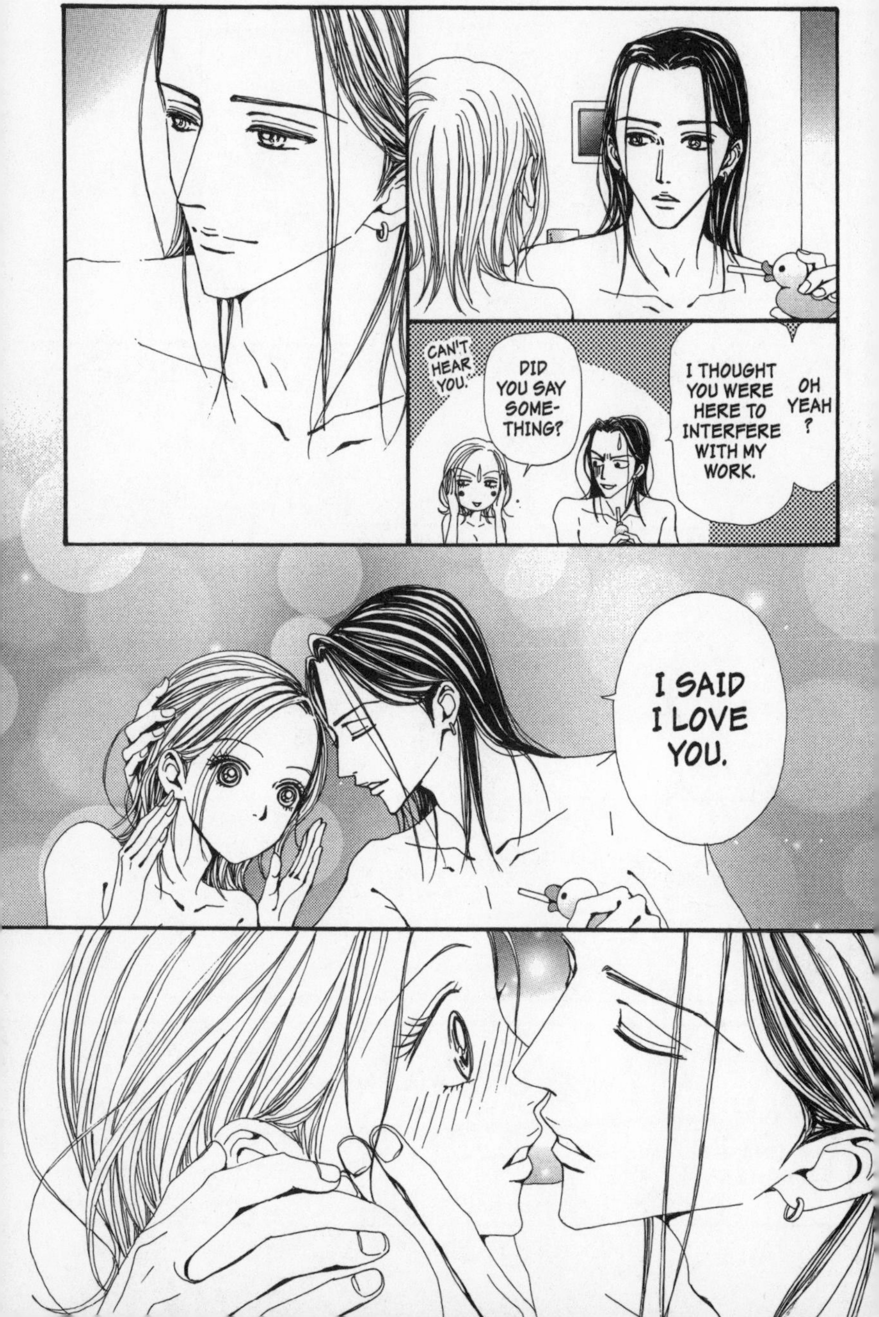
OH YEAH?
I THOUGHT YOU WERE HERE TO INTERFERE WITH MY WORK.
DID YOU SAY SOME-THING?
CAN'T HEAR YOU.
I SAID I LOVE YOU.

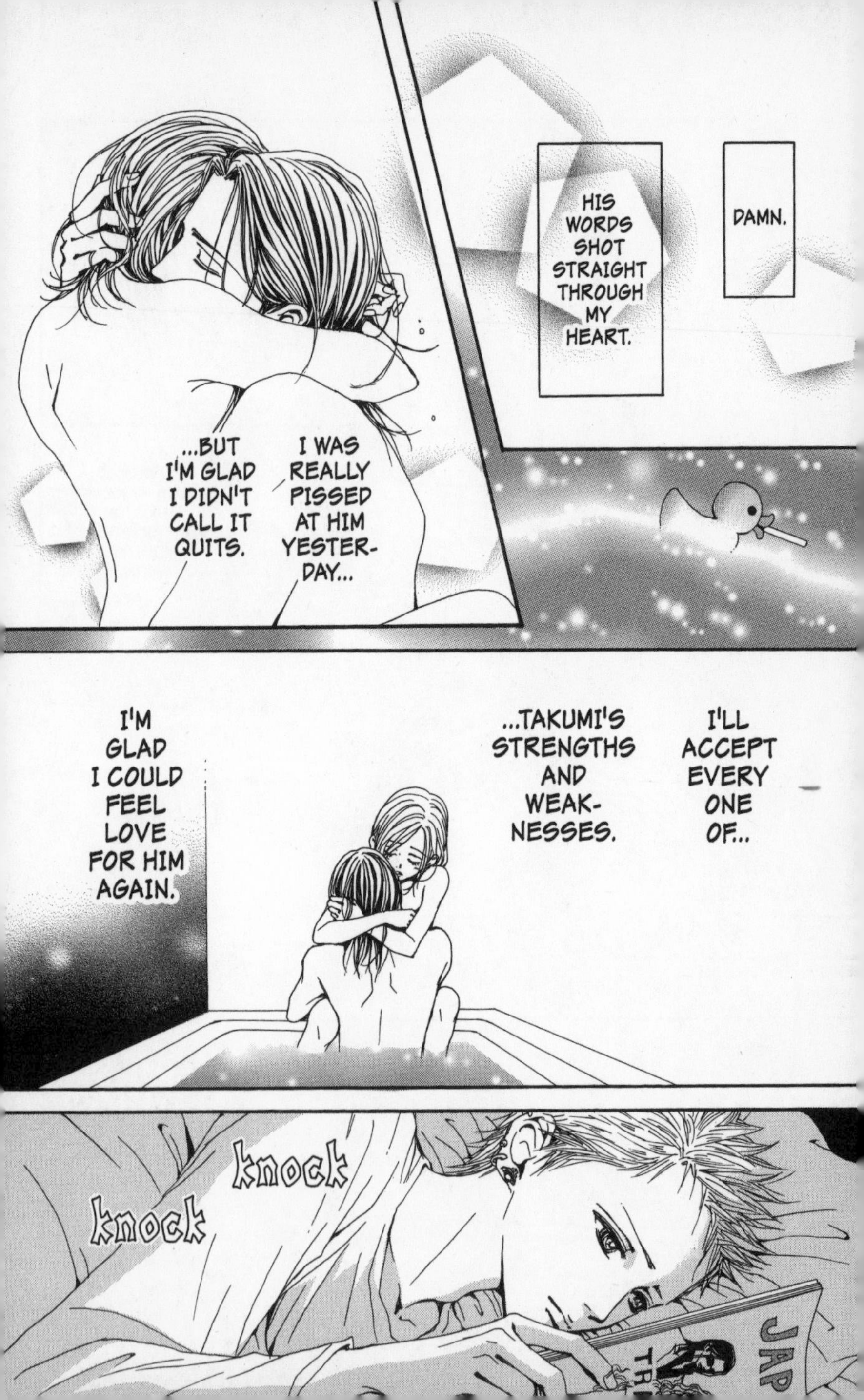
DAMN.
HIS WORDS SHOT STRAIGHT THROUGH MY HEART.
I WAS REALLY PISSED AT HIM YESTER-DAY...
...BUT I'M GLAD I DIDN'T CALL IT QUITS.
I'LL ACCEPT EVERY ONE OF...
...TAKUMI'S STRENGTHS AND WEAK-NESSES.
I'M GLAD I COULD FEEL LOVE FOR HIM AGAIN.
knock
knock

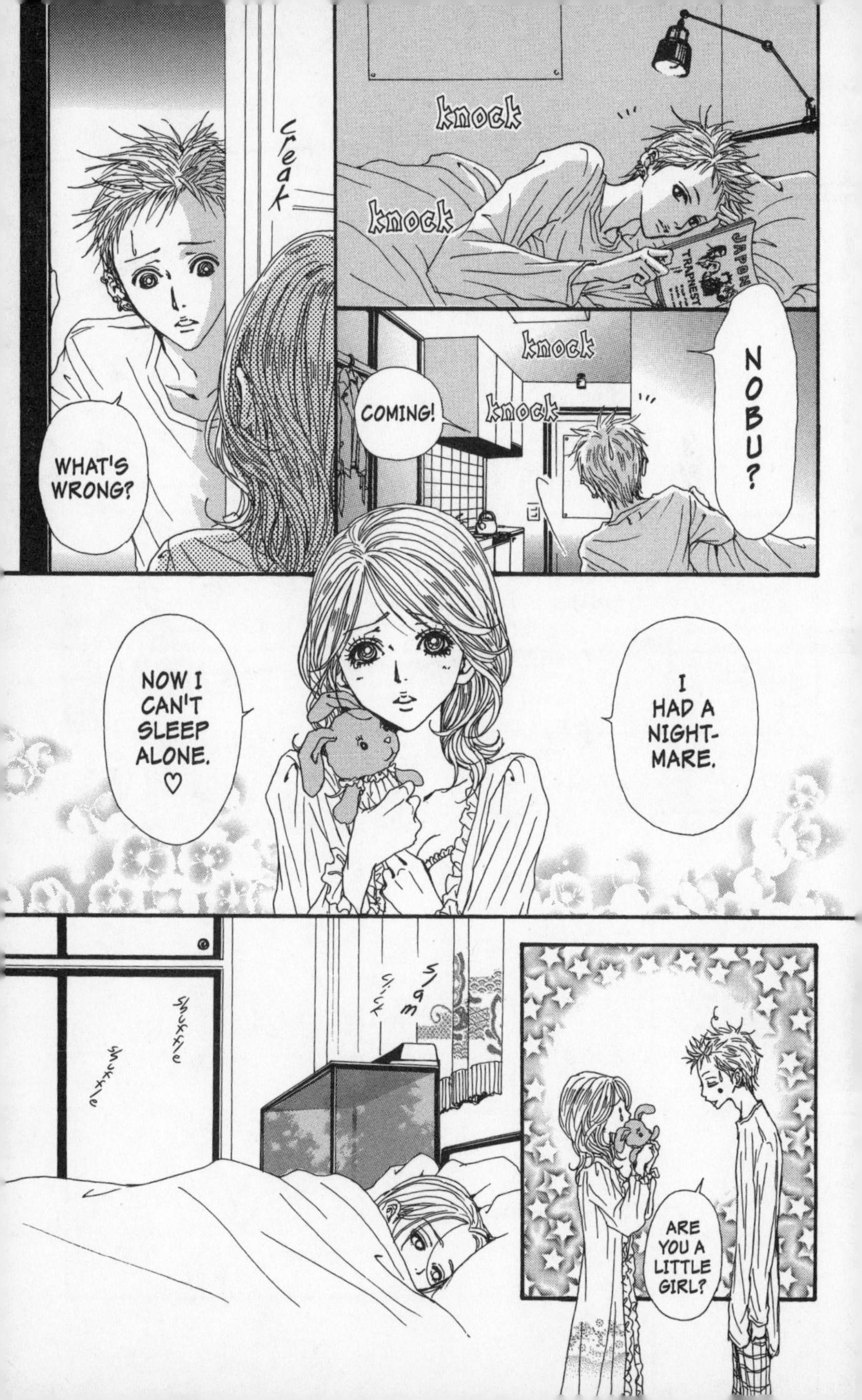
knock
knock
NOBU?
knock
knock
COMING!
creak
WHAT'S WRONG?
I HAD A NIGHT-MARE.
NOW I CAN'T SLEEP ALONE. ♡
ARE YOU A LITTLE GIRL?
slam
click
shuffle
shuffle

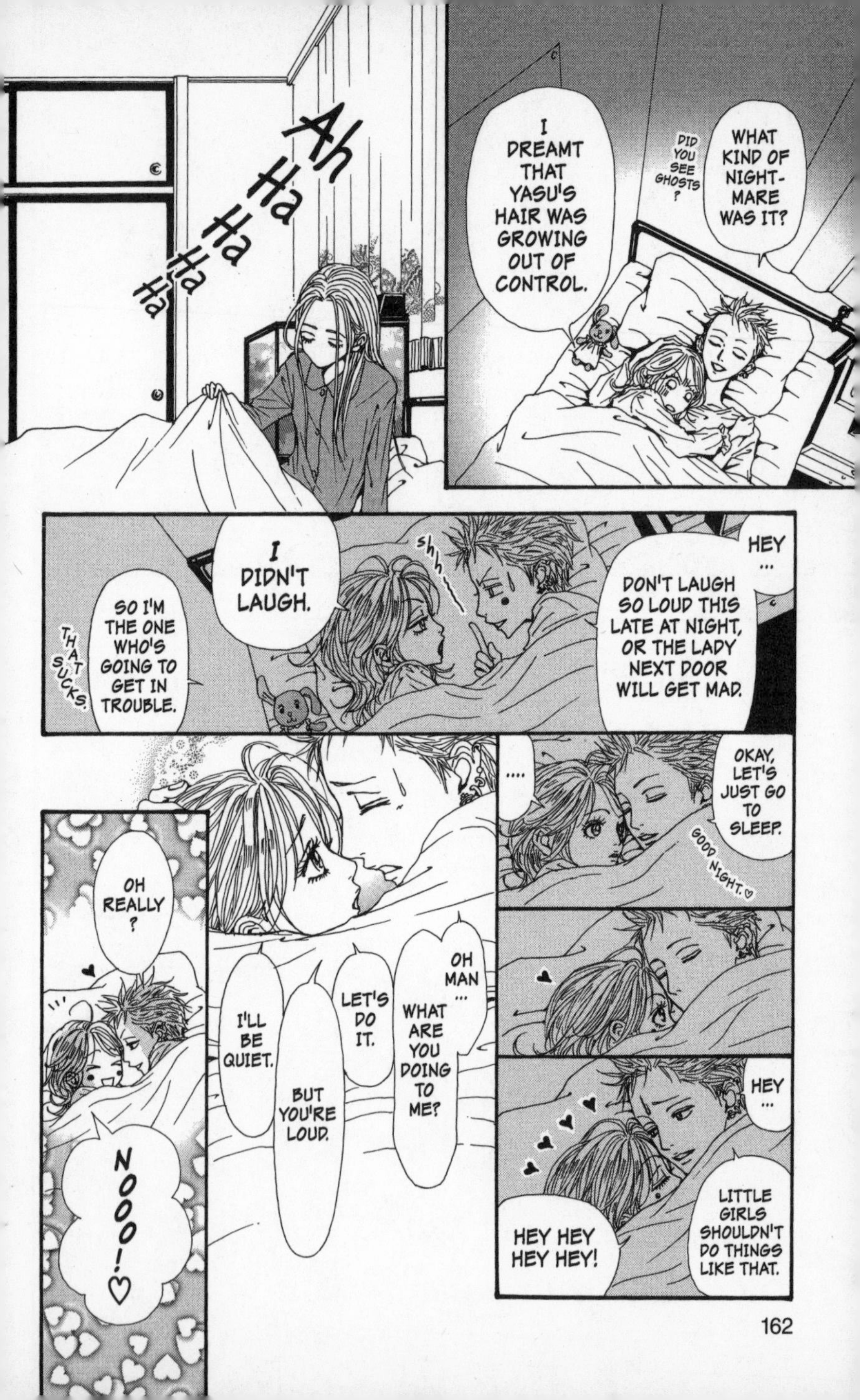
WHAT KIND OF NIGHT-MARE WAS IT?
DID YOU SEE GHOSTS?
I DREAMT THAT YASU'S HAIR WAS GROWING OUT OF CONTROL.
Ah Ha Ha Ha Ha
HEY ...
DON'T LAUGH SO LOUD THIS LATE AT NIGHT, OR THE LADY NEXT DOOR WILL GET MAD.
Shhh
I DIDN'T LAUGH.
SO I'M THE ONE WHO'S GOING TO GET IN TROUBLE.
THAT SUCKS.
OKAY, LET'S JUST GO TO SLEEP.
GOOD NIGHT.♡
....
HEY ...
LITTLE GIRLS SHOULDN'T DO THINGS LIKE THAT.
HEY HEY HEY HEY!
OH MAN ... WHAT ARE YOU DOING TO ME?
LET'S DO IT.
BUT YOU'RE LOUD.
I'LL BE QUIET.
OH REALLY?
NOOOO!♡

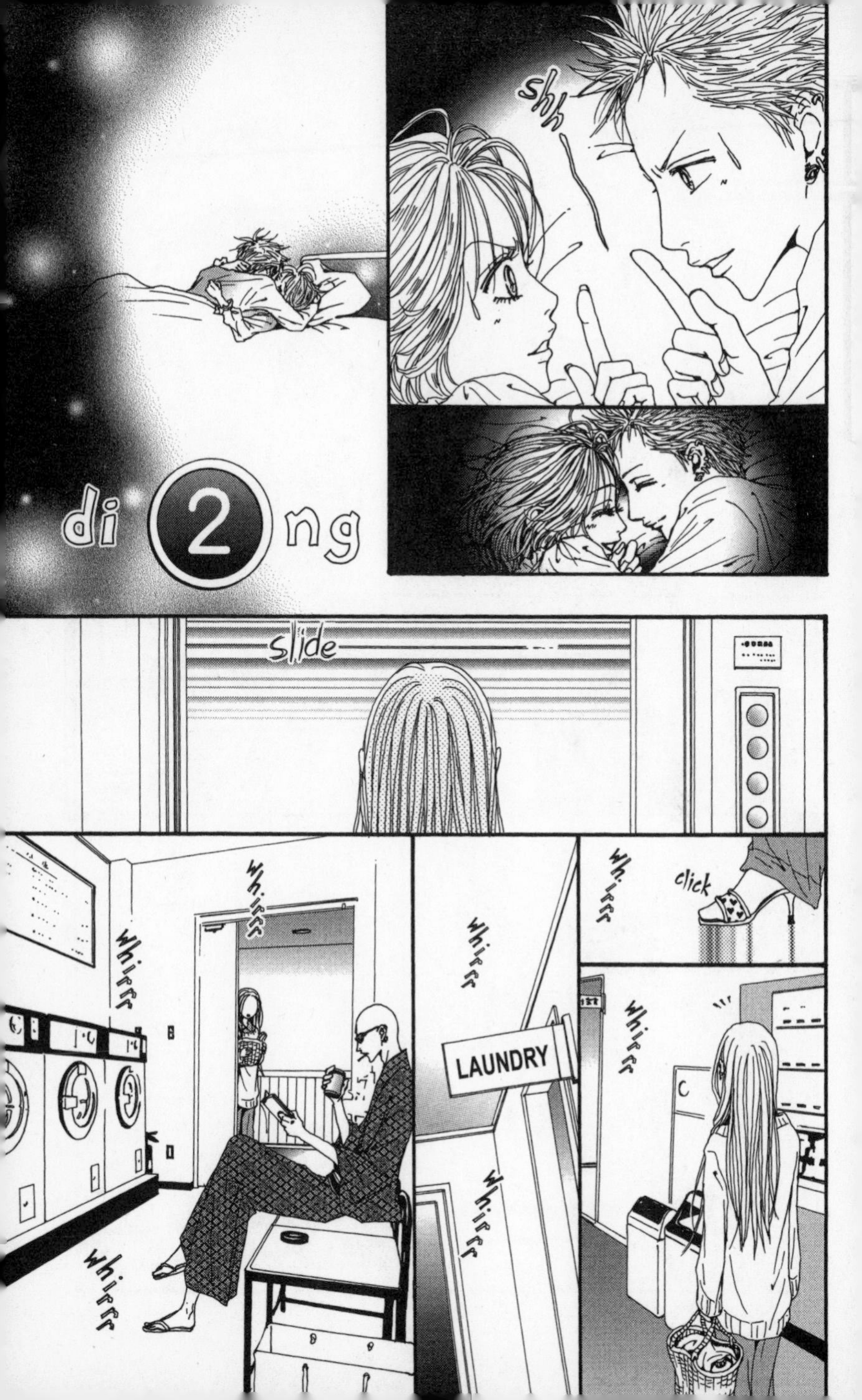
shh
di 2 ng
slide
whirrr
click
whirrr
whirrr
LAUNDRY
whirrr
whirrr
whirrr
whirrr

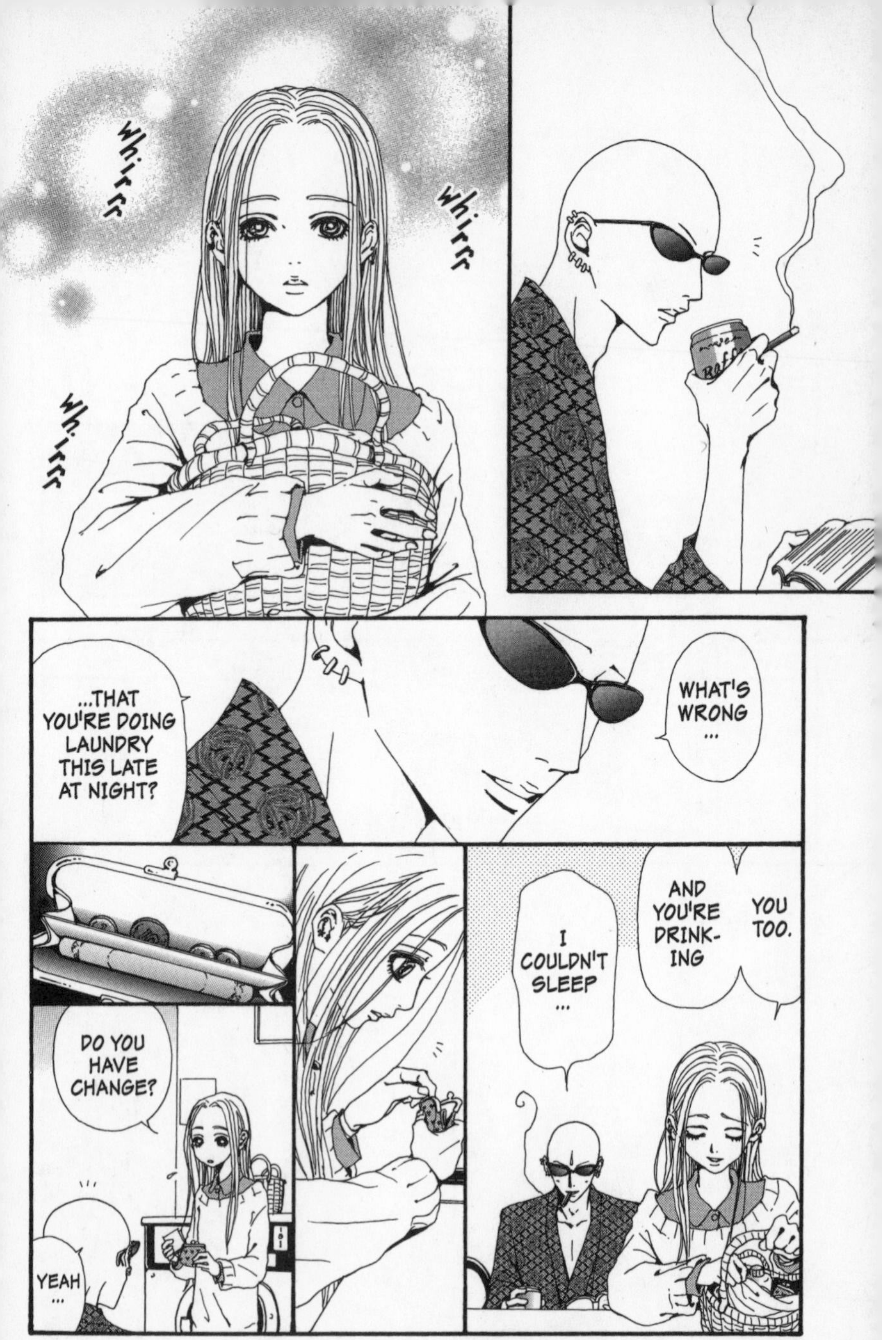
whirrr
whirrr
whirrr
WHAT'S WRONG...
...THAT YOU'RE DOING LAUNDRY THIS LATE AT NIGHT?
YOU TOO.
AND YOU'RE DRINKING
I COULDN'T SLEEP...
DO YOU HAVE CHANGE?
YEAH...

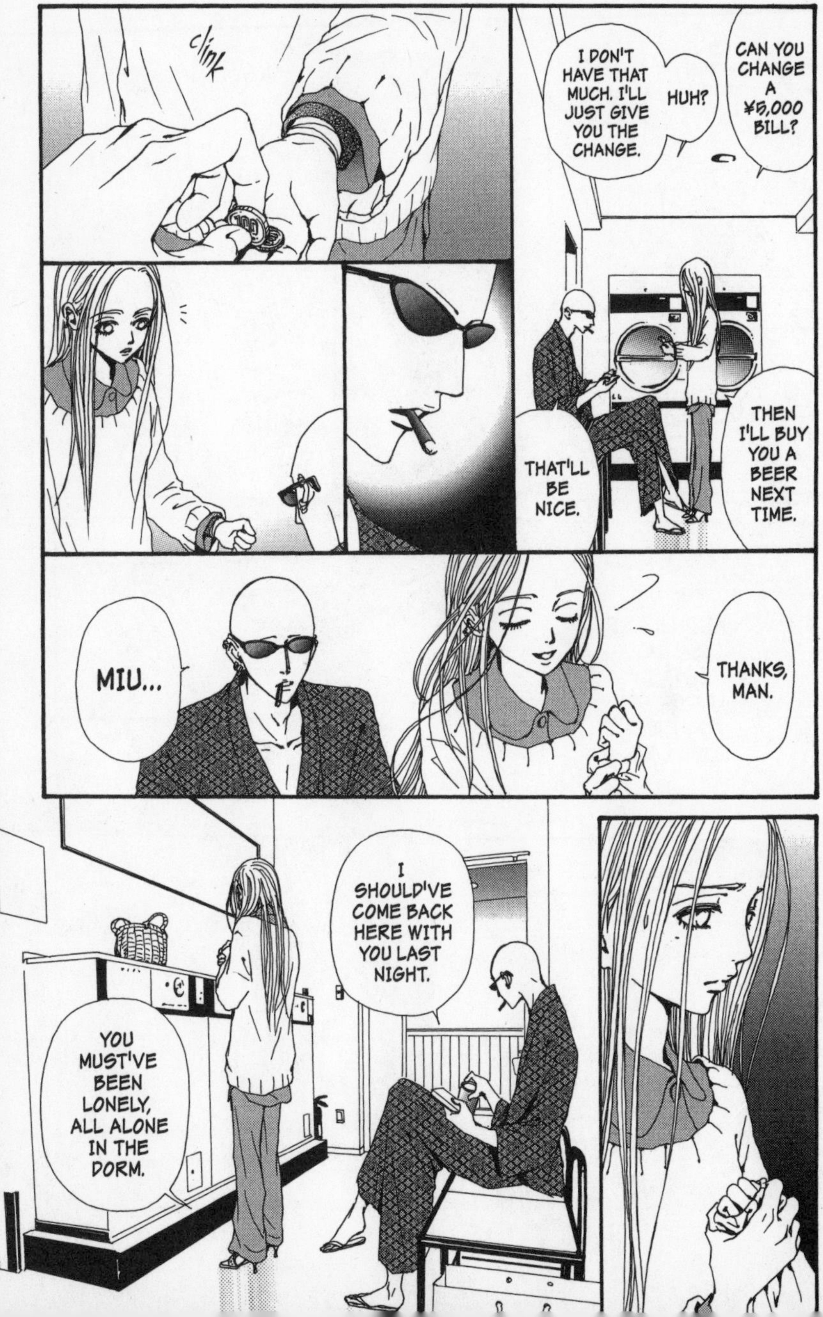
CAN YOU CHANGE A ¥5,000 BILL?
HUH?
I DON'T HAVE THAT MUCH. I'LL JUST GIVE YOU THE CHANGE.
THEN I'LL BUY YOU A BEER NEXT TIME.
THAT'LL BE NICE.
clink
THANKS, MAN.
MIU...
I SHOULD'VE COME BACK HERE WITH YOU LAST NIGHT.
YOU MUST'VE BEEN LONELY, ALL ALONE IN THE DORM.

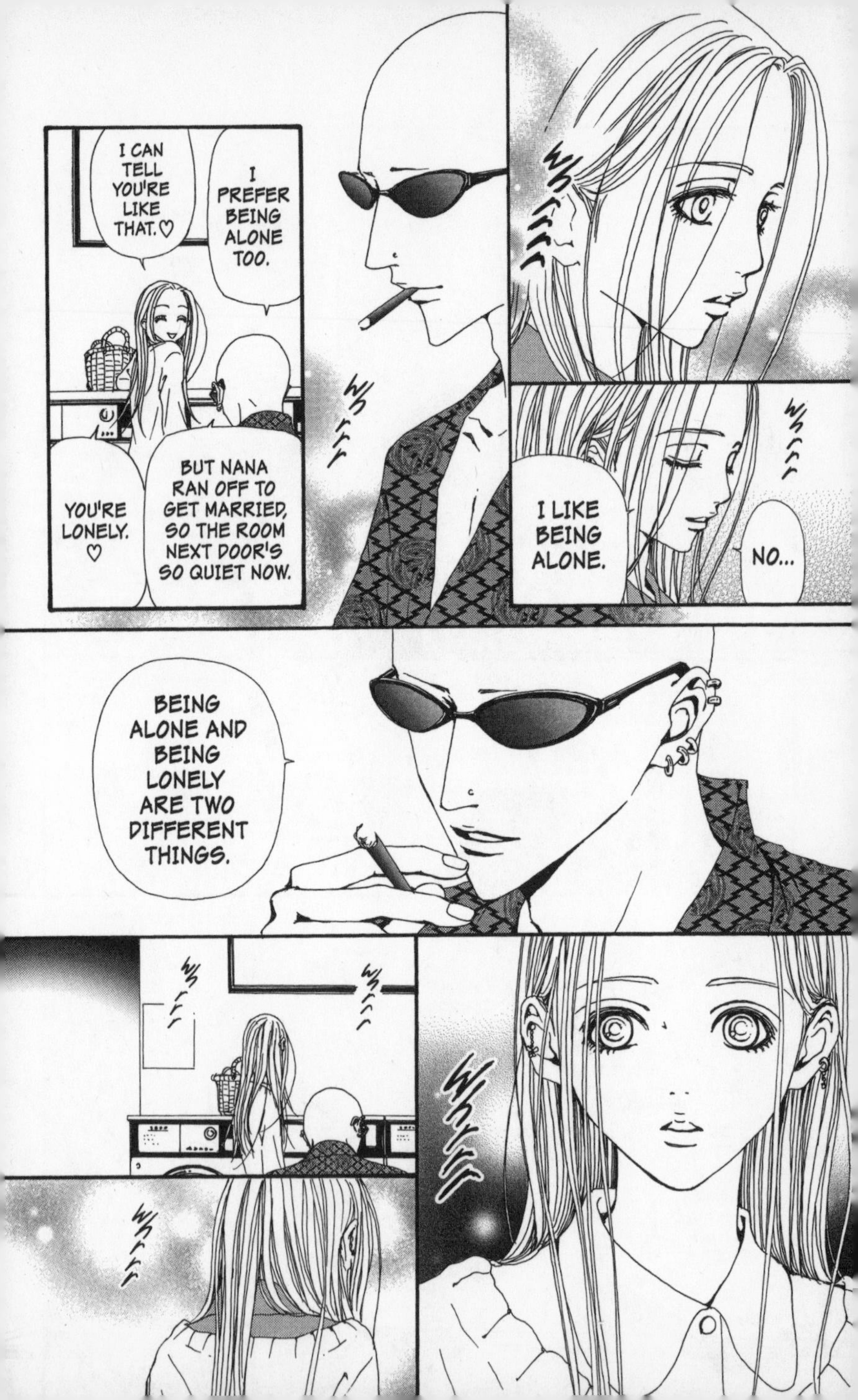
Whrrrr
Whrrr
NO...
I LIKE BEING ALONE.
Whrrr
I PREFER BEING ALONE TOO.
I CAN TELL YOU'RE LIKE THAT.♡
BUT NANA RAN OFF TO GET MARRIED, SO THE ROOM NEXT DOOR'S SO QUIET NOW.
YOU'RE LONELY. ♡
BEING ALONE AND BEING LONELY ARE TWO DIFFERENT THINGS.
Whrrrrr
Whrrr
Whrrr
Whrrrr

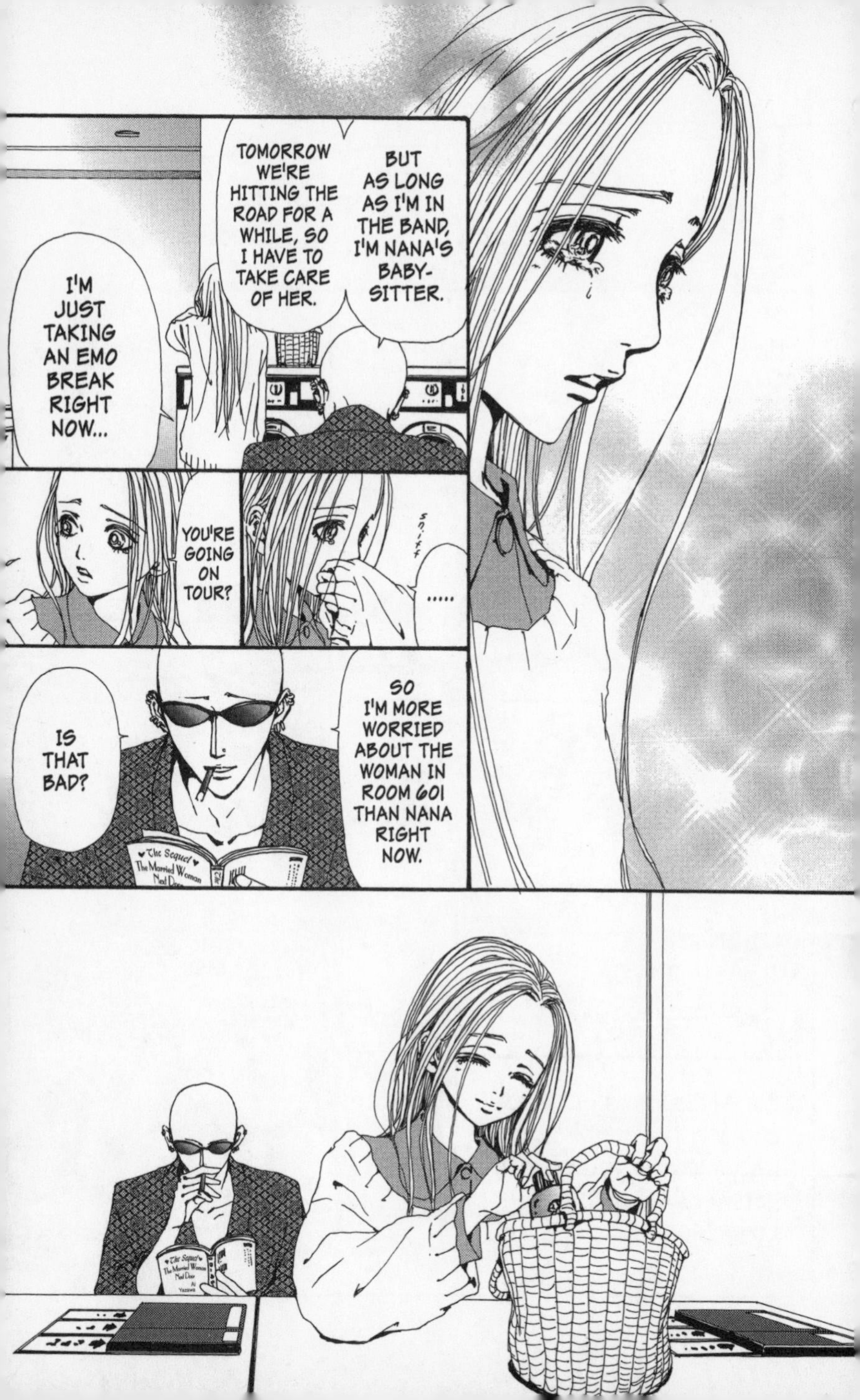
BUT AS LONG AS I'M IN THE BAND, I'M NANA'S BABY-SITTER.
TOMORROW WE'RE HITTING THE ROAD FOR A WHILE, SO I HAVE TO TAKE CARE OF HER.
I'M JUST TAKING AN EMO BREAK RIGHT NOW...
sniff
.....
YOU'RE GOING ON TOUR?
SO I'M MORE WORRIED ABOUT THE WOMAN IN ROOM 601 THAN NANA RIGHT NOW.
IS THAT BAD?
The Sequel The Married Woman Next Door Ai Yazawa

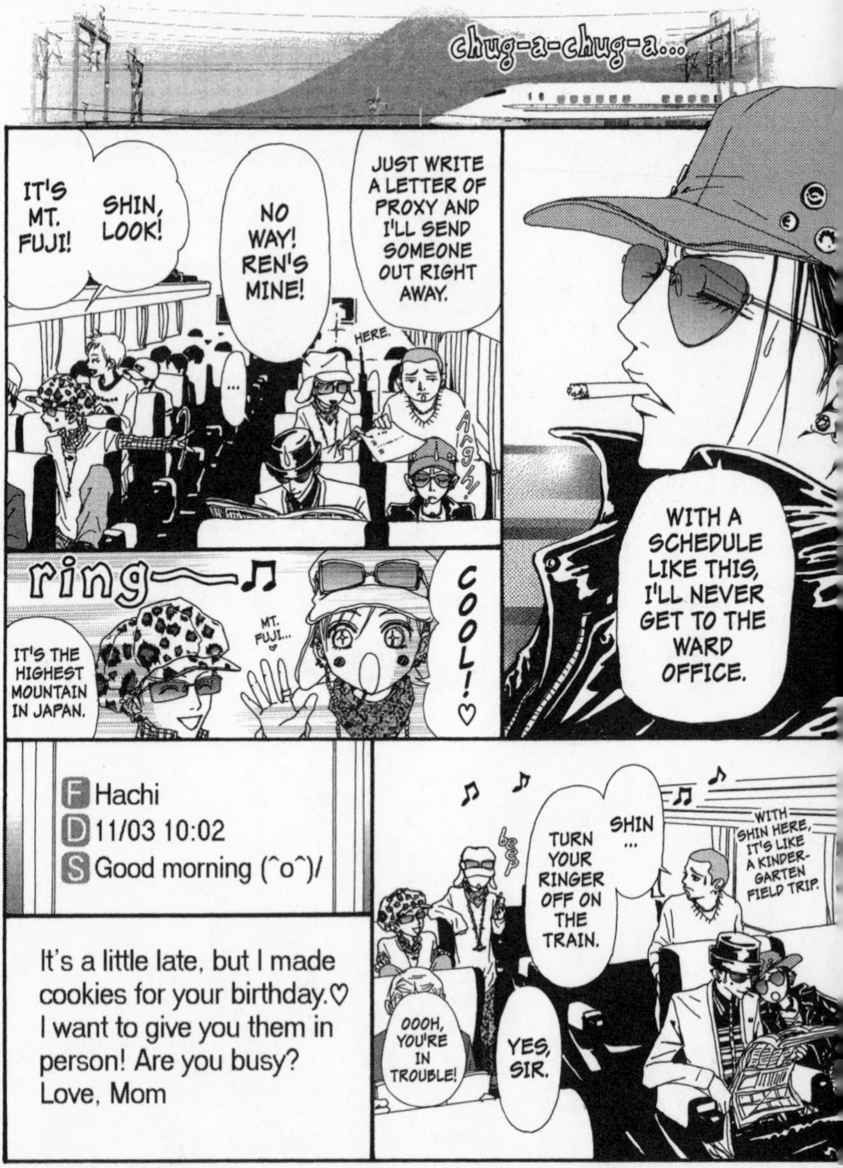
chug-a-chug-a...
WITH A SCHEDULE LIKE THIS, I'LL NEVER GET TO THE WARD OFFICE.
JUST WRITE A LETTER OF PROXY AND I'LL SEND SOMEONE OUT RIGHT AWAY.
HERE.
Argh!
NO WAY! REN'S MINE!
...
SHIN, LOOK!
IT'S MT. FUJI!
COOL!♡
MT. FUJI...♡
ring——♫
IT'S THE HIGHEST MOUNTAIN IN JAPAN.
WITH SHIN HERE, IT'S LIKE A KINDER-GARTEN FIELD TRIP.
SHIN...
TURN YOUR RINGER OFF ON THE TRAIN.
beep
YES, SIR.
OOOH, YOU'RE IN TROUBLE!
F Hachi
D 11/03 10:02
S Good morning (^o^)/
It's a little late, but I made cookies for your birthday.♡ I want to give you them in person! Are you busy? Love, Mom

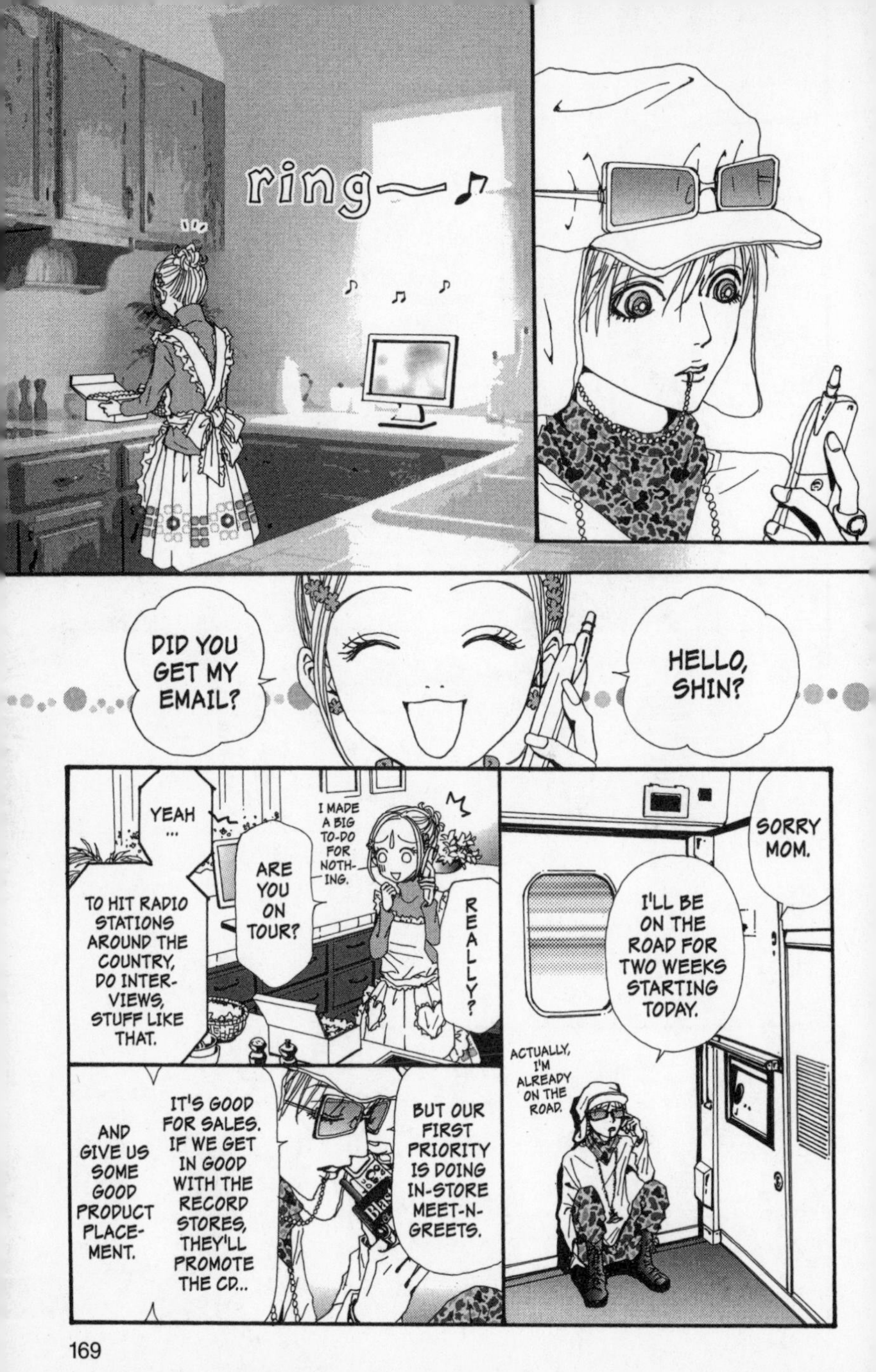

ring~♪
HELLO, SHIN?
DID YOU GET MY EMAIL?
SORRY MOM.
I'LL BE ON THE ROAD FOR TWO WEEKS STARTING TODAY.
ACTUALLY, I'M ALREADY ON THE ROAD.
REALLY?
I MADE A BIG TO-DO FOR NOTHING.
ARE YOU ON TOUR?
YEAH ...
TO HIT RADIO STATIONS AROUND THE COUNTRY, DO INTERVIEWS, STUFF LIKE THAT.
BUT OUR FIRST PRIORITY IS DOING IN-STORE MEET-N-GREETS.
IT'S GOOD FOR SALES. IF WE GET IN GOOD WITH THE RECORD STORES, THEY'LL PROMOTE THE CD...
AND GIVE US SOME GOOD PRODUCT PLACEMENT.

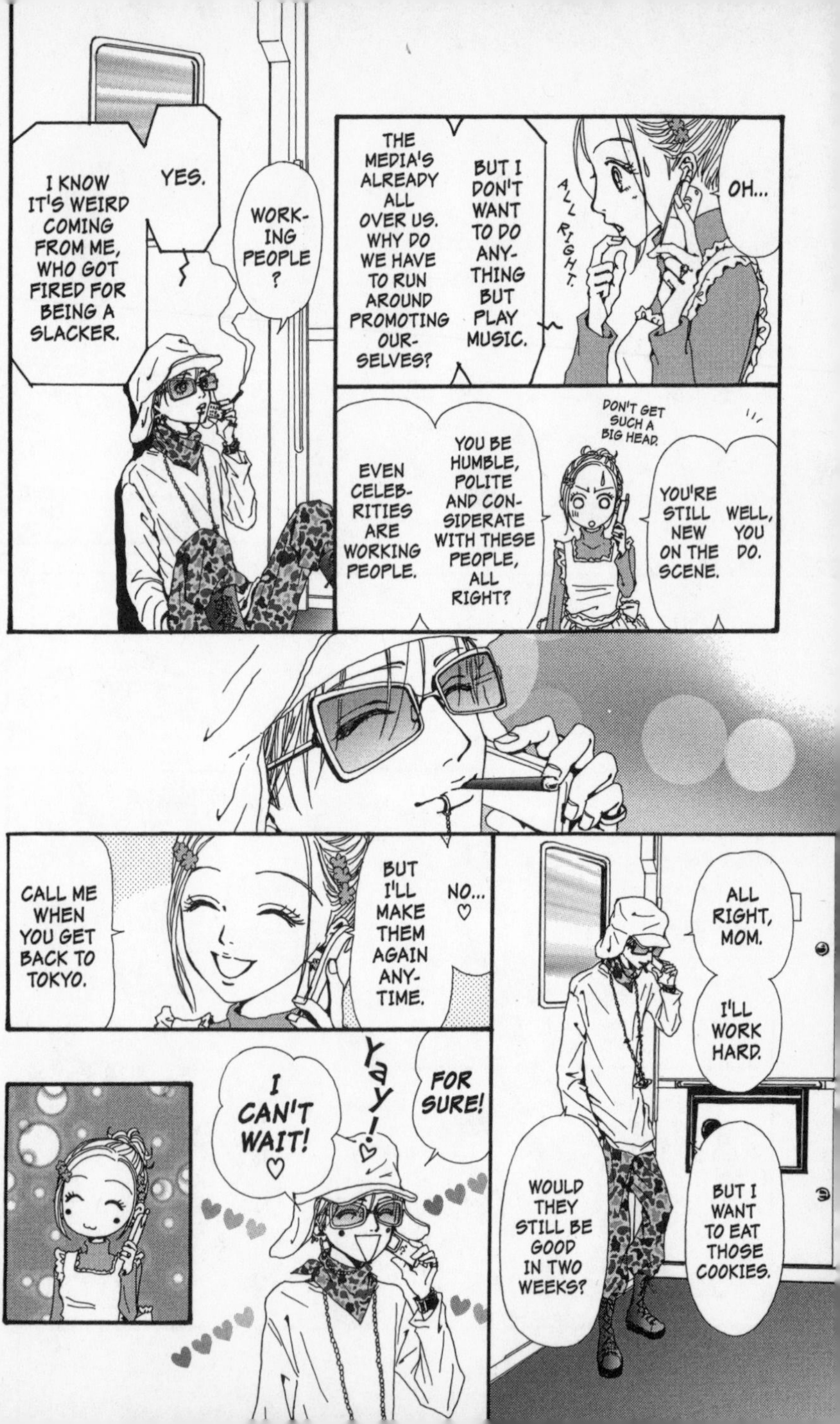

OH...
ALL RIGHT.
BUT I DON'T WANT TO DO ANYTHING BUT PLAY MUSIC.
THE MEDIA'S ALREADY ALL OVER US. WHY DO WE HAVE TO RUN AROUND PROMOTING OURSELVES?
WELL, YOU DO.
YOU'RE STILL NEW ON THE SCENE.
DON'T GET SUCH A BIG HEAD.
YOU BE HUMBLE, POLITE AND CONSIDERATE WITH THESE PEOPLE, ALL RIGHT?
EVEN CELEBRITIES ARE WORKING PEOPLE.
WORKING PEOPLE?
YES.
I KNOW IT'S WEIRD COMING FROM ME, WHO GOT FIRED FOR BEING A SLACKER.
ALL RIGHT, MOM.
I'LL WORK HARD.
BUT I WANT TO EAT THOSE COOKIES.
WOULD THEY STILL BE GOOD IN TWO WEEKS?
NO...♡
BUT I'LL MAKE THEM AGAIN ANYTIME.
CALL ME WHEN YOU GET BACK TO TOKYO.
FOR SURE!
Yay!♡
I CAN'T WAIT!♡

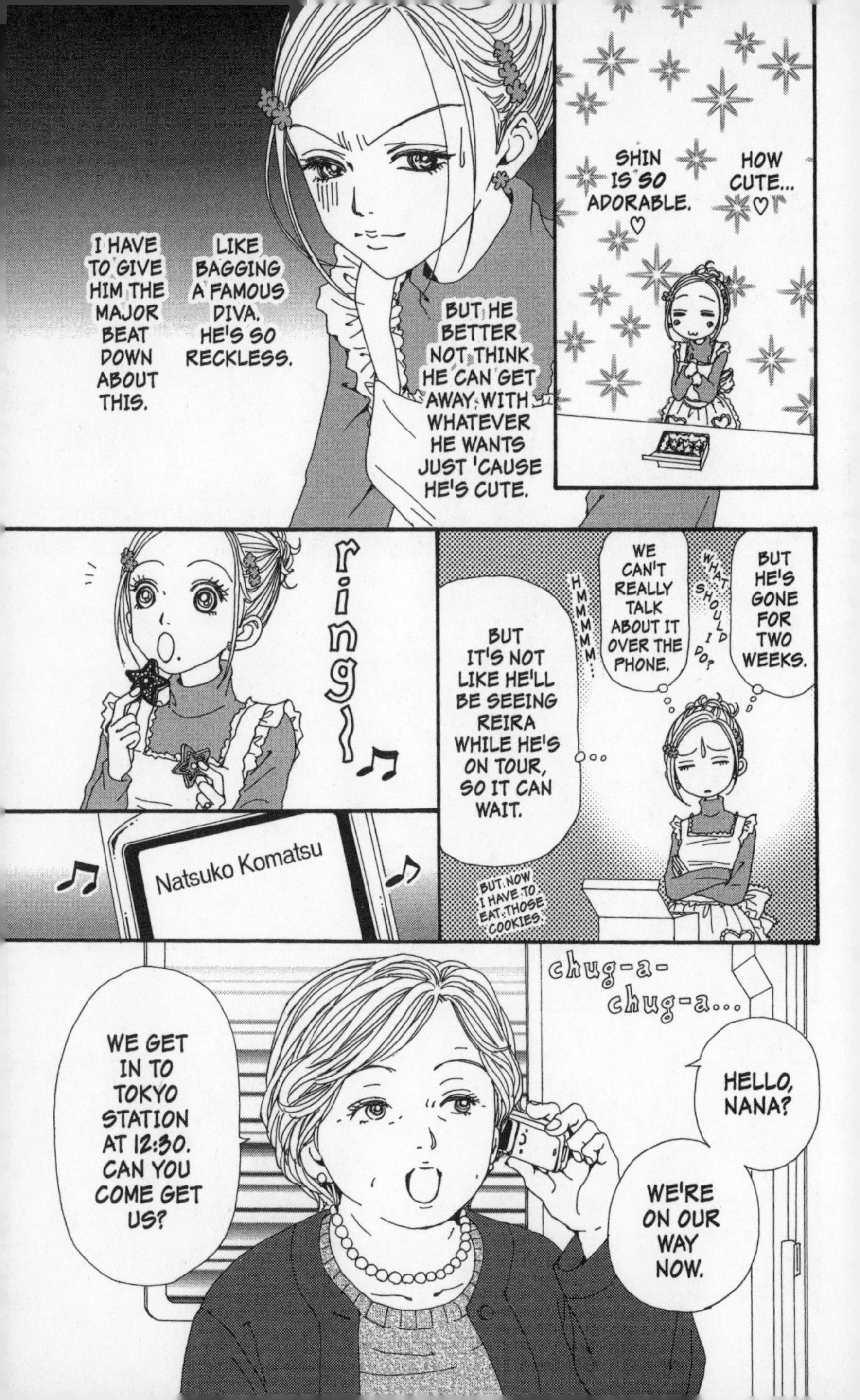
HOW CUTE... ♡
SHIN IS SO ADORABLE. ♡
BUT HE BETTER NOT THINK HE CAN GET AWAY WITH WHATEVER HE WANTS JUST 'CAUSE HE'S CUTE.
LIKE BAGGING A FAMOUS DIVA. HE'S SO RECKLESS.
I HAVE TO GIVE HIM THE MAJOR BEAT DOWN ABOUT THIS.
BUT HE'S GONE FOR TWO WEEKS.
WHAT SHOULD I DO?
WE CAN'T REALLY TALK ABOUT IT OVER THE PHONE.
HMMMMM...
BUT IT'S NOT LIKE HE'LL BE SEEING REIRA WHILE HE'S ON TOUR, SO IT CAN WAIT.
BUT NOW I HAVE TO EAT THOSE COOKIES.
ring~
Natsuko Komatsu
chug-a-chug-a...
HELLO, NANA?
WE'RE ON OUR WAY NOW.
WE GET IN TO TOKYO STATION AT 12:30. CAN YOU COME GET US?

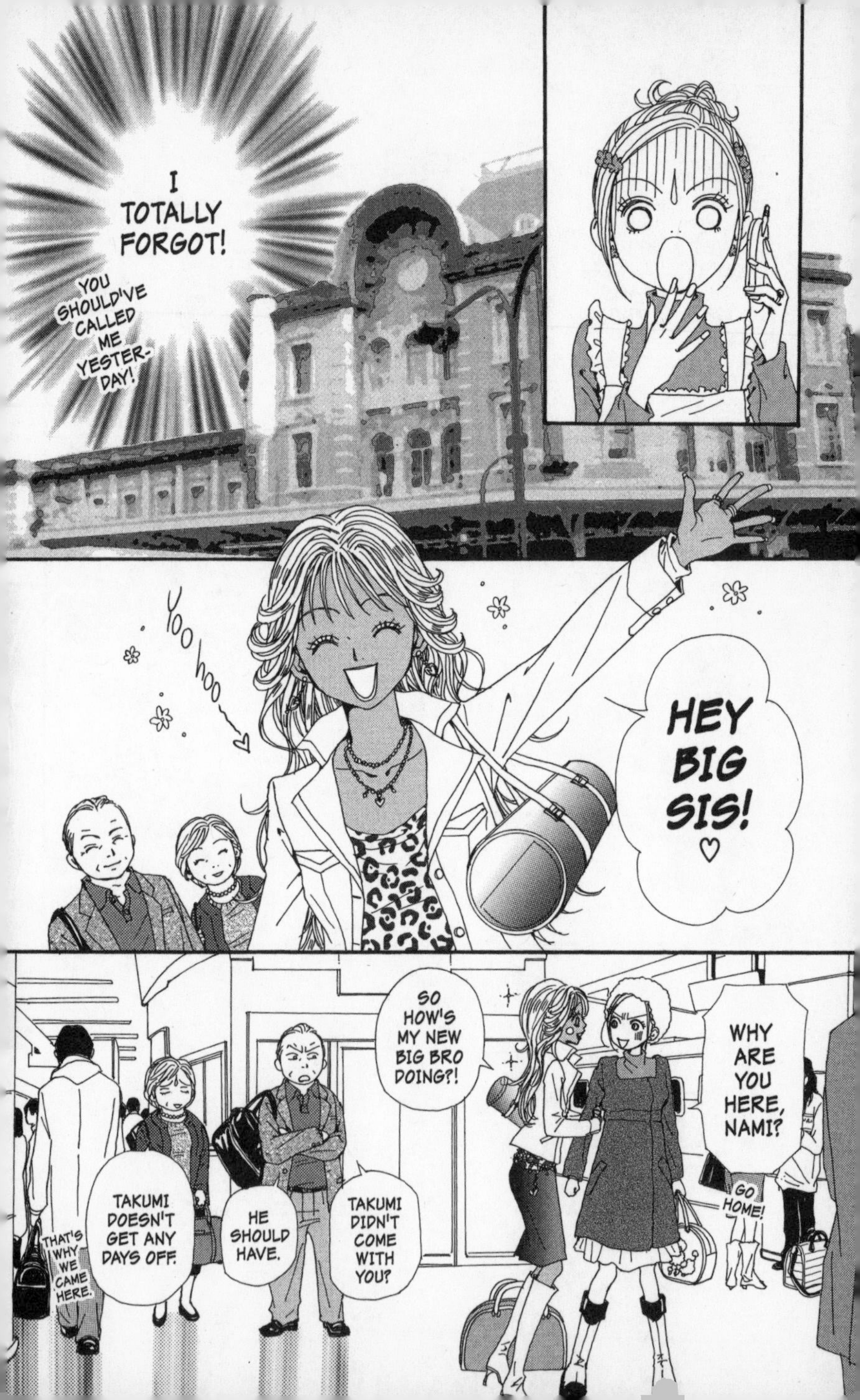
I TOTALLY FORGOT!
YOU SHOULD'VE CALLED ME YESTER-DAY!
HEY BIG SIS! ♡
Yoo hoo~♡
WHY ARE YOU HERE, NAMI?
GO HOME!
SO HOW'S MY NEW BIG BRO DOING?!
TAKUMI DIDN'T COME WITH YOU?
HE SHOULD HAVE.
TAKUMI DOESN'T GET ANY DAYS OFF.
THAT'S WHY WE CAME HERE.

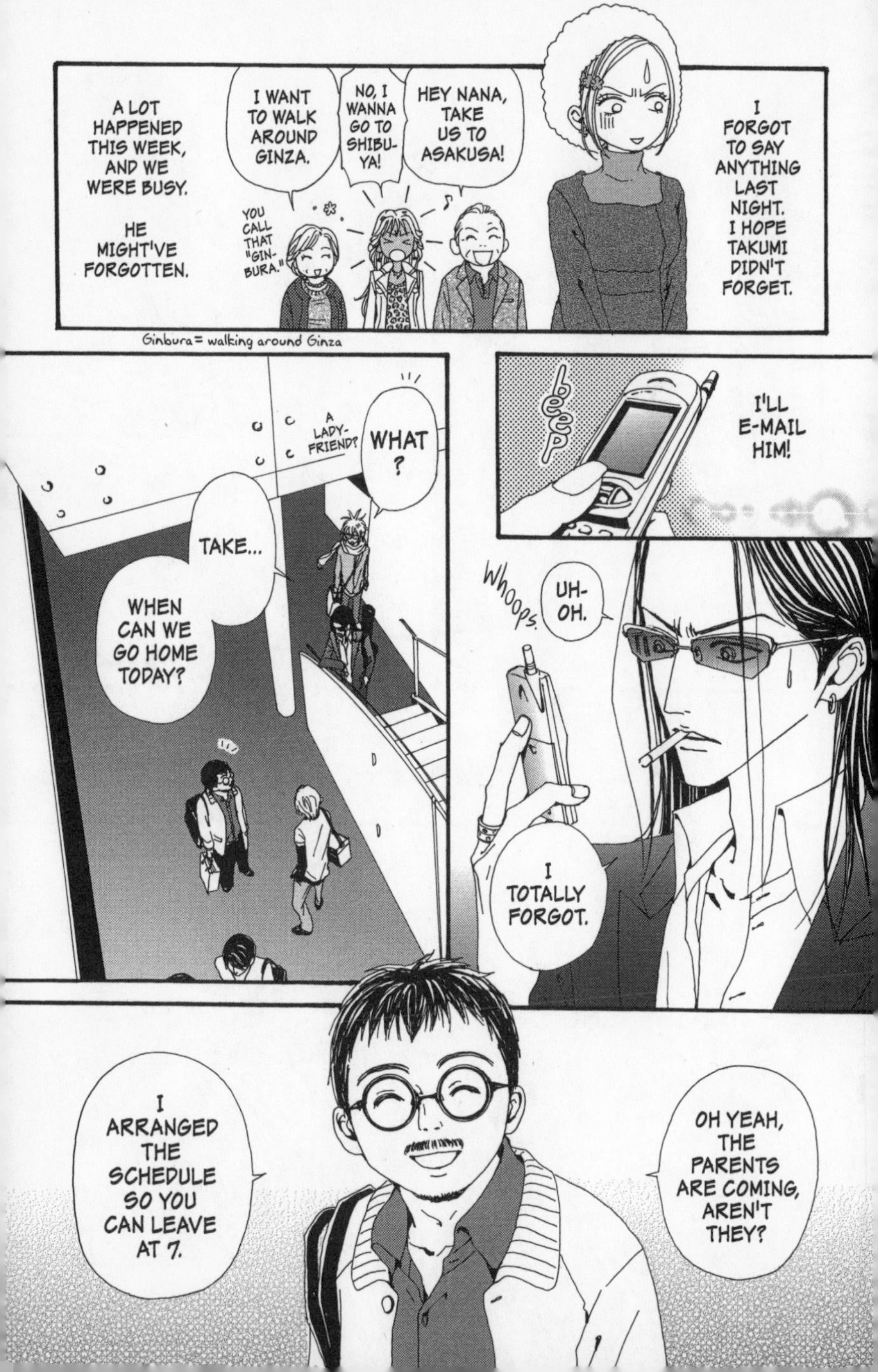
I FORGOT TO SAY ANYTHING LAST NIGHT. I HOPE TAKUMI DIDN'T FORGET.
HEY NANA, TAKE US TO ASAKUSA!
NO, I WANNA GO TO SHIBUYA!
I WANT TO WALK AROUND GINZA.
YOU CALL THAT "GINBURA."
A LOT HAPPENED THIS WEEK, AND WE WERE BUSY.
HE MIGHT'VE FORGOTTEN.
Ginbura = walking around Ginza
beep
I'LL E-MAIL HIM!
UH-OH.
Whoops.
I TOTALLY FORGOT.
WHAT?
A LADY-FRIEND?
TAKE...
WHEN CAN WE GO HOME TODAY?
OH YEAH, THE PARENTS ARE COMING, AREN'T THEY?
I ARRANGED THE SCHEDULE SO YOU CAN LEAVE AT 7.

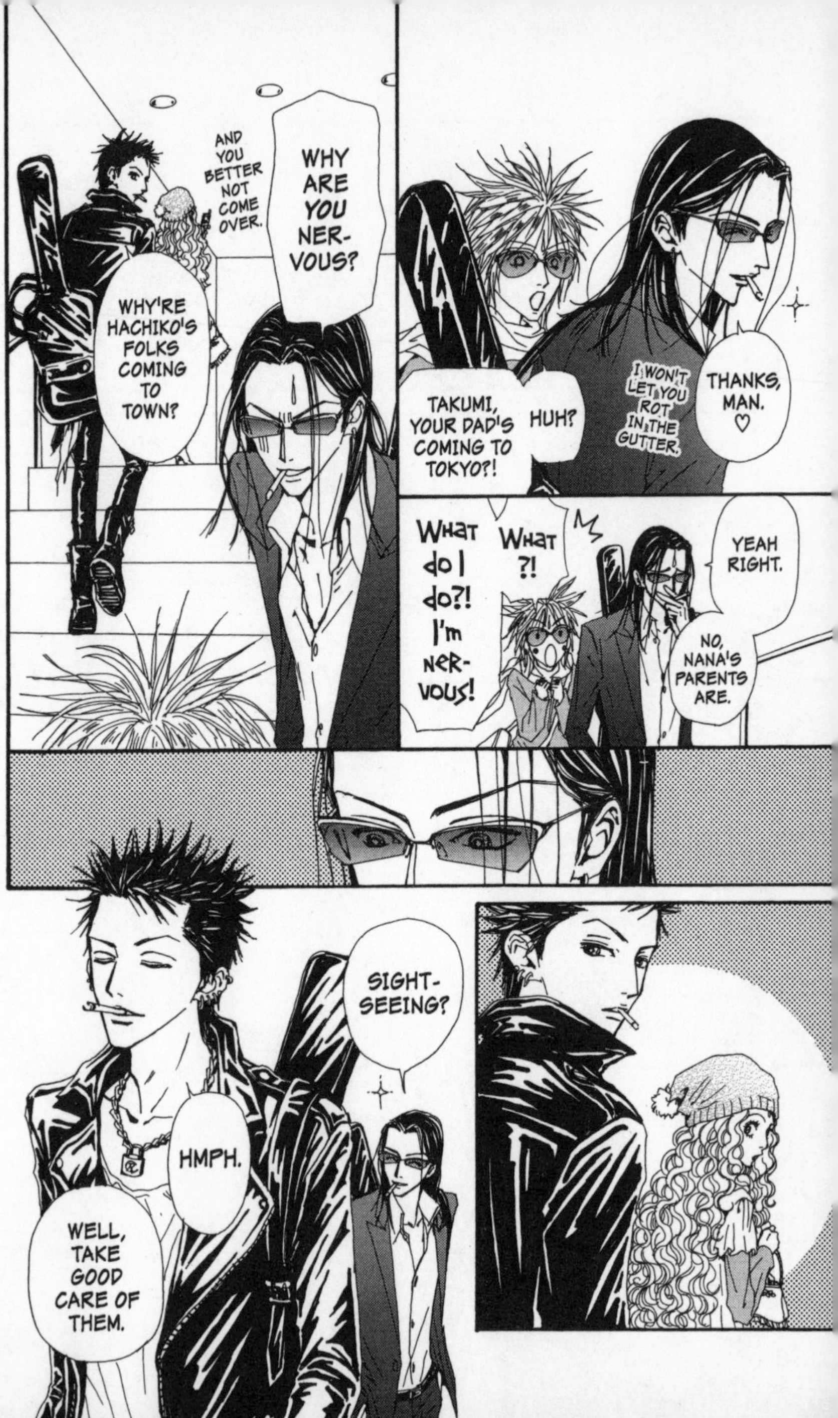
THANKS, MAN. ♡
I WON'T LET YOU ROT IN THE GUTTER.
HUH?
TAKUMI, YOUR DAD'S COMING TO TOKYO?!
YEAH RIGHT.
NO, NANA'S PARENTS ARE.
WHAT?!
WHAT do I do?! I'm NERVOUS!
WHY ARE YOU NERVOUS?
AND YOU BETTER NOT COME OVER.
WHY'RE HACHIKO'S FOLKS COMING TO TOWN?
SIGHT-SEEING?
HMPH.
WELL, TAKE GOOD CARE OF THEM.

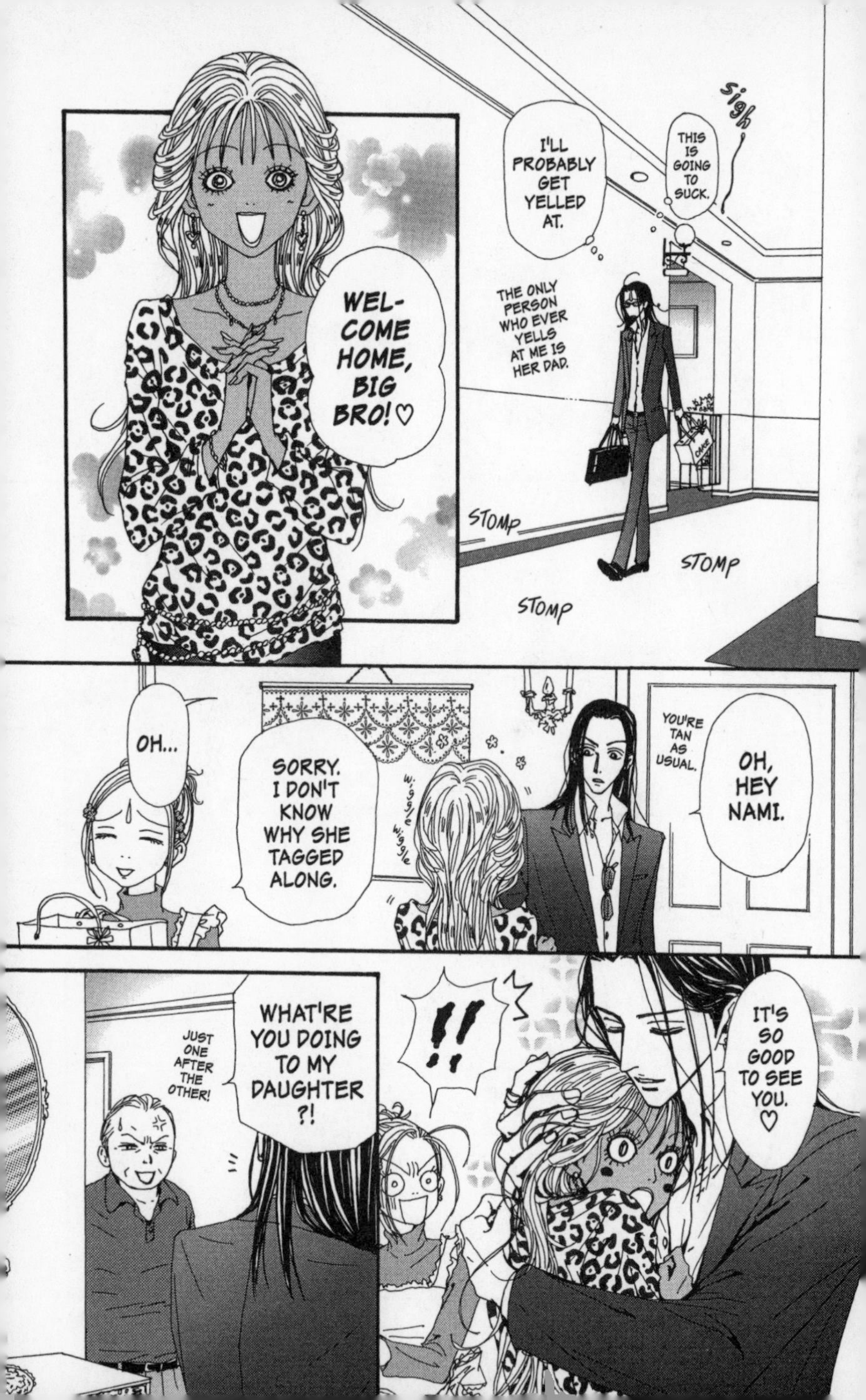
sigh
THIS IS GOING TO SUCK.
I'LL PROBABLY GET YELLED AT.
THE ONLY PERSON WHO EVER YELLS AT ME IS HER DAD.
STOMP
STOMP
STOMP
WEL-COME HOME, BIG BRO! ♡
OH, HEY NAMI.
YOU'RE TAN AS USUAL.
wiggle wiggle
SORRY. I DON'T KNOW WHY SHE TAGGED ALONG.
OH...
IT'S SO GOOD TO SEE YOU. ♡
!!
WHAT'RE YOU DOING TO MY DAUGHTER?!
JUST ONE AFTER THE OTHER!

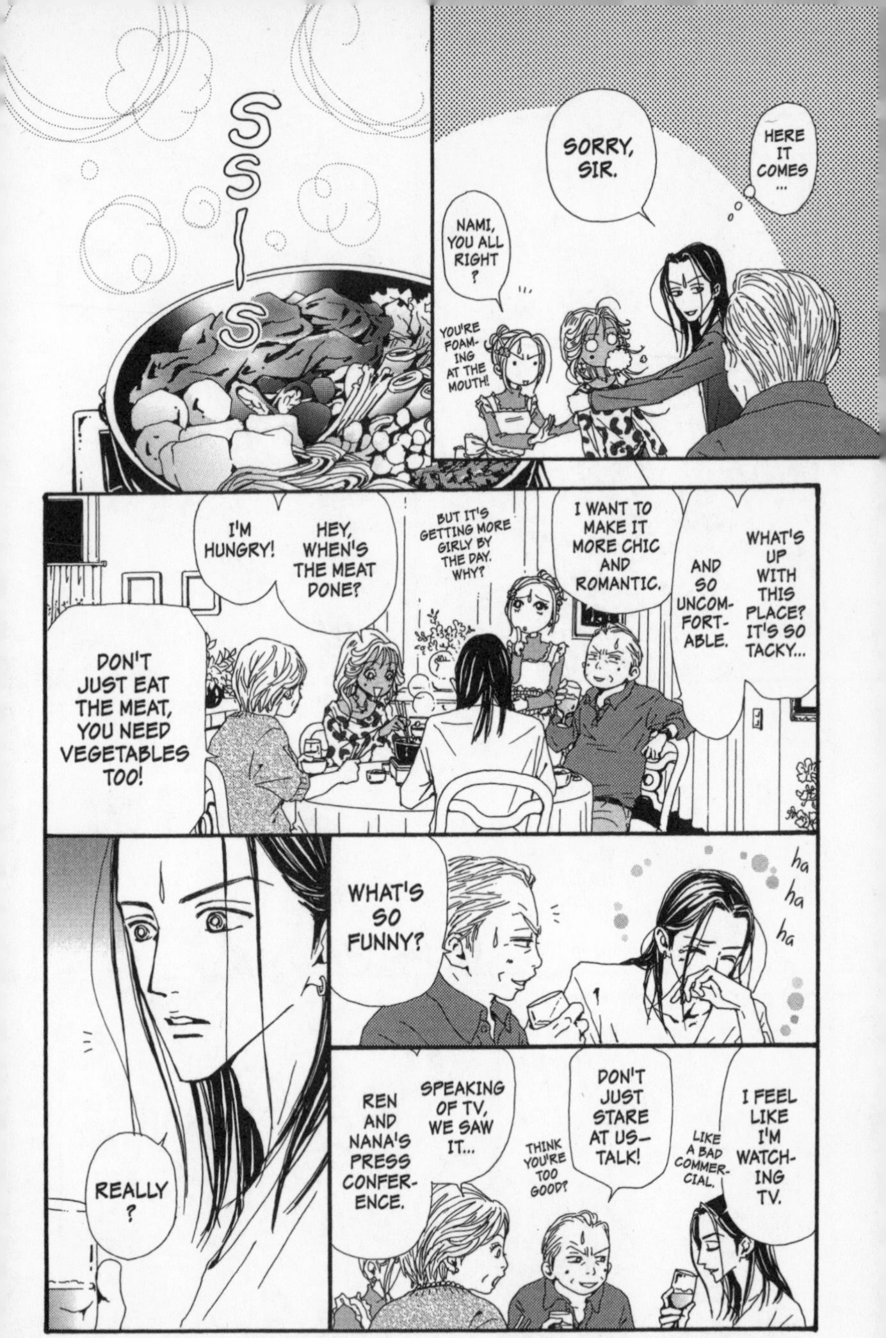
HERE IT COMES ...
SORRY, SIR.
NAMI, YOU ALL RIGHT ?
YOU'RE FOAMING AT THE MOUTH!
SSIS
WHAT'S UP WITH THIS PLACE? IT'S SO TACKY...
AND SO UNCOMFORTABLE.
I WANT TO MAKE IT MORE CHIC AND ROMANTIC.
BUT IT'S GETTING MORE GIRLY BY THE DAY. WHY?
HEY, WHEN'S THE MEAT DONE?
I'M HUNGRY!
DON'T JUST EAT THE MEAT, YOU NEED VEGETABLES TOO!
ha ha ha
WHAT'S SO FUNNY?
I FEEL LIKE I'M WATCHING TV.
LIKE A BAD COMMERCIAL.
DON'T JUST STARE AT US—TALK!
THINK YOU'RE TOO GOOD?
SPEAKING OF TV, WE SAW IT...
REN AND NANA'S PRESS CONFERENCE.
REALLY ?

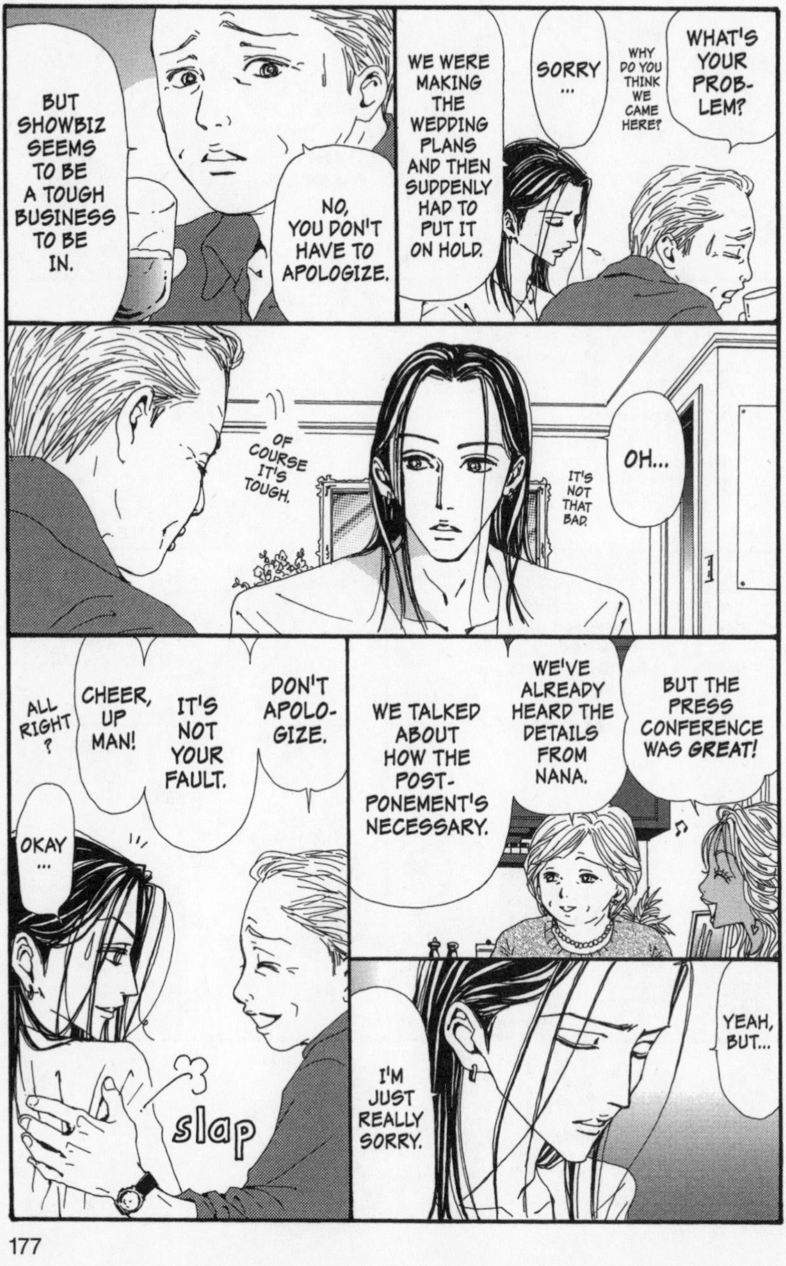
WHAT'S YOUR PROB-LEM?
WHY DO YOU THINK WE CAME HERE?
SORRY...
WE WERE MAKING THE WEDDING PLANS AND THEN SUDDENLY HAD TO PUT IT ON HOLD.
NO, YOU DON'T HAVE TO APOLOGIZE.
BUT SHOWBIZ SEEMS TO BE A TOUGH BUSINESS TO BE IN.
OH...
IT'S NOT THAT BAD.
OF COURSE IT'S TOUGH.
BUT THE PRESS CONFERENCE WAS GREAT!
WE'VE ALREADY HEARD THE DETAILS FROM NANA.
WE TALKED ABOUT HOW THE POST-PONEMENT'S NECESSARY.
YEAH, BUT...
I'M JUST REALLY SORRY.
DON'T APOLO-GIZE.
IT'S NOT YOUR FAULT.
CHEER, UP MAN!
ALL RIGHT?
OKAY...
slap

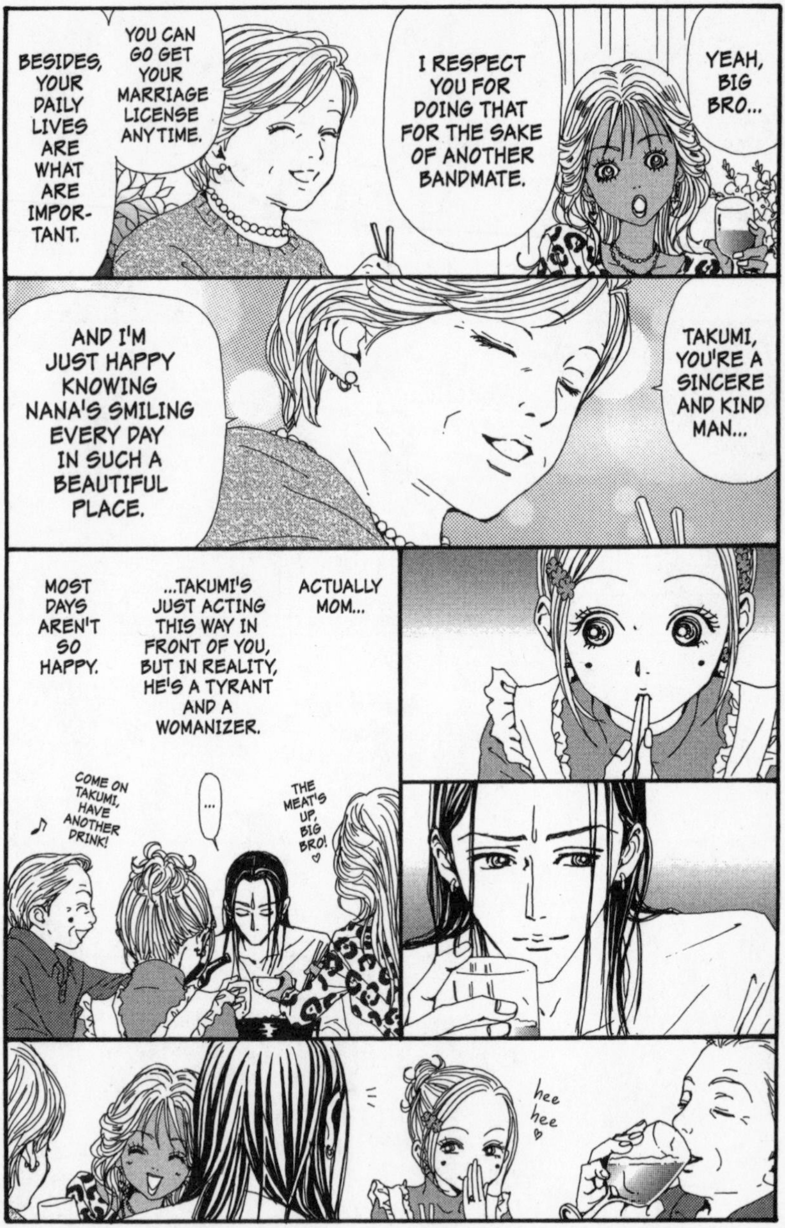
YEAH, BIG BRO...
I RESPECT YOU FOR DOING THAT FOR THE SAKE OF ANOTHER BANDMATE.
YOU CAN GO GET YOUR MARRIAGE LICENSE ANYTIME.
BESIDES, YOUR DAILY LIVES ARE WHAT ARE IMPORTANT.
TAKUMI, YOU'RE A SINCERE AND KIND MAN...
AND I'M JUST HAPPY KNOWING NANA'S SMILING EVERY DAY IN SUCH A BEAUTIFUL PLACE.
ACTUALLY MOM...
...TAKUMI'S JUST ACTING THIS WAY IN FRONT OF YOU, BUT IN REALITY, HE'S A TYRANT AND A WOMANIZER.
MOST DAYS AREN'T SO HAPPY.
THE MEAT'S UP, BIG BRO! ♡
...
COME ON TAKUMI, HAVE ANOTHER DRINK! ♪
hee hee ♡

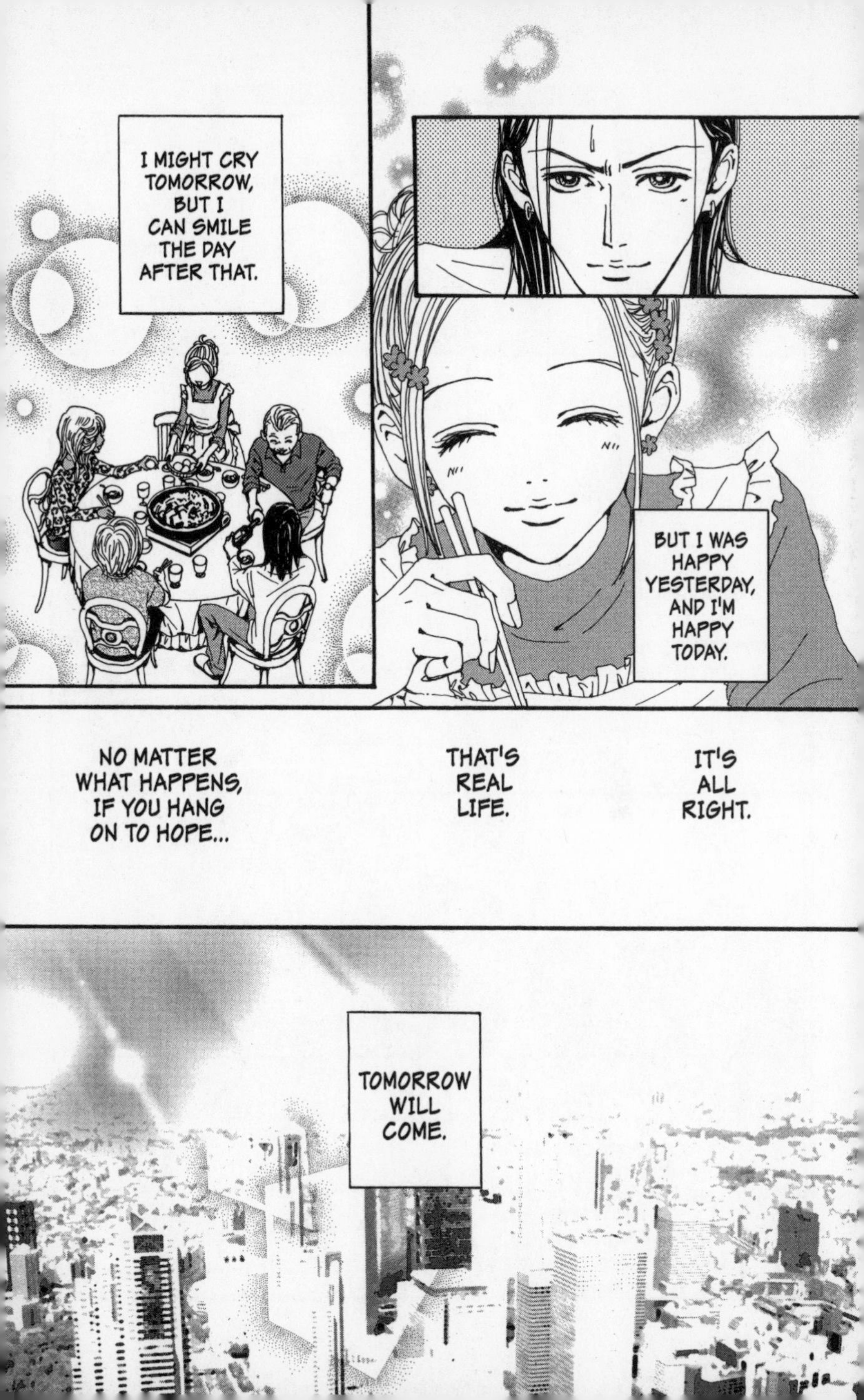
BUT I WAS HAPPY YESTERDAY, AND I'M HAPPY TODAY.
I MIGHT CRY TOMORROW, BUT I CAN SMILE THE DAY AFTER THAT.
IT'S ALL RIGHT.
THAT'S REAL LIFE.
NO MATTER WHAT HAPPENS, IF YOU HANG ON TO HOPE...
TOMORROW WILL COME.

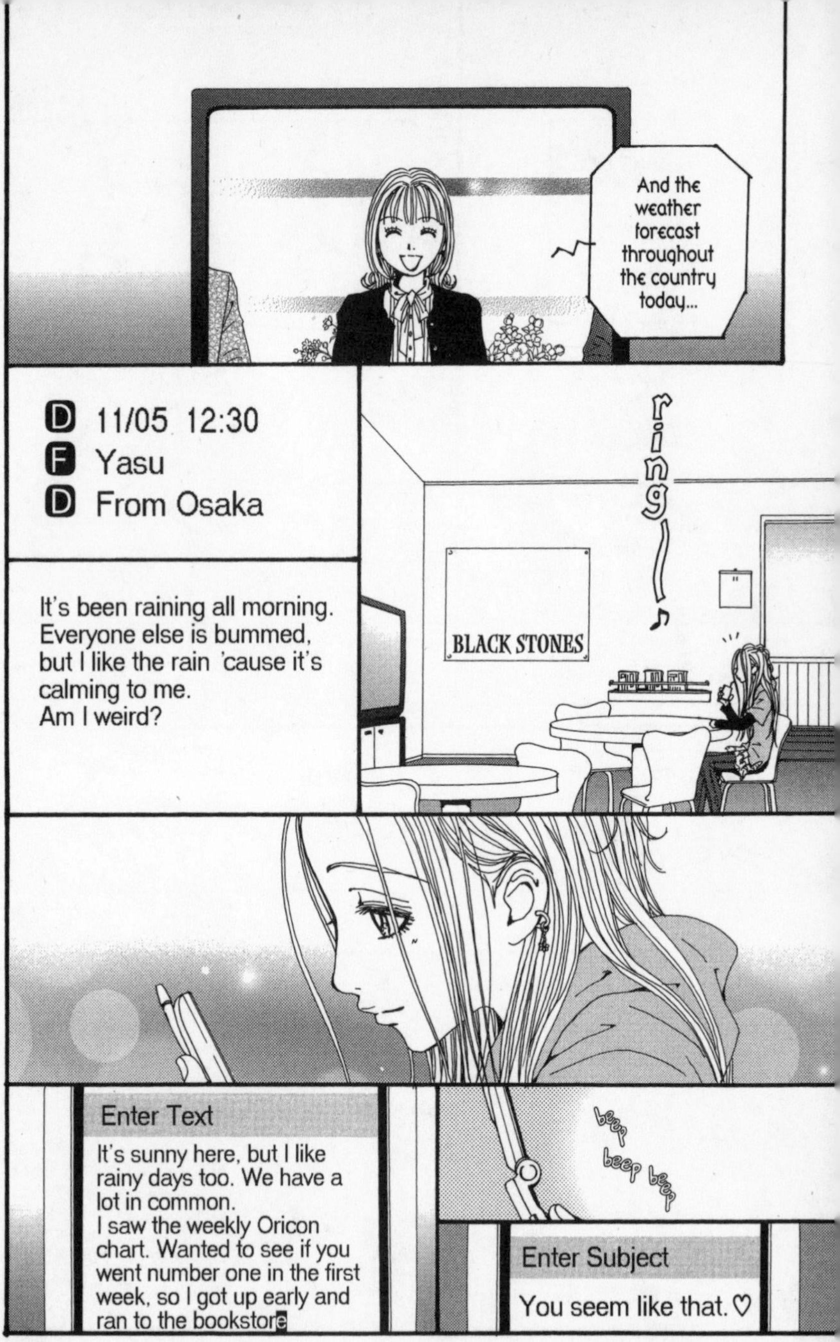
And the weather forecast throughout the country today...
ring—♪
D 11/05 12:30
F Yasu
D From Osaka
It's been raining all morning. Everyone else is bummed, but I like the rain 'cause it's calming to me. Am I weird?
beep beep beep
Enter Subject
You seem like that. ♡
Enter Text
It's sunny here, but I like rainy days too. We have a lot in common. I saw the weekly Oricon chart. Wanted to see if you went number one in the first week, so I got up early and ran to the bookstore

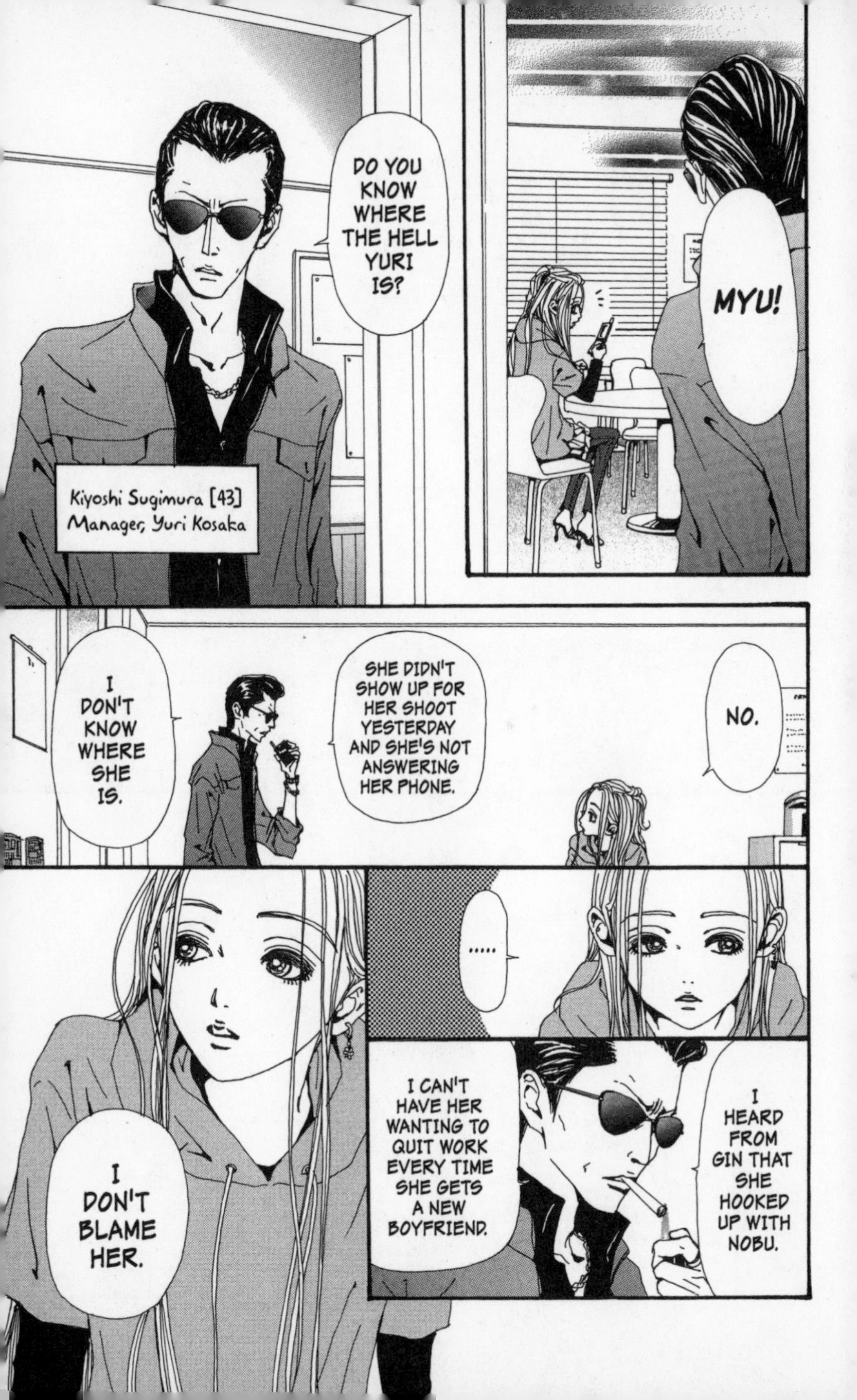
MYU!
DO YOU KNOW WHERE THE HELL YURI IS?
Kiyoshi Sugimura [43]
Manager, Yuri Kosaka
NO.
SHE DIDN'T SHOW UP FOR HER SHOOT YESTERDAY AND SHE'S NOT ANSWERING HER PHONE.
I DON'T KNOW WHERE SHE IS.
.....
I HEARD FROM GIN THAT SHE HOOKED UP WITH NOBU.
I CAN'T HAVE HER WANTING TO QUIT WORK EVERY TIME SHE GETS A NEW BOYFRIEND.
I DON'T BLAME HER.

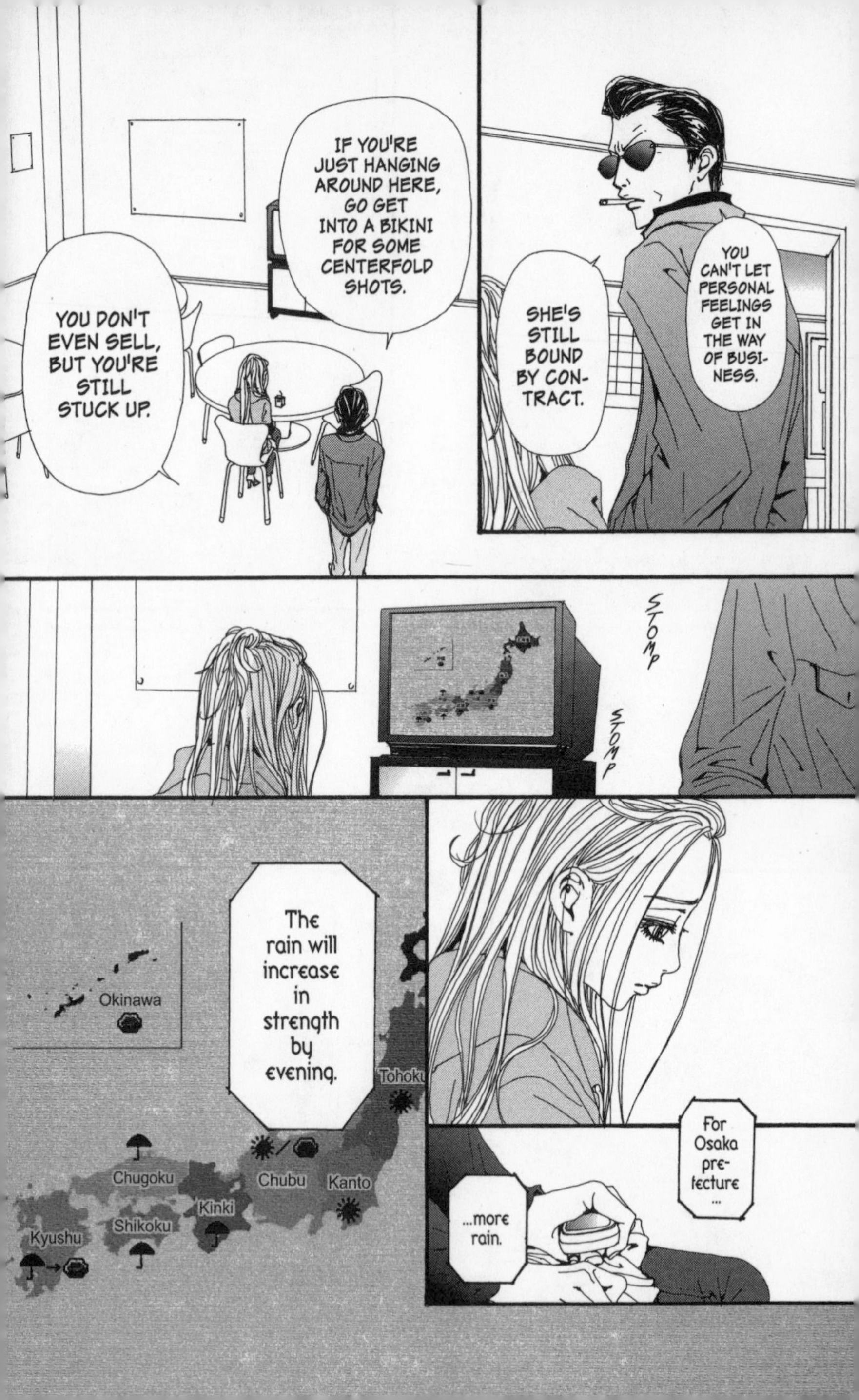
YOU CAN'T LET PERSONAL FEELINGS GET IN THE WAY OF BUSINESS.
SHE'S STILL BOUND BY CONTRACT.
IF YOU'RE JUST HANGING AROUND HERE, GO GET INTO A BIKINI FOR SOME CENTERFOLD SHOTS.
YOU DON'T EVEN SELL, BUT YOU'RE STILL STUCK UP.
STOMP
STOMP
For Osaka prefecture...
...more rain.
The rain will increase in strength by evening.
Okinawa
Tohoku
Chubu
Kanto
Chugoku
Kinki
Shikoku
Kyushu

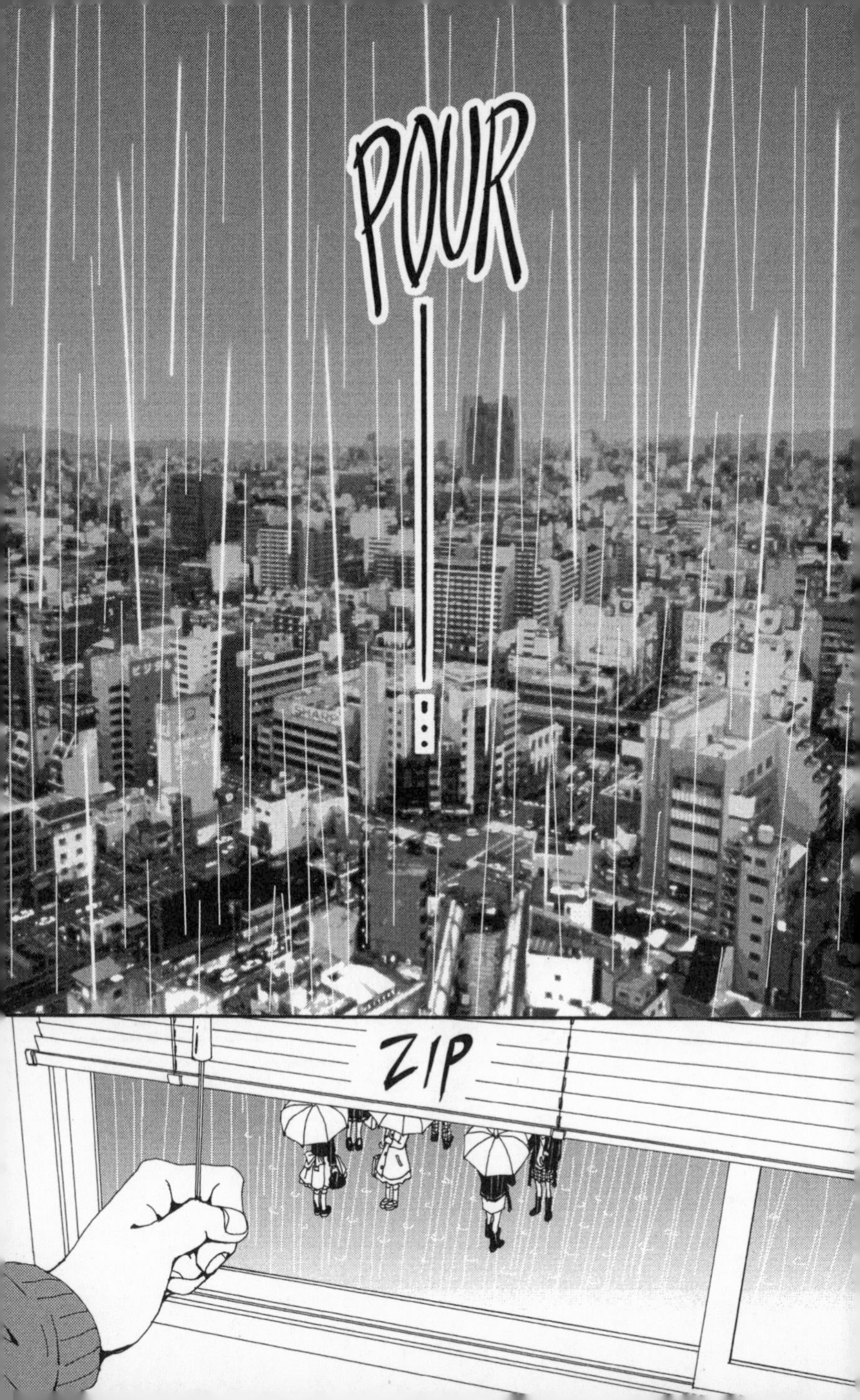
POUR
ZIP

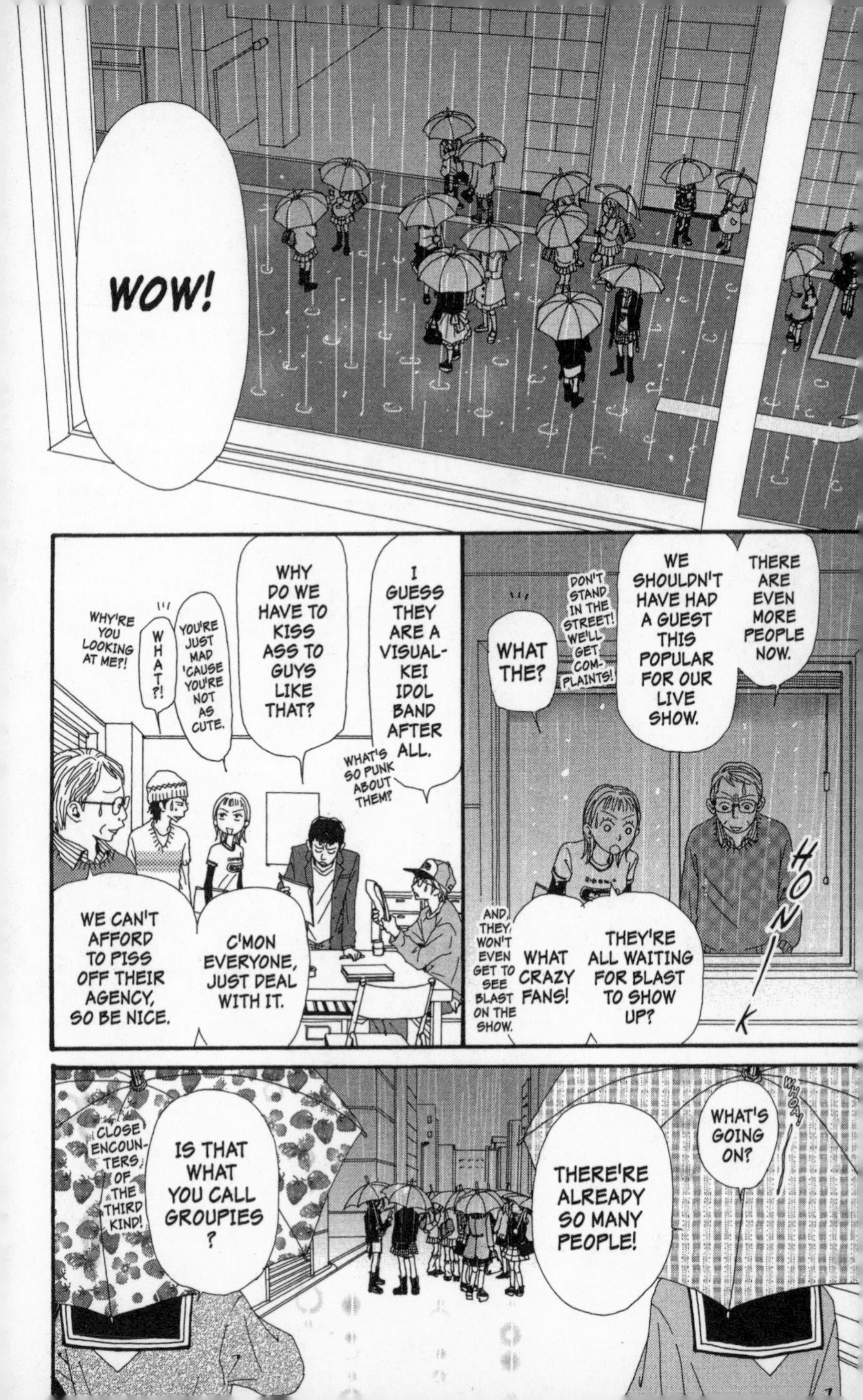
WOW!
THERE ARE EVEN MORE PEOPLE NOW.
WE SHOULDN'T HAVE HAD A GUEST THIS POPULAR FOR OUR LIVE SHOW.
DON'T STAND IN THE STREET! WE'LL GET COMPLAINTS!
WHAT THE?
HONK
THEY'RE ALL WAITING FOR BLAST TO SHOW UP?
WHAT CRAZY FANS!
AND THEY WON'T EVEN GET TO SEE BLAST ON THE SHOW.
I GUESS THEY ARE A VISUAL-KEI IDOL BAND AFTER ALL.
WHAT'S SO PUNK ABOUT THEM?
WHY DO WE HAVE TO KISS ASS TO GUYS LIKE THAT?
YOU'RE JUST MAD 'CAUSE YOU'RE NOT AS CUTE.
WHAT?!
WHY'RE YOU LOOKING AT ME?!
C'MON EVERYONE, JUST DEAL WITH IT.
WE CAN'T AFFORD TO PISS OFF THEIR AGENCY, SO BE NICE.
WHAT'S GOING ON?
WHOA!
THERE'RE ALREADY SO MANY PEOPLE!
IS THAT WHAT YOU CALL GROUPIES?
CLOSE ENCOUNTERS OF THE THIRD KIND!

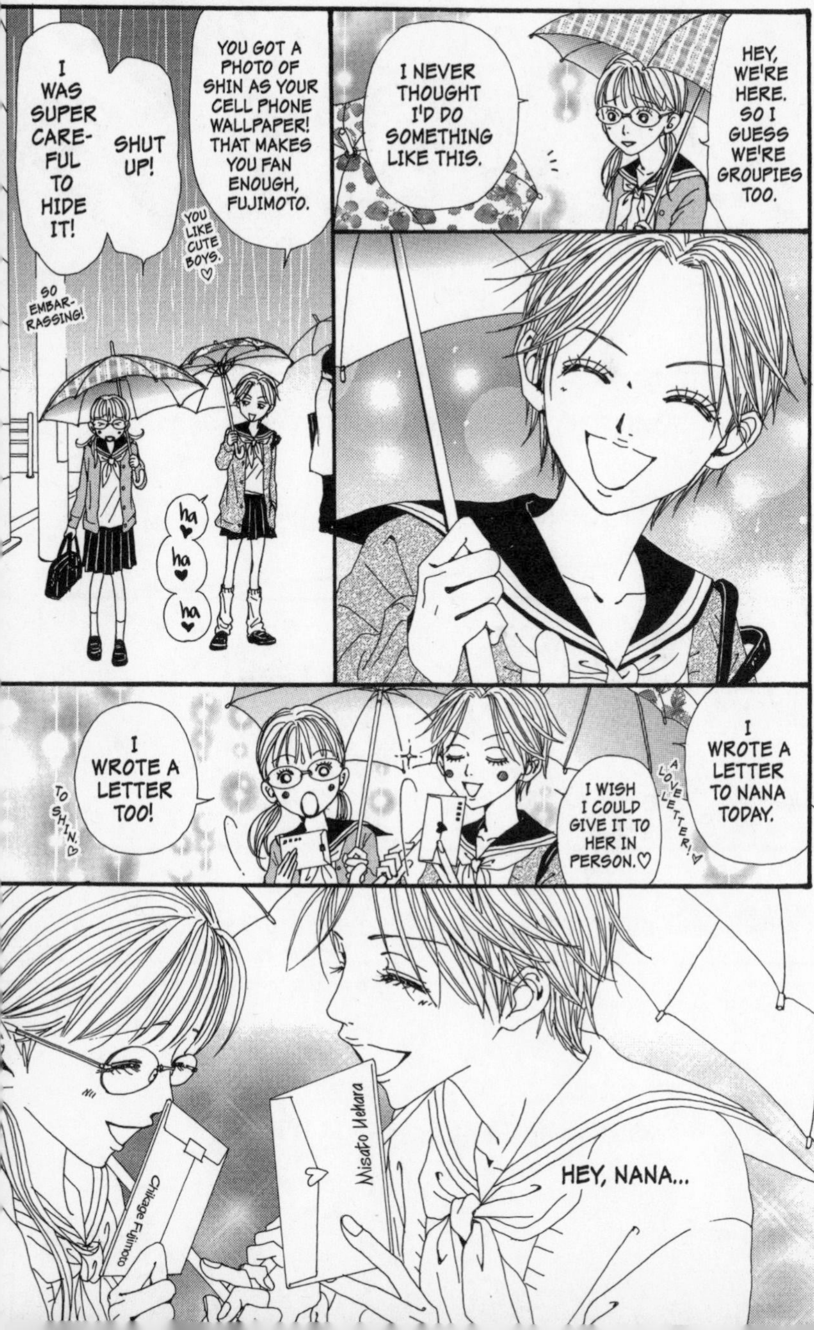
HEY, WE'RE HERE. SO I GUESS WE'RE GROUPIES TOO.
I NEVER THOUGHT I'D DO SOMETHING LIKE THIS.
YOU GOT A PHOTO OF SHIN AS YOUR CELL PHONE WALLPAPER! THAT MAKES YOU FAN ENOUGH, FUJIMOTO.
YOU LIKE CUTE BOYS. ♡
SHUT UP!
I WAS SUPER CAREFUL TO HIDE IT!
SO EMBARRASSING!
ha ♥ ha ♥ ha ♥
I WROTE A LETTER TO NANA TODAY.
A LOVE LETTER! ♥
I WISH I COULD GIVE IT TO HER IN PERSON. ♡
I WROTE A LETTER TOO!
TO SHIN. ♡
HEY, NANA...
Misato Uehara
Chikage Fujimoto

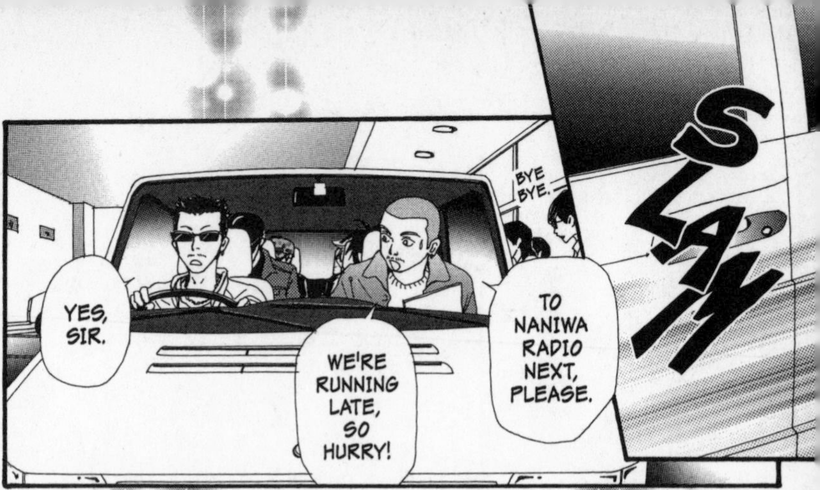
SLAM
BYE BYE.
TO NANIWA RADIO NEXT, PLEASE.
WE'RE RUNNING LATE, SO HURRY!
YES, SIR.

IF YOU DON'T LOSE HOPE, TOMORROW WILL COME.

I LEARNED THAT FROM YOU, NANA.

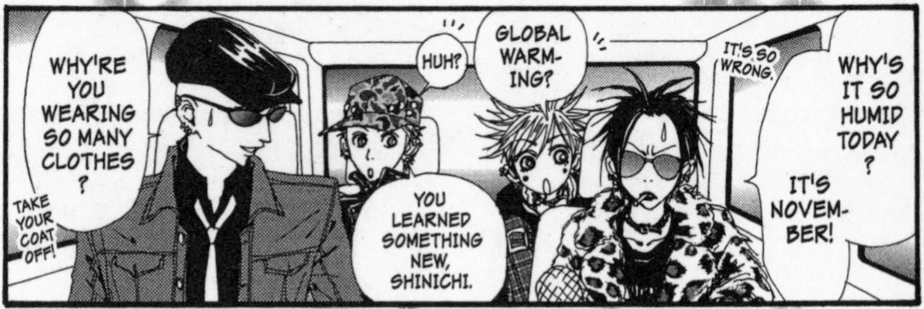
WHY'S IT SO HUMID TODAY?
IT'S SO WRONG.
IT'S NOVEMBER!
GLOBAL WARMING?
HUH?
YOU LEARNED SOMETHING NEW, SHINICHI.
WHY'RE YOU WEARING SO MANY CLOTHES?
TAKE YOUR COAT OFF!

BUT THE RAIN THAT DAY NEVER STOPPED.

IT STILL WETS MY CHEEKS TO THIS DAY.

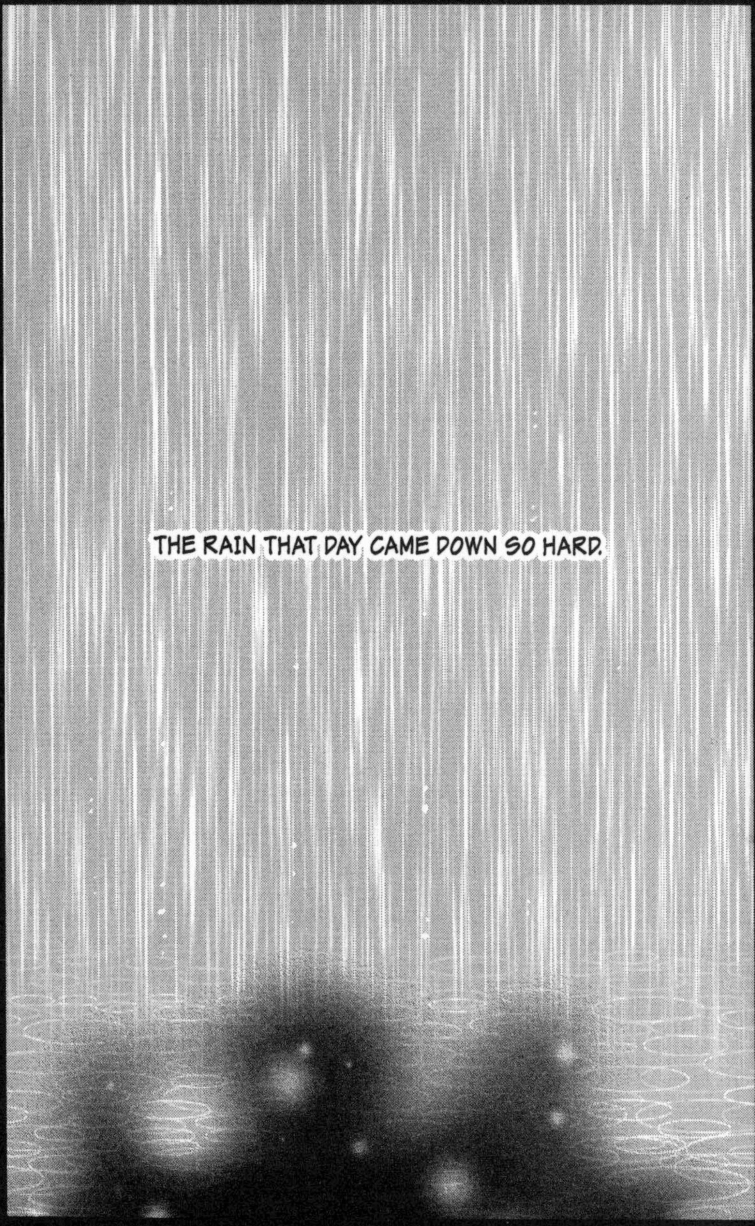
THE RAIN THAT DAY CAME DOWN SO HARD.

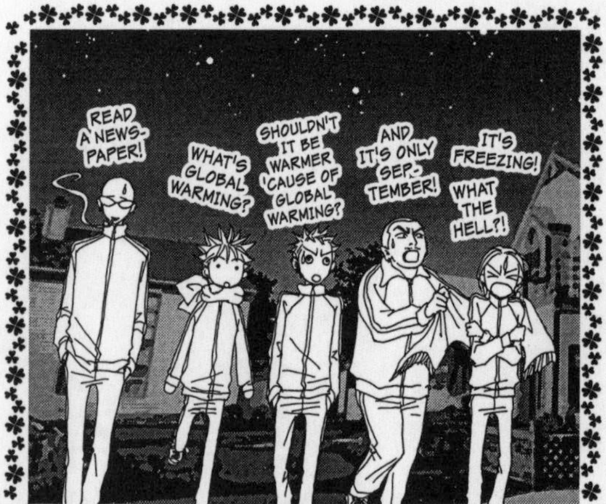
IT'S FREEZING!
WHAT THE HELL?!
AND IT'S ONLY SEP-TEMBER!
SHOULDN'T IT BE WARMER 'CAUSE OF GLOBAL WARMING?
WHAT'S GLOBAL WARMING?
READ A NEWS-PAPER!

Bonus Page

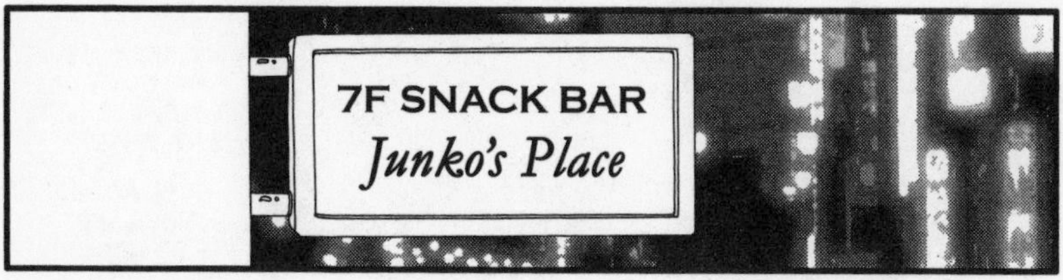

7F SNACK BAR
Junko's Place

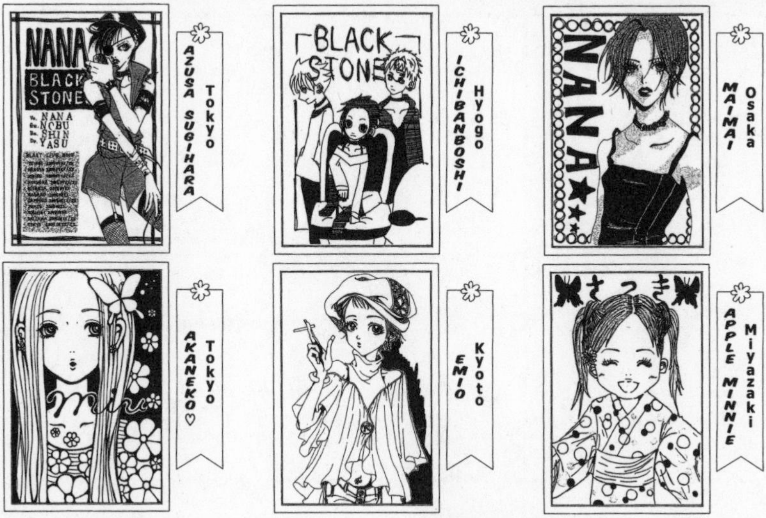

NANA
Osaka
MAIMAI
BLACK STONE
Hyogo
ICHIBANBOSHI
NANA
BLACK STONE
Tokyo
AZUSA SUGIHARA
さつき
Miyazaki
APPLE MINNIE
Kyoto
EMIO
mini
Tokyo
AKANEKO♡

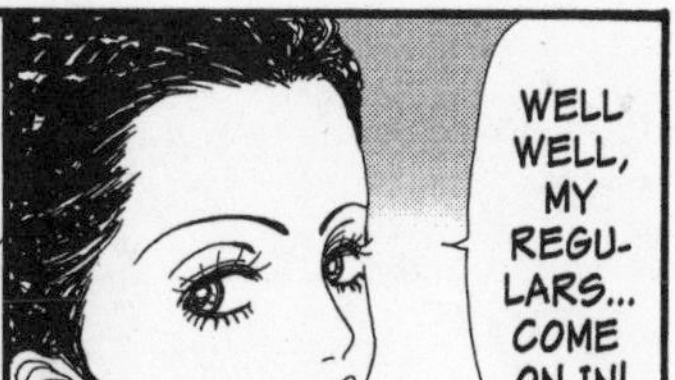

WELL WELL, MY REGULARS... COME ON IN!
Ai Yazawa

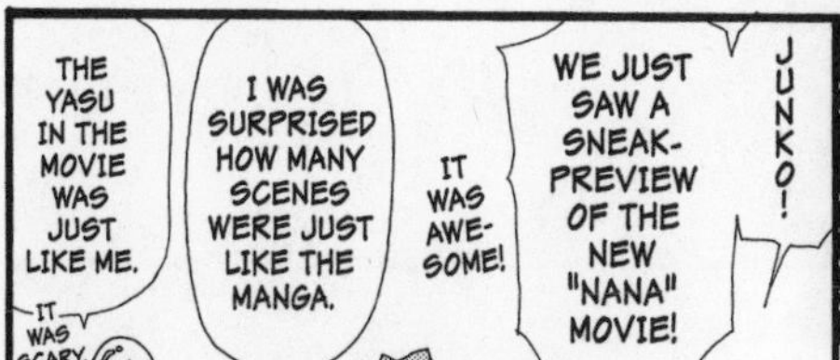

JUNKO!
WE JUST SAW A SNEAK-PREVIEW OF THE NEW "NANA" MOVIE!
IT WAS AWE-SOME!
I WAS SURPRISED HOW MANY SCENES WERE JUST LIKE THE MANGA.
THE YASU IN THE MOVIE WAS JUST LIKE ME.
IT WAS SCARY.
I WAS FEELING THE LOVE FROM THE FILM CREW.
IT WAS EMBARRASSING, LIKE I WAS WATCHING MYSELF.

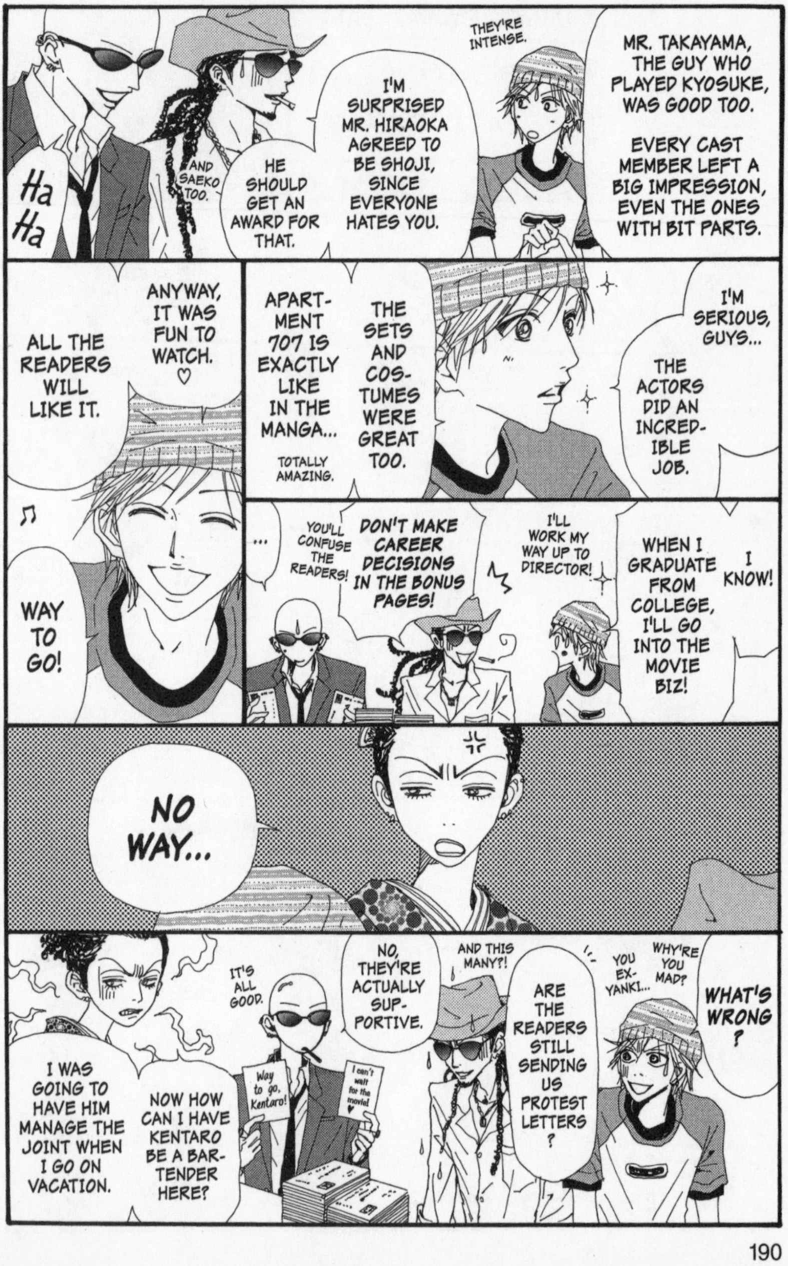
MR. TAKAYAMA, THE GUY WHO PLAYED KYOSUKE, WAS GOOD TOO.
EVERY CAST MEMBER LEFT A BIG IMPRESSION, EVEN THE ONES WITH BIT PARTS.
THEY'RE INTENSE.
I'M SURPRISED MR. HIRAOKA AGREED TO BE SHOJI, SINCE EVERYONE HATES YOU.
HE SHOULD GET AN AWARD FOR THAT.
AND SAEKO TOO.
Ha Ha
I'M SERIOUS, GUYS...
THE ACTORS DID AN INCRED-IBLE JOB.
THE SETS AND COS-TUMES WERE GREAT TOO.
APART-MENT 707 IS EXACTLY LIKE IN THE MANGA...
TOTALLY AMAZING.
I KNOW!
WHEN I GRADUATE FROM COLLEGE, I'LL GO INTO THE MOVIE BIZ!
I'LL WORK MY WAY UP TO DIRECTOR!
DON'T MAKE CAREER DECISIONS IN THE BONUS PAGES!
YOU'LL CONFUSE THE READERS!
...
ANYWAY, IT WAS FUN TO WATCH. ♡
ALL THE READERS WILL LIKE IT.
♫
WAY TO GO!
NO WAY...
WHAT'S WRONG?
WHY'RE YOU MAD?
YOU EX-YANKI...
ARE THE READERS STILL SENDING US PROTEST LETTERS?
AND THIS MANY?!
NO, THEY'RE ACTUALLY SUP-PORTIVE.
IT'S ALL GOOD.
I can't wait for the movie! ♥
Way to go, Kentaro!
NOW HOW CAN I HAVE KENTARO BE A BAR-TENDER HERE?
I WAS GOING TO HAVE HIM MANAGE THE JOINT WHEN I GO ON VACATION.

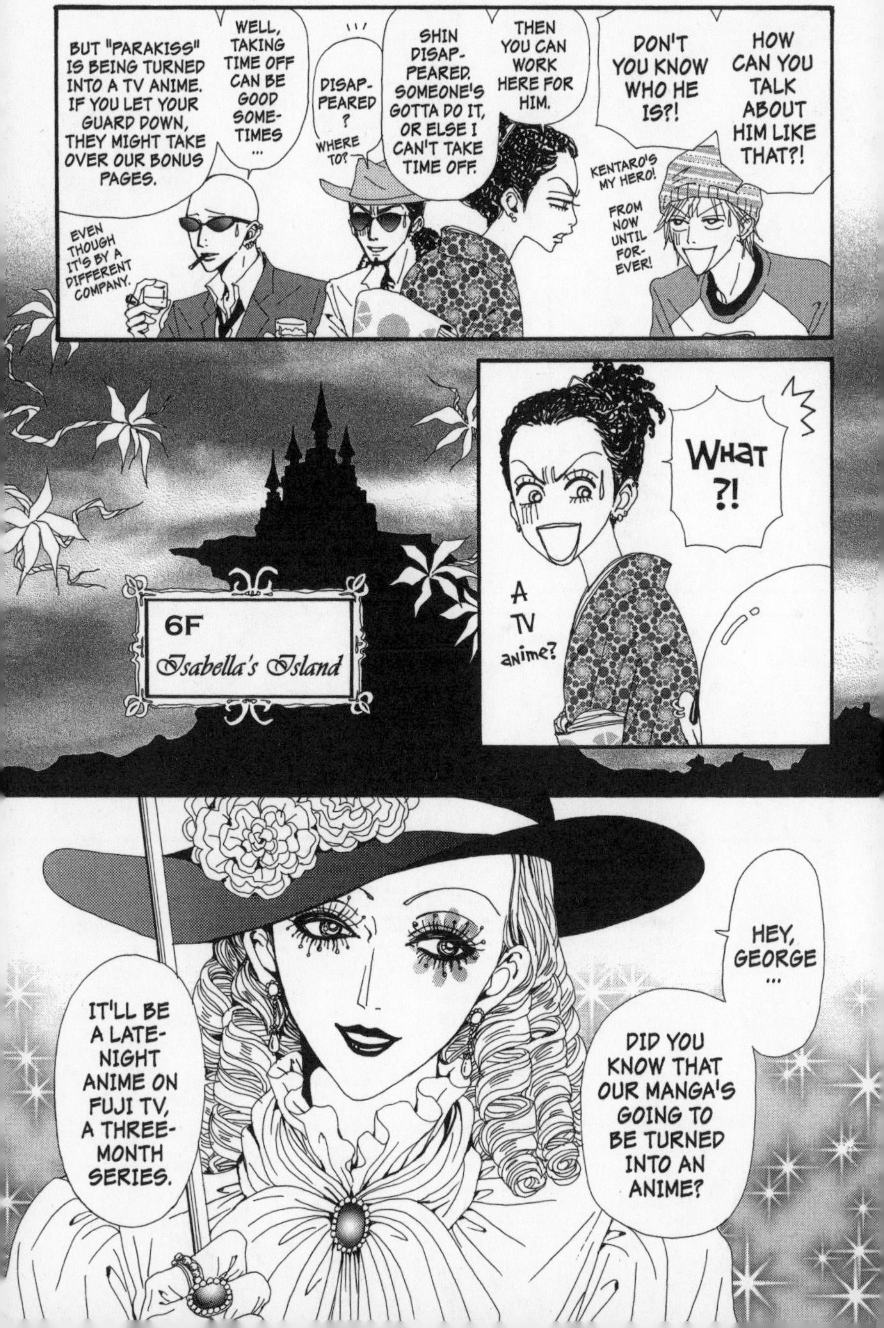
HOW CAN YOU TALK ABOUT HIM LIKE THAT?!
DON'T YOU KNOW WHO HE IS?!
KENTARO'S MY HERO!
FROM NOW UNTIL FOREVER!
THEN YOU CAN WORK HERE FOR HIM.
SHIN DISAPPEARED. SOMEONE'S GOTTA DO IT, OR ELSE I CAN'T TAKE TIME OFF.
DISAPPEARED?
WHERE TO?
WELL, TAKING TIME OFF CAN BE GOOD SOMETIMES...
BUT "PARAKISS" IS BEING TURNED INTO A TV ANIME. IF YOU LET YOUR GUARD DOWN, THEY MIGHT TAKE OVER OUR BONUS PAGES.
EVEN THOUGH IT'S BY A DIFFERENT COMPANY.
WHAT?!
A TV anime?
6F
Isabella's Island
HEY, GEORGE...
DID YOU KNOW THAT OUR MANGA'S GOING TO BE TURNED INTO AN ANIME?
IT'LL BE A LATE-NIGHT ANIME ON FUJI TV, A THREE-MONTH SERIES.

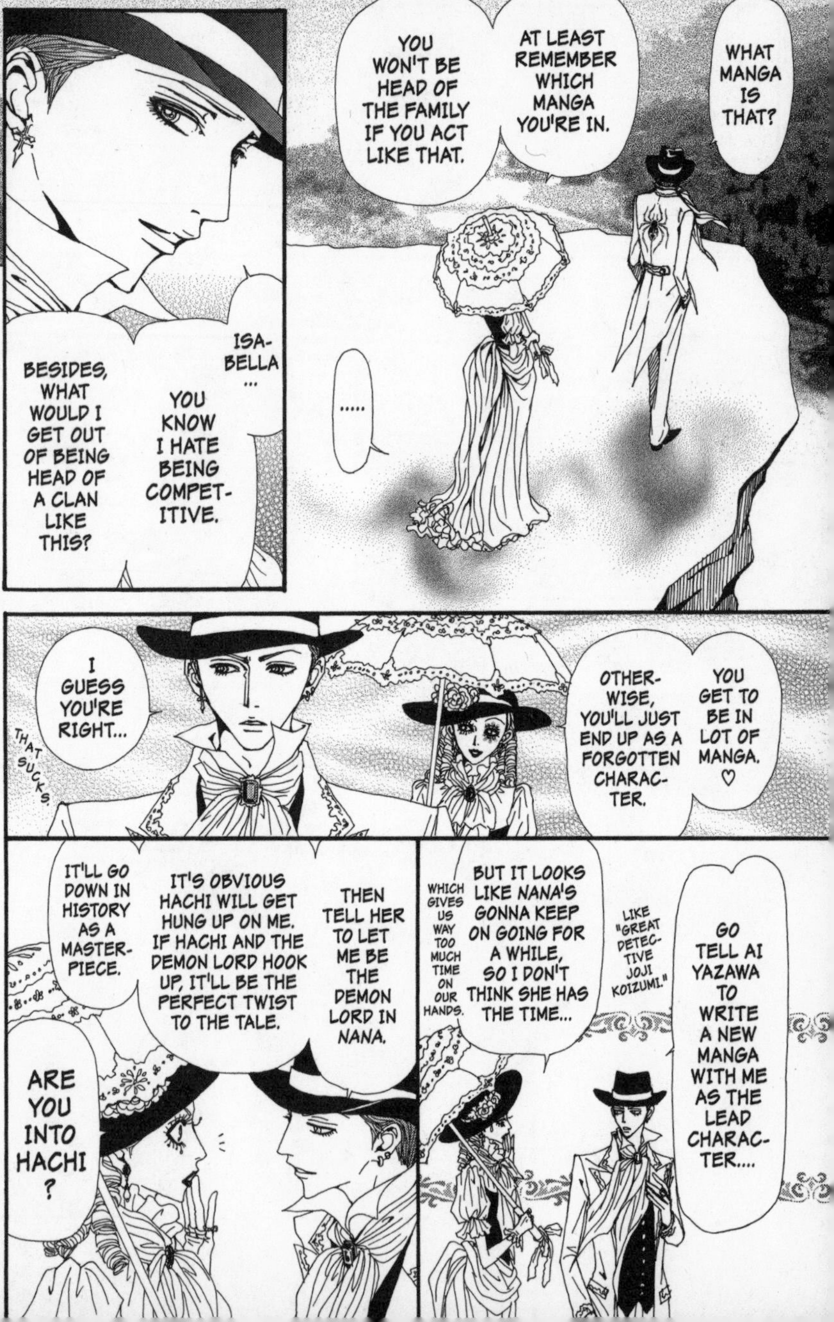
WHAT MANGA IS THAT?
AT LEAST REMEMBER WHICH MANGA YOU'RE IN.
YOU WON'T BE HEAD OF THE FAMILY IF YOU ACT LIKE THAT.
.....
ISA-BELLA...
YOU KNOW I HATE BEING COMPET-ITIVE.
BESIDES, WHAT WOULD I GET OUT OF BEING HEAD OF A CLAN LIKE THIS?
YOU GET TO BE IN LOT OF MANGA. ♡
OTHER-WISE, YOU'LL JUST END UP AS A FORGOTTEN CHARAC-TER.
I GUESS YOU'RE RIGHT...
THAT SUCKS.
GO TELL AI YAZAWA TO WRITE A NEW MANGA WITH ME AS THE LEAD CHARAC-TER....
LIKE "GREAT DETEC-TIVE JOJI KOIZUMI."
BUT IT LOOKS LIKE NANA'S GONNA KEEP ON GOING FOR A WHILE, SO I DON'T THINK SHE HAS THE TIME...
WHICH GIVES US WAY TOO MUCH TIME ON OUR HANDS.
THEN TELL HER TO LET ME BE THE DEMON LORD IN NANA.
IT'S OBVIOUS HACHI WILL GET HUNG UP ON ME. IF HACHI AND THE DEMON LORD HOOK UP, IT'LL BE THE PERFECT TWIST TO THE TALE.
IT'LL GO DOWN IN HISTORY AS A MASTER-PIECE.
ARE YOU INTO HACHI?

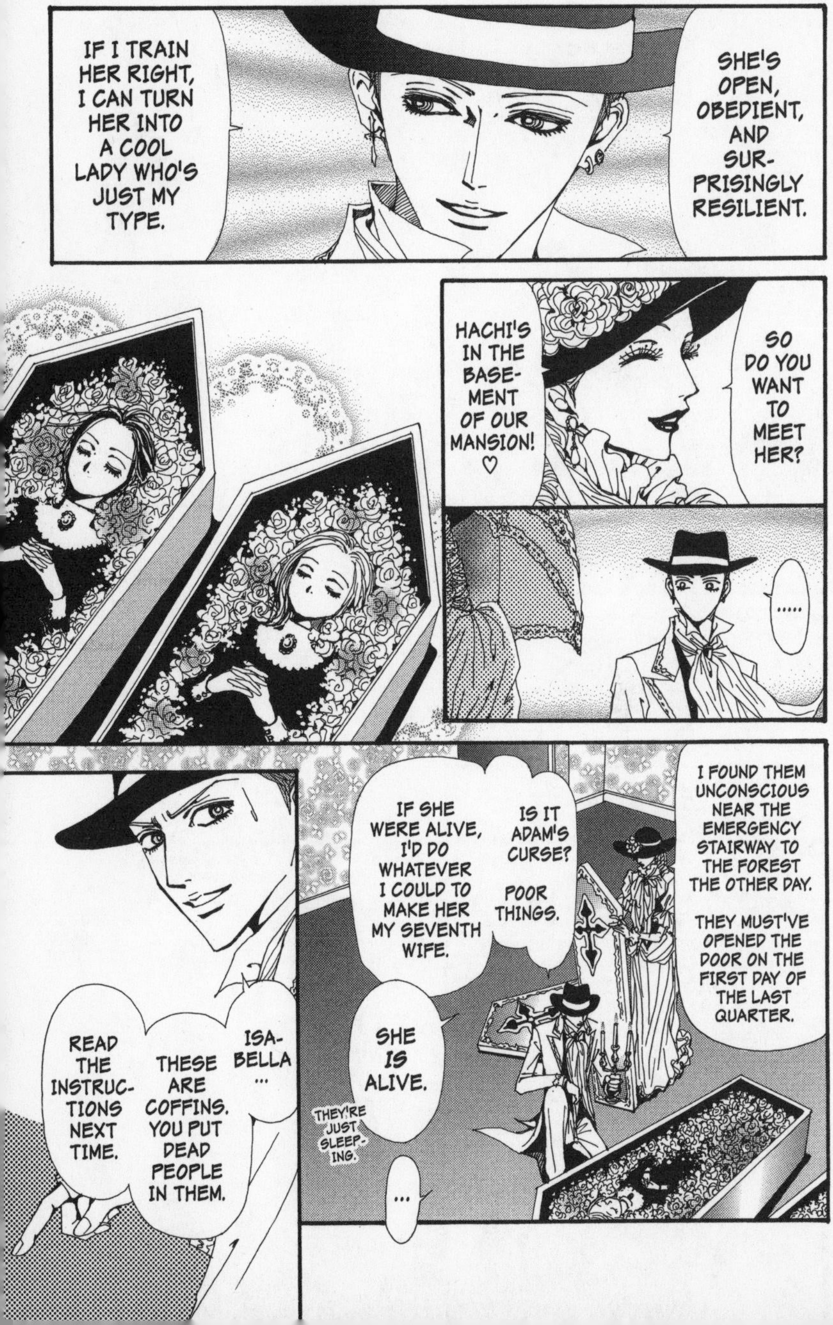
SHE'S OPEN, OBEDIENT, AND SURPRISINGLY RESILIENT.
IF I TRAIN HER RIGHT, I CAN TURN HER INTO A COOL LADY WHO'S JUST MY TYPE.
SO DO YOU WANT TO MEET HER?
HACHI'S IN THE BASEMENT OF OUR MANSION! ♡
.....
I FOUND THEM UNCONSCIOUS NEAR THE EMERGENCY STAIRWAY TO THE FOREST THE OTHER DAY.
THEY MUST'VE OPENED THE DOOR ON THE FIRST DAY OF THE LAST QUARTER.
IS IT ADAM'S CURSE?
POOR THINGS.
IF SHE WERE ALIVE, I'D DO WHATEVER I COULD TO MAKE HER MY SEVENTH WIFE.
SHE *IS* ALIVE.
THEY'RE JUST SLEEPING.
...
ISABELLA...
THESE ARE COFFINS. YOU PUT DEAD PEOPLE IN THEM.
READ THE INSTRUCTIONS NEXT TIME.

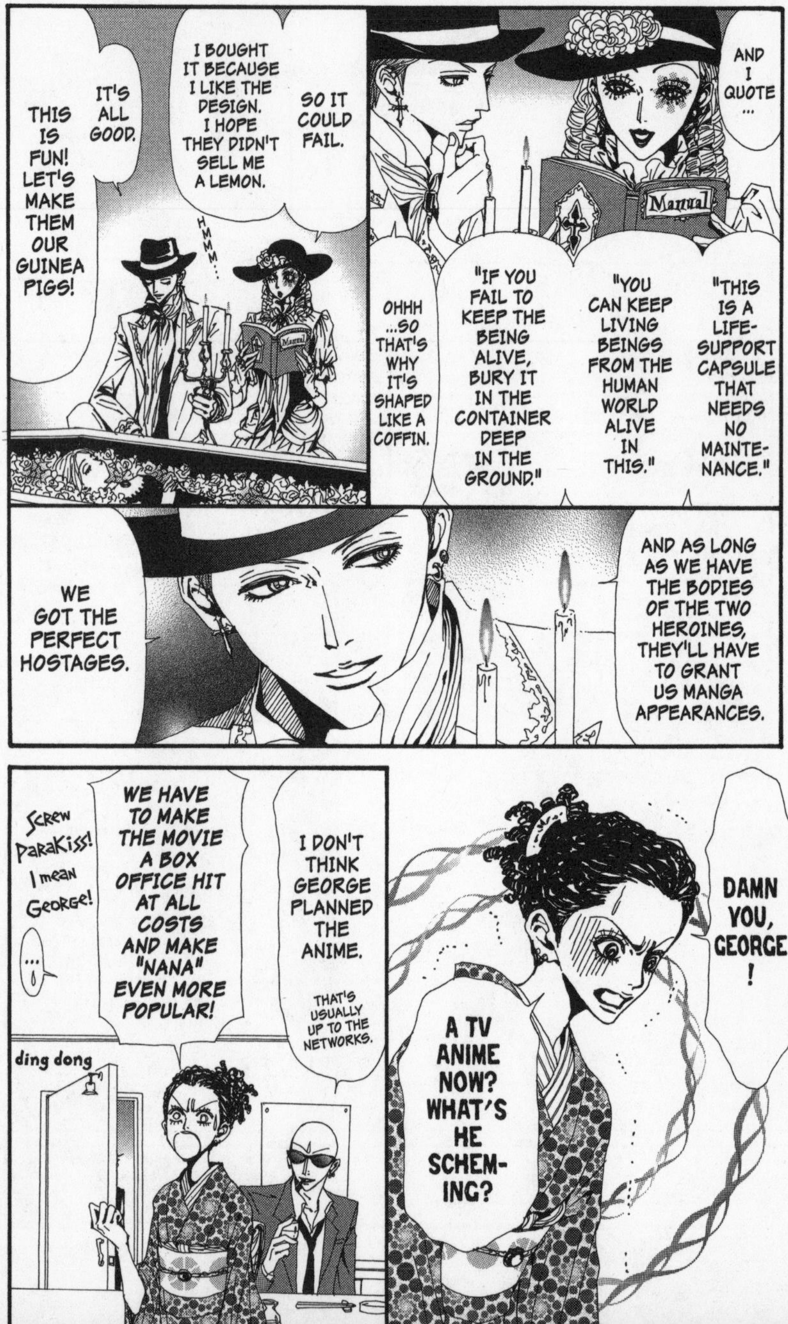
AND I QUOTE...
"THIS IS A LIFE-SUPPORT CAPSULE THAT NEEDS NO MAINTENANCE."
"YOU CAN KEEP LIVING BEINGS FROM THE HUMAN WORLD ALIVE IN THIS."
"IF YOU FAIL TO KEEP THE BEING ALIVE, BURY IT IN THE CONTAINER DEEP IN THE GROUND."
OHHH ...SO THAT'S WHY IT'S SHAPED LIKE A COFFIN.
I BOUGHT IT BECAUSE I LIKE THE DESIGN. I HOPE THEY DIDN'T SELL ME A LEMON.
SO IT COULD FAIL.
HMMM...
IT'S ALL GOOD.
THIS IS FUN! LET'S MAKE THEM OUR GUINEA PIGS!
AND AS LONG AS WE HAVE THE BODIES OF THE TWO HEROINES, THEY'LL HAVE TO GRANT US MANGA APPEARANCES.
WE GOT THE PERFECT HOSTAGES.
DAMN YOU, GEORGE!
A TV ANIME NOW? WHAT'S HE SCHEMING?
I DON'T THINK GEORGE PLANNED THE ANIME.
THAT'S USUALLY UP TO THE NETWORKS.
WE HAVE TO MAKE THE MOVIE A BOX OFFICE HIT AT ALL COSTS AND MAKE "NANA" EVEN MORE POPULAR!
Screw ParaKiss! I mean George!
...
ding dong

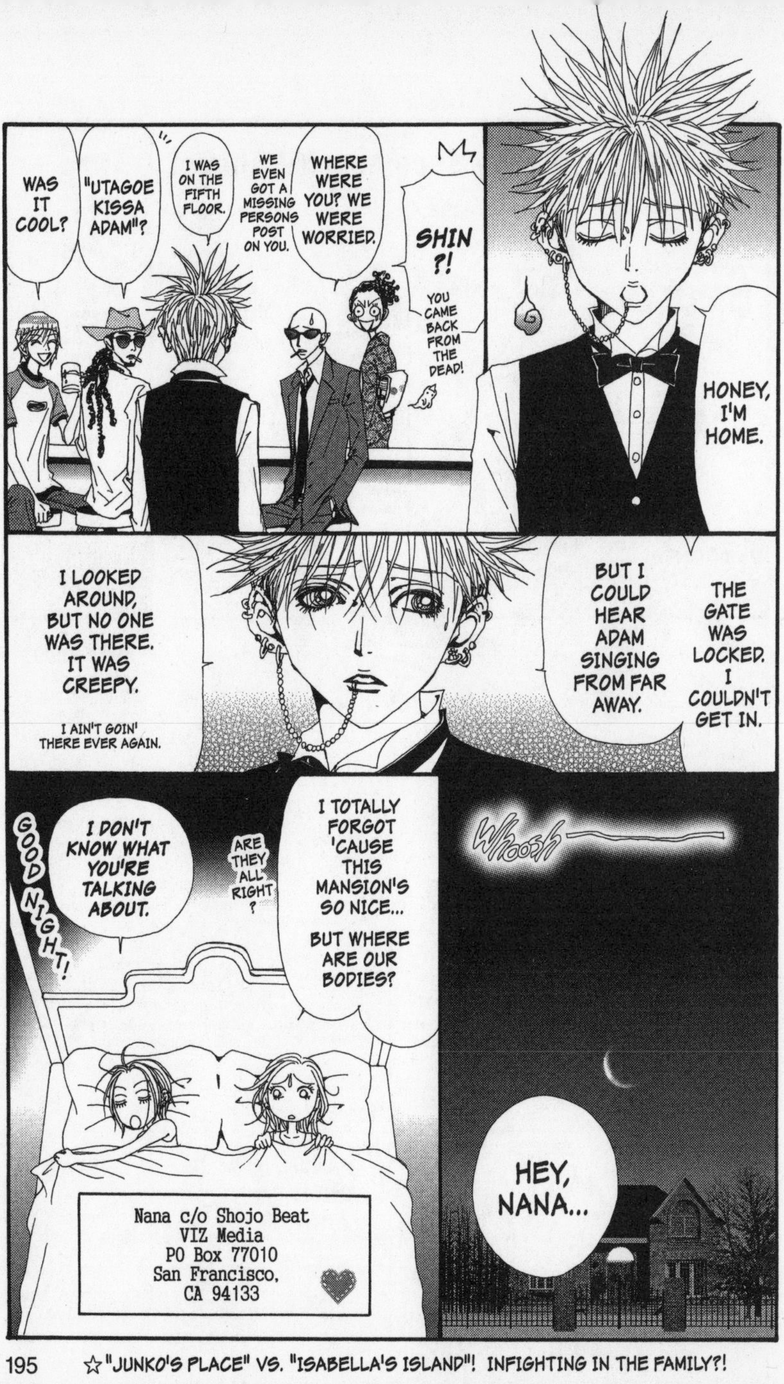
HONEY, I'M HOME.
SHIN?!
YOU CAME BACK FROM THE DEAD!
WHERE WERE YOU? WE WERE WORRIED.
WE EVEN GOT A MISSING PERSONS POST ON YOU.
I WAS ON THE FIFTH FLOOR.
"UTAGOE KISSA ADAM"?
WAS IT COOL?
THE GATE WAS LOCKED. I COULDN'T GET IN.
BUT I COULD HEAR ADAM SINGING FROM FAR AWAY.
I LOOKED AROUND, BUT NO ONE WAS THERE. IT WAS CREEPY.
I AIN'T GOIN' THERE EVER AGAIN.
Whoosh
HEY, NANA...
I TOTALLY FORGOT 'CAUSE THIS MANSION'S SO NICE...
BUT WHERE ARE OUR BODIES?
ARE THEY ALL RIGHT?
I DON'T KNOW WHAT YOU'RE TALKING ABOUT.
GOOD NIGHT!
Nana c/o Shojo Beat
VIZ Media
PO Box 77010
San Francisco,
CA 94133

 ☆"JUNKO'S PLACE" VS. "ISABELLA'S ISLAND"! INFIGHTING IN THE FAMILY?!

"PARADISE KISS" to Become a TV Anime!

George is Back!!

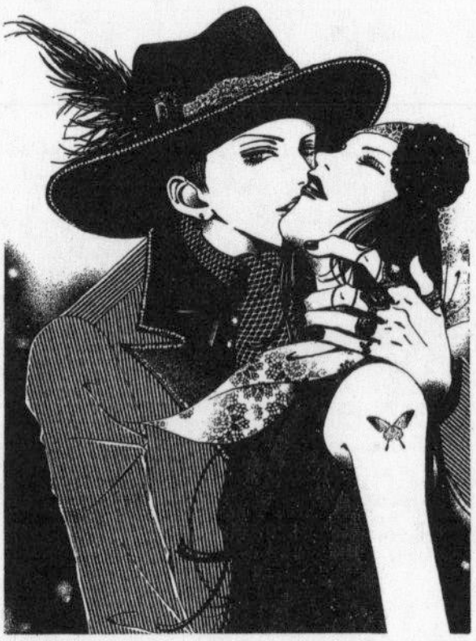

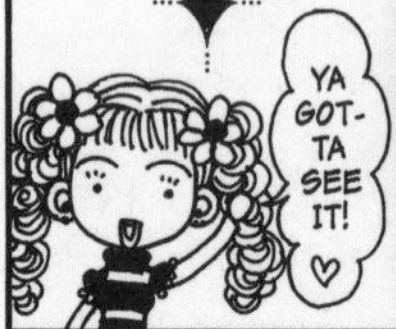
YA GOT-TA SEE IT! ♡

Airing every Thursday starting in October.

On Fuji Television at 24:35. ♡

※ Broadcast days and times may differ depending on where you live.

The Family Times

Aug. 12, 2005

"Gokinjyo Monogatari"

Wanna know how much it is?
¥53,865
(tax included)

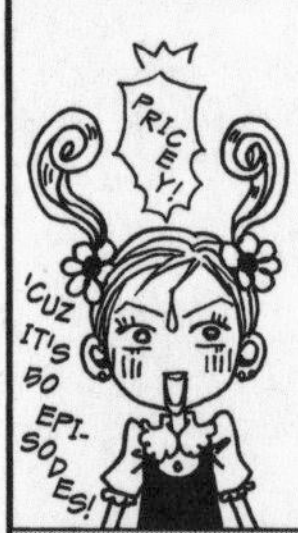
PRICEY!
'CUZ IT'S 50 EPISODES!

The beloved "Gokinjyo" anime will be back as a DVD box set! Wow! It includes all 50 episodes that were broadcast on TV! Nine disks that come with a special bag to put your make-up in! ♡

Released by Toei Animation/Super Vision

Anime DVDs

On sale September 28th!!

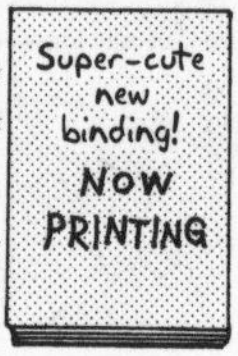
Super-cute new binding!
NOW PRINTING

127 x 188 mm special size
Suggested Retail: ¥1,260 (tax included)
Shueisha

"Paradise Kiss," which will be a TV anime, is the sequel to "Gokinjyo Monogatari." Please read "Gokinjyo" before "ParaKiss"! These volumes are the same size as the complete collection of "Tennai." They'll look good next to each other on your bookshelf! ♡

Complete Collection: 4 Volumes

On sale September 16th!!

"Have You Seen Me?"

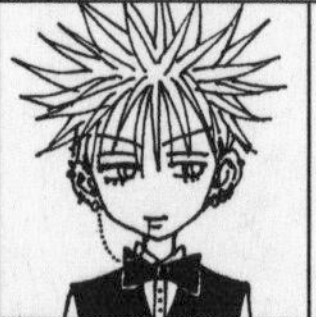

Shinichi Okazaki

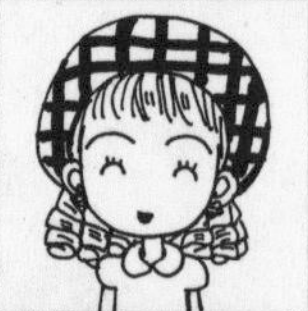

Misato Uehara (alias?)

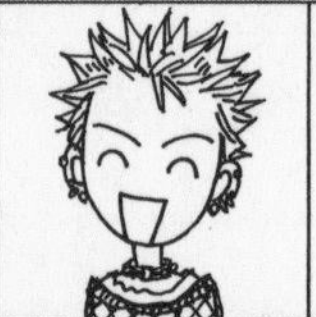

Nobuo Terashima

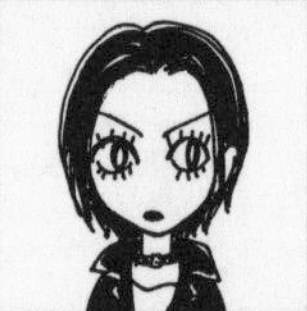

Nana Osaki

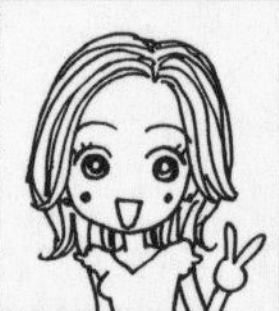

Nana Komatsu

The Family Times Aug. 12, 2005

NANA Trains on the JR Yamanote Line!!

FOR A LIMITED TIME ONLY

NANA trains will run in Tokyo's JR Yamanote line! 2 NANA-customized trains, a Nana version and a Hachi version, will go around Tokyo-to. You'll see super-sized NANA color illustrations on the doors and around the windows. Of course you can ride these trains. The inside of the trains are the same as usual, so don't freak out! Since it's only two trains out of all the trains running that line, you won't always be able to catch a NANA train—only if you're lucky! ♡ For your safety and that of others, don't go crazy and mob the trains or anything! So I guess you're coming to Tokyo for summer break?!

8/14 (Sun) to 9/9 (Fri)

Cookie

Hits the stands the 26th of every month!

♡ Sometimes comes with NANA extras! ♡

http://cookie.shueisha.co.jp/

Mekke!

Various Blast tour merch for sale!

BLACK STONES

The T-shirt Nobu's wearing on the front flap of this volume will be for sale soon! ♡

http://mekke.shueisha.co.jp/

Mobile Site - "Mobile NANA"

How to Access the Site!

Check out http://m.s-nana.com for instructions to log on with i-mode, EZweb, or Softbank (previously Vodafone!)

We love new members! ♡

If you're a NANA fan, sign up!

NANA screensaver images are updated every weekday! We got lots of stuff, like ring tone movie clips and email notice images. You can play pop trivia and vote in character polls. The first poll was "Who's the No. 1 guy you wanna have sex with?" So who won?! I can't sleep 'til I find out! ♡

Continuously updated! Official site "NANA Online"

Check out the latest information here!!

http://www.s-nana.com/

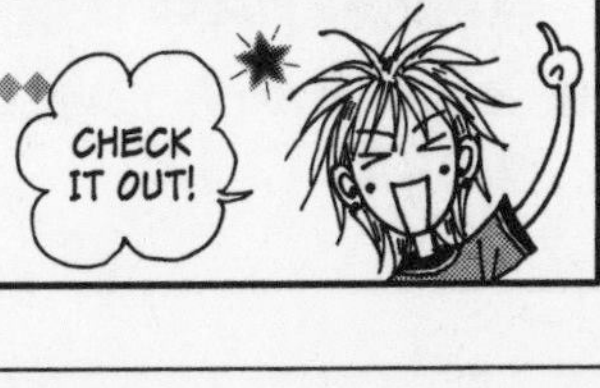
CHECK IT OUT!

The Latest "NANA" Movie News!!

"NANA" movie photo scrapbook

A4-size
Price: ¥1200 (tax included)
Shueisha

Available now!

A scrapbook that contains lots of rare photographs! It also includes interviews with Mika Nakashima (Nana), Aoi Miyazaki (Hachi), and Ai Yazawa (The Demon Lord?)!

"NANA FM 707," the making of the NANA movie, to be released August 26th!
(From TBS)

Super-cool, mainly featuring interviews with Ms. Nakashima and Ms. Miyazaki...♡ and of course our beloved Kentaro! A must-see!

[NANA – the novelization of the movie]

Shinsho-size edition
Price: ¥680 (tax included)
Shueisha

The novelization of the NANA movie, elegantly written by Ms. Kanae Shimokawa!

At the end of the novel there's the "Junko's Place, Virtual Reality," a special interview with Anna Nose (Junko), Yuta Hiraoka (Shoji), and Takehisa Takayama (Kyosuke)!

<**Author**>
Kanae Shimokawa

<**Script**>
Taeko Asano

Kentaro Otani

Experience the "NANA" movie premier event, "NANA TEN"!!

Starting July 30th in Tokyo (Harajuku) and Osaka, and later all over Japan! Maybe it'll come to your town? Check it out!

As seen in the movie
"ENDLESS STORY"

Starring YUNA ITO as REIRA

(Sony Music Records)

In stores Wed., September 7th!

Ms. Yuna Ito, who plays Reira, was chosen at the audition 'cause she sings great! ♡ This is her debut single. We'll be seeing a lot more of her!

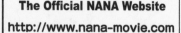

The Official NANA Website

http://www.nana-movie.com

Find out movie details here!

Theme Song "GLAMOROUS SKY"

NANA, starring MIKA NAKASHIMA

Lyrics: AI YAZAWA   Music: HYDE
(Sony Music Associated Records)

"What? Adam's doing the music and Principal Yazawa wrote the lyrics?!" If you thought something weird like that, you're already in with the Yazawa Family. In the manga, people refer to Blast songs as "something high school girls wouldn't sing at karaoke," but because this is the movie's theme song, it was created with love so anyone can get intimate with it. The lyrics are easy to memorize, so sing it loud at karaoke and score high! ♡

In stores Fri., August 31st!

The Family Times Aug. 12, 2005

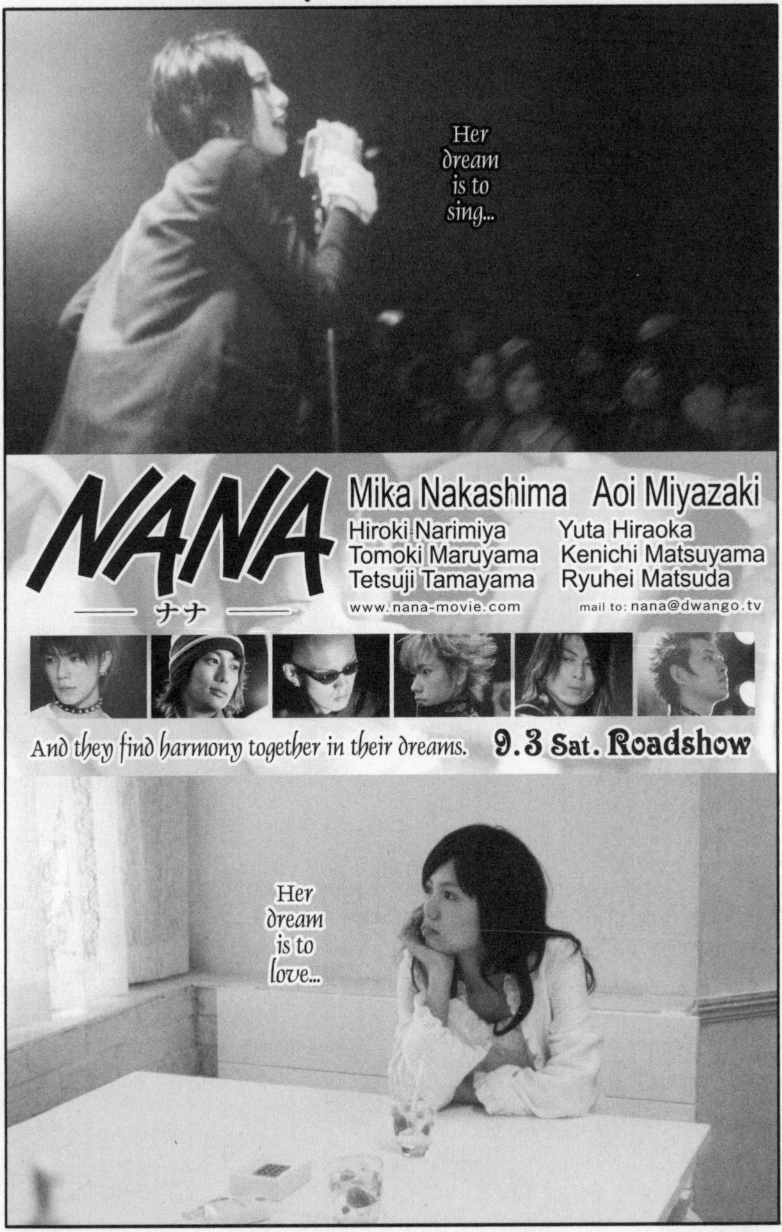
Her dream is to sing...
NANA
Mika Nakashima Aoi Miyazaki
Hiroki Narimiya Yuta Hiraoka
Tomoki Maruyama Kenichi Matsuyama
Tetsuji Tamayama Ryuhei Matsuda
ナナ
www.nana-movie.com
mail to: nana@dwango.tv
And they find harmony together in their dreams.
9.3 Sat. Roadshow
Her dream is to love...

☆ All products listed in this newspaper actually exist. Buy freely without fear.

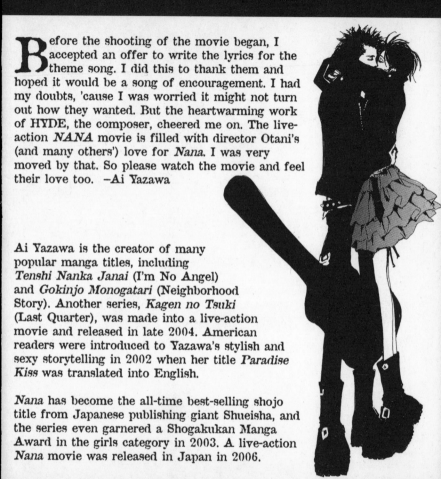

Before the shooting of the movie began, I accepted an offer to write the lyrics for the theme song. I did this to thank them and hoped it would be a song of encouragement. I had my doubts, 'cause I was worried it might not turn out how they wanted. But the heartwarming work of HYDE, the composer, cheered me on. The live-action *NANA* movie is filled with director Otani's (and many others') love for *Nana*. I was very moved by that. So please watch the movie and feel their love too. —Ai Yazawa

Ai Yazawa is the creator of many popular manga titles, including *Tenshi Nanka Janai* (I'm No Angel) and *Gokinjo Monogatari* (Neighborhood Story). Another series, *Kagen no Tsuki* (Last Quarter), was made into a live-action movie and released in late 2004. American readers were introduced to Yazawa's stylish and sexy storytelling in 2002 when her title *Paradise Kiss* was translated into English.

Nana has become the all-time best-selling shojo title from Japanese publishing giant Shueisha, and the series even garnered a Shogakukan Manga Award in the girls category in 2003. A live-action *Nana* movie was released in Japan in 2006.

Shojo Beat

NANA
VOL. 13

The Shojo Beat Manga Edition

STORY AND ART BY AI YAZAWA

English Adaptation/Allison Wolfe
Translation/Tomo Kimura
Touch-up Art & Lettering/Sabrina Heep
Design/Julie Behn
Editor/Pancha Diaz

Editor in Chief, Books/Alvin Lu
Editor in Chief, Magazines/Marc Weidenbaum
VP, Publishing Licensing/Rika Inouye
VP, Sales and Product Marketing/Gonzalo Ferreyra
VP, Creative/Linda Espinosa
Publisher/Hyoe Narita

Printed in Canada

Published by VIZ Media, LLC
P.O. Box 77010
San Francisco, CA 94107

Shojo Beat Manga Edition
10 9 8 7 6 5 4 3 2 1
First printing, November 2008

RATED M FOR MATURE

PARENTAL ADVISORY
NANA is rated M for Mature and is recommended for mature readers. This volume contains strong language and sexual situations.
ratings.viz.com

VIZ media

store.viz.com

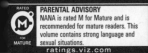

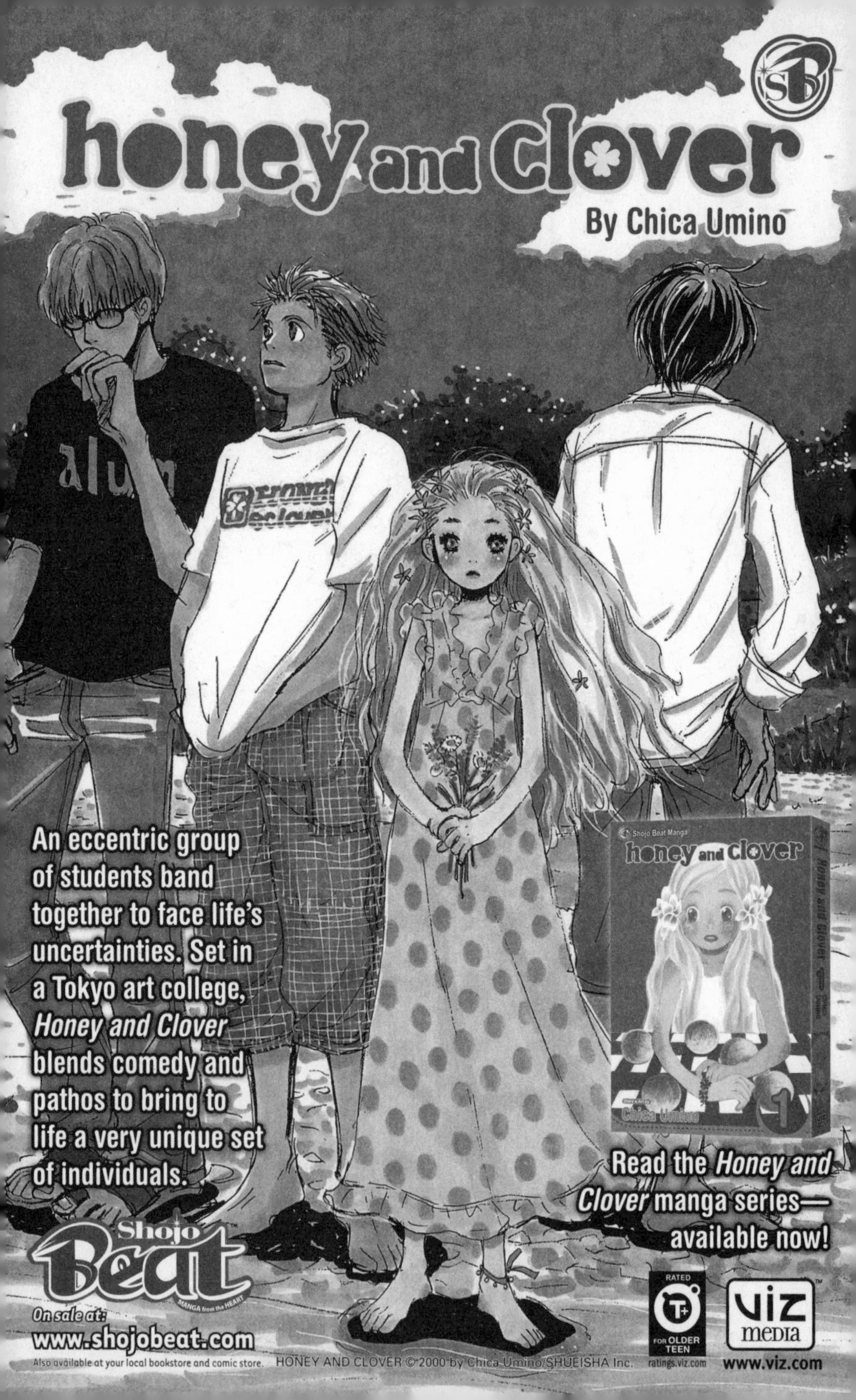

honey and clover
By Chica Umino
An eccentric group of students band together to face life's uncertainties. Set in a Tokyo art college, Honey and Clover blends comedy and pathos to bring to life a very unique set of individuals.
Shojo Beat Manga
honey and clover
Chica Umino
1
Read the Honey and Clover manga series— available now!
Shojo Beat
MANGA from the HEART
On sale at:
www.shojobeat.com
Also available at your local bookstore and comic store.
HONEY AND CLOVER © 2000 by Chica Umino/SHUEISHA Inc.
RATED
T+
FOR OLDER TEEN
ratings.viz.com
VIZ media
www.viz.com

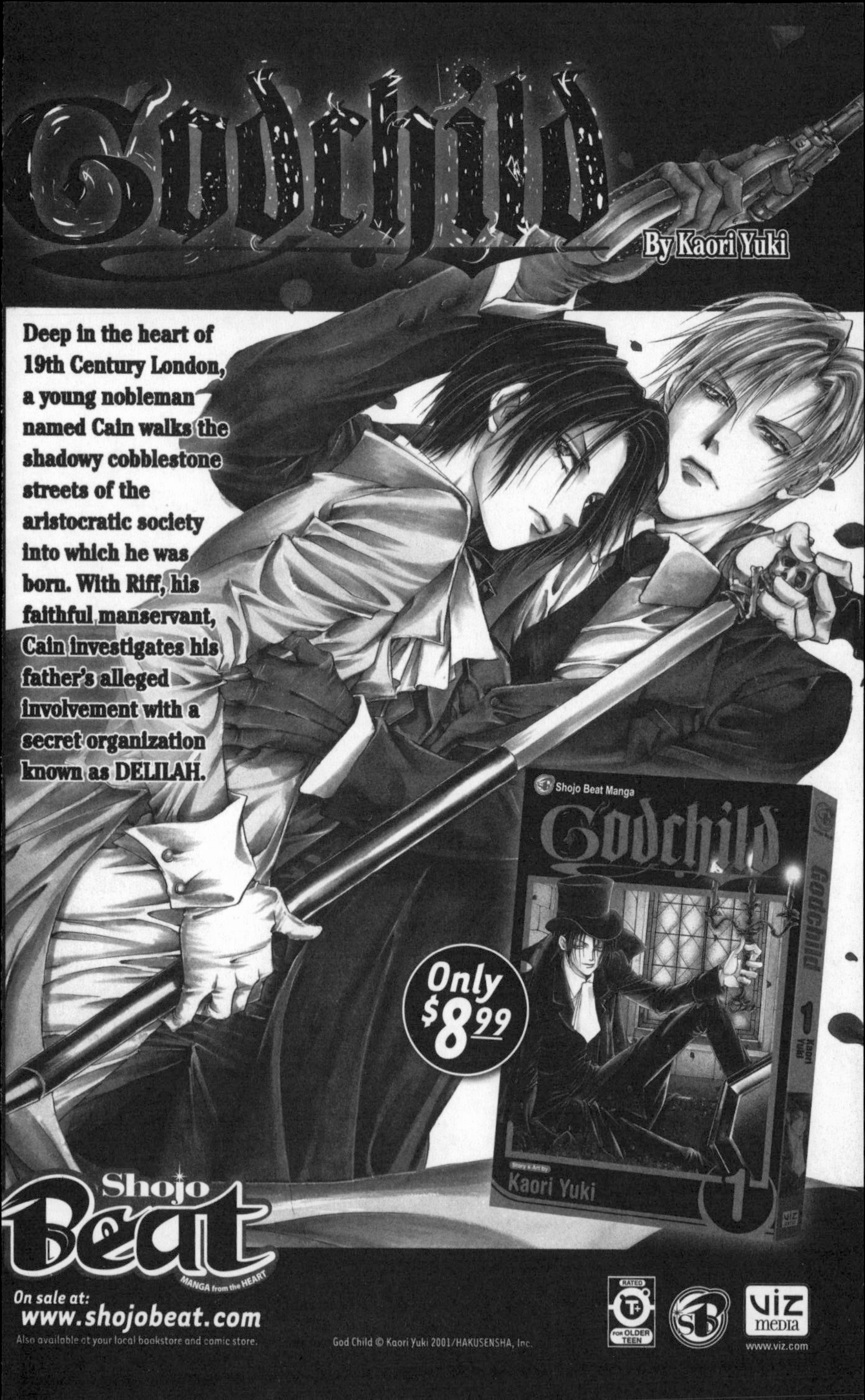
Godchild
By Kaori Yuki
Deep in the heart of 19th Century London, a young nobleman named Cain walks the shadowy cobblestone streets of the aristocratic society into which he was born. With Riff, his faithful manservant, Cain investigates his father's alleged involvement with a secret organization known as DELILAH.
Shojo Beat Manga
Godchild
Story & Art by
Kaori Yuki
Only $8.99
Shojo Beat
MANGA from the HEART
On sale at:
www.shojobeat.com
Also available at your local bookstore and comic store.
God Child © Kaori Yuki 2001/HAKUSENSHA, Inc.
RATED T+ FOR OLDER TEEN
VIZ media
www.viz.com

Tell us what you think about Shojo Beat Manga!

Our survey is now available online. Go to:

shojobeat.com/mangasurvey

Help us make our product offerings better!

THE REAL DRAMA BEGINS IN...

Shojo Beat™

MANGA from the HEART

The Shojo Manga Authority

The most **ADDICTIVE** shojo manga stories from Japan **PLUS** unique editorial coverage on the arts, music, culture, fashion, and much more!

12 GIANT issues for ONLY **$34.99***

That's **51% OFF** the cover price!

Subscribe NOW and become a member of the SB Sub Club!

- **SAVE** 51% OFF the cover price
- **ALWAYS** get every issue
- **ACCESS** exclusive areas of www.shojobeat.com
- **FREE** members-only gifts several times a year

Strictly VIP!

3 EASY WAYS TO SUBSCRIBE!

1) Send in the subscription order form from this book **OR**
2) Log on to: www.shojobeat.com **OR**
3) Call 1-800-541-7876